Double-Sided Witch

by
Margarita Gakis

This book is available in print at Amazon.com.

Digital Edition, License Notes

Double-Sided Witch
Book 3 of Covencraft

Copyright © 2015 by Margarita Gakis

Published by Castalian Springs Press

Cover by Steven Novak

Edited by Donna Serafinus

To my family - thanks for supporting and encouraging me!

CHAPTER ONE

Hiding in the closet wasn't new to Jade. Crouching down, making herself small - she was good at it. Or rather, *they* were good at it - Jade and Lily. When their father would drink, the closet was a refuge - a small, forgotten corner of their house that in his drunken stupor, their father seemed to forget about. If he'd had the clarity of mind that came with sobriety, he might have realized his daughter was a small child and couldn't actually leave the house. He might have realized that the dark closet, with its long shape, was the perfect place for a six-year old to curl up in the back, piling an old quilt on herself to make it seem like she was just another misshapen lump of detritus relegated to a bleak corner.

So no, being in the closet wasn't foreign or strange to Jade. What was strange was that she was an adult now. She should be long past the time where she felt the need to hide in the closet. She had magic. She could call fire to her fingertips, cast a circle of protection, or conjure a hex to lash out at demons. Jade shouldn't need to hide in the back of a closet, pressing herself into the cool drywall and waiting for daybreak. She ran her hands along the wall, finding the dimensions of the closet strange and wrong. The closet should be smaller, or she should be. She frowned, squinting in the dark. Now that she thought about it, she shouldn't be in this old closet at all, should she? If she was in a closet, wouldn't she be in the one in her little cottage at the

Coven? Why was she in the closet in her old bedroom? In a house she hadn't been back to in years?

It was that detail that first tipped her brain toward the inevitable realization that she was dreaming. That and the fact that she wasn't in the closet alone.

Jade looked down at the warm weight next to her where a little girl was curled up against her leg. The girl turned her face toward Jade and in that strange wrong-logic that dreams had, Jade could make out her features perfectly despite the dark. She found them to be a miniature of her own features, except for the eyes. Jade's eyes were a stormy grey - somewhat bland, actually, but for the fact that their light color tended to make people nervous when she gazed at them for too long. She'd been told she had eyes like a bird of prey. She didn't mean to glare at people, but the pale color of her irises sometimes gave that impression.

The little girl's eyes were apple green. The color of Lily's eyes.

"Are you her?" Jade asked, her voice sounding loud in the small space. The girl blinked up at her, her eyes glowing for a moment. "Are you back?"

A loud crashing sound outside the closet made them both flinch. The girl curled up into Jade and Jade tried to pull her closer, to bring her further back into the closet.

"He's out there," Jade whispered. She could hear their father cursing and shouting - breaking things, throwing things. The words were unintelligible - nonsense words from a dream.

Maybe it was because Jade and Lily had never understood what he was yelling about, or maybe they'd both forgotten over the years what he'd said.

The closet door was yanked open and the light burned her eyes. Jade squinted, unable to see. There was a shrieking sound and Jade could feel the girl being pulled from her - being dragged away. Jade couldn't make herself open her eyes, couldn't make herself see what was happening. She lashed out, clawing with her hands, trying to grab something, anything - a hand, an arm, a leg.

Her fingers wrapped around something too large to be part of the girl, but too slender to belong to a man. The light faded and Jade could open her eyes. Above her stood another version of herself - same long brown hair, pulled back into a ponytail, same impressive height, same fit build. Except the doppelgänger that stood before her had green eyes. Lily's eyes.

Jade's fingers tightened on Lily's arm. "Are you back? Say you're back!"

Lightning quick, Lily's fingers shifted underneath Jade's, grabbing Jade's wrist back tightly and Jade winced - she thought she could feel the bones grinding together. Lily was urgent, desperate. Jade could feel anxiety coming off her and it was so unlike everything she ever remembered of Lily.

Lily pulled hard on her arm and Jade struggled. "No, I'm sorry. I didn't mean to. I didn't know it wouldn't work. You made me."

"You need to come with me."

Hearing Lily speak, her voice the same pitch and cadence as Jade's own was strange and vertigo inducing. The grip on her arm tightened and Jade tried to pull back into the depths of the closet.

Lily looked behind her, over her shoulder. They were no longer in the house where they grew up, but were at the lake, at the Nature Preserve by the Coven. In the distance, a figure stood, dark and faceless, a swarm of birds swirling around her like an ominous fairy tale. Lily's grip on Jade's forearm was tight, her fingers digging in.

"I shouldn't have slept so long."

#

Waking up after one of her nightmares was like rising from a body of water. There was an initial shock of air as she sucked in a breath and then disorientation mixed with slight distress. Both bled away, leaving her feeling shaky and a little cold.

It was dark in the mornings now. This time of year, it seemed impossible that when she would get up at the same time during the summer, her bedroom would be already bright. She wouldn't need to turn on any lights to get out of bed and get her running gear on. But now, closer to midwinter, it was as though it were still night. The only light came from the glow of her alarm clock and even that made her squint at its partial brightness after the blackness of sleep. Like most mornings, Jade wanted to roll over and close her eyes. Maybe more lately because of the dreams. She'd been dreaming of Lily a lot lately. Every night.

Jade didn't know how to explain it. She'd never known how to explain it. She wasn't Lily and Lily wasn't her, and yet, they both lived in the same body. It wasn't a split personality or dissociative identity disorder or whatever the world was calling it now. She didn't know how or why it wasn't that. It just wasn't. They had never been one person. They had always been two separate people. Jade didn't remember anything but being that way. When Jade was little, she hadn't questioned it. It had always just been. Like other things she 'knew' as child - the only monster in their house was their father when he drank, her mother would always forget dinner on Tuesdays after her ladies lunch, and surely everyone was really two people that shared the same body. That way no one was ever lonely. Jade had no memory of a life that didn't include Lily. It was only once she got older that she'd realized the rest of the world wasn't the same.

It had been different for Lily. Lily could remember a time that didn't involve Jade. Jade could see the memories in her head still, even with Lily gone - murky, abstract images where it had been just Lily and her parents. Before the drinking and the yelling and the fighting. But when Jade tried to think of anything for herself that didn't have Lily, her head was just... empty and dark. Cold.

Intellectually, Jade knew everything she remembered, everything she described sounded like dissociative identity disorder. But she also had a sense that the definition didn't fit what they were. They never felt like one person. They were always separate, yet together, sharing one body except for their eyes. Their eyes shifted color depending on who was 'in control.' It was a subtle thing people never noticed, or if they did, they never said anything. As far as Jade knew, things like that didn't, couldn't happen with an identity disorder. They didn't often think about it. It just was. Always had been and always would be. Or so she thought.

Then Lily … went away. Thinking about that day, the last day she saw Lily and spoke with her, made Jade feel sick. She finally pushed herself out of bed for her run. She couldn't think about it. She wouldn't think about it. She would 'Scarlett-O'Hara' the problem. Only she wouldn't think about it tomorrow or the next day or the day after that. It made her chest clench, her heart pound, made her angry and anxious and just… empty. Alone. Incomplete. Like losing a limb, she was unsure of her new structure and balance. Everything was hard and different. Sometimes, late at night when the darkness of the day was pressing in on her, she would get crazy thoughts like maybe the morning would never come and sometimes she would wish that it wouldn't. She wished she would just fall asleep and never wake up. Some days she couldn't stand being alone.

As if sensing her thoughts, Bruce, her lizard familiar, leapt off the bed, where he'd been curled by her feet and butted his serpentine head against her leg.

"I know, Bruce. I've got you now."

His pink tongue flicked out and he made his customary 'pffft' sound. She wasn't sure what to make of him most days. It was extremely uncommon for a witch to have a familiar and Jade wished she could take credit for Bruce's presence, but he'd chosen her far more than she'd chosen him. Jade didn't understand their connection, but she knew she liked having him around, knew that he was somewhat magical, and also knew that he was a horrid little laundry thief. He loved to drag her workout clothes out of the laundry basket and make himself a little nest, burrowing under tanks, shirts and sport bras. Jade was both disgusted and a little touched.

Jade realized she wasn't really alone anymore. She had Bruce and maybe something more.

As Jade pet Bruce, feeling his serpentine skin under her fingers, warm and smooth, she remembered a moment when she'd been fighting Dex, a witch gone bad, trying to defeat his hex. Jade had felt something against her brain - a presence - Lily's presence - for the first time in years and it was just as it had always been - a cool tingle in her brain - calming, soothing and *there*.

Afterward, when Jade was safely by herself in her little cottage, she'd worked up the courage to stand in front of the mirror, like she'd done so many times in the past before Lily left, and spoke to her reflection. Jade asked the mirror if Lily was there. She asked for a sign. For a moment, so quickly she could have imagined it, one of her grey irises had turned apple-green. The color of Lily's eyes.

Jade didn't know what that meant. She'd tried to talk to Lily since then - the silent communication they'd always had with each other, unheard and unspoken, inside her head. There'd been nothing but emptiness and blankness in response.

Bruce head-butted her leg again and Jade realized she'd been standing stock still in the middle of her darkened room. "Sorry, sorry," she mumbled and then, "watch your eyes, Bruce," as she turned on the light. They both squinted at the brightness, blinking away the last vestiges of sleep. She pulled on her running outfit before she stumbled down the stairs, liking the way Bruce's heavy footfalls followed after her own. She headed straight for the coffee pot in the kitchen, firing it up, while Bruce took a detour to the window she'd spelled for him, hopping up and over the sill, spilling out to the ground outside. The magic on the window let him in and out as he pleased without it needing to be physically opened. Ah, magic. Not just for the fancy-pants things in life, but for practical stuff like letting your lizard familiar out without having to actually open a door.

Bruce toddled into the kitchen moments later, shaking himself like a dog. His Elizabethan lizard-collar flapped open and shut a few times and he came over to where Jade sat at the kitchen table. She flipped open her laptop and read her email reaching down to pat his head. When he tilted his head to the side, she pressed her fingers against the soft part of his neck, intending to give him a good scratch. She paused when she felt a small rough patch of skin under her fingers.

"Whatcha got here, bud?" she asked. He tilted his head even more, stretching his neck to the side, almost presenting the area. Jade ran her fingers over the scaly skin, peering closely. Despite the fact that he was a lizard, Bruce's skin was normally soft and supple. Although she hated to think it and would never, ever, *ever* say it out loud, (and certainly not in front of him), Bruce's skin was like an Italian leather handbag - buttery smooth and pliant. Finding a section feeling scratchy and uneven was new.

"Dry weather got you down? Do we need to get some of that udder cream they put on cows?" she teased. He pushed his neck out a bit more and she patted his head. "Okay, I'll keep an eye on it. If it gets worse, we'll go to the vet. I guess." She frowned. A vet might not cut it. "Well, Paris will know who we can see." If there was anyone who could help her familiar, Jade was sure it would be the Coven Leader.

Giving a longing stare toward the coffee pot, she tapped Bruce's head one more time. She knew that drinking coffee before her run was a bad idea - it was why she set it up so it would be ready upon her return. She was tempted every time to grab just a half a cup before heading out, but this early in the morning, it was like her body was hyper-efficient - if she drank even half a cup, she'd have to pee halfway through her run with Daniel and she was not going to end up squatting somewhere in the Nature Preserve, getting poison ivy in the summer or freezing her ass off in the winter.

Jade laced up her runners, donned her head lamp and darted out the front door, detouring to the back alleys until she got to an access point to the reserve. She used to just hop over the chain link fence, but she'd tried her hand at spelling the fence the same way she had spelled the window at home for Bruce and found that she could now come and go through the chain link as she pleased. She pressed against the metal, murmuring her spell and felt it almost melt away underneath her skin, or maybe into her skin, she wasn't sure. There was a slightly unpleasant tingle associated with it, but it was worth not going up and over the fence. She'd ruined a pair of running pants that way, tearing a really indecent and obnoxious hole in the soft fabric. She was mostly certain the spell was temporary and only remained active for a few minutes after she used it. Of course, if it turned out she was letting deer or moose or whatever out of the Preserve by accident she was going to deny all knowledge.

Daniel was waiting for her in his usual spot. He jerked his head at her, his own headlamp bobbing in the semi-darkness. It was still too early for the sun to be up and Jade was thankful for her multiple layers. She knew she'd be warm enough in a few minutes, but right now, it was pretty damned cold. Her breath plumed out in grey globes as she exhaled from her mouth and her nostrils burned from the chill as she inhaled. She bobbed her own headlamp at Daniel; morning greeting complete. As much as Daniel's boyfriend, Henri, was chatty, Daniel was not. If he were, Jade didn't think they could be running partners, at least not in the morning. She liked the company, or rather, the companionship, but appreciated the silence. Running with Daniel was blissfully conversation-free. It was his day to pick the music, so he fired up his MP3 player and they fell into step to the identifiable beat of the

Black Keys. She was yawning her way through their first mile, willing her body to fall into the semi-trance like state it often did while she ran. The 'thump-thump' of their footfalls, the beat of the music, and the cadence of their breathing all started lining up, but just when Jade thought she might drift into 'the zone,' her mind would jerk back to last night's dream. Like a record scratch - jarring and harsh - she was zipped back. She could see Lily standing over her, feel her tugging on her wrist. Jade shivered in the morning air and told herself it was just the reaction of the sweat on her face evaporating in the cold morning air. Pushing all thoughts of Lily down, she listened to the music, focusing on the lyrics and the bass line. As the next song started up - a heavy hip-hop tune - she wondered what kind of bass setting Daniel must have his speakers on because she could feel the beat in her chest. A heavy, wet thumping.

Then she realized that it wasn't the music causing the feeling in her chest. It was the lake.

Jade had first passed by the lake with Paris as they walked through the Nature Preserve to work on Jade's circle casting - casting magical spells within the confines of a circle. It could boost power, protect a witch and enable them to work on more complicated spells. At the time, she'd felt something tugging at her - pulling at her insides. Paris had led her toward the lake, thinking maybe they could work on Jade's water magic, but on the way there, she had felt sick. Even now, she couldn't articulate it. Her hand had reached out of its own volition to clutch at the back of Paris' coat, stopping him from going any further. Getting closer and closer to the lake had felt like being sucked into a gravity well. The closer she got, the harder it was to stop; as though something deep inside her was being pulled against her will. Paris mentioned there'd been an accident at the lake years before and many witches in the Coven had an aversion to the area. She hadn't asked what he meant and he hadn't offered. She was both sorry and grateful; Jade wasn't sure she wanted to know what other witches felt when they passed by the lake. She'd rather not think of it at all.

It made no sense that Jade should feel a similar sensation from the lake now. She and Daniel were on the other side of the Preserve from where Paris and Jade had been. She never felt the lake on this side of the Preserve until today. Her chest felt like a hollow drum, her skin stretched tightly across the cavernous emptiness. The thumping sensation she felt was as though someone were striking the surface with deep, hard blows, sending the reverberations rippling through the space, rattling the edges. While running always made her breathe hard, today she felt like she couldn't catch her breath, couldn't get in enough oxygen. Her legs slowed down until she was stopped, bent over, hands on her knees, trying to breathe. Her lungs felt small and inadequate, unable to pull in enough air. The light from her headlamp made a circle on the ground in front of her, illuminating the dry twigs and desiccated leaves that littered the pathway. She focused on the bright area in front of her, willing her lungs to open up. There was a hot press against her chest and she fumbled with her gloves, pulling one off so she could dig under her coat and sweater. Her salamander charm, the one Paris gave to her, was hot to the touch. She pulled it away from her skin, pinching it between her fingers.

"Rough run today?" Daniel asked. He'd stopped a few paces in front of her and turned back, jogging little circles around her while she panted. She rubbed at her chest. Some running days *were* easier than others, but this was different.

Without warning, she dry heaved, making a choking-gagging sound. Daniel immediately stopped, standing still beside her.

"Hey, hey," he said, placing a hand on her back and rubbing a small circle. "You okay?"

Jade nodded, still gasping. *Focus*, she thought. *Breathe in and out. In and out.* It seemed like the silver weight of the salamander increased for a moment and then released. She wasn't sure if the charm was magical. She'd thought that it was only symbolic, but as she clutched it in her hand now, she felt safer, calmer. Slowly, it felt as though some kind of wall was coming up in her mind, blocking the sensation of the lake. Between the comforting warmth of the charm and the sudden scent of citrus, the empty-drum feeling ebbed and her body no longer felt like it was betraying her with its weakness. She stayed bent over and focused on the feeling of Daniel's hand on her back, feeling the pressure through the layers of her long-sleeved shirt and coat.

"You must really be in the inner circle now. I didn't even flinch when you touched me," she joked.

He huffed with laughter. "We'll work you up to hugs."

"Hey now, let's not get crazy."

He laughed again, the sound warm and friendly. "Seriously. You okay?"

She nodded again, this time managing to stand upright. He stepped back, out of her space. It was one of the reason's she was so comfortable with Daniel. Jade always got the feeling he respected her space. That and he was gay. He didn't want anything from her. Or rather, he would never want from her something she couldn't or wouldn't give.

"Yeah, I don't know what happened."

"You sick?"

"No, I don't think so. Just... tired lately. Not sleeping well." It was mostly the truth.

Daniel nodded. "Well, let's cut it short today. It's all fun and games till someone dry heaves."

"And then it's a sport."

"Or a reality show."

Daniel turned around on the little pathway and started walking back the way they came, keeping his pace easy. They worked their way toward the outer edge of the Preserve, away from the lake. Jade took several deep, icy breaths, almost relishing the way the cold air bit at the soft tissue of her lungs as she did. By the time they were back at Daniel's car, it was hard to remember she'd ever felt sick in the first place.

As per their usual routine, Daniel drove her home, instead of Jade hiking her way back through the alleyways and paths. Back at her cottage, he turned to her one last time.

"You sure you feel okay now?"

Jade rolled her eyes. "Yes. I didn't even really get sick. I just got all…" she made a churning motion with her hands.

He studied her for a moment, as if weighing the truth of her words. "Let me know if you want to take any of our other running days off this week. It's okay to have a rest period."

"I'm fine. Just tired."

He made a 'hmm' noise, as though he'd wait to see how she was himself. "All right. See you at work."

She got out with a wave, watching his car pull away. The sun was just barely coming up, making the sky dirty grey-blue with touches of pink and orange. She knew by the time she saw Daniel again at the Counter-Magic offices, it would be pinky-orange with the arc of the sun crowning.

Heading up the walkway, she checked in with her demon locks, more out of habit than any real need. It wasn't like she had a lot of visitors. The locks would keep anyone out other than herself, Bruce and now Paris. She had to add him one day and just hadn't bothered re-configuring the locks. Her steps slowed as she reached her front door. The magic felt sluggish and slow in her mind. Normally, it was a big puzzle box and Jade could feel the gears of it turning and twisting as she moved through the space - like it was stretching open around her and then sagging closed again. This morning, it was like the gears and cogs were cold, like the weather - moving slowly and with protest.

Or maybe it was her. It might be because she was tired. Jade wasn't sure. While she had been proficient enough to cast the spell, she didn't know enough about demon magic to be able to troubleshoot why her locks weren't acting the same. Maybe the spell needed touching up? Maybe it was responding to how she felt? Maybe this just happened to demon magic in the winter? She'd have to check Sakkara's demon grimoires.

It's not like she could (or would) ask Paris. While his mother, Sakkara, had been a beloved Coven Leader and seemingly good mom (if the way Paris turned out was any indication), she was also quite the demon spell hoarder and conjurer. Sometimes (okay, most times) Jade felt bad for how much she liked demon magic given how adverse Paris was to it. Not only did he, and the Coven, consider demon magic taboo, Jade didn't think he'd ever really gotten used to the idea that his mother had regularly practiced it and had been damn good at it. Finding not one, but three demon grimoires in Sakkara's handwriting had been a blow to him.

Jade would have to go through the books on her own and see if she could find a reason why her locks were acting weird. Or maybe they would be better tomorrow. But she wouldn't ask Paris about it. Not yet.

Bruce came charging out of the kitchen when Jade came in, like he was surprised it was her at the door. He pushed his way past her, sticking his snout

out the front door and giving a deep, hard sniff. A laugh escaped Jade at the sight of him wiggling his lizard-nose back and forth.

"Getting some fresh air? You know you can go out the window for that."

He huffed as if he was expelling something out his nose and then turned, sauntering back inside. His long, scaly tail swished behind him as he made his way to the stairs and then started hobbling up them.

"All right then," Jade muttered, closing the front door. She watched Bruce labor up the stairs enviously. No doubt he'd crawl back into bed, or into a pile of her laundry and go to sleep. Jade didn't have such luxury. It was time for a cup of coffee and then getting ready for work. Her cube at Counter-Magic awaited.

#

After taking the bus to work, Jade always wanted to wash her hands. Maybe her face. Maybe all her clothes. Ugh, public transit. Gross. Plus it was really inconvenient to pick up coffee before work when you took public transit. It meant finding a bus route that stopped by a coffee shop, getting off, getting coffee and then waiting for the next bus. No, thank you. So after her cup at home, Jade resigned herself to wait until she, Callie and Henri went for their usual ten-thirty coffee break in the Coven's cafeteria. The coffee wasn't bad and it gave Jade something to break up her morning.

She needed to get her car and bring it to the Coven.

She'd been getting ready to move to the Coven. Honestly. But then Dex, one of the other Coven Leaders, had gone all dark side and Jade ended up getting involved. Okay, she threw herself into the mix, but she knew Dex was bad news from day one and guess what? She'd been right and it was thanks to her that he hadn't gotten his bat-shit crazy paws on Sakkara's demon grimoires.

If only the Coven were grateful about it. They seemed *mostly* grateful. Partially grateful. Reluctantly grateful. They gave Jade sideways glances and not-so-covert looks for the most part. Jade could feel the equal parts of discomfort, distrust and grudging gratitude in their expressions. It wasn't Jade's fault that in the process of stopping Dex, Coven magic got sort of broken and Paris had to reset it.

According to the Coven, it *was* apparently Jade's fault that Paris reset Coven Magic to resonate with Jade's personal magic. A magic that was slightly different than what everyone else had been born into. Of course it was.

Jade couldn't help that. Her magic was just her magic. At first, people seemed intrigued by the difference. It was like a shiny new car that had the new car smell. But now, the new car was making a clunking noise that couldn't be fixed, it guzzled gas like it had a hundred cylinders and the dealer was saying no take-backs.

Jade was the only one who was proficient at 'driving' it. She felt bad. Sort of. Obviously it was great for her because her magic was what she was used to. It must totally suck for everyone else trying spells they'd been using for years only to have them fizzle out, or blow up in their faces. Literally. Penny Simpson had a bad experience with a scrying spell she'd done for years and her eyebrows hadn't grown back yet. Hannah, their sometime-resident magic expert, said the residual magic had to dissipate on its own before the hair follicles would resume their natural cycle.

Still, it's not like that was Jade's fault. But try telling that to Penny and her horridly drawn-on eyebrows. Yeesh. Penny should just... not do anything with them. Although that would mean she'd have to walk around with that perpetually surprised look people with no eyebrows have.

Whatever. It wasn't life-threatening. No one had died. No one would die. Probably. So long as they didn't go crazy with their magic until they got it figured out, it would all be fine. She was trying to help by reconfiguring spells at Counter-Magic, but even if she hadn't been helping, she couldn't force them to like her.

Plus, she didn't need to be liked. Being liked wasn't important in the grand scheme of things. Right? Still, when she walked into the Coven and Henri, already at his reception desk, looked up and gave her a big smile and wave, she felt warm and pleasant in her chest. He had his headset on, taking a phone call, but he still managed to point at his watch and mouth 'ten-thirty?' and then mime drinking a coffee. Jade nodded, passing by his desk on her way to Counter-Magic. Once there, she took off her coat, straightened her keyboard and then settled down in her chair. Time to work.

She had some emails waiting for her - a couple of minor spells that Coven witches had been using, but couldn't get working since Coven magic had been reset. Jade's job at the moment was to slog through spells that were failing, see if she could figure out why, and tweak them. She liked it. It wasn't as much fun as demon magic, but it was puzzle solving and no two were the same. She worked on easy and simple spells assigned to her by Daniel or Josef after they had reviewed the Counter-Magic Incident Report log. Coven members called in, their issues got logged and then assigned out to appropriate witches. Sometimes spells went wrong due to bad ingredients or improper casting. Sometimes people just weren't as good as they thought they were. Counter-Magic ensured that nothing too horrible happened to the Coven and that things were mostly put right in the end.

Except for Penny and her eyebrows.

Jade was just glad she was finally getting work, even if it was simple fire creation spells, house-cleaning charms gone awry or positive mantra magic not working. At the end of the day, she could point to the number of emails she'd resolved and say, 'Yeah. I did that.' Simple, but gratifying.

Daniel came in about ten minutes after her and raised his eyebrows in question. Jade guessed he probably wondered if she was feeling well after her dry heaving incident that morning. She gave him the thumbs-up and then went back to her spell work, trying to untangle why Lucy DeWinter hadn't been able to scry for her favorite necklace yesterday. Or rather, why she'd found four lost socks and a ball of dryer lint instead. Jade wasn't sure if she wanted to first figure out how Lucy could find her necklace, or if she should figure out how to cast a spell that would perpetually locate lost socks. She hated losing socks.

Ten-thirty rolled around faster than Jade expected and she grabbed her purse to head to the cafeteria. Callie and Henri were already there, at their usual table, heads bent together. Callie's fine blond hair was pulled back into a simple French braid and Jade wondered if she should or could try something similar with her own hair. Maybe she could ask Callie to try it out on her. Did women do those kinds of things when they were adults? Or was that a 'teenage sleepover' thing, complete with requisite pillow fight and giggling? Absently, she reached up and tugged on her usual ponytail, tightening it at the crown of her head, feeling it swing as she grabbed her coffee, pulling at her scalp. She never did anything with her hair other than pull it back. Hair was a hassle.

Henri and Callie both had their smartphones out, looking up from their screens as Jade sat down, half-heartedly stirring cream into her coffee.

"Oh good, you're here. What are you doing the day after tomorrow. At night?" Callie asked immediately.

Jade frowned. "Nothing. Why?"

Callie smiled, her brown eyes going wide with excitement. "Booty yoga!"

Jade felt her insides go a little cold. "What?" she asked weakly.

"It hear it's amazing," Henri said, voice colored with enthusiasm. "It's all the poses that target your booty. Lifts your butt. Makes you look like a dancer. It's like hot yoga and booty boot camp with some Pilates thrown in."

Jade took a sip of her coffee. "That sounds horrible."

Callie rolled her eyes. "You promised you'd try a fitness class with us. We've picked. Booty yoga. Seven p.m. I'll pick you up at quarter to."

Jade hoped she hid her nose wrinkle behind her coffee cup as she took another drink, wracking her brain for some reason she could get out of it. She'd already said she wasn't doing anything. It's not like she could lie now. Besides, she didn't have anything believable to lie about. She didn't have a social life before she moved to the Coven, never mind after. She woke up, sometimes she ran with Daniel, then she worked. She read books and streamed TV on her laptop. She fiddled with demon magic and tried to learn some regular spells. She talked to Bruce. Such were her hobbies.

Henri waved a hand. "It's going to be so good for you. Runners always have really tight hips and lower back. I'm going to try to drag Daniel as well. He never stretches after he runs with you. He's going to snap an achilles tendon or something, I swear."

"If you get Daniel to booty yoga, I'll buy you coffee for a week," Jade told him.

"Deal." They shook on it.

They exchanged the minutiae of their lives. Henri brought up the last episode of the sci-fi show they were all watching.

"No, I'm telling you, Peter is the alien and they're going to kill him when they find out. They need to write him off the show. The guy who plays him just got offered the lead in that sexy remake of Frankenstein."

"Spoiler alert!" Callie yelled, slapping him on the arm.

"It's not a spoiler! It's speculation," argued Henri.

"Wait, how are they going to make Frankenstein sexy?" Jade asked.

"Meh," mused Henri. "It's cable TV. They make everybody good-looking and mostly naked."

"That has nothing to do with Frankenstein!" Jade protested.

"I repeat, cable TV." Henri took a sip of his coffee, giving Jade knowing eyebrows from over the rim as he did. "It doesn't matter what the original story is."

"Well, be that as it may, it's not Peter. Jackie is the alien."

Callie made a face. "Jackie? What makes you say that?"

Jade stirred her coffee and then gnawed on the stir stick. "Didn't you see her face when Dr. What's-his-name was trying to put the moves on her?"

Callie and Henri both shrugged. Callie leaned in. "She didn't look interested."

"That wasn't disinterest. That was disgust. Little lip-curl, slight nose-wrinkle." Jade touched her lip and her nose as she spoke. Jade knew what disgust looked like. She spent a lot of time schooling it off her face when she was hit on.

Callie thought about it. "I'm going to have to watch that again."

"Plus, whenever the doctor stands too close to her, she moves back."

"I never noticed that," Henri mused.

Jade nodded. "She's totally not into it."

They chatted for a bit longer before heading back to their respective jobs; Henri to reception, Callie to the library and Jade to Counter-Magic.

Just before Jade sat down at her desk to get back to work she used a bit of magic to lob a paperclip at Daniel, clipping him lightly in the back of the head.

"What was that for?"

"You're about to owe me your eternal gratitude," Jade said.

"Eternity is a long time."

"Okay then weekly gratitude and maybe some coffee. Henri's going to try to get you to booty yoga this week. Day after tomorrow at seven. Make plans with someone else or suffer the consequences."

Daniel frowned. "What the hell is booty yoga?"

"I've no idea but, apparently, I'm going to find out. Save yourself."

He nodded, already pulling out his phone and texting someone to make plans, she assumed. "Someday they'll sing songs about this act of friendship."

"I'm a peach. I know."

Jade settled back into work, stopping only to grab something from the cafeteria for her lunch and eating at her desk, for which her keyboard suffered mercilessly. She used a quick air spell to blast out the crumbs that she lost under the keys, but couldn't get a lonely staple out from underneath the 'CTRL' button. She didn't have enough finesse with the magic to focus that finely. Yet. She was determined to keep at it. She'd get it. Someday.

At the end of the day, her boss, Josef, came out of his office and headed straight for her cube. Jade immediately checked that all browser tabs she had opened earlier looking at boots and some leggings were closed and the only programs she had up were email, word processing and link in to the Coven library database. Not a shopping tab in sight.

"Jade, I was hoping to ask you a favor."

With his impressive height, he towered over her even when she was standing, and she was five-ten. While she sat at her desk, she felt a little like Alice in Wonderland - looking way up after taking the 'drink me' shrinking potion. Josef was one of those super fit older guys - like a Patrick Stewart or Clint Eastwood type. Tall and lean. But he wasn't one of those men that used his bulk to loom over people. Jade never felt that he was trying to bully her with his size or his attitude. In fact, she was surprised by how comfortable working with him was. She really liked the vibe he put out. He'd asked for her specifically to join Counter-Magic after she'd decided to stay with the Coven. She'd never officially asked him why, but Paris had indicated that Josef had said he got a 'good feeling' off Jade and was impressed with her power.

"Uh, sure," she said, feeling a little nervous. She liked Josef, but when your boss asked you a favor, was saying 'no' ever an option? She was pretty sure she would be committed to whatever he wanted before he even asked.

"Most witches have never had a chance to see a familiar in person. I was wondering if you would bring your lizard by the Coven."

"Bruce?" she asked inanely, as if she had more than one lizard. "You mean for a show and tell?"

Josef nodded. "If you're both okay with it."

Jade shrugged. "I guess so." She had a horrible thought. She'd have to ask for a ride from someone. There was no way she'd be able to get Bruce on the bus. It was too crowded in the morning and he'd get stepped on. Or squished. Or he'd hiss and spit at people. "Oh crap," she muttered.

"Problem?"

Jade waved her hand. "Uh, just logistics. But, yeah, I'm sure I can bring him in. And then just… show him around?"

"If that's okay by you. I didn't get a chance to learn much about him while he was here briefly before," Josef said, which was a nice way of putting it. When Jade had rescued Bruce from the sewer, he'd been stuck in a pipe, causing a magical kind of blockage. Jade happened to be the witch that freed him and he sort of imprinted on her, breaking away from Josef and Counter-Magic and finding his way to Jade's cottage. He'd been there ever since. "I understand he's fairly tame?" Josef asked.

Jade nodded. "Definitely. He sleeps in the house, eats crumbs from the table. He's kind of like a dog. Except he can do magic." She paused for a moment to consider. "And he spits. And hisses. And sometimes flips up his lizard collar." She made flapping motions around her neck to illustrate. "Plus, you know. Really big lizard."

Josef seemed amused by her descriptions. "Well, I think the other witches in the Coven would really appreciate a chance to see a familiar close up and maybe interact with him. And you. Both of you."

Jade nodded slowly. She wasn't an idiot. She knew she wasn't a favorite around the Coven, no matter how Josef was trying to phrase it. "I'll bring him by. Any particular day you were thinking?"

"No, whenever works for you and your familiar."

"Bruce."

"Pardon?"

"That's his name. Bruce."

Daniel poked his head around the cubicle. "Because he's green and gets angry. Bruce Banner."

"Cubicle etiquette dictates that you pretend not to be hearing this conversation," Josef said dryly.

"But then how would we all learn all the gossip we do and spread it around?" Daniel asked with a wicked grin.

Josef turned back to Jade. "I appreciate you agreeing to bring him. "

"No problem," Jade said.

Josef headed back to his office and Jade turned to Daniel.

"Hey, think my lizard will fit in your back seat?"

CHAPTER TWO

Prior to resetting Coven magic, if Paris had been asked how his Coven would respond to the challenge of learning a new norm, he would have said he was sure they would handle it with grace, diligence and strength of character.

He truly hadn't expected this level of complaint. Or, if he were honest, bitching. It made him question whether he was the right person for the job of leading the Coven. This was another instance of what was becoming a trend. He was continually being surprised by the actions and reactions of his Coven members.

He didn't regret resetting Coven magic to Jade's natural resonance. Indeed, he hadn't had a choice. The spell Dex cast on the entirety of the Coven had warped its usual tone and when Dex's spell had been broken, Paris had acted in the moment - wanting to immediately to bring it back in alignment with working, functioning magic. It just happened at the time that Jade's magic had been the only magic working. He hadn't had another option. He wished the rest of the Coven realized that.

It would do more harm than good to toss the latest reports from Counter-Magic and Research and Development into the fireplace, but the idea was certainly tempting. Although Josef personally had little problem with Jade's magic, his department, Counter-Magic, was facing significant workload issues with all the incidents reported from the other witches of the Coven. No one seemed to be adjusting quickly or easily to the shift in the balance. Witches who primarily used Earth spells found their magic sluggish. Those who used Fire found it too responsive, likely due to Jade's own proficiency with it. Those who used scrying, psychomanteum and tarot said their results were unpredictable and confusing. Those who used Water were dismally desperate; they couldn't get a thing to work, finding their spell work collapsing around them. While Counter-Magic took calls for magic that needed work or fixing, the incident log had recently turned into some sort of complaint line, with witches calling or emailing in only to protest the new magic, even when they were able to make their spells work.

Paris wasn't sure if he should issue a formal statement or not. He would *not* be resetting Coven magic. At the moment, he had no way of knowing if he could get it back to the way it had been before. He could be trading one problem for another. Additionally, he found his own spell work... interesting, now that it lined up with Jade's magic. He'd always been powerful, but now it seemed like there was something… more. Something else, just beyond his reach. He'd always known he could be doing more powerful spells, if only he had the time to study and research them. But now, he felt as though they were just out of the corner of his eye. Waiting patiently for him to turn his head and catch sight of them.

Paris didn't consider himself power hungry nor a vain man, but there was certainly something alluring about the new Coven magic. It was no wonder Jade was so cocky in her power and so sure of trying new spells if she felt this way all the time. Hannah had mentioned her own magic hadn't felt so fresh in years. She was quite sorry leaving the Coven to head back to her Council duties, wistfully waxing on about all the magic she'd not done in years but was itching to try again with the new 'normal.'

The desk phone ringing distracted him from his thoughts and he pushed them away, turning his mind back to Coven business.

"Paris, here."

"Paris, it's Josef."

"Good morning. How are things in Counter-Magic?"

"Mostly the usual. I've got a couple of kids that ended up turning themselves blue. Not sure if it's the new magic or if it's just kids and their spell work being shoddy. No serious damage. The parents have decided to let it wear off on its own as a lesson to the kids. Although one of the fathers wants Counter-Magic to get involved, claiming it must be because of the magic reset. It's winter season picture time in school and I think his son is a bit of a prince-type. Raising hell complaining about his pictures being ruined."

"What are your thoughts?"

"That family is... difficult. The kid needs some blue-faced pictures in his life. Might sort him out a bit."

Paris smiled wryly, hearing Josef's chuckle over the phone. "I remember having to wait out a spell gone bad that turned one of my eyes lazy. Horrid six weeks."

Josef laughed even louder. "I remember that. Your mother would come into the Coven offices every day and tell us what you'd run into - poles, animals, other witches."

Paris groaned in embarrassment. That was the problem when your mother had been Coven Leader before you - everyone knew you as a child and still remembered all your infractions.

"She'd been absolutely adamant that it recover on its own and wouldn't let me wear an eye-patch to cover it up. I still have the scar from the stitches I needed from when I accidentally tripped over that rabid dog."

"If I remember correctly, that rabid dog was a twelve-pound schnauzer."

"It was fourteen pounds and their claws can be quite sharp if not kept well," Paris mused. "But, I assume you're not calling to discuss some truant schoolchildren. What can I do for you this morning, Josef?"

Josef sighed and Paris could feel the tone of the conversation change. "Well, I'm getting more complaints."

"You're Counter-Magic. There are always complaints. Spells gone awry, spells overlapping where they shouldn't, spells not working correctly. But you don't generally call me about them."

"No. No, I don't. These complaints are about the lake."

Paris felt his good humor drain out, replaced by slight confusion. The lake area in the Nature Preserve was well-known among the Coven, or perhaps 'notorious' was a better description. An accident years ago had left the area magically tainted. The lake had previously been a popular picnic and recreation spot, but after the accident, many of the Coven's witches abandoned it, feeling as though the area had been corrupted or changed. Some witches wouldn't work magic anywhere near the area, some witches *couldn't*. Most complained of an 'off' or 'spoiled' sensation and gave the area a wide berth. Other alternate areas had become popular in the Nature Preserve as a result and now the lake area tended to be abandoned year-round. It was something Coven witches never had to clarify when speaking. All they had to say was 'the lake' and everyone understood.

"What sort of complaints?"

"Witches out in the woods for nature walks or spell casting are feeling 'weirded out' further out from the lake than usual. Spells not working in some parts of the Preserve that used to be okay. Then, just recently, the kindergarten class was out last week doing a nature walk. It was one of the nicer days and we don't get many of those this time of year. A few of the kids started crying and wouldn't stop until they left. That led to some parents heading out and noticing more power in the area than usual."

"Power?" asked Paris. "People don't usually get a sense of power from the area. A bad vibration or sensation maybe. But power usually is indicative of working magic."

"I know."

Paris paused for a moment, choosing his wording carefully. "These complaints must be serious if they've reached you." The accident in the lake area had involved Josef's family. Over the years, it had become customary for witches to be cautious around him and make an effort not to mention any discomfort the lake area caused.

"Yeah," Josef said, his tone regretful. "To be fair, I think Daniel was keeping a log of all the complaints and was going to investigate it himself, but after the kindergarten kids, it was hard to keep a lid on it. Also, I think more people feel uncomfortable talking to me about it than I actually feel myself."

"I think most people just want to be respectful of your loss and not remind you unnecessarily of it."

"I'm sure that's true, but it's not like I ever forget about it."

"No, I'm sure you don't." Paris shifted in his chair. "I understand of course if you'd rather pass this along to someone else. I can certainly ask one of the other Department heads to investigate this for you. Perhaps transfer someone temporarily to work on it."

"I appreciate the offer, but that's not why I called."

Paris blinked, taking in Josef's words. "Oh, I see. If not that, then is there another problem?"

"The problem is, I think the issue at the lake has something to do with Jade."

"Jade?" Paris repeated. "I'm afraid I don't follow."

"Well," Josef began, dragging the word out slightly. "The complaints coming in say the disturbances at the lake feel like her magic."

Paris was glad he was on the phone and not in person because he was certain the look on his face was less than professional. "I've just reset Coven magic to Jade's power. I'm sure everything feels like her magic at this point. It's an adjustment and I understand witches are struggling, but I'm positive this change will prove good for us."

Josef chuckled in his ear. "No need to sell me the party line. I've been a Coven member for years and worked for your mother before you. I recognize the buzz words when I hear them."

Paris' lips curled slightly at the older man's tone. "That bad, huh?"

"You might have gotten some younger ones with that speech, but this isn't my first rodeo."

"I suppose not. So, I take it then this is *not* just the Coven adjusting to the new norm."

"I don't think so," Josef answered. "If it were just the complaints about magic in general feeling 'off,' then I would be inclined to agree with you - the Coven needs time to adjust. But it's not just complaints about magic. It's complaints about the lake area and the Coven doesn't really have a reason to attribute anything in that area to Jade."

"Other than the fact that Jade stopped Dex out in the Preserve," Paris interrupted and then wanted to chastise himself. As Coven Leader, he was supposed to remain neutral. Thankfully, Josef was an older Coven member and wasn't perturbed by Paris' outburst.

"You're correct - Jade did do some magic out in the Preserve to stop Dex. But unless I'm mistaken, not in the vicinity of the lake."

Paris paused. Josef was completely correct. While Paris and Jade had travelled out into the Preserve to work on some of her magic skills, and Jade had stopped Dex's attempt to re-cast a Hex on the Coven out in the forest, she'd not been around the lake area when she'd done it. In fact, when Paris had brought Jade out to the Preserve to work on her magic, Jade had felt a strong aversion to the lake area - much further out than Coven witches generally felt anything.

"No, you're not mistaken. Jade wasn't at the lake area when she stopped Dex. She was further north."

"That and the reaction of the children. While the adults in the Coven may have some issues with their magic being reset to a new norm, the kids aren't likely to have the same problems. They're usually still figuring out their powers and it's all new to them. They may hear things from their parents, but I don't think overhearing gossip and grousing is likely to make them burst into tears."

Feeling the need to play devil's advocate, Paris hedged, "They could still be reacting to something they heard."

"They could," Josef agreed. "But I don't think so and neither do you."

"No," Paris said quietly. "No, I don't."

There was a silence over the phone for a moment before Josef said, "I can head out there and check it myself, if you like."

Paris felt a fondness swell in his chest for the older man. Josef had avoided the lake area for years. While Paris couldn't be absolutely certain, he didn't think Josef had been back to the lake since the accident that led to a death in his family.

"I heartily appreciate the offer, but that won't be necessary. I think given the circumstances and the likelihood of this somchow being tied to Jade, I should head out there myself and see what I can learn."

"I can send Daniel. I know as Coven Leader you don't have a lot of free time to go gallivanting around in the Preserve. He's one of my best and if there is anything… sensitive out there, he'll be quiet about it."

Paris smiled at Josef's kind offer and tone. "I'll keep that in mind, but I think for now, I should handle this. I'll let you know what I find out. But, I would appreciate it if you could set up some perimeter spells - you or one of your agents. Just to monitor the area."

"I'll try, but I'm not sure if they'll work. Sakkara already set some powerful wards in the area. I was wondering if something about this was causing them all to fail."

Paris paused at the mention of his mother's name. "I don't recall that. I don't recall that at all."

"I'm not surprised. You were young when the incident at the lake happened."

"I think I was eight or nine. Old enough to remember," Paris replied. Additionally, his mother often took him with her when she did magic for the Coven, wanting him to learn by example and watching. "What sort of wards? I've never felt anything like her magic out there."

"If I understood correctly, Sakkara set them to neutralize some of the bad energy surrounding the area. Her own magical essence was probably cancelled out in the process. I doubt if anyone from the Coven gets a sense of her magic at all out there. I'm worried that with the Coven starting to sense Jade's magic out there, she's somehow nullifying your mother's wards. Or maybe your mother's wards have finally failed. It has been years."

"Yes, her magic was strong, but it wouldn't be indefinite. I had no idea she'd set anything out there."

"She was very kind after everything that happened," Josef said, his voice soft and a little faraway. "She really tried to help my family and stopped by often. But…well, you know how it all went."

Paris knew enough to know that there really wasn't anything to say to make the passing of loved ones easier, not even years after the fact. "I hope she was able to offer some comfort."

"She tried," Josef said amicably, and Paris recognized it for what it was - an acknowledgement of the act, but a statement that during grief, not much can help.

"I know you have some of her spell books in Counter-Magic. Perhaps if you sort through those, I'll go through her other grimoires and we can try to find the wards she used. If they held up for this long, perhaps all we'll need to do is reset them."

"Sure," Josef agreed. "I'll look through the indices for them. Although," his voice turned fond. "I must say, with all of our magic resonating at Jade's frequency, it might not work."

"You don't sound too upset about that," Paris said.

"Well, she's a firecracker for sure. And I admit, this new frequency makes me feel a little bouncy and young. My magic hasn't felt like this since I was a teenager."

Paris found himself smiling at Josef's tone. "No problems with your own magic then?"

"Oh, a little tweaking here and there, but I've not had any major problems. Certainly nothing like the rest of the Coven. I'm really enjoying it actually. It's like a puzzle."

This time Paris laughed. "Well, that's why you're the right man for Counter-Magic, I suppose. All right, I'll plan a trip out to the Preserve and look through the spell books of my mother's that I have. I'll check in with you if I learn anything."

They exchanged a few more casual pleasantries, rounding out the conversation. Despite the light note it ended on, Paris felt uneasy when he hung up the phone. Everything seemed to circle back to Jade. And his mother.

It wasn't like Paris to avoid problems and yet that's exactly what he'd been doing. He'd avoided thinking about what he'd seen after Jade stopped Dex. Jade stopped Dex from re-casting a spell on the entire Coven by using a large amount of her power and siphoning some of his. Immediately after, she'd had fallen to the ground, dazed and confused. When she'd looked at Paris, he had the notion that she didn't know who he was. Her eyes, normally a clear, distinct grey color, had been a bright, vibrant green. Paris had no idea what it meant.

Of course, a witch changing her eye-color was a knock-off spell - something young witches did for fun, the same as putting on new clothes or trying out eyeliner. But when it had happened, Jade had been in no condition to be tossing out frivolous spells. She'd just managed a rather significant demon hex against Dex, attempting to bind his magic. There was no reason for her eyes to have changed color, no matter how quickly they shifted back.

There was one other thing that kept him lying awake nights, worrying. When Dex had been fighting with Jade, Dex had tried a blood spell on her, a named blood spell, and it hadn't worked. When Paris had found them, Dex had been yelling at Jade, enraged. He shouted it should have worked because Dex used Jade's real name, Lily.

Jade answered that 'Lily' had never been her name. Which meant she lied to Paris. Jade told him 'Lily' had been her name and she changed it when she was twenty-one. She'd been somewhat defensive at the time, claiming Paris could look up the paperwork if he liked. Paris never told Jade that he had investigated her claim and he'd seen the legal paperwork that officially changed her name. Either Jade lied to Paris, or she lied to Dex. But why?

It was also the *way* Jade had answered Dex. 'It was never *my* name,' she'd said, with the slightest emphasis on the word 'my.' Paris wondered if he'd made the emphasis up and had even gone so far as to use a memory spell to bring the moment back, so that he could observe it as a third party. He saw Jade, on the ground, inside a magic circle of flames. Dex off to one side, spitting out a blood curse and then turning ugly and deranged as it didn't work.

"That's your name, your real name. I read your file. Your name used to be Lily."

"It was never my *name."*

At the crux of his avoidance was that Paris wasn't sure what to do about it. He needed to know if there was something about her that would affect the Coven as a whole, but his instinct was that if he pushed Jade, she'd back herself right out of the Coven altogether. In his mind, when he thought of her inclusion in the Coven, he sometimes saw her as a lean, hungry coyote, circling a warm fire where there might be food. Wary and timid, but fierce -

ready to attack if threatened. Paris couldn't afford to have Jade leave the Coven. The Supernatural Council, made up of all types of magical and supernatural creatures, demanded witches be tied to a Coven. Witches could leave the Coven proper and live further away, but they could still only perform sanctioned magic and usually had familial or other ties to the Coven. A sort of long-distance Coven relationship. If Jade left, Paris had no doubt she'd sever ties to the Coven. She had no real ties as of yet. The problem was, Jade wouldn't be able to keep from practicing magic. She had too much power to simply turn it off. Even if she tried, it would start bleeding out from her - which was how they'd found her in the first place - hemorrhaging magic out because it had no where else to go.

He knew he needed to talk to Jade about all this, but first he wanted to gather more information. He just wasn't sure how to go about it. As of yet, he hadn't mentioned any of this to Hannah to seek her guidance or advice. He felt as though this was something more personal and sensitive. He didn't want anyone else to know and he also couldn't keep running to Hannah when there was a problem with the Coven. While she'd provided invaluable guidance when he first became Coven Leader, it was at the point where he needed to pull away and be the Coven Leader his mother had always groomed him to be.

His mother was another point of contention. Paris didn't like that he kept learning new things about her. To be sure, no child ever really knew everything about their parents. Children often think they are the only things in their parents' worlds but that's never the case. They have lives and responsibilities outside of their children, to which children are not privy. However, Paris had thought that he was more in tune with his mother because of her role as Coven Leader and how she included him in what she did in order to pass the role to him.

As a child, his mother always had a sort of frankness with him. He was sure other parents and adults may have thought her cruel at times with her honesty, but he remembered being relieved and reassured by her bluntness and truth. One of the things she was famous for saying was that nothing could surprise her more than the fact Paris wasn't born a woman. Coven Leaders tended to be female and, unless something unusual happened, it was a hereditary position passed down from mother to daughter. When Paris had been born, the Coven assumed this was one of those unusual happenstances and the position of Coven Leader would finally leave Sakkara's family and be passed along to someone else. However, Paris' first and only tarot card reading, at seven, indicated he *would* be Coven Leader. After that, Paris began accompanying his mother on Coven business, and would often do his homework in the very office that was now his at the Covenstead. Thinking back of all the time he was with his mother, he'd thought, naively he supposed, that he knew all there was to know about her.

Then Jade found the demon grimoires in his house. Spell books hidden there for years that he'd never known about, with a letter inside from his mother.

'I'm sure you'll think less of me knowing I practiced demon magic. All I can say is, I did what needed to be done. My intentions were always the best, even if my methods were not.'

Now, finding out his mother had set wards at the lake was a little thing, a minor thing, but it bothered Paris that he hadn't known. He'd been to the lake area including just recently with Jade. He'd never gotten any sense of his mother's magic while out there. He'd thought himself rather attuned to her magic, his own being similar to hers. He didn't like that he'd been unaware of her wards. It made him wonder what other magic she'd done of which he wasn't aware.

His first order of business should be to head out to the Preserve and see if he could determine if her wards were failing and if not, then perhaps gain some knowledge about the 'bad' feeling witches were getting from the area.

But before that, Paris wanted to see Jade.

#

Jade configured her demon locks to let Paris in, but it didn't mean he was completely immune to or ignorant of their presence. He paused at the foot of the stone pathway that led up to her cottage, feeling the press of them. As he stepped forward, they shifted and shirred, letting him by. They felt slower than he was used to, sluggish. He didn't have long to consider it before the front door opened and Jade stood there, waiting for him. She was in casual clothes, although to be honest, he'd only once seen her in something other than jeans and a shirt and that had been at the Coven Ball where formal attire was required. He remembered that she'd seemed somewhat awkward and stilted in her shiny, silver dress, absently tugging on the thigh-length hem as if she could make it longer if only she gave it enough tugs. He hadn't thought it was too short, but he did wonder how she managed to walk in her sky-high heels. Tonight she was barefoot as she stood in the doorway, her bright pink toenails and the faint scent of nail polish broadcasting what she'd been up to.

"I felt the locks announce you," she said by way of greeting, her toes wiggled slightly as she spoke.

"They feel different," he replied, coming up the final steps and standing in front of her, pausing in the doorway.

She frowned. "I thought it was just me. You feel it too? It's like they're... unsure?"

"I don't get that much of a sense of them. More like slow."

"Hmm." Her toes curled under bit. "I'm not sure what that means. They've felt off lately and I don't know if..."

"What?" he prompted when she trailed off.

Jade shook her head. "Nothing. Come on in."

The scent of her magic was thick in the house and he'd no doubt that while catching her at the end of her pedicure, he'd also caught her in the middle of some spell work. Jade's magic had a scent of cloves and some kind of flower he couldn't identify. Not lavender, nor roses - those he would recognize. This was something else - floral but sweet. Not cloying, only just... there.

"Casting spells?" he asked as he doffed his shoes and hung his coat up on her coat rack.

She looked a little sheepish and he wondered what exactly she'd been practicing. "Uh, yeah. But I don't know if it will work."

"Would you like me to take a look at it?"

Her fingertips twitched at her side and she glanced toward the coffee table where he could see some spell books laid out. "Maybe."

A set of thumping footsteps drew Paris' attention to the stairs and Bruce came barreling down, his long body almost forcing him tail over head as he ran enthusiastically down the treads. He knocked into Paris' legs, sending Paris stumbling back a few steps.

"Bruce! Company!" Jade chastised, seeming embarrassed at his display.

"That's all right, I don't mind," Paris answered. He bent over and pet Bruce a few times on the head. "Hello, Bruce. It's good to see you as well."

Bruce's tongue flicked out, hitting Paris quickly on the hand, leaving a small, damp spot. Paris managed to wait until Bruce turned his face to look up at Jade before discretely wiping his hand on his pant leg. Though he was fond of the creature, he didn't like the wet feeling Bruce's tongue left behind.

"So, what kind of spell are you working on?" Paris tried to keep his tone light, casual. Jade was prone to trying demon magic and although she was quite good at it, demon magic still gave him a wrong-bad feeling. He'd had years of hearing his mother caution against it - paradoxical given what turned out to be her propensity for and skill with it. He casually sniffed the air again but didn't scent anything demon-like. He could smell only cloves, peppermint and something spicy. He sent his magic out, like feelers in the air, circling.

Jade turned around at him sharply before she sat down on the sofa. "It's not demon magic."

"I didn't say anything."

"Please. I can feel your magic checking the area out." She motioned in the air with her hands. From the coffee table, she grabbed the spell book she'd been using, holding it up for him to see the cover. "It's from this book."

Paris glanced at the cover quickly, happy to see it was a primary level spell book from the library. She handed it over to him, flipping it open to the spell in question - a spell to calm dreams. He could see why the smell of cloves was so strong. Not only was it the scent of Jade's magic, but the spell called for five whole ones. He also noted cardamom, peppermint oil, salt and some candles. He glanced down at the table and saw she had large quantities of everything, far more than the spell called for.

"Planning on casting it for the entire Coven?" he asked, eyeing what she had out.

Jade looked bashful. "No, but... more is more, right?"

"Not always."

"But if less is more, just think how much more 'more' will be," Jade said, a faint joking tone in her voice - forced and slightly hollow.

"Are you having problems sleeping?"

Her shoulders slumped. "Sort of. I just... I thought... I hoped that I could cast some magic to help me just sleep more peacefully."

"Are you restless or are you having nightmares?"

She stilled at his question and he immediately worried. He'd only been asking casually due to the nature of the spell, but her body went tense and she leaned slightly away from him.

"Maybe a little of both."

Paris nodded. "I see. And have you tried this spell before?"

"No. I didn't really think about trying something till this morning. But I don't know. Maybe it's a bad idea."

Jade moved forward like she was going to start cleaning up the supplies.

"No, no," he said, holding a hand out to stop her. "If you're feeling... troubled at night, let's try this spell together and see if it helps."

She sagged a bit. "I tried it twice already, but it just... doesn't feel like it's working?" She fiddled with the salamander charm, running it back and forth along the chain like a nervous tick. "I mean, I normally get some kind of... ping?" Her eyes looked at him for confirmation and he nodded. He knew what she meant. When a spell worked, it aligned with a witch's personal magic, and it felt like it 'set' in place. Jade continued. "But I haven't got that. Or maybe it's more like there's a ping, but it's not the right one."

Paris nodded again. "Okay, give it a go with me here and I'll see if I can figure out what's wrong."

It was Jade's turn to nod and she took a deep breath, dropping her talisman back against her neck. It was slightly foolish of him, but he felt a little prideful that he always saw her wearing her talisman. He'd spent careful consideration on what he should chose for a charm for her, finally settling on a salamander. Not only was a salamander traditionally associated with fire, which Jade wielded well, it was also a symbol of courage and loyalty. Both were qualities he'd come to identify with Jade. He'd worried after he'd given it to her that she'd think it some strange trinket and put it in a drawer somewhere, never to be seen again. He'd yet to see her without it.

Jade picked up a white candle from her coffee table and lit it, placing it in a large candleholder that was adorned with a generous saucer to catch the wax drippings and hold the other ingredients. She took the mint oil and added a few drops to the saucer, then some salt, then a few of the cloves and then finally she crushed a cardamom pod and scooped the seeds out with her fingernail, flicking her fingertips three times to land them in the saucer. There were words for the spell, but she didn't need to glance at the book Paris was holding. With her near perfect recall for printed matter, she'd only had to read the words once to have them well memorized.

Paris felt her magic coil about her, like an eager puppy waiting for its master to throw a ball. Despite what she'd said about it not working, when Jade finished the words and sent her magic out to the ingredients, Paris fully expected the spell to take hold. She'd done everything well; all her ingredients were of good quality and her magic was focused and even.

However, it was as though her magic glanced off the ingredients and shot off on an angle. There was a sort of resonance, as she'd indicated, but nothing like the spell should have given off.

Jade turned hopeful and expectant eyes on him. "Well?"

"I don't know," Paris admitted. "I thought it would work."

"Ugh," she moped. "This is such a bust."

Paris looked down at the spell book again, reading over the ingredients and the words. He picked up each of her ingredients, checking the manufacturing dates and giving them all a little sniff to see if there was anything amiss. Jade had completed everything correctly, and it was a beginner level spell. She wasn't reaching beyond her knowledge. Given her proficiency with everything else, this should have been a simple task for her.

Setting all the ingredients back down, he took one more deep inhale, trying to get the overall scent of the spell. As he did, he caught the scent of something else. Vanilla. He looked down at her table and found none.

"Do you have any other candles or that wick-less wax? The scented kind?"

"No, should I? I thought those were bad and they messed up spell work. I only buy the kind you suggested - the plain, natural ones. I think this one's even organic." Jade pointed at the candle in front of her.

"What about your perfume?"

She shook her head. "I'm not wearing any today. I can get the kind I use though, if you want to see it."

"Does it have vanilla in it?"

Jade pursed her lips. "I don't think so. Wait, let me google it." She pulled her smart phone out and tapped quickly. "No. Currant, apple, jasmine, moss, oh, wait it says vanilla is an undertone."

Paris shook his head. "I thought I smelled vanilla around the magic. Your perfume would likely have to be primarily vanilla for me to smell that, unless you spray it all around," he said wryly.

"Not at the price I pay for it."

He sniffed the air again, but this time couldn't find the faint scent of vanilla.

Paris checked over the book again. As the head librarian, if Callie got a number of complaints about spells in a book not working, or being 'bad' or configured incorrectly, she would often make small notes inside the cover, warning the next person who checked the book out. Paris didn't see any of Callie's careful, and no doubt archival safe, markings.

"Let me see if I can cast it."

Jade blew the candle out and handed it to him, unlit, with a soft cotton cloth for him to use to wipe it down to 'rinse' off any residual magic. She took the candelabra into the kitchen and he could hear her washing it, also ridding it of any lingering charm. By the time she came back with it, clean and dry, he had set the book open in front of him and had his ingredients ready. He took a calming breath and then worked the spell.

Right as he was saying the last words, he felt it. There was something pushing against his magic, testing it, checking it. But it didn't feel malevolent. It felt inquisitive and cautious. He reached out his own magic to test it back and felt it scurry away - like a spooked deer in the forest. He finished the spell, feeling it 'click' into place.

Jade fell back against the sofa, discouraged. "I can tell that worked for you. What a bust. I must be doing it wrong."

"Hmmm." Paris said, leaning forward and blowing out the candle. He wasn't sure that was the problem. What he'd sensed from the magic testing his was that, once it realized it wasn't Jade working the spell, it backed off, content to let Paris cast the spell on himself.

Someone was keeping Jade from working the spell. Someone Paris must know - the brush of magic was familiar. He couldn't quite place it, but he was positive he knew it. He was equally positive it knew him in return. Another mystery involving one of his Coven members and Jade. He schooled his expression into his best neutral Coven Leader face.

"Why don't we try something else for tonight and what we can get to work?"

"Yeah, okay." He could tell by her tone and expression that she was disappointed. She brightened up for a moment. "Oh, there was one in there for making your own runes. I've collected some rocks and gotten some stones. Maybe we could try that?"

He smiled. "That's an excellent choice to add to your repertoire."

"Okay, let me go grab my stuff."

As she ran upstairs, Bruce, who'd been waiting outside in the foyer, sidled into the room coming to stand on his short, squat legs in front of Paris. He looked up at Paris expectantly, like he was waiting for something.

"Can I help you, Bruce?"

"Pfffft." Bruce's tongue flicked out and then he looked pointedly toward the kitchen.

"I'm sorry, I don't understand." Paris felt a little silly talking to Bruce, but he did seem to have some sort of intelligence, albeit an animal one.

Bruce made the 'pffft' sound again and tossed his head. This time his glare was more accusing. Paris was about to ask him another question when Jade came back in with some bags.

"Bruce, leave Paris alone. Go sit in front of the fireplace." As she spoke, a fire lit up in the hearth. It appeared that although someone was blocking Jade from the dream spell, nothing was blocking her from casting fire. The flames lit up easily, and Paris sensed nothing amiss in the magic - the essence of Jade's power was clear and strong.

Jade knelt on the ground and pushed all the previous spell casting materials off to one side before dumping out a bag of rocks and stones on the wooden coffee table with some indelible markers in varying colors and some spray sealant from the craft store. Paris picked up some of the rocks she had, rolling them over in his hands.

"These are quite nice," he said, picking up a few more. "Where are they from?"

"Some are from the Preserve, some are just from around the Coven and some I already had. We've always liked rocks. Had a bit of a collection." She was smiling as she spoke, setting out the rocks in a line on the table and pulling out the spell book that had the instructions for making the runes.

Paris rolled the stones in his hand. These ones must have been part of her collection. They had a strong sense of 'Jade' about them.

"Who's 'we?'"

Jade stilled, the smile fading from her face. "Oh, I don't know why I said that. I meant me. I've always liked rocks."

Paris nodded even though she didn't look up at him to see him do it. "I see," he said lowly. He was glad he'd taken the time to come over tonight. Between her wanting to cast a spell for her dreams, the spell not working and her words, it would appear that he should be spending more time with Jade. Something was amiss, he just wasn't sure what.

Watching her now, she seemed like she was waiting for him to push her more on what she just said. She was fiddling with the rocks, shifting them in their line up needlessly, swapping their places. He put the stones he'd been holding down.

"All right, let's see what instructions you've gathered for your rune making."

He saw her shoulders relax and even though he knew he was only putting off the inevitable, he was glad that he could help her with this simple task tonight.

CHAPTER THREE

With the frequency of her nightmares and the failure of the dream spell, Jade knew she could expect a nightmare that night. It took a long time for her to fall asleep, a coil of dread settling in her stomach while she lay in bed. But, the body needed rest, whether the brain wanted it or not. Jade knew she would eventually fall asleep. She had no desire to try and push the limit of how long she could go without sleep. Like most former post secondary students, she'd already played that game. Eventually, sleep won. Paris stayed, helping her with her runes, until about nine. She'd laughed, watching him get indelible marker on his fingers. Then when he helped her take the rocks outside to set with the craft spray, he'd been like a child in an arts and crafts class - careful, but slightly awkward. Of course, he'd come back into his element when it was time to cast the protection spell on the runes - magical charms that would keep them from soaking up negative energy. Jade had no problems with those little spells and it had been both a relief and an annoyance. She was glad she could still cast new spells, but disappointed she couldn't get the dream protection charm to work.

After Paris left, cleaning up from the rune making had taken time and Jade stayed up to put a load of laundry through the washer and into the dryer. She still hadn't gone back to her apartment to get her things and doing laundry had to be a regular occurrence or she ran out of underwear and socks. She was dragging her heels about going back to her apartment. With everything that had happened since she came to the Coven, she just wasn't sure if she was ready to sever that link to her old life.

Finally falling into a dream was almost a release - like hearing a second shoe fall, or the instant right after you'd been dreading a hiccup and you'd had it, before your body realized it meant you still had the spasmodic problem. The dream, like most of Jade's recent dreams, involved the Preserve, or more specifically, the lake. Jade sometimes felt that when she thought of the lake, it should be capitalized. The Lake. She'd never liked water, never learned to swim. Lily knew how and had gone a few times. Jade made sure she was far, far away when that happened, retreating deeply into their shared mind. It was almost like sleeping. Almost.

But since Jade had gone to the Preserve with Paris and passed by the lake, she found herself dreaming of it more and more. Sometimes in her dream, she only walked by it - getting an ominous and looming feeling. Sometimes she got close, standing a few feet away. Sometimes, like today, if she were any closer, she feared she'd be in it.

Underwater.

Jade stood on the dock that jutted out from the shore. She'd never seen the lake in person. She and Paris had only started heading in the general direction of it before Jade had been overcome by a sick, heavy feeling, her upper lip breaking out in a cold sweat. She'd made him stop and they'd not returned. It wasn't like she'd been avoiding the area. Paris had taken her into the Preserve to work on her magic and at one point, he had thought they could go to the lake to work on her water magic, which was dismal at best. Having been 'distracted' by stopping Dex, they hadn't gone back. Jade admitted, she was dreading Paris bringing it up. She didn't want to go back to the lake. But she wasn't sure if she wanted to say it out loud and have Paris ask why. She made sure to have other spells and charms she wanted to work on when they got together.

But now, in her dreams, like many of them before, the lake was in front of her. The dock swayed and swung slightly beneath her feet and she kept her knees soft in order to move with it. In her dream it wasn't winter, like it was now at the Coven - it was spring. The trees were bare, but if she squinted, she could make out small buds cropping up on the branches, tiny dots of green against the dark bark. A flock of birds poured out of a tree, their shapes black spots against the sky. Sparrows, though Jade wasn't sure how she knew that. One of them swooped close and perched on her shoulder, as if she were some kind of fairytale maiden, lost in the woods.

Breathing in, the air had the smell of crisp promise that comes in the spring, different from the sharp cold that was winter. But the water... the water would be cold, so cold. Jade doubted the lake ever truly got all that warm. It was too deep. She had a sense of its depth from where she stood on the dock. Peering down at the surface of the lake, she could imagine it stretching far below. The deeper it went, the colder it got. She could see her reflection in the water - wavy and jumbled - distorted by the uneven surface of the water. She looked closer. There was something wrong with her reflection. Something not right. She bent over, teetering on the dock. There was something over her shoulder. There was something behind her. No. Not something, someone.

Before she could shout or move, she felt hands at her shoulders and she was falling. The water so cold, she involuntarily gasped when she hit it. She choked on it, sputtering and resurfacing to get another breath. But there was a shape above her. Was it Lily? Jade could just barely make out long, dark, hair and only the impression of a face. Surrounding the face was a flock of birds. More sparrows.

Jade awoke with a start and then yelped, jumping a step backward as she found herself in her bathroom, standing in front of the mirror instead of safely tucked her bed. She'd woken up in the closet before but she'd never woken up anywhere other than the bedroom. She heard a loud thumping and turned just as Bruce came stampeding to the open doorway of the bathroom, hovering at the entrance. He looked around and spat three times. Not seeing any threats, he dropped his butt to the ground with a thunk. He was so long, he didn't have much of a butt to speak of and his entire lower half slouched down when he sat.

Jade looked around, trying to figure out how she'd gotten to the bathroom. She must have walked in her sleep - something she hadn't done for a long time. She looked at the mirror, taking in her too pale skin and the circles under her eyes. She looked sickly - like a vampire doomed to too long indoors.

One of her eyes flashed green for a split moment and her breath hitched. Apple green. The color of Lily's eyes. It was there and then it was gone. She stumbled back with surprise, Bruce making a 'pfffft' sound. Slowly, she moved forward, closer to the glass. She reached a hand up, touching her fingertips lightly to the mirror, the surface cold and hard under her skin. She licked her lips nervously, afraid to speak.

"Are you there?"

The glass cracked under her hand, splitting the skin on two of her fingers. She yelped, pulling her hand back in surprise and pain.

Bruce stuck his tongue out. "Pfffffft"

Jade turned to look at him. He didn't look overly concerned. Jade had seen him mad and angry before, certainly when Seth, the demon, made an appearance, but whatever was happening now, Bruce wasn't upset about it. As she looked at him though, at his luminous eyes, she thought he did seem... concerned? He blinked at her twice and then turned his head, presenting his neck, where his dry patch of skin was.

"Yeah? You're hurt too, hey?" she said, hearing the shakiness in her voice and hating it. She was dripping blood into the sink, stark red patches against the white porcelain. Jade turned the faucet on and held her fingers under the water while she rummaged around the medicine cabinet with the other hand for bandages.

"We'll be okay, buddy. Just flesh wounds."

Jade bandaged her fingers quickly, having to use several bandages to cover the round shape of her fingertips. Finger wounds were the worst. She'd have to bring bandages with her to work and change them out over the day as they got dirty or wet. Wet bandages were gross - all clammy and cold against the skin.

She shivered and pretended it was just from the thought of dealing with dirty bandages all day long and not the lingering cold from the dream. As she worked on her hands, she could see her misshapen reflection in the broken mirror - doing the same things she was doing only in reverse. A strange doppelgänger.

Had the figure in her dream been Lily? Was she back? And if so, was she angry with Jade? Jade remembered the arguments they'd been having, right before Lily disappeared. Circular, circuitous, always whirling around the same topic.

Go away, you're distracting me. It's my turn.
I don't have anywhere to go.
Just sleep. It's time you slept.

You sleep. You haven't slept in weeks.
Neither have you.

Bruce hit her leg with his tail, a solid 'whap' against her skin that jerked her out of her thoughts. She'd been standing there with the water still running, staring at blood on the white porcelain of the sink. Not a lot of blood. Not like before, when Lily left. She shut her eyes. This wasn't the time to think about this. She looked up at the small clock on the wall of her bathroom.

"You're right. I'm going to be late for work." She left the bathroom, pulling the door shut behind her, hoping it would keep her from seeing the broken mirror with her distorted reflection.

#

Given what he'd felt when Jade had been trying to cast her dream protection spell, Paris took it upon himself to cast some rudimentary protection runes over Jade's cottage as he was leaving the previous night. They were simple ones his mother had used and Jade likely wouldn't even notice them. He felt duplicitous in not telling Jade he was doing it, nor *why* he felt the need to. He felt as though he needed to gather more information first. Someone had stopped Jade from casting her dream spell, but hadn't stopped her from doing any other magic that night. That same someone hadn't stopped Paris from casting the dream spell on himself, although in the middle of Jade working on her runes, he'd gone to her kitchen under the pretense of cleaning up the spell items and tried to cast it for her and found it similarly blocked. Whoever it was, they didn't want

Jade to have a peaceful night's sleep. That was eerily disturbing to Paris.

When Jade had first come to the Coven, Paris had been shocked to discover Matthew, one of their weaker witches, had entered a demon deal to try to steal Jade's magic. After that, Paris learned about Dex and Veronica betraying not only their own Covens but Paris' as well. Paris had always believed in the cardinal rule of witches: do what you will, though it harm none. Now, he was wondering how many witches truly followed that rule and if he was naive for ever assuming it was all witches everywhere.

Paris wondered if whoever was responsible for stopping Jade was also responsible for the magical disruption out at the Preserve.

Once at the Coven the next morning, he waited until he saw Jade's icon on the internal link system light up indicating she was at her desk and online. He ran out quickly to the local coffee shop he knew she favored and ordered her a large latte - something he'd seen her order for herself once or twice. Once back at the Coven, he detoured from his office and headed toward Counter-Magic, spotting her at her desk, typing away on her keyboard.

As if sensing she was being watched, Jade looked over as he came. Her eyes immediately fixed on the two cups he was carrying.

"One of those better be for me."

"Or?" he teased, handing her the larger of the cups. Jade sniffed it once and, happy with what she smelled, took a sip. She smiled, a blissful look on her face.

"Mmmm. Cafe Crema latte. They make the best ones."

Paris took a sip of his tea latte and had to agree. It was rather good.

"To what do I owe this honor?" Jade asked, taking another drink of her latte. "Not that I'm complaining, mind you. If you want to stop by everyday with coffee, have at it. But... do you need something?"

He could see how it was completely suspect - it wasn't as though he popped by regularly with coffee. Looking around, Paris could see Daniel in Josef's office through the glass door, showing the older man something on the computer screen. Possibly reports on the Preserve area. Since no one else was close enough to Jade's cubicle, Paris felt safe in asking a direct question.

"How did you sleep last night? Any bad dreams?"

Jade fiddled with the coffee sleeve, as though it were in the wrong position, twisting it around. "Sort of."

Paris frowned. When Jade did too much magic, she would say she 'had a headache' - as though it were that simple, even though the overuse of her magic could cause her to bleed from the nose, or from the ears. He had a strong suspicion that Jade saying she had 'sort of' of bad dreams was akin to her replying that she'd had a troubled night. Watching her continue to fiddle with her coffee cup, he noticed bandages on two of her fingers.

"What happened there?"

She swallowed. "Oh, just… a minor accident. You know how it is."

"No, I don't," Paris replied, not that easily put off. "Was that last night or this morning?"

"This morning. Curling iron. It happens. Price of beauty."

Paris took in Jade's ponytail - straight as usual. He wasn't so certain she didn't at least own a curling iron, but he was fairly certain if she *did* own one, she didn't use it often. She lied so quickly and convincingly. If he hadn't been looking for anything amiss, he likely wouldn't have noticed. He wanted to press it, but didn't think that the middle of Counter-Magic was the right time.

"If you want a healing spell to help your fingers along, let me know. My mother had a wonderful poultice for burns. I think Dr. Gellar uses it in medlab, actually. Keeps infection rates low."

"Thanks, I'll keep that in mind."

"Well, I just stopped by to see how you were. I best return to my office."

"Heavy hangs the head that wears the crown, hey?"

"Just so. Please let me know if any more of your spells don't work, and come by and see if me if you want to try something new."

"You bet."

Paris wasn't at all surprised when the day passed and Jade didn't pop by his office once. She was more likely to text or email if she decided to do any more magic, although he did feel a tad disappointed. By five o'clock, he decided he put off his next errand long enough and took off early to head to the Preserve. The Nature Preserve had a number of entrances for Coven and town members to use - some with pathways for walking or hiking, some with picnic benches and fire pits for cooking. There were even a few small camping areas that could be reserved for those wishing to take a short vacation but not go very far. Jade's cottage was close to an entrance where Paris knew she and Daniel went running regularly, but the entrance closer to the lake was further away and he used the drive to let his mind wander over work, Jade and the rest of the Coven. Paris remembered to send a quick email to Josef to let him know where he was going and that he would let Counter-Magic know if there was anything of interest.

Paris turned off the paved road, his car jostling and rolling unevenly on the gravel that led into the Preserve area. The sky was already going dark. He really should have left earlier. This time of year didn't leave much daylight for being outdoors. Although it was past Winter Solstice and the days were getting longer, it was happening slowly and they were still firmly within winter's stiff grip. The weather around the Coven was mild compared to other places, for which Paris was grateful. He didn't think he could stand having to dig his way out of a snow drift every morning in addition to being in the dark.

The trees were barren, reaching for the twilight sky, casting their arms in long, grey spindles. As he stepped out of the car, his breath plumed out in grey puffs before disappearing into the darkness. He pulled a high powered flashlight out with him and flicked it on, heading toward the pathways. He said a quick spell for his intentions, letting the forest know he was coming and asking it to look after him. The last thing he needed was to trip over a branch or a root and break a leg. Hopefully, Mother Nature was feeling kind and generous despite the cold and would keep him safe. He was glad for his coat and gloves, although he would have done better to bring a hat. His coat collar came up to cover the bottom part of his ears, but the night was sharp and he felt the tips of them growing cold.

As Paris walked, he turned over the bits of information he knew. Jade was having problems sleeping, having nightmares. Someone stopped her magic, but not his. There were reports coming in from the lake tied to Jade's magic. He hoped no one in the Coven was foolish enough to try to keep Jade from using magic simply because they were worried about the lake or angry about the new Coven norm. But if that were the case, they'd likely be trying to stop Jade from all magic and not just the spell she'd done last night. Indeed, nothing had interrupted their rune work.

He was still fairly far out from the lake when he felt it - a brush of magic against his. Like the reports coming in Counter-Magic had said, it did feel like Jade's magic, but he could also feel why the children would have cried. It was... chaotic and... raw. When Paris first met Jade, her power had been completely untrained, but even then, it hadn't felt like this. This felt... hurt. Sad. Scared. It made the hair on the back of his neck rise. Paris had never gotten a sense of Jade's magic like this. He didn't even know her magic could feel like this. He realized his steps had slowed and he was moving forward at less than half his previous pace. The closer he got, the worse the feeling became. He felt anxious himself - as though the forest had eyes, all of them malevolent and turned his way. A sharp scent caught his attention and he sniffed. Licorice. He'd never smelled that as part of Jade's magic before. He didn't know anyone in the Coven with that marker. It was quite distinct. Paris took another deep breath. Licorice and vanilla. Vanilla was quite common among the Coven members. A lot of witches had it as a secondary, tertiary or quaternary scent. But the licorice was unique.

Another ten minutes in and he felt the deep pull of the lake. While large bodies of water always had some kind of magic in them, the lake's had been amplified and affected by the tragedy involving Josef's family. Witches could usually tell if there was a lake, river, or other large body of water close by from the natural pull of the element. But the lake in the Preserve had a stronger current to it now. It *dragged* at witches, not so much calling their power as tugging and yanking at it sharply. It usually affected those with an affinity for water the most. The less strong a witch's water magic was, the less they would feel the lake. Paris had been quite surprised when Jade felt the lake from so far out. She was quite poor at water magic with no affinity for it. She was extraordinary with fire, strong in air, and moderately talented in earth. But her water magic was weak.

Now, though, the pulling, tugging sensation from the lake was mixed up with the feeling of Jade's magic and Paris was assaulted by it. Jade's magic overwhelmed him, though she was nowhere near the lake. The smell of licorice grew stronger as he got closer and when he finally cleared the tree line and could actually see the lake, he thought the taste and smell of licorice would be embedded permanently in his soft palette.

Paris closed his eyes and sent little tendrils of his magic out, searching for the familiar feeling of his mother's magic, searching for the wards Josef had said she set. Though it had been years, he knew he would recognize it if it were there to be found. He wanted to examine them and see if they had just expired from age or if they had been broken, perhaps on purpose.

When he did sense his mother's magic, he sighed. The feel of it was still the same after all these years, so familiar and well known, bringing with it the memory of being safe and comforted. Paris turned his flashlight to the left and followed the faint trace of her magic until he found where she cast the original ward. He reached out to one of the tree trunks, knowing as he did that she would have carved the ward in the bark. He'd seen her cast wards many times and she favored etching them into permanent structures for endurance. The beam of the flashlight danced over the trunk, dipping into the nooks and crannies. He finally found it - the distinctive marks of a ward carved into the bark, the inherent magic keeping it from fading, even after all these years. But covering the ward, blacking out parts of it were dark lines. Paris reached out and touched them. Scorch marks. Not from magic. He didn't sense any other spell work and working magic on a ward would be dangerous - it would be hard to predict how it would react. No, these marks were done with something meant to destroy the wards, meant to make them fail. Maybe a small blow torch.

It was definitely deliberate. Though he was sure he'd find more of the same things as he searched, he sent his magic out to find the rest of his mother's wards. He located three more - one set in each cardinal direction. All of them had been scorched, the magic burned out of them purposefully.

His mother's wards being destroyed would explain the lake feeling stronger, but it didn't explain why it felt so much like Jade's magic, unless it was just a residual affect of Paris resetting Coven magic to match Jade's. Perhaps whatever lingered at the lake was trying to tune itself to Jade, the same way the rest of the Coven was. Maybe that tuning was going badly. Paris wasn't sure.

He might need to bring Jade out to the lake. If there were something wrong because of how he reset Coven magic, her magic would be the best to deal with it. Paris would be able to guide her and perhaps help with some spell casting, but Jade would have the best chance at fixing something that was amiss with her own natural resonance. She wasn't going to be happy about it. He remembered how reluctant she'd been when they'd started approaching the lake the last time they'd been out at the Preserve. Given everything that was going on with her currently, he hated to ask for more, but she could possibly be the quickest and easiest solution.

Now if Paris could just convince her of that.

#

Jade wracked her brain trying to figure a way out. She thought about magic, about lying, about brute force, but she couldn't come up with anything that would work.

She was at Booty Yoga and couldn't escape.

"Do you have your own mat?"

The perky woman behind the counter hadn't stopped smiling since Jade approached the counter. She smiled as she gave Jade the disclaimer form. She smiled as she took payment. She smiled as she offered Jade a newbie pass and now she wore a smile and an expectant expression as she waited for Jade to answer. It was unnatural to be so happy.

"Uh, no."

"No problem! You can use one of our mats. Rental fees are two dollars. Unless you'd like to buy a mat. They are thirty dollars each. But! If you purchase a pass with a mat, that drops down to twenty-five."

"I'll just rent the mat for tonight."

"No problem!" she repeated. "But I've a feeling you're going to love it. It's a great workout."

Jade curled her lips in what she hoped was an approximation of a smile. Callie and Henri better already be here. If Jade walked in that yoga room and didn't see them, she was out. She felt slightly jostled and anxious in the front area, surrounded by women who obviously knew each other. They greeted one another, also smiling, catching up with each other's days. There were too many people in such a small area for Jade's liking. She paid for her workout (and her mat rental. Jesus, mat rental. Like they couldn't let her use it for an hour. She was going to give it back) and then followed the overly perky woman for a quick tour. Finally, Jade was left on her own to head for the yoga room. As she pulled the door back, she was hit with a thick wave of heat that had her eyes crossing. Good lord. She was expected to stay an hour in this room? Was there a medical kit on standby just in case?

Callie must have been on the lookout for her because she waved Jade over the moment she stepped inside. She and Henri had situated themselves at the front of the room, which was covered in floor to ceiling mirrors. Jade felt her step falter. She had managed to avoid looking in any larger mirrors since her accident the other day. She did her makeup in the morning by using a small compact mirror, only needing to focus on her eyes or her cheeks or her lips - one feature at a time. Jade managed another approximation of a smile, catching sight of herself in the mirror. It definitely looked more like a grimace. She ducked her head low as she made her way up to the obvious spot between Callie and Henri.

"We saved you a spot," Callie said. Unlike the woman at the counter, Callie's smile didn't make Jade nervous. It was a warm, easy grin that Jade was familiar with and found comforting.

"Thanks." Jade spread out her mat and, after checking how Callie and Henri had set themselves up, put her water bottle at the top. "Uh, is it supposed to be this hot?"

Henri nodded. "Yep. It helps your muscles relax and stretch out. Really good for the poses. It also helps you sweat out all the toxins in your body."

"It's going to be really good for the full mummification of my corpse." She could already feel sweat breaking out along her hairline and upper lip. She hoped she was wearing enough deodorant. She should have put more on before coming. Thank God she'd just washed these clothes.

"It's too moist for that," Henri said with a sassy grin. Jade had to laugh. He was right.

"Most people say you get used to it after a couple of classes," Callie added.

"Oh. Happiness." Jade wasn't sure she wanted to get used to it. She was fully dressed in a sauna. She would sweat like a pig. It would be gross and to top it off, she was paying for it.

They had a few more minutes of idle chat before their instructor, a tall, willowy brunette, came into the room, introduced herself and asked if there were any newbies. Callie and Henri's hands shot up like the woman had asked for volunteers at a wine tasting. Jade waved her hand, feeling awkward and on the spot. The brunette, Andrea, walked them through the class etiquette, some quick terminology lessons and then finished off her introductory speech with, "…and if you feel faint you can just lie down. If you do leave the room, gimme some kind of a signal so I know you're okay, unless you're rushing out because you're sick."

"Sick?" Jade asked, a niggling suspicion in her brain.

Andrea nodded solemnly. "Some people vomit the first time due to the heat, but give it a few goes; your body will adjust."

Jade turned to Callie, her glare accusing. '*Vomit*?' she mouthed. Callie gave her a weak smile and a half shoulder shrug. Jade turned to Henri who was obviously avoiding her gaze, staring straight ahead at the mirror. She poked him in the shoulder.

"Vomit?" she hissed.

"Oh, don't be such a baby," he whispered back. "You've stopped a demon and a madman. A little hot yoga isn't going to kill you."

"I'm not afraid it will kill me, I'm afraid it will make me vomit."

He shushed Jade, finger coming up to his lip. Her eyes widened. Oh, he did *not* just shush her. She was about to say something else when Andrea dimmed the lights and instructed them all into the first pose. Jade looked pointedly at Henri and dragged her finger across her throat. He rolled his eyes.

It went about as well as Jade expected.

Which is to say, after five minutes she could feel the sweat rolling down her neck, skimming down her spine and sinking into the waistband of her pants. She studiously avoided looking in the mirror but that didn't keep her from looking at Henri and Callie. Jade imagined she looked like a variant of them - red faced, dripping sweat, face contorted in grimaces as they held poses. Although, she could see how this would give her a killer ass.

Her glutes and hamstrings were on fire. At one point, the entire class was holding what the instructor called a chair pose. Gone was the mild mannered persona who introduced herself at the start. Now, Andrea had a sharp tone, hollering that they could squat lower, they *would* squat lower, and they would *hold it.*

Jade glanced over at Henri and saw her squat was lower than his. "I'm winning," she whispered.

"It's not a competition!" he hissed back.

Jade shrugged, throwing off her balance and she stumbled-stepped, falling to her knees hard. Henri only managed to slightly mute his guffaw and Jade had to laugh at herself along with him. This was ridiculous. She was horrible at yoga.

At the end of the hour they got to lie down in what was appropriately called 'corpse pose.' It was the best pose of the class, in Jade's opinion. She was soaking wet, her legs were shaking and there was a promise of a cool lemongrass towel in a few minutes. Andrea was leading them through some kind of guided meditation. It was the same sort of thing that Paris wanted her to try, in order to focus her magic. Jade was crap at it. She couldn't clear her mind, couldn't focus on her breathing, couldn't stop being distracted by anything that happened around her. Someone coughed. Someone else shifted. The heater kicked on (again, my God it was hot enough, but that thing kept running).

After a few minutes, Jade felt like she was doing better. She did feel a little more relaxed. Maybe there was something to all this yoga business. She was tired, hot and she should be hosed down before leaving, but she felt good. She listened to Andrea talk about inhaling and exhaling and instead of dismissing it, Jade tried to do as instructed. She breathed in and out, thought about the oxygen circulating in her body, thought about how heavy her body felt, how tired she felt. It was a good kind of tired. A clean tired. She was drowsy and started to feel like she was drifting. Her body felt like liquid, sinking into the ground. Or maybe the ground was liquid, and she was merging with it, becoming one viscous puddle.

Andrea's voice sounded further and further away. Jade could hear her heart beating in her ears, loud and thick. Her breathing slowed down, her breaths got shallow. She was so heavy. She was so tired. She wasn't so much falling asleep as falling away, drifting from the surface into the depths.

Like being in water.

Like drowning.

A loud crack made everyone in the room gasp and a few people shrieked in surprise. Jade had heard that sound, but not only that, she'd *felt* it. Something had broken. Something had snapped. She was afraid to open her eyes but knew it would look weird if she didn't. She cracked open her eyelids, her gaze opening immediately to the area in question.

The wall of mirrors was broken - spider-like lines of fractures splintering through each pane. Jade cringed internally. She'd done that. She didn't know how, but she knew it had been her. Or maybe not exactly her. More like... Lily.

Jade wanted to run, to hide, but she couldn't move. Any moment now, Callie and Henri would turn to her and say that it was Jade's magic that had done that. They both knew what her magic felt like, what it smelled like. The room was full of chatter, the calm that had existed only moments before gone, driven away by the cracks in the glass.

"Is everyone okay?" the instructor asked. General assent rose from the room and Jade could only be relived that no one was hurt. She was also relieved that no one seemed to be blaming her. Yet.

"God, that's so weird! What the hell happened?" Callie asked.

Henri sniffed the air and Jade froze like a wild rabbit spotted by a predator. "Do you smell that?"

This was it, she was screwed.

Callie sniffed too. "Is that grapefruit? Who's magic is that?" Callie looked around. All the students were doing the same thing - slightly sniffing the air and looking around in bewilderment.

Jade cautiously sniffed the air too. It *was* grapefruit. Grapefruit and cinnamon. She didn't think she'd smelled that before.

Henri shrugged. "I don't know anyone whose magic smells like that. You?"

Callie shook her head and when they both looked at Jade, she dumbly shook hers too. Andrea was asking everyone to calmly leave, noting that they could pick up a voucher for a free class at the front. She'd also report the incident to Counter-Magic and asked that the students not discuss the incident amongst themselves until they called in their details. It was the Counter-Magic standard line

- don't mix up your details by discussing with others until you've reported the incident. Hearing the familiar words calmed Jade enough to push to her feet, leaving her rented mat on the floor and stumbling after Callie and Henri.

CHAPTER FOUR

Another night. Another nightmare. If she slept and didn't have one, Jade would be suspicious and edgy, she supposed. After coming home from yoga and resolutely avoiding any reflective surfaces, she killed time streaming vids on her laptop before finally heading up to bed, feeling dread pool in her stomach with each step. Bruce trotted along after her, sniffing the air. His tail made a whirring sound as he swished it back and forth. He crawled under the bed at first, but after a minute or so, popped back out and then pushed the closet door open with his snout. He had a little nest in there with a pillowcase, a throw pillow from the sofa and Jade's caffeine t-shirt - one of her favorites. She guessed it was more his now.

She wondered how long it would take her to fall asleep, but she refused to keep checking the clock. All she knew was that she was back in the Preserve, the sparrow from her previous dream perched on her shoulder. It had a high-pitched chirp, but Jade thought all birds might. It wasn't like she was any kind of expert. She heard a high-pitched sound, it sounded like a chirp, it must be a bird sound. That was the extent of her knowledge.

The sparrow's feet were sharp on Jade's skin, digging into the flesh of her shoulder. With how small the sparrow was, Jade couldn't see it out of the corner of her eye, but if she turned her head a little, she could catch a glimpse of it. If she turned her head too far to see it better, she felt dizzy and had to look straight ahead again.

Up ahead of her were the dock and the lake. As she walked toward them, she looked down and saw her bare feet. Where were her shoes? What was she doing outside without shoes? Even though she knew it was a dream, the lack of footwear bothered her. It was so impractical.

Other than the sparrow on her shoulder, Jade didn't hear any other sounds from the forest. No crunching of leaves as squirrels ran, no other birds talking, no rustle of branches. She dragged her hand across the rough bark of one of the trees she passed and then pulled her hand back sharply when pain bloomed across two of her fingers.

Blood. It blossomed bright red against her pale skin, like water over the petals of a delicate flower. As she turned her hand, a few fat drops ran down her fingers, then her palm and started crossing her wrist. She had to look away then. Blood on her hands, on her wrists always made her think of the day Lily left. But that wasn't what this dream was. These were only the cuts from the mirror, when she thought she saw Lily. Nothing more, nothing less.

She didn't have any other wounds on her. Still, she couldn't stop herself from turning her hands over, palms up and checking her arms. No wounds, just smooth skin with the hint of blue-green veins underneath.

Her fingers throbbed in time with her heartbeat and she found herself pausing in her walk toward the lake, distracted by the pulse. One-two. One-two. One-two.

The sparrow dug its feet into her shoulder and she winced. She started moving forward again.

This time on the dock, her body knew how to sway along with the slight movement. Keeping her balance felt easier than before. She walked to the end and then curled her toes over the edge, feeling the rough, worn wood under her feet. It was foolish of her to be standing so close. She couldn't swim.

In the first dream she'd had of Lily at the lake, back when Jade had been worried about Dex, Lily had been underwater, her eyes closed, her arms reaching up, like a ghostly stalagmite stretching for the surface. Jade stared at the spot where Lily had been before, but there was nothing out there now. Just the flat surface of the cold water. It reflected back broken fragments of the sky and the surrounding trees - the picture jumbled and odd.

The sparrow nibbled at her neck and Jade raised a hand to flick it off or push it away. It unset her balance and she felt herself falling toward the water. Time slowed in the impossible way it can in dreams and she was able to turn, putting her back to the water. She was out of step with time, tipping backward so slowly that it seemed she would have forever to dread and fear hitting the water. She could see a shape on the dock. It must have been standing behind her - a cloaked figure, the face hidden by black folds, like a grim reaper. It stood still and solemn, neither helping nor hindering. Behind that figure was Lily - her eyes, so green, so wide. She was like Jade - moving so slowly she was nearly frozen. Her hair moving around her face like lazy smoke. Her hand stretched out toward Jade, as though she wanted to stop her from falling. Her mouth was open, mid-shout, but there was no sound. Nothing from the forest, nothing from the cloaked figure, nothing from Jade herself.

Except her heart. One-two. One-two. One-two. An absurd number of beats in her ear as she fell backward, the water moving up to meet her.

Jade woke up, again not in her bedroom, but in the kitchen, halfway to the back door. Her heart stuttered in surprise and she shook her head to clear it. Feeling wetness on her fingers she looked down. Tiny red droplets of blood were dripping from her bandage-free fingers, leaving small crimson spots on the kitchen linoleum. The time on the microwave said two in the morning - way too early for her to be up and only about an hour or so after she'd gone to bed. She looked slowly around, hoping a reason for her being in the kitchen would come to her. None did.

Mechanically, she went through the motions of cleaning up the blood she trailed on the floor, following little bloody droplets all the way out of the kitchen, through the living room and up the stairs to her bedroom. Thank God she didn't have carpet. What a disaster. It was easier to focus on the mess that could have been instead of thinking about her dream.

Back in her room, she found her old bandages by the side of the bed and could only guess that she'd ripped them off in her sleep. A quick peek in the closet showed Bruce sleeping like the dead - his belly rising and falling heavily. It made her smile. It was relaxing to watch him sleep.

It took a few more minutes to rebandage her fingers and then she was back in her room. She paused just as she was about to get into bed and instead, grabbed one of her pillows and a blanket. Heading back to the closet, she poked her head in.

"Scooch over, Bruce. Stop hogging all the space."

#

Jade was touched when both Callie and Daniel offered up their cars to drive Bruce to the Coven. Since Daniel already did Jade a couple of solids a week by dropping her off after their run and in fact, would have to turn around after dropping her off in the morning just to come back and get her and Bruce an hour later, Jade accepted Callie's offer of a ride.

Thankfully, that morning's run had been free from any dry-heaving moments, although Jade did feel like death warmed over. Having her sleep interrupted was taking its toll. Daniel and Jade took another pathway for their jog, one that Jade suggested. It hugged close to the perimeter of the Preserve instead of travelling deeper into the forest. While it kept Jade from getting sick, it didn't hide the fact that she was struggling to keep up with Daniel. They were usually evenly paced, but Jade felt like she was running through mud. Daniel slowed his pace down and Jade barely had enough oxygen to thank him for it. He'd dropped her off with a careful look, promising to see her at work.

Back at her cottage, Jade showered, changed and then asked Bruce if he wanted to go take a ride with Callie to the Coven. Jade would swear on a stack of bibles Bruce actually preened at the question. He did a little butt-shimmy-wiggle and then bounded toward the foyer. Jade laughed at his exuberance.

"We still have to wait for Callie to arrive, buddy."

Bruce's head drooped and he planted his butt in the foyer while Jade made her way to the kitchen. Bruce seemed genuinely excited to go to the Coven. Why, Jade wasn't sure. He was just going to meet people. Unless he was excited about that. Which would honestly be surprising because in other ways, he was a lot like Jade.

Jade was halfway through her morning coffee when Bruce decided to abandon his vigil in the foyer and come into the kitchen. He whacked Jade's chair with his tail, causing her to spill coffee on her (thankfully) black pants.

"Nice." She looked around for a napkin, but then decided a few drops of coffee on black slacks wouldn't show anyway. Bruce hit her leg again, this time with his flank.

"What's up? If this is about more bacon I told you that was a special treat. We can't have that all the time. It's bad for our hips."

He presented his neck to her, like he had before, tipping his head off to the side and bluntly showing her the skin under his chin. Frowning, Jade set her cup down and scooted her chair forward, bending over to cradle his face and tip his head up further. The dry, scaly patch was worse - spreading out across his neck. She touched it carefully and he blinked quickly a few times.

"Does it hurt now?" she asked, keeping her voice low. His tongue came out quickly, touching her wrist. "Hmm. I think that means yes." She looked it over again and then sat back in her chair. "Okay, wait right here."

She ran upstairs and came back with a small travel sized container of aloe vera and vitamin E cream. She squirted a bit on her fingertips (avoiding her bandages) and held them out for Bruce to sniff.

"Okay if I put some of this on?"

His snout came closer, wiggling slightly as he sniffed the cream. She could almost see him considering it.

"I'll ask around and see if I can make a witchy-type one, but I'm afraid until I do, this is the best I've got."

He exhaled once sharply and then again presented his neck, which she took as permission. Jade carefully smoothed the cream into the scaly skin, trying to ensure even coverage, but not wanting to over-saturate the area. Bruce turned his head and Jade was able to get a better angle.

"There we go. Looking a bit better."

Maybe this was all Bruce needed - for Jade to put some cream on him a couple times a day. She laughed unexpectedly. "I'm sorry, Bruce, but I gotta say, I never pictured this in my future when I joined a Coven."

Bruce's tongue flicked out at her once more before he turned his head sharply to the front door, moments before Jade did. She could feel Callie pressing up against her demon locks, stuck down by the street.

"Guess our ride's here."

Bruce bounded to the front door and wiggled his butt while he waited for Jade to get her shoes and coat on. As soon as she opened the door, he tore down the steps and pathway, heading directly for where Callie stood by her car.

"Sorry, couldn't get any closer. I was about to text."

"No worries. I should probably change the spell to let you through, but it's been acting weird lately."

Callie shrugged. "It's not like I can't text you. Or yell."

Jade snorted. "I'm sure the neighbors will love that. Will you yell out 'STELLA!' like we're in that play?"

"I'll do my best Brando impression. All five-feet and two inches of me. By the way, I have treats!" Callie waved a box of donut holes proudly.

"Bruce, look! Treats for humans and lizards!"

Callie tossed one in the air and Bruce, in a surprising show of agility and speed, leapt up and caught it - his pink tongue flicking out and wrapping around the donut hole. He hopped into the back of Callie's car, where he eagerly pushed his face in between the front seats and started nosing at the coffees in the cup holders. As Jade got in the car, she tapped him on his snout.

"Dude, I like you a lot, but that's my coffee."

Bruce turned his eyes on Callie and Jade wanted to laugh at the doe-eyed expression he was giving her. It was eerily akin to the same cow-eyed expression that Callie was capable of with her large brown eyes.

"Aw, he's so cute! I should have brought him a small coffee too."

"He doesn't need coffee," Jade protested, taking a sip of her own.

Callie snorted. "I don't know, Jade. Familiars are supposed to be very much like their witches. With how much you love it, Bruce might need it to survive." Her tone was light and teasing and Jade smiled at it.

By the time they were walking through the front doors of the Coven, Jade could already tell that Bruce was going to be a spectacle. Bruce trailed behind her - his loping, awkward gait making him waddle slightly. As they entered the Covenstead, Jade heard a chorus of sharp breaths and braced herself to protect or defend Bruce in case anyone was afraid of or antagonistic toward him. Instead, a witch Jade knew by sight but not by name immediately rushed over, hunkered down and met him eye-to-eye.

"Look at him! What a cutie!" the witch exclaimed, she reached out tentatively to pet

Bruce's head looking up at Jade, for permission or assurance, Jade wasn't sure. Jade nodded once and Bruce flicked his tongue out at the other witch, making his 'pffft' sound.

The witch laughed a bit, smiling widely and then pet him on the head, marveling at the texture of his skin. "Oh, I didn't know he'd be soft!"

Bruce, the traitor, was totally eating it up. His eyes slitted shut in bliss as he deigned to let some stranger pet him. After that, some kind of seal was broken and more witches came up. Jade and Callie couldn't even get past the foyer of the Covenstead to make it to Henri's reception desk - too many people had crowded into the limited space.

Jade thought at first Bruce's popularity was due to the fact that familiars were so rare - no one had ever had much of a chance to meet one before. But, after watching the serpentine wiggle of Bruce's long body as he preened under the attention, she realized he was a bit of a diva and was totally hamming it up.

When Jade usually walked in through the main doors of the Covenstead on her own, people turned all right, but it was more with sideways glances and hairy eyeballs. She'd never once been the subject of cooing and fawning. The forced smiles and greetings Jade got were a far cry from the 'oohing' and 'ahhing' Bruce was inspiring.

"It's nice that he's so friendly," Callie said, standing just off to Jade's side. Callie flicked her pale, fine blonde hair over her shoulder in a wide fan and then bent down to give Bruce a pat on the head. Bruce gazed up at her adoringly. Callie probably solidified her position in Bruce's little lizard heart with all the donut holes she fed him on the car ride over.

"What kind of lizard is he?" someone asked.

Jade shrugged, vaguely recognizing the witch from Supernatural Relations. "He doesn't really match up to anything. I think the herpetologist figured he was closest to a bearded dragon, but he's almost seventy pounds - way too big to actually be one."

All that time spent lost in the sewer, feeding on magical bits and bobs, had probably done strange things to Bruce's anatomy and growth. Nobody knew exactly what Bruce was or had been before he'd turned into what he was now.

"He seems so tame!" someone else exclaimed.

"Yeah, he's a prince," Jade said dryly, watching as Bruce flapped his Elizabethan lizard collar, causing the small crowd of witches gathered around to startle as a group, and then surge in for a better look. Bruce preened and then flopped sideways, showing his pale yellow belly. One of the women reached out and patted his supple, sturdy belly soundly and Bruce flopped his tail with a loud thump on the marble floor.

"Oh my God, you're such a sook," Jade said lowly. She didn't think anyone heard her but from the way Bruce rolled his eyes toward her, he totally did.

It didn't escape Jade's notice that while the Coven members had crowded the foyer, they were wholly focused on Bruce and ignoring Jade. Maybe not deliberately. Jade was the recipient of some small smiles and hesitant looks, but for the most part, people were more interested in her lizard than her.

There was a metaphor for her life in there somewhere; Jade just couldn't figure it out.

One of the male witches who was crowding around Bruce reached out a hand and Jade saw he was too close to Bruce's scaly spot.

"Wait-"

She only managed to get the one word out before he brushed his hand a little too roughly over Bruce's sore spot. Bruce reared up, Elizabethan collar maxed out, and snapped at him with teeth. Everyone jumped back - well, everyone except Jade. The foyer had gone silent; the witches looked from Jade to Bruce with hesitant eyes.

"He's got a sore patch there. Don't touch it," Jade said, crouching down next to Bruce. He leaned heavily against her. All seventy pounds. She had to put one of her legs awkwardly out to the side to take the weight. He seemed slightly embarrassed, whether by his sore patch or because he snapped and didn't mean to, Jade wasn't sure.

"What is it?" Callie asked, coming to kneel next to Jade, keeping a good distance from Bruce.

"I don't know," Jade answered truthfully. "I only noticed it recently. It just showed up. It's getting bigger." Jade turned from Callie to the witch Bruce had snapped at. "Sorry, I should have warned you guys."

"That's okay," he said, a little tremor in his voice. "I shouldn't have surprised him. I guess."

Bruce looked around at the Coven witches with a sort of questioning gaze, as if wondering where his admirers had gone.

"If you don't bother that spot, he's fine," Jade said. There was a sort of shuffle in the crowd and then people started coming forward, this time much slower, giving Bruce tentative touches. When Bruce resumed his relaxed posture complete with slitted eyes and deep breaths, it seemed like everyone, including Jade, relaxed.

Jade stood up, stepping away from Bruce, with Callie following suit, letting the Coven witches have their look at him.

"I guess I should take him to see someone, but I'm not sure if he should go to a vet or what. Maybe I could use a spell to make him a cream or something? Is there anything in the library on familiars getting sick?"

Callie paused, her face going frozen for a moment and Jade felt a flash of worry. As head of the library, Callie was the expert on all the books kept downstairs in the Covenstead's former dungeon. If there was a book about familiars being ill, Callie would know about it.

"What? Do you know something?"

Callie shook her head, brushing imaginary dirt off her pants. "No, it's just odd for a familiar to be sick, that's all. I'm sure it's fine. Maybe it's just a dry patch now that he's out of the sewer."

"Yeah," Jade said lowly, not entirely convinced. Bruce had rolled onto his back again, getting a belly rub.

"I'll pick some books out of the library for you. You may even be able to help us update some of them once you get used to having him as your familiar."

"Excuse me, do you think we could take him up to HR department?" asked another one of the witches. Jade didn't know her name either. She was always better with office numbers and people's jobs rather than their names. "I mean, if you don't mind?"

Jade looked back and forth between Bruce and the young witch. "Uhhh, sure. If he wants to go." Jade pursed her lips and looked down at Bruce. "So, go on with them for a bit. Have fun." She made little shoo-ing motions with her hands. Bruce flipped back onto his stubby feet and started trotting away from Jade.

"Thanks!" said the witch brightly. "I'll bring him back! I just thought everyone would like to get a chance to see him."

Jade smiled, feeling the skin on her cheeks tight. "Sure. Make the rounds. He likes people food, so if anyone leaves their lunches out, he'll filch. Be careful."

Bruce tossed a look over his serpentine shoulder, eyeballing her for tattling on him. She fought the urge to stick her tongue out as she headed over to Henri's desk. Henri glanced sideways as Bruce passed, trying to look like he wasn't afraid and failing miserably.

"I know he's your familiar, but he's weird!" he said, voice a comical stage whisper. Jade laughed softly, seeing Callie smile as well.

"Yeah, he is. I mean, he's a seventy-pound lizard thing that I found in the sewer. Weird doesn't really even begin to cover it."

"Can he do magic on his own?" Henri asked, his long neck craning as he hunched his body over his desk to watch Bruce labor up the stairs. It was definitely an exercise in physics - Bruce's stout but lengthy body easily spanned about four or five steps. As he moved, his short legs weren't always visible. It gave the impression he was gliding up the stairs.

"Uh, no," answered Jade. "I mean, I don't think so. He gets cold and I have to conjure up a little fireball for him to curl up around. I think if he could do it on his own, he would."

"I'm going to have to read up on familiars," said Henri. Bruce had finally made it to the top of the first set of stairs and disappeared around the corner. For all that Jade groused about having him, she missed the scaly beast when he was gone.

"Me too," Jade said.

"Coffee at ten thirty in the caf?" Callie asked.

"Of course," answered Henri quickly. "But if they're making those cinnamon things again, we have to drink it somewhere else. They smell too good and I can't keep buying one and pretending like I'm going to split it with Daniel when I get home. Once in a while is fine, but I passed that benchmark five cinnamon buns ago. And now *my* buns are paying for it."

Jade made a kind of grumbling sound along with Callie, but she knew they were all in agreement. No more cinnamon buns for anyone.

"Hey, how are you doing?" Henri asked. "Daniel said you're having a hard time keeping up during your runs?"

"Is nothing sacred?"

Henri snorted. "Stuff said in the sacred trinity of you, me and Callie is safe. But all your desperate secrets like your per mile pace and how many sprints you do a week is up for grabs. He mentioned last time you were sick and this time you struggled. You feeling okay?"

"Aw!" Callie said, interrupting. "I feel bad for making you go to Booty Yoga now!"

"Just now? You didn't before?"

Callie smiled. "Nope."

"Seriously, are you sick or is our resident heroine just tuckered out from saving the world?" Henri joked. Jade managed a wane smile.

"If we're gonna take turns saving the world, it's totally someone else's next," Jade said.

Callie laughed. "I promise the next time someone makes a deal with a demon or tries to take over the Coven, we'll step up to the plate and take care of it."

"Speak for yourself," said Henri. "You know in thriller movies when they say to someone 'Stay in the car!' and that same dumbass gets out of the car?" He shook his head. "That's not me. I'm staying the hell in the car. Let the professionals deal with it." Henri regarded her for a moment with that far-off glazed look he got when he was reading auras. Jade's shoulders tightened under the scrutiny. Aura-reading wasn't something she'd ever tried herself, being far more interested in spell casting and demon magic. Henri was somewhat of an expert aura-reader and Jade never had the courage to ask him what he saw when he looked at hers.

This time, he frowned.

"Are you feeling okay? Are you sure you're just tired?" he asked.

This could be it. Her opportunity to share some of her troubles. Weren't Callie and Henri her friends? She liked them, liked spending time with them. Maybe Jade should take the plunge. Ugh, bad time to use that word. It made her think of water, which made her shudder. It was probably a bad idea to talk about it now anyway. In the foyer. Where anyone could hear. Jesus, she really was losing it if this was the moment she almost decided to tell the truth.

Jade shrugged. "Yeah, just tired. You know." *Maybe going crazy but whatevs, no biggie.*

His eyes glazed over again with his far-off look as he examined her aura. Based on the look on his face, she knew he didn't believe her.

Jade averted her eyes, nervous. "I should get going. There are some Counter-Magic things that Josef wants me to look at. I think he figures since the Coven's magic is set to me, I might be able to sort some stuff out faster."

"Must be nice to have some real work, hey?" Callie said brightly. "It's tough when you're new and you haven't quite settled in yet, but now it seems like you've got some stuff on your plate that you'll be good at."

Jade managed a smile, her face feeling tight and a little brittle. "Yeah, for sure. Better than reading the training manuals over and over."

Callie laughed. "Oh my God, those things are so old! I can't believe they made you read them."

"Well, gotta put the new girl through her paces, I guess."

"Okay," said Henri, wrapping up their conversation with a quick handclap. "Coffee in the caf at 10:30. First one there buys."

"You say that and then you suspiciously always run late," Callie said, eyebrows raised.

Henri looked shocked and outraged. "I can't help it if I'm busy. Every time I try to get away from my desk, the phone rings."

Callie rolled her eyes. "Yeah, yeah," she said, a smile on her lips.

"Fine, last one there buys," Henri said, raising his own eyebrows to see if that was acceptable to Callie. Her smile broke out wide and bright.

"Deal!"

Jade spared one last look up the grand staircase, hoping Bruce faired well during his day trip to the Coven.

CHAPTER FIVE

Even though Jade had been drinking more coffee lately to make up for the lack of sleep, she still found her brain feeling foggy as she entered the Counter-Magic offices. At this point, she wanted to ask the cafeteria if they could jerry-rig kind of an upside-down latte. She could rest her head on the counter and they could pour milk and espresso down her throat. She just had to work on the fact that those drinks were usually made at something like one hundred and forty degrees Fahrenheit. It had potential, except for the scalding temperatures and likelihood of getting her face burned off.

But until that glorious day when they rolled out Upside-Down Lattes and Espresso Shots, all she could do was steel her spine and plaster on her best fake 'I'm ready for the workday' face. She stopped briefly outside the office and put on some dark lipstick. That usually tended to scare people off.

Daniel was already on the phone, typing away. He looked up from his cube when Jade came in, giving her a quick jerk of his head. He beat her into the office every day even though he had to drop her off after their run before he headed home. Jade blamed sexism. She had a lot more 'working parts' to her daily routine - hair, makeup. Daniel probably just hosed himself down and went back out the door.

Daniel got off the phone just as Jade sat down. "Isn't that your werewolf haute couture outfit?" He looked her up and down.

"Yes," she said. "Most comfortable outfit I've ever worn to a party." In early January, she'd been invited to meet the local werewolf pack and celebrate their Wolf Moon. It turned out werewolves were kind of picky, not only about who they socialized with, but with what those people wore. They'd sent her some pure cotton, un-laundered black slacks and a shirt, letting her know she could wear her own boots. Jade had sort of been expecting some kind of fete with fancy dresses and high heels, but that wasn't how the wolves rolled, at least not for the Wolf Moon. Instead she'd gotten to don a cute little wolf mask and go running with them in the woods. It had been fun. She'd also been offered a job by their Alpha, Lucia. Jade had turned her down, content to stay at the Coven and continue magic, but she kind of got the feeling that Lucia would bide her time and ask again. Jade wasn't sure how many times she could tell the Alpha 'no.' "I'm a little short on clothes right now. Most of my stuff is still back at my old apartment."

He made a face. "Are you kidding me? You haven't you moved all your stuff to the Coven yet?"

Jade grumbled as Daniel shot her an incredulous look. She was going to get around to moving her stuff. She was. She just needed to… plan it out. Go and do it.

"You've been here months. You have a job. You have a house. You pay taxes."

"I know," Jade said. "I'm going to do it. I will! It just hasn't been a priority, what with demons and rogue witches and stuff." At his continued look she added, "I've been *busy*!"

"Do you need help? Henri and I can head back to your place and help you pack up."

Jade glanced at him a dubiously and he smirked.

"Okay, so I can help you pack and Henri can sit there and drink lattes and tell us we're doing it wrong. Seriously, is it that you don't want to do it alone?"

"No," she lied. Sort of. It wasn't a total lie. It was mostly truthful. She wanted to go alone, but she wasn't sure how she felt about being alone in the apartment, packing up all her things, all Lily's things. She wouldn't have any witchy stuff to distract her. No Counter-Magic Call Log, no coffee breaks with Callie and Henri, no Bruce padding around looking for a heat vent to sleep on top of.

Jade could probably bring Bruce with her but if she was honest, she'd need the space in her car to bring all her stuff back and a seventy pound lizard wasn't exactly space-economical.

Oh, *her car*. She thought of it longingly. No more asking for a ride. No more feeling indebted. No more taking public transit to and from the Coven. No more trying to get groceries on the bus.

No more needing a ride if Callie wanted to go for a drink. No more being stuck someplace because the bus only ran every thirty minutes.

"Fuck, I really need to get my stuff," she said, swiping a hand over her face, mindful of mucking up her mascara.

Daniel gave her a knowing look. "You really do. Pick a day, stick to it. If you need time off work, I'm sure Josef will give it to you."

"Yeah."

"I'm serious about the offer. If you want or need help, let me know."

"Thanks." Jade felt all kinds of awkward. Daniel really did mean it and she didn't quite know how to accept that kind of generosity.

"No problem." He looked around the office, focusing on the area by her feet. "Where's your lizard."

Jade rolled her eyes. "Ugh, he's Mr. Popularity. Some witches asked to take him up to HR and show him off."

Daniel laughed at her tone. "He doesn't mind being away from you?"

Jade shrugged. "I guess not. I mean he hangs out at home when I'm not there and he seemed okay to trot off this morning."

Daniel placed a hand over his heart, batting his eyelashes. "Ah, they grow up so fast. I remember when you pulled him out of the sewer and he howled when you left."

"Well, thankfully he seems to have grown out of that. Callie said she's going to look for some books in the library on familiars so I can read up. I may have to take him to a vet or something. He's got this dry patch of skin."

"A lizard. With dry skin," Daniel deadpanned.

"His scales are normally very soft! And this patch just sort of showed up!"

Josef, her boss, came over to where she and Daniel stood next to Jade's desk, casually interrupting.

"I see you two are working hard," Josef said with a wry tone.

"Hardly working," Daniel said back with a sharp wink.

"I thought you were bringing your familiar in today?" Josef asked.

"He was stolen for show and tell. I think he's making the rounds," Jade answered. "He'll either make a break for it and escape when they aren't looking or they'll start feeding him and I'll lose him forever."

Josef crossed his arms in a casual pose while he stood by her desk. "Did I hear you say you wanted to take him to the vet?"

Jade felt embarrassed now. It was probably nothing. "Yeah, he's got this scaly patch and I don't know why. I thought maybe he would need some kind of lizard cream or something? Do they make that, do you think?"

Josef frowned and Jade felt wary at his expression.

"What? Is that bad? Do you think he's sick?"

Josef shook his head. "No, I'm sure it's fine. It's just… well, familiars don't generally get ill or have ailments. Their health is usually quite robust."

"Oh, well maybe it's just because he doesn't live underground anymore or something."

"Of course," Josef replied. "I'm sure it's something simple like that. Let me know when he arrives, I'd like to see him."

"I'm sure you'll know. Just leave your lunch or a cup of coffee on the ground and he'll find you."

Josef chuckled at bit at her statement, but before he left, he added, "I know you've been working on re-configuring some spells. I've been getting good feedback on them. I think you're ready to advance to more complex ones. I've had a couple of complaints come in that I had to put off because I couldn't rework the spells myself. Think you'd like to give them a try?"

Wow, that sounded way more interesting than reviewing minor spells and tweaking them like she had been. "Yeah, I can totally do that."

"I'll forward you the emails and notes I've gotten. When you're done, type up the new spells along with a report and send it back to me."

Jade nodded enthusiastically. "Definitely. I can do that." She felt a little thrill at the idea of starting a new project.

"I imagine it will take you some time to go through the spells. If you need any ingredients, you know where to find them." He gestured at the large back area of Counter-Magic that held cupboards, cabinets and shelving. While Jade had used some items from there, it had always been after someone had gotten them for her. Josef was pointing to the area now and indicating she could go get stuff herself.

Jade couldn't stop nodding her head and even though she didn't mean to speak, she found herself blurting, "Yep. I can do that," she repeated.

"I know you can," Josef said kindly and she winced wryly at herself. She was obviously a little eager. "And bring your familiar by when you get a chance."

She smiled and it felt more natural and genuine than any other expression she'd had all day. "Okay." As Josef walked away, Jade took a deep breath and then settled down at her desk, almost trying to will the email from Josef to pop into her inbox.

#

It was almost lunchtime when Paris was distracted by an unfamiliar sound. He paused working on his computer to look up and around his office, trying to place the noise. It stopped and then started up again - a scritching-scratching sound coming from outside his office. Paris pushed his chair back and padded over, opening the door and poking his head out.

In a flash, Jade's lizard familiar darted inside his office, nearly bowling him over. Looking down at the front of this door, Paris could see claw marks marring the formerly pristine wood. Jade's lizard paused in the center of Paris' office and did a strange sort of shimmy - his entire body going through some kind of a wiggle that started from his nose, worked its way through his Elizabethan Collar and then ended with his long, serpentine tail whipping back and forth. He looked up at Paris expectantly, as though he were waiting for something.

"Bruce," Paris intoned, closing the door firmly and hoping he was interpreting Bruce's gestures correctly. "I'm glad to see you as well."

Bruce let loose another full body shimmy and then did a strange wobble-walk over to Paris' fireplace, giving Paris a significant look. Paris felt his lips curl in a smile. "Ah, yes. I believe Jade mentioned your desire to be warm."

Paris murmured a quick fire incantation, setting a small blaze alight in the fireplace. Bruce sidled up to the grate, and flopped over onto his side, presenting his belly to the flames and tossing a grateful look over his shoulder at Paris. Paris made a move to go back to his desk and Bruce let out a strange kind of squawk.

"Was that a bark?" Paris asked incredulously. It had been not quite a dog bark, but perhaps as close as Bruce could come to it. Bruce stared at Paris, again seemingly waiting for something. Paris took another step toward his desk and Bruce made the sound again. Experimentally, Paris took a step back toward Bruce and the fireplace. Bruce's tail thumped on the ground. Paris took another step closer to Bruce again and thumped his tail once more, like a happy canine.

"I see how it is. Feeling a tad lonely?" Abandoning his work, Paris sank down in one of the Queen Anne chairs in front of the fireplace. Bruce kept his eyes on him the entire time, watching him unblinkingly. The way the light hit his irises made them appear mirrored at times, almost flashing. Bruce shifted so that his back was pressed up against Paris' leg, a heavy, warm weight. While

Paris had extensive academic knowledge of familiars, Bruce was the only one he'd known in person. Paris wasn't sure if all familiars were odd and enigmatic or if it was just Bruce's nature. He did feel a fondness for the creature. Bruce had saved Paris from one of Dex's spells and he also resonated with the continual pulse of Jade's magic - similar in feeling and in scent. Paris knew if he breathed deep, he would smell flowers and cloves.

"I didn't know Jade was bringing you by today," Paris said. He should feel foolish addressing Bruce, but reminded himself familiars were more than just animals. They had to be highly intelligent and somewhat magical themselves to be candidates for witch magic. Aligning himself as Jade's familiar required some kind of conscious choice on Bruce's part. Paris had no doubt that Bruce was as attached to Jade as Jade often seemed to be to him. "Did you lose her? Does she know you're here?"

"Pfffffffft." It was long and drawn out, Bruce's forked tongue flicking out of his mouth and tapping once against Paris' pant-leg. Paris reached forward carefully, giving Bruce ample time to turn or pull away as he did. When he didn't move, Paris touched the soft, supple skin of Bruce's neck, petting him lightly. Bruce preened and Paris felt... content. Bruce's trust and acceptance of Paris was akin to Jade's trust and acceptance of him as well. A familiar generally echoed its witch's feelings. Seeing Bruce's eyes slit slightly shut as he relaxed next to Paris was gratifying.

Bruce turned, rolling further onto his back, away from the fireplace and toward Pars. He tipped his chin up and Paris laughed at first, thinking Bruce was angling for some kind of belly rub, until he noticed it was more like Bruce was presenting something to him. Paris leaned in and looked at Bruce's neck, running his fingers down the skin. He paused upon finding a leathery, scaly patch that was not at all like the rest Bruce's smooth underbelly.

"What have you got here?" Paris said quietly, coming out of his chair to hunker down on the ground next to Bruce. One of Bruce's clawed feet came up and rested against Paris' knee while he examined the lizard's neck, his talons light and careful. A heavy feeling settled in his stomach as he trailed his fingertips lightly over the area. The skin was cracked and slightly hot to the touch. Paris had the feeling that if he pushed, it would split open and bleed. He gave it a bit of a press, checking for any swelling under the surface.

One of Bruce's sharp talons poked through Paris' trouser-leg and Paris flinched.

"Did that hurt?"

Bruce seemed intent on watching him - his silver-green eyes staring hard. Paris frowned as something else caught his notice. He leaned closer, as close as he could get to Bruce's head, looking into one of his reflective eyes. In his left eye, slightly off center of his iris, there was a cracked line of color - apple-green. It was a sharp contrast to the rest of Bruce's silver-green and moss-colored iris. As he stared, the crack seemed to glow for a moment and then disappear - Bruce's eye going back to a solid shade.

Bruce stared at Paris profoundly, as though willing him to understand.

The problem was, Paris had no idea what it meant. But, he knew that particular shade of green. It was the same color that Jade's eyes had been the day she stopped Dex.

"What does it mean, Bruce?" Paris said, keeping his voice quiet.

Another sound at his door had him turning his head, only this time it was just a simple knock, a precursor, before Callie opened the door and poked her head in. She looked like she was about to say something, but then she caught sight of Paris on the ground with Bruce splayed out in front of the fire place. She smiled.

"So this is where he is."

"Was he lost?"

Callie shook her head as she came in, closing the door behind her. She pulled her phone out of her pocket and started typing away on the keyboard. "No, not really. I had coffee with Jade about an hour ago and she mentioned he hadn't come back from being borrowed by HR. She didn't seem too concerned, but she got that pinched look around her eyes that she gets sometimes?" Her voice intimated a sort of question and Paris nodded. He knew the look of which Callie spoke. "It was a quiet day in the library so I thought I'd take a look around and see if I could find him. Some people had seen him wandering about here and there and a few people tried to get closer. He seemed to really like the attention at first, but I hear he got sort of standoffish as the morning went on. Then he started full on evading people."

Paris chuckled. "Sounds a little like his mistress."

Callie laughed, coming closer and pocketing her phone. "Yeah. I sent Jade a text to let her know he's here. He seems pretty popular. I think most witches wanted a chance to see him, see what he's like. I don't even know the last time the Coven saw a familiar. I remember seeing one when I was little. Some kind of bird creature. It would perch on its mistress' shoulder and just looked so…" She sighed longingly. "I begged my parents for a bird for years, just hoping that I could make it perch on my shoulder like that." She knelt down in front of Bruce and Bruce's tail thumped happily against the carpet. He let Callie pet his head and then run her fingers under his Elizabethan collar.

"Familiars are rare. Most witches haven't had contact with one."

"I was reading up on familiars in the library today, trying to pick out some books for Jade."

"I'm sure she'd love to read more about him."

"Yeah. Oh, you've found his patchy spot," Callie said, indicating where Paris was petting Bruce, his hands moving around the rough, scaly bit under his neck.

"Yes, he showed it to me."

"You know a bit about familiars, don't you? You did that paper on them in school, didn't you?" Callie asked, her voice indicating it wasn't so much of a question as a prodding for information.

"Yes," he answered, his fingers, checking over Bruce's underbelly for any other strange areas. "They only show signs of illness when their witch is sick."

Callie nodded, patting Bruce on the head. "That's what I was trying to look up today. I knew they showed signs of distress when their witch was ill, but I wasn't sure if they could be sick on their own."

"Not generally," Paris said, keeping his voice low.

"Jade's noticed it already. She wants to take him to a vet."

Paris gave a low 'hmm.' "I would take him to Hannah before I went to a vet," he replied, thinking of their oldest and wisest member. Hannah knew more about magic than anyone else in the Coven. Possibly more than anyone realized, Paris was sure. If there was something to do be done for Bruce, she would know, or would be able to find someone who did. "Unfortunately, she's out of town on Council business."

"Should we…" Callie trailed off, sitting back on her haunches. "I mean, I guess we shouldn't even worry about treating him. He's not the one who's sick." She paused and then looked up at Paris. "Is he?"

Paris gave Bruce's neck another long stroke, careful of the sore spot. "No, he's not."

"Is it… does it mean… well, is it only physical sickness? Like could it just be that Jade has really bad allergies or is getting a bad cold?"

Paris thought about the shift in Jade's eye-color when she fought Dex. About her nightmares, about the sense of someone outside her house doing magic.

Then there was Bruce's intelligence to consider. Paris thought of the way Bruce had come to his office, directly presenting his neck and then staring Paris in the eye as his own iris pulsed with a strange green shade.

No, this wasn't something trivial like Jade having a cold or the flu. It was something serious enough that not only was her familiar ill, he'd felt the strong urge to come and show Paris.

But, Paris wasn't ready to say that out loud yet. He felt as though to do so would be betraying a sort of confidence. He wanted to speak to Jade about it first.

"Perhaps."

"What should we tell Jade?" Callie's eyes were large and dark as she stared at Paris.

With one last pat on Bruce's head, Paris pushed himself up and settled back into the Queen Anne chair, Callie mirroring his actions and seating herself on the other side of the fireplace. Looking somewhat satisfied, Bruce stretched out further in front of the fire, each one of his talons coming slightly further out of his forefoot before slipping back as he relaxed again. "The truth. That if Bruce is sick it means that there's likely something wrong with her."

Paris' cell phone buzzed from his pocket, vibrating loudly with a harsh 'tzzzz.' Bruce rolled his head back and stared at Paris accusingly, as though the sound had disturbed his naptime. Paris regarded the screen fondly when he saw the text from Jade.

I hear you have my lizard. Has he destroyed anything?

"I bet that's Jade, checking in on Bruce," Callie said, her voice amused.

"Yes, wanting to know if he's destroyed anything." Paris typed a back a quick 'no' and then added that Bruce was just lying down in front of the fireplace.

He's a sook. He hates winter. I don't know how he survived the sewer. If he's bothering you, I can come get him.

"She's seems to be concerned he's being a bother."

Callie smiled. "I think that's her way of saying she's worried about him and wants him back. She seemed nervous bringing him this morning."

Paris typed back that Bruce wasn't a bother and was welcome to stay in Paris' office as long as required. "She likes knowing where he is. She probably feels connected to him, even if she doesn't realize it. He's certainly connected to her. Familiars tend to take on the characteristics of their witches and sync up with them emotionally. They tend to like the same things."

"Are you saying Jade would like to be stretched out in front of a fireplace as well right now?" Callie asked, a smile on her face.

Paris smiled back. "No, but if I put a cup of coffee down in front of Bruce, I've a notion he'll drink the entire thing and go looking for the pot."

"He did try to steal Jade's coffee this morning."

"He probably has a 'what's yours is ours' mentality when it comes to her things."

Paris' phone buzzed again and he scanned the text. "She's on her way up to get him."

Callie took a deep breath and pushed herself out of the chair. "I guess that's my cue to leave. Unless you'd like me to stay while you talk with her about Bruce?" Callie turned her eyes onto him, searching his own for an answer.

He shook his head. "No. But perhaps you could ensure those books you found are ready for Jade, should she want additional information after we speak."

Callie nodded and then in a burst of movement, leaned forward and gave him a big hug. She'd always been the more tactile of the two of the, ever since they were children. He hugged her back, grateful for the support. She pulled back after only a moment, crouching down to pet Bruce on the head.

"Bye, Bruce," she said lowly before giving Paris a quick wave of her fingers and leaving his office.

Paris looked back down at the lizard, stretched out languidly. "I don't suppose you have any advice on how to address your mistress?"

Bruce poked his tongue out. "Pfffffft." He turned his gaze from Paris and flopped his head back down on the ground.

"That's what I thought."

#

It wasn't like Jade had been called to Paris' office because she'd done something wrong or was in trouble. She'd offered to go of her own free will to get Bruce. Also, she was an adult. Even if she *had* done something wrong, which she hadn't, and she *was* being called down to Paris' office, she still shouldn't feel like a truant school child being summoned to the principal and told to wait outside the door.

Except she totally felt that way.

Jade didn't see Paris' assistant, Suki, which wasn't anything new. Although Jade had received emails from Suki and had once spoken to her on the phone, she'd yet to see her in person and hadn't completely abandoned the idea that she was some kind of sprite or fairy. No matter how much Callie laughed when Jade suggested it.

It was weird. The woman seemed to get a lot done in a day, and yet was never at her desk.

Jade knocked quickly three times on the door, waiting to hear Paris' invite before entering. She immediately caught sight of Bruce, stretched out languidly in front of the fireplace, a small fire there for him. Given the lack of wood or other material in the fireplace and the faint scent of Paris' magic when Jade sniffed - mint and sandalwood - she guessed that Bruce had suckered Paris.

"He totally made you cast that fire spell, didn't he?" Jade asked, crossing her arms over her chest and eyeballing Bruce. Bruce didn't roll over and look at her, but he did let out a decidedly loud huff of annoyance.

"I recalled you saying he gets cold easily and he pointedly looked at the fireplace."

"You are such a sookie baby," Jade said directly to Bruce, crossing over to him and then sitting down in one of the Queen Anne chairs. She leaned over and patted his belly, liking the firm 'thunk' it made when she did. Bruce's tongue flicked out at her quickly and then disappeared back in his mouth. He never opened his eyes to look at her, content to soak up the warmth.

"Lucky bastard. No working for you," Jade said, scratching her nails lightly over the one spot on his belly she knew he liked. "Did you have fun this morning?" She turned back to Paris. "I hope he wasn't bothering you. I let him go off with some other witches and I kind of thought they'd either bring him back or he'd find his way to me when he was done, but I guess he didn't."

"It wasn't a problem. He's an extraordinary creature. I don't mind if he stays here for a while," Paris replied, coming over to sit in the chair opposite Jade. Jade watched him move out of the corner of her eye without taking her gaze from Bruce. Sometimes she preferred watching Paris on the sly instead of straight on.

With everything going on lately - joining the Coven, then Dex and now Lily and the dreams, Jade didn't feel like she had enough time to sit down and eat breakfast let alone think about other things. Things like how the other night, when Paris came over, he'd sat next to her on the couch. Or things like at the Coven Ball, how Paris had leaned in and kissed Jade on the cheek. He'd meant it as a sort of teasing, fond gesture, and she got that, but having him so close to her in that moment, the feeling of him almost taking up all the space around her and of knowing that she must equally be taking up the space around him... it made her nervous. There were parts of herself that she'd thought were closed up for good - locked down and secured. She had purposely closed off those parts and she was fine with it. She wouldn't necessarily say she was happy with it, but it was the way things were, the way she wanted them to be. Now, sitting across from Paris, being able to smell his magic in the air and being in his office where so much of his essence was soaked into the room, she felt twitchy and on edge. Maybe... scared. She didn't want to think the word, but she also couldn't ignore it. It was a horrible time for her to even entertain such thoughts. Maybe her whole life was a horrible time to entertain such thoughts. Lily would probably know what to say to Paris, or know what to do. Jade just felt like a gangly pony - awkward, fumbling, limbs in all directions.

Bruce's tail flapped on the ground, wiggling a little bit and her eyes darted over to follow the movement. She patted his belly a few more times and then sat back in the chair. She could feel Paris' magic in the fire just off to her side and she tentatively pushed at it, poking around the edges. She felt an answering response from it and wasn't sure what it meant at first, but when she reached out with her magic again, she almost felt like she could suck the spell into her. Bruce twitched as she did it and Jade looked up at Paris questioningly.

"You can take it over, if you like."

Jade hadn't been aware that magic could transfer between witches, but as soon as Paris said it, she realized that she did feel like she could scoop it up. She carefully reached out with her magic, her power feeling fat and clumsy next to his. It was like trying to pick up a fine china teacup while wearing oven mitts. She sensed Paris pushing the spell toward her and then with a sort of swooping feeling in her stomach, the spell settled into her, the flames flaring up for a moment before flickering down again.

"There. You have it now."

Jade felt her shoulders straighten at the tone of pride in Paris' voice. She only had two seconds to enjoy the feeling before Paris spoke again.

"I'm glad Bruce found his way here. I'd like to talk you."

"I was sick that day," she said automatically. It was her standard response - half joking, half serious. She'd used it on Paris once before and his lips quirked.

"You're not in trouble. It's a little about Bruce as well, actually."

"You said he didn't destroy anything." Jade looked around the office for any signs that Bruce had done damage. The carpet still looked perfectly plush and beige everywhere, except for the one spot Jade knew was trapped underneath the chair she was sitting on, where Henri had once spilled a latte. She wasn't about to sell Henri out though. Paris' large, dark wood desk sat in front of the bay windows, looking pristine and well kept. The curtains hanging from the windows didn't seem disturbed, although to be honest, they did look a little worn.

Ugh, her lack of sleep was giving her 'squirrel brain' - when her mind just jumped from one thought to the other with no concept of attention or linearity.

Jade refocused her thoughts. "Everything looks okay. Did he eat your lunch? Or maybe chew your shoes? Scratch your outfit?" Jade asked, looking over Paris quickly and finding him well presented as always - grey turtleneck, dark slacks, dark shoes. But when she looked up at his face, his sharp blue eyes were watching her carefully and she had the fleeting thought that she was being watched by a hawk or other large bird of prey. He was looking for something, watching her. She narrowed her eyes in return. "What?"

"Bruce came into my office and showed me a bad patch of skin on his neck."

Not knowing why, Jade reached up to touch her own neck, her fingers pressing into the soft flesh there. "Yeah. I noticed it. I was going to see about taking him to a vet or one of those whatchamacallits. Herpetologist? Like the one you were going to bring in when we first found Bruce."

"I don't think that will be necessary."

"Okay," Jade said, wary. "Do you know what's wrong with him?"

"Usually when a familiar shows signs of distress or illness it's because its witch is distressed or ill."

Jade's eyes darted to Bruce, who still had his eyes closed, blissfully sleeping in front of the fireplace. "I wouldn't say he's distressed," she answered, deflecting the statement from being about her.

"No, but he did come here to show me his neck, and you were concerned about it yourself."

"Well, I wanted to put some cream on it or something. He keeps showing it to me." Her stomach sunk low into her belly, a heavy feeling swirling inside it.

"I think he knows that whatever is wrong with him, it's tied to you."

"But I'm not sick." She held her hands in her lap carefully. Her eyes darted down to Bruce. He was watching her, unblinking. Was his scaly patch her fault? Jade wasn't physically sick, but mentally...God, she had the sudden urge to laugh, her body flooded with anxiety and no way to outwardly release the energy. If Bruce was tied to her *mental* status, he was screwed.

"If Bruce is showing signs of illness," Paris continued, "it's likely because you're ill or sick. His body is forming a response to it."

"But I feel fine." Her voice came out weak and soft. She wouldn't have even believed it herself.

Paris didn't say anything in reply at first, just calmly stared at her with those almost too-blue eyes.

Jade thought of the dreams she'd been having - dreams of Lily, of the lake. Of water and cold. Dreams of feeling heavy and weighted down. She thought of waking up in the closet, then the bathroom, then the kitchen, not knowing how she got to any of those places.

She thought of the mirrors cracking. First at her cottage. Then at yoga. She'd been managing to avoid large mirrors since, but how long could she keep that up?

"I'd like you to go see Dr. Gellar."

Jade wanted to protest and clamped down on the immediate knee-jerk reaction to jump out of the chair and assert she was fine. It would only look worse. Besides, maybe there was something that could be done.

She looked at Bruce, watching him snooze by the fireplace. His belly moved up and down in rhythmic breathing and she counted the motion. Up and down. Up and down.

"If I were sick, what would happen to Bruce?"

"He'd likely get more ill until you started getting better."

Better. That was just such a loaded word. Jade didn't even know what it would mean. 'Better' as in 'no longer thinks she's two people?' 'Better' as in 'not constantly having nightmares about sparrows and the lake and Lily?' 'Better' meaning 'no longer wonders if she should be committed?' A bit of nausea rose up in her and she took a deep breath to stifle it.

"Okay. I'll go see Gellar." Jade started picking at one of her cuticles, her nails digging into the dry skin, pulling it away from her finger. It immediately began to hurt, but she couldn't stop. She'd end up making it bleed.

"Would you like me to go with you?" Paris asked.

Jade shrugged, not knowing if she wanted to say yes or no. The skin on her finger tore and sure enough, bright red popped up as it bled. She curled her fingers into a tight fist. "Uh. Sure. Or if you're busy you don't have to."

"I can make time for this. If I'm mistaken and Dr. Gellar finds you're not sick, I'll bring in a herpetologist for Bruce."

That made Jade feel better. If they didn't find out anything, Bruce would still get to see someone. She nodded, focusing on trying to unclench her fingers.

"I'm sure Dr. Gellar could fit you in today. Why don't I call down and then we can go together?"

"Okay. Let's go see Gellar."

CHAPTER SIX

No one liked going to the doctor. Jade knew she wasn't rare in her opinion on the matter. People only went to the doctor when they didn't feel well, so it was a good bet that most people already felt crummy before they ever stepped foot in the doctor's office. The crappy thing about the medlab in the Covenstead was that it doubled as a clinic, so it had that permanent 'hospital' smell - bandages and antiseptic. Sometimes Jade thought she could even catch the metallic scent of blood, but that could just be sense memory from all her trips to hospitals and emergency rooms when she was younger.

Ah, childhood. The not-so-good times.

Dr. Gellar herself was nice. She was professional and kind. Jade had the sense she really listened to her patients and it seemed like she was more than happy to fit Jade in without an appointment. Jade was silent as Paris explained the situation - Jade's familiar was showing signs of potential illness which indicated Jade herself was ill and could Dr. Gellar please look Jade over?

It was hard not to feel like a child while Paris did the talking, but at the same time, Jade felt uncharacteristically shy about voicing her concerns - especially with Paris standing right there. It's not like she was normally chatty with health care, but she wasn't about to start adding in any details with an audience. She was usually able to articulate her symptoms well and didn't play them up or down, but right now, she felt like if she opened her mouth she didn't know what would come pouring out.

Bruce remained in Paris' office. Neither Paris nor Jade thought it was a good idea to bring Bruce to medlab. Paris probably thought it was unsanitary or something, but Jade just didn't want him to end up smelling like hospital. Plus, there were a lot of sharp things. She liked knowing he was happily still in front of Paris' fireplace - unless he got bored and started poking around Paris' office. If she'd been left alone in Paris' office, it was what she would do.

Gellar was efficient and had Jade ensconced in a small examining room within a few minutes, handing over the requisite medical gown and leaving her to change. Jade held it up and turned it back and forth a few times wondering if she wanted the ties in the front or in the back or if it mattered. She settled on ties in the back, leaving her underthings on and hopping up on the medical table. With only the medical gown and her socks on, she was sure she made quite the picture. Classy. She pulled out her smart phone and killed some time surfing the net and checking her apps until Gellar came back in.

"Sorry about the wait, I just had a few other patients I had to finish up with."

Jade tossed her phone, watching it land on the pile of her clothes on the chair. "It's fine."

"Before we get started on anything new, I'd like to check in on your older injuries. How's the wrist? Any problems since the cast came off?"

Jade shook her head. The break she'd sustained after first coming to the Coven had healed well enough. Jade could say with some dark humor that, while it was the first time a demon from another dimension had broken one of her bones, it wasn't the first time a monster had done it. Her father held that dubious honor.

"Fine."

"No lingering aches? No weakness?" Gellar questioned.

"Nope."

Gellar smiled. "Good. And the scars from the demon, how are they healing?"

Jade knew she made a face at that, thinking about the five claw marks on her chest. "They're fine," she said. "Healed up. Just... pink and... well, I guess most people are pretty pale in the torso area, so they stick out. They're noticeable. Not that anyone's seeing me naked. Not that I *want* anyone to see me naked," she blurted out, her brain flashing quickly back to Paris and him kissing her on the cheek. She squirmed in her chair. "Or *don't want* anyone seeing me naked or-" She had to take a steadying breath to cut herself off. She wanted to clap her hand over her mouth. "They're fine."

"They'll start to fade with time." Gellar paused and then gave her a knowing look. "But, given your little outburst," Jade cringed, wishing she could snatch the words back, "are there any prescriptions I can fill for you while you're here? Contraceptives?" she asked, looking down at Jade's medical file briefly.

"No," Jade answered quickly, feeling her cheeks go hot. "Nothing."

"Okay. You know where I am if you change your mind." Gellar easily let the subject drop and Jade was grateful. She didn't think she had it in her to go down that road right now.

"Have you had any further adverse reactions to magic? Headaches, losing consciousness or bleeding from your nose or ears?"

"You make it sound like it happens all the time. It only happened twice," Jade protested. "Once because a demon was trying to pull me into their dimension and then once because I had to use a metric ton of magic to stop Dex's spell on the Coven."

Gellar looked slightly bemused at Jade's tone. "And if you keep pushing your magic too hard too fast, it will keep happening. So, anything since?"

"No," Jade replied, feeling like a kid that got busted stealing cookies. "I've been good with my magic, and nobody's needed saving from demons or witches gone bad. But you know, it's still early in the week."

"What is it that the witches say? Don't tempt Mother Nature?" Gellar asked, eyebrow raising. She wasn't a witch herself and being surrounded by so many other magical people, Jade sometimes forgot that Gellar was mortal, like Jade used to be. Or maybe never was. Sometimes when Jade thought about Lily and their childhood, she wasn't sure which was true.

"So, how have you been feeling in general?"

Jade blinked at Gellar's question, wondering how to answer. "Fine. I guess."

"Not exactly a rousing response."

Jade drummed her fingers against her knee. Gellar put her medical file down at the foot of the bed and leaned a hip against it.

"You know, anything you tell me stays with me."

"Yeah, but you work for the Coven."

"I'm paid by the Coven, yes, but I'm still a doctor. I keep doctor-patient confidentiality."

"What about Paris?" Jade asked, her eyes darting over to the door, behind which Paris was likely waiting.

"Paris is the Coven Leader and if something were affecting the entire Coven, a sickness or an illness, then I would have to tell him. But if something's only affecting one witch and is more of a personal nature, then he has no right to any information."

"But if Bruce is sick, doesn't it mean it has to be magic in origin?"

"Not necessarily," said Gellar. "Bruce may be ill because you are ill and he's tied magically to you. It could be something simple like you have eczema or allergies. Or maybe you're anemic. Or maybe this is the extraordinarily rare instance when a familiar is ill and it's not tied to a witch and we *do* need to treat Bruce."

"Or maybe something's wrong with me." Jade's voice was quiet in the sparse room. She wished she'd kept her sweater. She was cold.

"Maybe."

Jade wasn't sure if she was ready to tell the truth, the whole truth and nothing but the truth but maybe... maybe she could be honest. About pieces. Just to see where this all went. She took a deep breath.

"I'm having trouble sleeping."

"How so?"

Jade shrugged, staring down at her socked feet, kicking them a bit. "I seem to fall asleep easily enough, but I've been having a lot of dreams. Vivid dreams." In her mind's eye, she could see the green-blue water of her dreams, feel the pressing sensation of weight bearing down on her, feel the sluggish response of her limbs. When she heard things in her dreams, they had the dulled, sloshing tones of things heard underwater - muffled and thick. "I feel like I don't get any rest. When I get up, it's like I haven't been asleep, but I know I have been."

"You're going to bed and getting up at the same time?" asked Gellar.

"Mostly. I mean half an hour here or there."

"Do you wake up in the middle of the night? Is your sleep fragmented?"

Jade paused. "I... think so."

"You seem unsure. Do you think you've been waking up? Are you waking up enough to remember being awake?"

"I must be getting up because..." Jade cut herself off, hesitant to talk about the closet.

"Because what, Jade?"

"I wake up in the closet," she said quickly, trying to get the words out fast, like ripping off a bandage. "It's something we used to... I used to do a lot. Sleep in the closet. I go to sleep in my bed, but I wake up in the closet. Once I woke up in the bathroom. And once in the kitchen. That was new. It used to just be the closet."

Out of the corner of her eye, Jade could see Gellar lean in, her entire presence seeming to ooze concern and comfort. "And you don't remember waking up to get there?"

Jade shook her head.

Gellar glanced down at Jade's medical file, flipping through some of the pages. "Did you sleepwalk as a child? Or have night terrors?"

Jade felt her whole body pause, remembering hiding in the closet as a child, hearing her father, drunk, ransacking the house. He'd be looking for more booze, looking for more money to buy booze, or just looking for something to hit. While she knew it wasn't what Gellar meant, she couldn't help but flash on the memories when Gellar asked the question.

"No? I mean, I had nightmares like most kids, I guess. And maybe once or twice I might have walked in my sleep, but I don't recall it being a common thing. And never those terror things. Those are the things where you wake up screaming right?"

Gellar made a see-saw motion with her head. "Sometimes. It's similar to nightmares, but more dramatic. Sleepwalking is more common in children. Adults that suffer from it tend to have a history of it carried over from their childhood. The problem with sleepwalking is that it's more likely to occur when sleep deprived. If you're having poor sleep, you may sleepwalk, further disrupting your sleep. Is there anything else that's troubling you?"

Jade thought about the image in the mirror - seeing her iris go green for a moment. She thought about the strange feeling she had in her brain - the gravity well just outside her conscious thoughts - a feeling she'd always associated with Lily. She didn't feel ready to say those things out loud.

Jade shook her head. "No, nothing else."

Gellar regarded Jade for a moment, letting the silence sit, giving Jade a chance to add in or change her mind. When that didn't happen, Gellar nodded once to herself and then spoke again. "Let's take a look at your numbers."

She took Jade's pressure and pulse, then checked her ears, eyes and throat. She held the requisite cold stethoscope to Jade's chest and made her breathe in and out - which always left Jade feeling a little out of breath even though she didn't really have to do anything. Gellar reached out to touch Jade's neck and Jade flinched back at first before offering a wry lip curl and then staying put as Gellar checked her lymph nodes. Gellar had a few more questions - digestion, monthly cycles, diet and exercise, etc. and Jade didn't really know what to tell her. Fine, regular, good and okay. Jade's health had always been robust and she wasn't prone to illness. She didn't eat great and didn't work out seven days a week, but she also wasn't at the drive-thru eating fast food every day and she was running at least three out of four days.

Gellar pursed her lips. "I'd like to run some basic lab tests - CBC, iron, check your electrolytes, that sort of thing. Let's have you come back in a couple days for the results. If we find anything, we can go from there."

Jade shrugged. "Okay." What was she going to say? No? What if there was something wrong with her? Something physical, something totally unrelated to Lily and magic. People got sick all the time. Young people, seemingly healthy people, people with no symptoms.

Gellar was fast with the blood draw, doing it herself and not calling in a nurse or a tech. She was quick to find a vein and only had to poke it once, and Jade suspected she wouldn't even bruise from the needle like she sometimes did. Gellar pocketed the vials of blood in one of the deep slots of her lab coat.

"I'll leave you to change, but as I said, lets get you back in a couple days so we can go over the results of your blood work and maybe re-assess some additional testing. How about early next week?"

Jade nodded dumbly, already sliding off the table and making her way to her clothes. Gellar placed a hand on her shoulder and gave it a squeeze and although Jade wasn't generally used to people touching her, she found she didn't mind. Gellar's hand was strong and solid.

"Try not to worry, Jade. We'll figure this out."

She gave Jade a slight smile and made her way out of the room. Jade stood there for a moment, fiddling with her bra, trying to get it right side up and proper side out, Gellar's words in her head - 'we'll figure this out.' We. Jade was part of a 'we' now, something she had to keep reminding herself. Jade was part of the Coven - even if said Coven didn't always seem to be full of warm fuzzies for her, she *was* a part of it. It wasn't just her alone anymore.

#

Paris looked up expectantly at Dr. Gellar as she came out of the examination room making quick notes in what was presumably Jade's chart. He'd been randomly flipping through one of the magazines left in the waiting area, not really paying attention to what he was looking at, but feeling the need to have something in his hands. He closed the magazine, pinching it between two fingers as he stood to face Dr. Gellar.

"Well, doctor?"

Dr. Gellar came over to him, a wry look on her face. "You know I can't tell you anything for two reasons. One: I've only just had a look at Jade and two: doctor-patient confidentiality."

"But if it's something magic in origin..." Paris began, hoping Dr. Gellar would pick up on the thread.

"If it's something magic in origin, then yes, you will be the first to know and I'll likely need help dealing with it or treating it with magic. But until we learn anything, I'll treat it as a medical concern and that means no sharing."

Paris took a breath and let it out. It was totally expected and yet the exact opposite of what he wanted Dr. Gellar to say.

"She might share with you if you ask her," Dr. Gellar said cryptically.

"So there is something to share?"

Gellar shook her head and nearly rolled her eyes at him. "If you want to know, ask her. I've got lab tests to run," she said, patting her pocket lightly. Paris was left standing in the middle of the waiting room, staring awkwardly at the door. Jade came out, moments later, still tugging her t-shirt down, giving him a quick glimpse of her pale midriff. He could see the dark pink slashes that were left over from her run-in with a demon. She hiked up her jeans on the way over, and then hopped on one foot as she adjusted one of her sneakers. She tended to favor casual clothing compared to some members of the Coven and since they had no official dress code, it wasn't an issue. He recognized her t-shirt with the chemical compound for caffeine depicted on the front. It must be one of her favorites - she wore it often.

Paris forced a smile to his lips, thinking on Gellar's advice. "How did it go?"

Jade paused midstep, hopping once more as she fixed her shoe before finally getting both feet back on the ground. She shrugged. "You know. Blood work, questions. Blah, blah. A regular trip to the doctor's."

Paris nodded thoughtfully, wondering how to ask if she had anything else to share. As it turned out, he needn't have worried. It seemed all Jade needed was a bit more silence to finish her thoughts. She pursed her lips, and then continued.

"With the bad dreams I've been having, I haven't been sleeping well. I bet all my electrolytes are off or something. Cortisol or adrenaline, all out of whack." She waved a hand, her eyes darting around. "But, you know, everyone has insomnia now and then."

Now *that* tone Paris understood. Jade quite often expressed a thought that she wanted reassurance on.

"Most people do have insomnia now and then, yes," he said, knowing he'd said the right thing when her shoulders relaxed, no longer looking like they were attached to her ears.

"Right? And it's been pretty wacky around here with demons and Dex and Veronica," Jade added, hesitating slightly before she said Veronica's name.

Paris bristled slightly, trying to mask his reaction. Having once been involved with Veronica, it stung that he hadn't ever guessed she would be the type to deal with demons. She'd never been as powerful as other witches, but he never thought she'd make a deal to increase her abilities.

"It's definitely been a trying time," Paris replied, his voice low. Jade was right of course; even without his worry over what was going on with Jade and Bruce's strange scaly patch, it had been a difficult time. It wouldn't be strange if she were suffering from insomnia or the like. He just didn't think that was *all* she was suffering from.

"Yeah," Jade said, picking at one of her cuticles. "I don't suppose you've heard from Veronica, hey?"

Paris shook his head. "No. I don't expect to."

"I kinda thought maybe she'd reach out to you, either to ask about your mom's demon grimoires or to ask me about Seth."

The way Jade casually spoke of the demon made him want to flinch. Paris grew up with a healthy aversion to demons. His mother had drilled him on how dangerous demons and their magic were. It was why he was so stunned when he found out his mother had regularly dealt in demon magic. She'd been adamant his entire life that demon magic was to be avoided at all costs. Before Jade joined the Coven, Paris honestly and, perhaps, naively thought that no one dealt with demons any longer. Then he found out that one of his own Coven members, Matthew, dealt with a demon trying to steal Jade's power. And then Veronica - dealing with a demon to boost her power so that she could never have her Coven Leader position taken from her. That deal still had the bitter taste of betrayal for Paris. He and Veronica had been close. To find out that she'd not only made a demon deal, but that she'd colluded with Dex to cast a spell on his entire Coven, including Paris, had been harrowing.

"I think that Veronica knows me well enough to know I would never entrust her with any grimoire of my mother's. Demon or otherwise."

"Not even if it could get her out of a demon deal with Seth?" Jade asked.

Paris paused, wondering what he *would* do if Veronica came to him for help. "If she did contact me and asked, I'd prefer you and I go over the grimoires ourselves and we could provide any reasonable leads or spells to her."

In contrast to Veronica, Paris trusted Jade implicitly with his mother's demon spell books. Jade kept one at her house, studying it in her off hours. She was far more proficient at demon magic than Paris. Indeed, more proficient than any witch in the Coven. If there was something to be found that could assist Veronica, Jade would be the one to find it. They could then pass it along to Veronica, if she ever surfaced again. She'd not been heard of since she left Paris' Coven.

"In addition, it's not as though we know a great deal about... Seth," Paris said, hesitating over saying the demon's name. He could still hear his mother's voice in his ear, 'Speak of the devil and who shall appear?' Seth once told Jade that all she had to do was say his name, with intent, and he would cross over from his dimension. Paris wasn't comfortable with the vagary of that statement and wanted to hunch in on himself whenever he had to say the demon's moniker, which thankfully, wasn't often. "Other than him showing up when you first arrived and trying to intimidate you into a deal, he's not really been an issue."

The way she bobbed her head and avoided his gaze made the hair on the back of his neck tingle.

"Has he?" Paris put a little oomph behind his words, trying to get every ounce of his authority behind it.

Jade toed her shoe against the floor causing the rubber to give a squeak. "Look, I was going to tell you."

He put one hand up to his eyes, his other hand crinkling the magazine he was still holding, the paper slick and fragile under his fingers. He had not been expecting this, although in hindsight, perhaps he should have.

"But it's not like I had a lot of spare time what with stopping Dex and everything, if you recall," Jade said, crossing her arms over her chest. Damn it, there was that sharp tone of hers. Jade seemed to have a rule - the best defense was a good offense and her offense was pretty damn good. "It wasn't like anyone was lining up to believe me when I said Dex was out to get us. Which he had been, with his freaky blood spells and," she uncrossed her arms for a moment to waggle her fingers in the air, "memory voodoo. So, I didn't really have time to mention that Seth was showing up in my pantry-"

"Your pantry?" Paris repeated, incredulous.

"I told you I don't keep any food in there!" Jade made it sound as though that should have cleared the whole issue up in the first place.

Paris pinched the bridge of his nose. "Goddess protect you." He made a tired 'go on' motion. "Please continue."

She shrugged, arms still tight against her chest. "I don't really have anything else to say. Seth likes to show up. He thinks he's wooing me or buttering me up and he maybe helped me with that demon rune I cast on myself." At the look Paris gave her, she straightened her shoulders and eking every millimeter out of her spine to put her only a scant two inches under his height. "Nobody else was able to help at the time, if you remember." Jade pointedly looked at him. He didn't have a leg to stand on for that accusation. He hadn't believed her when she accused Dex and even though he'd apologized for it, it was still fresh enough that he should steer clear of the topic if possible. He also hadn't been able to assist her with the demon rune she'd cast on herself that would expose liars. "So, if Veronica contacts you," Jade continued, "given that her deal is held by Seth, she might like to know that he does show up in my pantry. Occasionally. Sometimes. It's not like I encourage it."

Paris could hear the paper in his hands tearing as he tried to keep his voice calm and level. "Will you please let me know if he shows up again?"

"Sure."

"Has *he* been contributing to your insomnia? Is there anything else you're not telling me?" This could change things entirely. If Jade still had the demon showing up, possibly working magic…

"Seth?" Jade asked, voice incredulous. Paris winced at the easy way she said his name. "No. I mean, it's not exactly comforting that he shows up in my pantry, but the house is warded so he can't show up anywhere else. Besides, I'm pretty sure he just wants me to deal. As long as I keep not doing that, he's kind of a known quantity." She smirked. "I guess he really is the devil I know."

"I would feel better if you kept me apprised of his appearances."

"I said I would."

"Anything else bothering you?"

A weak laugh burst forth from her lips, seeming to surprise her as much as it did him. "Um, no." She shook her head. "Just same old stuff as always."

Paris frowned. It wasn't really the answer he'd been hoping for. "I hope you know that if something is troubling you, I'm happy to help, if I can."

Jade nodded, staring down at her feet, her ponytail swinging to and fro as her head bobbed. It was pretty clear she was humoring him so he let it drop.

"You probably have Coven-y Leader things to do. Shaking hands, kissing babies. You can go, if you want."

"Your health is important to me, Jade."

"No, I get that. It's just... I've got stuff at Counter-Magic and... things."

It was so clearly a dismissal and done so awkwardly, he wanted to wince for her.

"I suppose you have been gone from your desk for a while."

"Yeah and I'm not high up on the food chain like you."

Paris felt his lips curl into a slight smile. "No, bit of a grunt, you are." He gestured with one of his hands, realizing he was still holding the magazine from the waiting room. Jade snorted as she caught sight of the cover.

"A little light reading?" She smirked.

He glanced down at the cover, a slim model proclaiming she knew all the secrets to weight loss, great sex and eternal happiness. He dropped the magazine back on one of the side tables, wanting to brush his hands off. To be honest, he hadn't noticed what he was picking up and flipping through while he'd been waiting for Jade. He'd been too worried about what was going on behind the closed medical examination room door to focus on what he'd picked up.

"Yes. However did I run the Coven before without that wealth of knowledge? Surely no one will be able to resist me now that I know all the secrets of body language and low-carbs."

Jade laughed, letting herself be corralled somewhat by him, heading toward the exit of the medlab. The sound was warm and bright and he leaned toward her to soak it up.

"Don't be hard on yourself, English. Next month's issue will come out and all of it will be proven wrong and you'll have to learn some other heretofore unknown tidbits."

"How will I keep it all straight?"

"That's why they pay you the big bucks."

#

Back at her desk, Jade tried to push the visit to medlab out of her head. There wasn't anything she could do about it now. She could sit there and borrow trouble from the future, wondering what her lab results would be, or she could try and get some work done. She texted Paris to check if Bruce was still in his office and Paris replied back that he was, still sleeping in front of the fireplace. Jade felt a quick surge of pride, realizing she'd been able to keep the fire spell stable for him even through her trip to medlab and from the distance of the Counter-Magic offices. She hoped Bruce was okay. She worried about him. He clearly knew something was wrong and was trying to communicate that with Jade - first showing her his scaly patch and then, when that didn't work, showing Paris. Paris texted back again, asking if he should bring Bruce down and even though she missed him and would love to have him sit by her feet while she worked, she knew he'd be happier in front of the fireplace. She typed out a quick text back.

Let him snooze. I'll swing by when Callie's ready to give us a ride home.

Jade lost track of the day, caught up in trouble-shooting a more complex spell than she was used to. Feeling like she'd finally been given something more than a 'rookie' task made Jade want to nail this spell. She had quickly learned when she started that while her knowledge of magic was still growing, she had a good intuition and she trusted her gut. However, there was no getting around that she just didn't have as much experience as other witches. She'd gotten used to querying the Counter-Magic's databases for similar spells, but in this case, she didn't find anything that felt like a 'match.' Finding nothing in the database meant she'd have to check the shared drives. Ugh. Nightmare. They were disorganized and haphazard with no one controlling the files. Everything about them made her want to start organizing them, even if she wasn't paid to do it.

She started poking around, opening some folders and files and doing some keyword searches. The spell she was working on had to do with heating up water and she knew she was going to have a hard time with it. Her water skills were horrible and she had no desire to work on them at all. But, if she avoided fixing this spell, it might lead to questions she didn't want to answer about why she wasn't solving it. She couldn't say, 'You know, I just get this hinky feeling in general about water magic, so I thought I'd avoid it all together. Why, no. I don't want to talk about it.' So, Jade was going to figure it out, fix it and then move on.

The problem with the shared drive wasn't usually no results, but too many. Searching for 'water' was like going to the grocery store and asking for 'food.' A lot of items came back from the query, but one word kept catching her eye.

Lake.

Her mouse pointer hovered over a spreadsheet that the search tool indicated had several hits regarding the lake. It was created this month and worked on just ten minutes ago. Should she click? It definitely didn't contain any information on the spell she was working on, so she didn't need to open it. Her finger twitched on the mouse. Did she need anymore fodder for her nightmares? She fiddled with the salamander charm on her necklace, running it back and forth on the chain. Was she being ridiculous? It probably wasn't anything to be worried about. It was probably some kind of ecological study or environmental report.

Something horrendously boring and full of mundane data. Right? Right.

Jade double clicked on it, holding her breath while it loaded. When the spreadsheet opened, she felt sick in her stomach and her throat was tight.

It was a Counter-Magic complaint log about the lake. Witches were complaining the lake area felt 'worse' than usual or 'stronger.' It was hardly quantitative and, since Jade was new to the Coven, it didn't tell her much. She didn't know how witches felt about the lake before. She started reading and felt her stomach take a further dive when her name came up in conjunction with the bad feelings people were having. Checking the dates of the log, she saw the calls and complaints started right after Coven magic had been reset. Jade glanced around, checking that no one was watching her or walking by her desk while she was reading the spreadsheet. Although, she thought, if someone tried to open it while she had it open, it would show as locked under her username. She closed it quickly and took a copy to open on her own computer.

The complaints started slowly but had increased. Her fingers trailed across the screen lightly as she read the spreadsheet from side to side, noting the date, the witch that called in and the details of their complaint. The complaints came in regularly and then started spiking - becoming more prevalent late at night or early mornings.

Around the time she would be asleep, or rather, having a nightmare.

That couldn't be her fault though, could it? She wasn't actively doing any magic at night, she was sure of it. Also, she preferred the demon grimoires, finding their spells more precise and measurable. She was extra careful working with those, knowing that slip-ups with demon magic were likely to be worse than other kinds of spells. She had proper wards up, checked in with Paris before she did anything and always completed the spells as written. To be any more careful, she'd have to be in a full on bubble suit inside a padded cell.

Hmm. Given her mental state, maybe thinking about padded cells wasn't such a good idea right now.

The complaint calls coming in detailed how witches felt more of her magic out by the lake, and felt it in a dissonant way. Jade knew most of the Coven was a little sore about their magic not working the same as it had before and part of her wondered if this could be sour grapes.

Although she was hesitant to admit it, it didn't seem so. The way the complaints were entered in, they seemed almost…. cautious. Careful. As though people had been hesitant to call in and didn't want to be any more forceful than they had to be. It was frustratingly vague, but Jade had already once vented to Daniel about the Counter-Magic complaint line. She didn't understand how people who had been witches their whole lives didn't have any better descriptors other than, 'it's weird now,' or 'I don't know, it's just different.'

Daniel had agreed it was one of their failings for sure. It was hard for witches to quantify magic. They tended to be rather intuitive and feelings-based about it and lacked any kind of quantitative measurement.

Reading the comments about the lake area, Jade recalled Paris once told her the area usually made people uncomfortable - ever since an accident several years prior. Now, it appeared it was making people even more uneasy and seemed to be pulsing with Jade's magic.

Jade rubbed the back of her neck, feeling the hairs there twitching. Looking at the words people used when describing the lake, they felt the opposite of how Jade felt. Witches complained the lake was giving off 'strange' energy, putting out 'bad' feelings. It was all about the area pushing something 'out.' Jade got the feeling the lake area was sucking something *in*. Like a black hole or gravity well, continually pulling, hungry for more.

Jade was cold and clammy. She stopped reading the spreadsheet and sat back in her chair.

"What happened out there?" Jade asked, murmuring aloud. Jade joined the Coven as an adult, instead of being raised in it. There were things, events, and histories that everyone else knew or had absorbed growing up that she had no idea about. She chewed on her bottom lip, worrying it between her teeth and tasting her lipstick. She leaned back in her chair, able to just barely see around the cubicle wall and catch a glimpse of Daniel's back. Should she just ask? Was it taboo? These complaints seemed to be about her magic and she was having nightly dreams about the lake. Didn't she have a right to information so she could defend herself?

"I can feel you staring at my back," Daniel said suddenly and Jade flinched. She grabbed the first thing within her reach, a small pad of post-it notes, and lobbed it at his spine.

"That's creepy when you do that. Did you use magic for it?"

Daniel turned around in his chair, a grin on his face. "Nope. Your chair squeaks when you lean back. Besides, what's creepier? You creeping on me or the fact that I can tell when you're doing it?"

Jade rolled her eyes on him. "Fine. I'm creeping on you," she said, keeping her voice low. "I found this log about the lake area and complaints about me and my magic."

Daniel paused and blinked a couple times. "Wow, you don't beat around the bush, do you?"

"Would you like me to try? Hey Daniel, what's new in the few minutes since we talked? Nothing? No kidding. By the way, there's this log on the Counter-Magic shared drives about me that I didn't know about. Can we discuss?"

Daniel shook his head, as though he found her amusing. "I think I prefer the straight talk to that painful attempt at being diplomatic."

"Me too. So. What's this log about?"

"It's just a log, Jade. We've had some complaints about the area and people say that they get an impression of your magic."

"The entire Coven is getting an impression of my magic right now," Jade said defensively. "I can't help that Paris reset Coven magic and used me as the template."

"I know," Daniel said, keeping his tone even and neutral. It was the same tone that Jade used on people when they were being unreasonable. She bristled.

"Why didn't anyone tell me about this?"

"We don't tell everyone everything that happens at the Coven, Jade. There's too much going on."

Jade eyeballed him with a look. "Lame answer. My name is all over that thing."

Daniel looked over at where Josef's office was, like he was checking on the man. Jade couldn't help but glance over her shoulder too.

"What?" she asked.

Daniel looked slightly grim. "No one around the Coven likes to talk about it. But there was a drowning out there. We don't have a lot of deaths in the Coven. I mean, we have regular accidents or simple mortality - car crash, bad cholesterol, that kind of thing. But it's… rare for witches to die in accidents involving nature. A lot of it has to do with our magic. We're tied to the elements and we are quite good at manipulating them. In turn, Mother Nature tends to respect us so long as we respect her. Death by fire, asphyxiation, or drowning isn't common. And of course, it's worse when it's a child."

Jade felt her stomach roll over. "A child drowned out there?"

Daniel nodded at her question. "Yeah." Daniel looked around again, checking there was no one close by. He scooted his chair in closer to Jade and she leaned toward him. "Josef's niece. She was about four."

In her mind, she could picture a small, diminutive form, sinking beneath the surface of the lake. Tiny arms, tiny legs, weighed down by cold water. A small burst of her power felt like it popped somewhere inside her, surprising her enough to flinch. From Daniel's quick jerk backward, it did the same to him.

"Sorry," Jade said quickly, pulling in her power. She rolled her neck, trying to loosen the tension.

"No problem. It's upsetting," said Daniel. "It's why we don't talk about it."

Jade's eyes darted over to Josef's office again. It hit her that she didn't know much about him. She liked him well enough and was happy working for him, but knew zip about his personal life.

"I didn't know he had a family."

Again Daniel looked grim. "He... doesn't. Not anymore. It was just his sister and her kid. And when his niece died his sister kind of... gave up I guess."

"What happened to her?"

Daniel gave a half-shrug. "It's kind of like a magical wasting away? We're so tied to nature and our magic, and it was like... her force of will just gave up."

Jade didn't know what to say. "That's sad."

"Yeah. After the accident the lake area was avoided out of respect. Later on, as time passed, people tried to go back and use the area again, but they noticed the area felt 'off.' Things like that leave a mark, you know? On witches and on nature. Bad vibes." He shook out his hands as though those same bad vibes were attached to him for speaking about them and he needed to rid himself of the energy.

"And now people are complaining that it feels like my magic out there too," Jade added. She worried her bottom lip again, feeling a sting of pain at a spot she'd worked over too much with her teeth. "I'm not doing anything. At least..." she hesitated and then pushed through, "at least, not on purpose." She thought about her dreams and Lily, about how the timing of her nightmares lined up with the complaints. She thought about Bruce's strange scaly patch and the possibility that she might be sick.

Daniel nodded. "I know."

"Does Josef?" Jade asked, hating how her voice came out hesitatingly. "I mean, is it weird for him to have something strange going on there now?"

Daniel paused before answering. "Maybe. It's hard to say. He plays it pretty close to the vest."

Jade looked at her computer screen, seeing the long list of complaints that had come in. "Are there any other spreadsheets with my name all over them?"

"No."

She swiveled her head to look at Daniel. "I'd rather know now then find out later."

"I promise, we're not keeping secrets from you."

Not like I'm keeping from you, Jade thought, the words coming sudden and unbidden into her head. She was a total hypocrite - feeling hurt and angry that they had a log with complaints about her when she was keeping so much more from them. Maybe she was totally at fault. Maybe she was losing her mind and this was how it was all starting - visions of Lily, dreams of Lily, magical consequences she couldn't control.

"Hey," Daniel said, tapping her on the arm, bringing her back from her thoughts. "Don't worry about. We'll get everything sorted out."

There it was again - 'we.' Coven members were so quick to use it. They were ready to see themselves as a unit, a functioning group. Jade found uneasy comfort in the word. Like a new pair of boots that felt fine at first, but two hours later had blisters breaking out and bleeding. Her stomach felt like lead - too much caffeine and anxiety and not enough food.

"Yeah," she said weakly, trying to approximate a small smile. "I'm sure we will."

CHAPTER SEVEN

For about half an hour after Paris came back from medlab, he watched Bruce. It wasn't that he was worried about the creature; it was more the novelty of him. When Paris entered his office, Bruce's tail twitched twice and he blinked open one eye. That watchful pupil followed Paris from the doorway to his desk. Bruce waited until Paris sat down before shutting his eye and adjusting himself slightly in front of the fire, scooting closer. Paris was surprised the flames were as bright as they were. He thought Jade's magic would have faded as her distance from the office increased, first with their trip to medlab and then on her way back to the Counter-Magic offices. He fully expected to have to recreate the flames upon his return. However, they glowed a lovely shade of yellow-orange and seemed to be serving Bruce well, keeping him warm.

Even though all Bruce did was sleep, he was still intriguing to watch. Paris took in his long, serpentine belly with his short, stout legs, each claw on his foot tapering to a fine point at the end. He had slightly hooded eyes, making him look a little perturbed, even as he slept. He twitched as he dozed in front of the fire, much like a dog would - legs jerking slightly, tail moving faintly. After thirty minutes, Paris forced himself to turn away and get back to work. Watching Bruce sleep wasn't accomplishing much, although it was quite relaxing.

After an hour, a low growling sound brought Paris' attention back to the creature. It took him a moment to realize that Bruce was snoring in his sleep. Long, deep inhalations followed by short, sharp exhalations. Bruce snored air into his snout and then puffed it out, just the tip of his pink tongue lolling out of his mouth. Paris knew he shouldn't, but he took his phone out and snapped a picture, thinking to share it with Jade at a later time. Her fierce, magical familiar, sacked out, drooling on the carpet.

The flames in the fireplace burst alight suddenly, sending a wave of heat across the office. In one deft movement, Bruce flipped up to all fours and exhaled sharply out his snout, making a loud snorting sound. Paris sent his own magic out and felt it push up against Jade's power, a quick, sharp flare that was gone almost as soon as it had come. Bruce turned accusing eyes on Paris, as though he were somehow responsible for what had happened and Paris fought the urge to explain himself to a lizard. Bruce gave a bark-like sound and then rushed the closed office door, scratching at it with one of his talons, leaving several long gouges in the wood before Paris was able to get over and open it.

Bruce bolted out, his talons making a clackety-clack sound on the tile floors. Intrigued, Paris hurried after him.

Bruce was a lizard on a mission and witches wisely got out of his way. Of course, Paris thought if a seventy-pound lizard suddenly seemed to be rushing him, he'd dodge out of the way too. Bruce went down the stairs so quickly, Paris feared he'd go tail over teakettle, but he managed to keep all four legs facing downward.

The kindest way to describe the sound Henri made when he saw Bruce go zipping by his desk was a shriek. Paris would have called it a squeal, but it was a tad too guttural for that. Unperturbed, Bruce sailed on by, heading straight down the corridor to the back of the Covenstead where the Counter-Magic offices were. Paris was afraid at what he might find when he finally caught up with Bruce.

Rounding the door to Counter-Magic, he was just in time to see Bruce race up to Jade and head-butt her leg.

"Bruce! Where's the fire?"

Bruce butted his snout against her leg again and Jade reached down to pet his head. She looked up and caught sight of Paris hovering in the doorway.

"What did you do to him?"

"I did nothing," Paris protested immediately. "He was sleeping, there was a burst of flame from the fireplace and he came tearing down here as though the very devil were behind him."

Jade looked sheepish, wincing. "Sorry about that, buddy. Magic got a little out of control."

Paris wasn't sure if he was outraged or not that she was apologizing to Bruce and not him. "Something wrong?"

Jade raised a shoulder in a shrug. "Nah. Just… distracted for a moment and lost my spell. It's all fine now."

"You've been quite good at controlling your magic lately," Paris said, hoping the leading sentence would give her an opening. She only nodded a bit, keeping her head down toward Bruce.

Bruce perked up, his head turning toward Josef's office and, after his talons skidded on the tile floor a few times, shuffled to his feet and then darted over, scratching at the door.

"Yeah, that's a habit we're going to have to work on breaking," Jade said, following after him.

Josef was already opening the door by the time Jade came over to fetch Bruce. Josef looked around for the sound of the scratching, much like Paris had done earlier.

"What have we got here? Oh, hello. You must be Bruce." Josef hunkered down to get closer to the lizard.

Bruce's tail wagged back and forth wildly, the long length of it making huge sweeping arcs across the floor. It knocked into two chairs and almost one witch before the young lady deftly jumped up like she was skipping rope, averting near disaster. Josef reached out to pet Bruce and Paris was surprised when Bruce also presented Josef with his scaly patch, as he'd done up in Paris office.

Josef reached out to touch it. "What have you here?"

"Oh! Don't touch it. He gets-"

Jade stopped herself suddenly when Josef laid a hand on Bruce's spot. Bruce dropped his butt onto the ground with a thud and then rolled over onto his side so Josef could have a better look.

"Oh." Jade looked completely stunned.

"Problem?" Paris asked her.

"I just thought… earlier today someone else touched it and Bruce got snippy. But…" she waved a hand toward Josef and Bruce.

"He seems fine with me looking at it," Josef said. He trailed his fingers lightly over the scaly spot.

"Yeah." Jade crossed her arms over her chest, looking perturbed.

Josef peered closely at Bruce's sore spot, pressing at it lightly. He turned his gaze up to Jade, eyes narrowing slightly. "Are you feeling all right?" he asked, voice quiet enough so that the rest of the office wouldn't hear.

"Um. I'm working on that," Jade managed to say.

"Have you seen anything like it before?" Paris knew Josef had a wealth of experience and it was possible he knew something.

Josef nodded. "A long time ago. When I was a boy. My grandmother had a familiar. An owl."

Paris wanted to ask what happened to Josef's grandmother and her owl but had a feeling there was a reason the older gentleman hadn't shared the details.

"You've seen Dr. Gellar?" Josef addressed the question to Jade and she nodded. "Then I'm sure it's well in hand," Josef replied. "This fellow reminds me a little of her owl. Same kind of eyes."

Bruce sneezed suddenly, Elizabethan collar fanning out and then flapping shut. He flipped up to his feet again and then without ado, trotted away to Jade's desk, curling into himself underneath and dropping his head down for a nap.

"And that's that," Jade muttered.

Josef stood. "Do you need any time off?"

Paris thought that might be a good idea but Jade shook her head. "No. I like to be busy."

"Okay. Let me know if you change your mind." Josef's phone rang from inside his office and he excused himself with a quick nod to both Paris and Jade. Jade fiddled with the salamander charm on the chain around her neck, running it back and forth.

"I meant to ask if you'd like me to stop by tonight and perhaps work on some magic," said Paris. "Perhaps we can find another spell for your dreams."

Jade chewed on her lip. "Okay."

"I can even give you and Bruce a ride back to your cottage."

"You know his talons are sharp, right? You have leather seats."

Paris smiled. "I know. I've faith in him."

Jade looked dubious. "I can't afford to fix them if he tears them."

Paris chose to ignore her comment. He felt quite confident that Bruce wouldn't damage anything. "I'll see you at reception at around five."

"Yeah, okay."

#

Jade kept a close eye on Bruce the whole way to her cottage. He was stretched out across Paris' backseat seemingly happy to have a little nap as they drove.

"I'm sure he's fine. It can't be good for your back to be twisted like that," Paris said, keeping his eyes on the road as he drove.

"It's fine."

Bruce flicked his tongue out at her, catching her right on the nose. Jade grunted in annoyance and only then turned to face forward.

Once back at her cottage, Jade made a quick dinner for them of some left over chicken and Caesar salad. It wasn't much, but Paris seemed to enjoy it. She wasn't much of a cook, but she could assemble food pretty darn well. After dinner, they moved back into her modest living room. Bruce stretched out in front of the fireplace (his belly full from the remains of the chicken that didn't get used in the salad) and before he even had to look pointedly at either of them, Paris conjured a nice, bright flame for him. Bruce wiggled closer to the fireplace in appreciation, sighing happily.

"Is your sleep still troubled?"

Jade thought that was a nice way of putting it, thinking of the dreams of water and Lily. "Yeah. I keep trying that spell but no luck."

"Hmm. No other problems with your other spell work?"

"Nope." She thought about the broken mirror upstairs and at the yoga studio. Should she mention it? What would she say?

"I've a spell I'd like us to try tonight. A hex bane oil. It's supposed to disperse bad energy. I thought we could brew it and then anoint your house. See if that helps."

It sounded interesting to Jade. "Sure. What do I need?"

It took a few minutes to gather the spices and other ingredients from her kitchen and then cleanse the coffee table for spell work. When she'd started working with magic, Jade had been surprised how much she liked the ritual of things - the routine. Cleansing areas before working, careful measurements, staying focused, keeping tidy. They all made her feel calm and focused - things she hadn't felt for a long time.

Although, it was getting harder to keep her focus around Paris. Jade found her mind drifting from the spell work to watch his hands as he measured herbs. Or she found herself breathing in deeply when he worked magic to catch the scent of mint and sandalwood. Tonight was no different and she had to shake her head once or twice to refocus on what they were doing.

Making the hex bane oil took over an hour and then it took longer still to travel to each room in the small cottage and anoint it. Just as Paris was about to enter into the master bath, where the cracked mirror would definitely draw his attention, Jade reached out and grabbed his sleeve, tugging at it.

"Oh, I… I haven't cleaned. I can do that room later."

He watched her for a few seconds and she forced herself to stay perfectly still.

He finally nodded. "All right."

Jade didn't think the cottage felt all that different after the anointing, but if it kept her from having any more nightmares, she didn't care. After cleaning up their spell work, Paris hovered in her doorway for a few seconds. Jade could almost feel him trying to find what he wanted to say and she was scared of what would come out of his mouth. Would he ask her about her dreams again? Did he have bad news about Bruce? Something he realized or remembered about familiars being sick? When he finally did speak, she was both relieved and disappointed.

"I hope you sleep well."

She managed a tight nod in return and then froze as he reached out and rested a hand on her shoulder, trailing it down her arm and wrapping around her fingers for just a moment. Was she supposed to do something? Say something? Her fingers twitched against his and he let go. She wasn't sure if he took her slight movement as acceptance or rejection and she didn't know what to say when she didn't know what she meant herself.

After closing the door, she heard the clacking of Bruce's claws on the floor, announcing his presence behind her. Even then, she still startled when he head-butt her leg.

"Shut up. I didn't know what to do."

"Pffffft."

Heading upstairs, she resolved to quickly anoint the master bath, make her lunch for tomorrow and then head to sleep.

Despite the application of the hex bane oil, Jade wasn't surprised to find herself back in a closet for this nightmare. She didn't know which nightmares she disliked more - the lake or the closet. The lake's ominous and vast presence disturbed her, but the closet... the closet made her think of her childhood.

She could hear her father outside the door, arguing with her mother. Was it still arguing when one person did all the shouting and yelling and the other person just sat there silently and took it? If there was one word that would describe her mother, it would be 'silent.' Silent in the face of her father's anger, silent while her husband terrorized her daughter, silent while the world kept spinning without her input.

Jade felt a hand on her leg and looked down. The little girl was back. Was it her or was it Lily? Was this her subconscious talking to her, or was it someone else?

"I'm glad you're back," the little girl said. Her eyes were green. Even if the half-light of the closet with the only illumination coming through the small slats in the doors, Jade could make them out. Not herself then, Lily. "I've been trying to talk to you."

"What do you mean?" Jade asked. Outside the closet something broke and she flinched, her attention distracted.

"Don't pay attention to that. It's just a memory. It can't hurt you." The little girl, Lily, moved closer, crowding into Jade's space. "It's the Sparrow Lady you have to be careful of."

Jade turned back to Lily. "What are you talking about?"

"You know. At the lake."

"I don't want to talk about the lake." Jade shook her head and pulled back.

"You never want to talk about the lake, but you have to," Lily persisted. She was thin, bony elbows and knees digging into Jade's legs as she moved, climbing on top of her. "I should have made you talk about it before."

Another sound from outside the closet caught her ear, only it wasn't the usual sounds she heard while hiding. Those were glass breaking, wood smashing, people yelling. This was something else.

Birds. Sparrows.

Jade looked at Lily. Her small face was grim. "It's easiest to get to you when you're asleep. For me and for *her*."

Something hit the wooden slats of the closet and Jade flinched back, her eyes fixed on the closet doors. She could see something flapping outside, trying to get in. Bird wings. Sparrows. They were chirping, their high-pitched noises harsh and painful.

Lily's little arms came around her. "I shouldn't have slept so long."

Her lips were close to Jade's ear, her small body tucked in close - warm and soft. Jade put her arms around her, pulling her closer.

Jade thought back to the last time she'd talked to Lily and that awful, awful day. "I'm sorry. I didn't know I was sending you away." Another 'thunk' against the closet door had her cowering back. The flapping of wings matched the furious beating of her heart. She worried that if she spoke, her words wouldn't come out loud enough to hear. "What is it?"

"It's her. She's trying to find you. The Sparrow Lady."

Jade's mouth was dry. "What does she want?"

Lily's lips thinned, her young face seeming impossibly grim and stony. "I don't know." Her eyes met Jade's. "I shouldn't have slept so long," she repeated.

One of the slats ripped away from the closet door, sending a beam of light into the dark space. It burned Jade's retinas, making black spots appear in her vision. Jade blinked hard against the brightness, trying to keep her eyes open. The beak of a bird was worrying away at another slat. Another beak joined it. Then another. And another. All it would take was for them to remove one more slat and there would be room enough for a bird to come in.

Lily's voice was loud in her ear. No longer the voice of a child, this time, it was the voice of a grown woman.

"Wake up, Jade. I'm coming right behind you."

#

Jade woke up, no longer confused at finding herself in the closet. Bruce was pressed up against leg, growling a little when she shifted and poked him with her knee. The alarm was blaring from outside the closet and Jade had to stumble out and fumble around in the dark to turn it off. She should have turned it off for the weekend, but she forgot. Stupid mistake. It sucked when she had the opportunity to sleep in and then squandered it. She flopped down on the bed, feeling it jiggle and bounce a moment later when Bruce hopped up and settled beside her. All the blankets were in the closet, but she snagged her bathrobe from the foot of the bed and covered her shoulders. Bruce pressed his back against hers, adding to the warmth. His spiny, slightly boney spine should have been uncomfortable mashed up against her, but she liked it. Even though she didn't fall back asleep, she wasn't quite ready to get out of bed. She lay there for about an hour in the lazy, drifting space between awake and unconscious. In that state, her brain pulled all the things she worried about into one big pot - magic, the lake, Lily, sparrows, the Sparrow Lady. Once or twice, she thought she heard her name called and jerked awake, but dozed again when she realized there was no one there.

She finally pushed herself up and turned on some lights, pausing when she noticed her shoebox. She kept it under the bed, always tucked away safely, but now, it was on the floor beside the nightstand with its lid flipped open. Jade slid out of bed to the floor next to it. Someone had gone through it. Jade liked to leave it in a certain order, but there were things out of place and jumbled. It must have been her, while asleep and sleepwalking. No one else could get into the house, not with the demon locks. The collection of rocks was out of the box; all the shiny baubles and sharp-edged pieces lined up off to one side. Jade put each one back carefully.

Bruce hung his head over the side of the bed, staring balefully at Jade. His tongue flicked out, touching the box quickly.

"If she's back, then she should just come back. If she's not..." her voice trailed off. If Lily wasn't back, then Jade was probably halfway to certifiably insane. Hell, even if Lily was back, Jade was probably still halfway to certifiably insane. She knew the Coven had sanitariums for witches with mental problems - it was where they had sent the witch who tried to kill Jade when she'd first come to the Coven. Obviously, there were problems with insane people having magic. She'd probably get sent to a place like that. She wondered if it would be like a modern hospital and she tried to picture it her head, but all she could come up with was the vision of a large, looming, creeping stone structure that had been prominent in a horror movie she'd once seen.

She flipped the shoebox closed and stuffed it back under the bed. She wasn't a danger to anyone. It was just some small things out of place. Nothing major. Coffee. Coffee would make everything better. She pushed herself up, slid her arms into her bathrobe and headed down.

Bruce followed making low-level grumbling sounds the entire time.

"You don't have to get up when I get up," Jade said. It was nice to have him as company and she could admit that during the week days when she got up and Bruce didn't, she would stare at him enviously while he snoozed away.

At the bottom of the stairs, he stopped, body freezing like a pointer dog about to dart into the forest.

"What?" she asked, pausing herself.

A voice came from her kitchen, creamy and smooth, like liquid caramel. "I can hear you out there, Possum."

Jade stopped so quickly, one of her feet was actually in mid-air. Ugh. Seth.

Bruce bolted from the foyer to the kitchen, long talons skittering on the hardwood floor. His motion startled Jade into moving as well. She got to the kitchen to find Bruce in front of the pantry, hissing and spitting at Seth. Seth was hunkered down, trying to entice Bruce closer.

"Come on, horrid thing. Come here. I want to know what you're made of."

Bruce spat three times at Seth in a way that reminded Jade of little, old, Eastern European grandmothers.

"Leave him alone, Seth."

Seth straightened, alighting his dark, obsidian eyes on Jade and for a moment she felt dizzy. He blinked once or twice and smiled.

"Sorry, possum. Hard to remember to dial it back amongst you mortal types." He waved his hand dismissively. She didn't know if demons had to shower and change their clothes or if Seth changed his outfits because he felt like it. Today he was in dark jeans and a gaming t-shirt with sneakers on. It looked eerily similar to what Jade herself liked to wear and she eyeballed his clothes dubiously.

"I think I own that shirt," she said before she thought better of it.

Seth grinned. His smile would be considered drop dead handsome on a mortal, but coming from him, it made Jade feel greasy and grimy. "I do like your style in general, so I'm taking a page out of your fashion booklet. Or postcard really, since you've hardly got any clothes here at the Coven. Ooooh, that sounds naughty!" Seth exclaimed, laughing. Bruce flinched, spitting again.

"What do you want?" Jade was just tired. Tired of demons, of magic going wrong, of bad dreams and not sleeping, and just... being tired.

"Oh you wound me, Possum, to the core. Can't I just show up and see how you're doing?"

"You know how I'm doing, Seth. Creepily, you seem to know it before I do."

Seth smiled, eyes narrowing in on her. "Yes, you do have a *je ne sais quoi* that I'm attuned to, although, it's not as *ne sais quoi* as you might think."

Jade sighed. "Just tell me what you're here for."

Seth trailed a finger around the door jamb of her pantry, unable to cross the doorway. Jade warded the entire house against him except for the pantry. At least then she knew where he was likely to show up.

"Excellent work with Dex," Seth said, apropos of nothing.

"He got away." It stung. Although Jade had been close to binding him with a demon spell, Dex had managed to escape using some kind of teleportation magic. From what she'd read in the

Coven grimoires and Sakkara's demon books, it wasn't a spell without consequences. Although none of the books nailed down what those consequences were.

"He did," confirmed Seth, nodding a little before his face went downright gleeful, "but it was glorious. Teleportation." Seth gave a pleasured shudder. "Fantastic if you're a demon, but practically turns you inside out if you're not. I haven't seen disfigurement like that since…" Seth's voice trailed off, his eyes going wistful and soft. "Not since the dark ages."

Jade felt sick at Seth's words, wondering what had happened to Dex after he disappeared. She'd been happier not knowing anything.

"Well," Seth said, pulling his attention back to Jade. "It's always quite lovely to see you work, possum. So far you've produced two disfigured witches and I must say I'm waiting on tenterhooks for your next trick."

"I don't do it on purpose."

"I know!" Seth crowed. "That's what makes it all the more fabulous. You don't mean to cause so much damage but you do. That's what happens when you put too much power in one place."

She felt some of her power slip out in anger and one of the mugs in the sink popped loudly and cracked, falling to pieces.

Seth made an almost comical face. "What a faux-pas. Still haven't quite got it under control yet, have you?" He studied her closer. "Or is it that there's just too much going on upstairs?" Seth tapped at his own temple, staring meaningfully at Jade.

Bruce skittered backwards, away from the pantry, coming close to Jade, pressing his tail against one of her legs. The weight of him, warm and heavy against her side bled away some of her anger and anxiety. Seth always lived in 'creeping-her-the-fuck-out' territory. Jade was fighting above her weight class with him. She knew it, and he knew it too. Jade was smart, but Seth was just a whole other level apart from her. Maybe he wasn't actually smarter, maybe it was because he was a demon and he had no boundaries. She wasn't sure and she didn't want to find out.

"You like to show up when you think you have information I want. What is it you know this time?"

He smiled, his teeth white and sharp. "You know me so well. Oh, possum, we could have such fun together." He rubbed his hands together. "Still think making a deal is a bad idea?"

"Yes." Her word was flat, blunt. Seth barked in laughter making Bruce hiss and raise a claw at him.

"Oh, so feisty, the both of you. A witch and her familiar. A matched set. Although, it's more like three of a kind, isn't it?"

Jade bristled. He was hitting a little too close to home.

"It's becoming a problem, I know," Seth said, propping his hip against the doorway. "And you're just dying to ask what I know, what I've been hinting I know about you, about Lily, ever since we met. But you know the terms. That information will cost you a deal."

Jade frowned. Seth had come to her when she first arrived at the Coven and told her another witch was after her power. Then he'd come again when Dex had put a spell on Coven magic. Seth had even helped her with a demon rune. Now that she thought about it, he was kind of a blabbermouth, but he was always resolute that information about Lily warranted a deal. "Why?"

"Pardon?" Seth's dark eyebrows came together. He'd not been expecting her question.

"Why is it only when you're talking about information on Lily that you ask for a deal?"

Watching him watch her, Jade felt like a small, furry creature standing in wide open plain, with birds of prey circling.

Seth smiled. "Clever possum."

Instead of making her feel better, she felt worse. Unease coiled in her stomach like a cold, dead snake. When Seth smiled at her, it was like looking down a long, thin tunnel - the world around her went dark, sounds went flat, the air felt thick. Jade shook her head, trying to throw off the feeling of being thick and fuzzy.

"I want you to remember who your friends are, possum."

"What?"

"Other people, other … things may be interested in you, may try to turn your head with shiny baubles and pretty tricks. I want you to remember who helped you out when you needed it. Gratis."

Her jaw dropped. "Are you talking about yourself? You've been nothing *but* self-serving. Everything you do is because there's something in it for you. I may not know exactly what it is, or when you're getting it but I'm not stupid."

Seth sighed, shoulders sagging dramatically as he shook his head. "That's the problem dealing with the smart ones. No trust." He eyed her steadily. "Think of all the things I could have done to you but didn't. Horrific torture, both physical and mental. You, your witch friends, your little lizard thing. But I haven't touched a hair on any of your heads." He looked down at Bruce. "Or scales as the case may be. Why, you ask? Because I like you, possum. And I consider us friends."

The idea scared Jade. Being Seth's enemy would be worse than being his 'friend,' so she should be grateful. Probably. Mostly. It made her shoulder blades itch.

"Why are you telling me all this now? What's about to happen?" Seth liked to show up right before things started going pear-shaped.

He waggled a finger, making a sort of tsk-tsk sound. "No spoilers. Just... keep our friendship in mind."

Before Jade could argue, he was gone. A strange shimmer rising from his body, like heat waves coming off a pavement. Bruce waddled over to the pantry door, raised his snout high and sniffed. He spat three more times and then waddled away, a haughty swing in his step.

Jade wished it was as easy for her to turn her back on the place Seth stood, but it wasn't.

CHAPTER EIGHT

Feeling shaky from dealing with Seth and her impending nervous breakdown, Jade needed to get out of her head for a while. Saturday wasn't always a running day, but she wanted something that would tire her body out, burn off some anxiety and clear her head. She pulled on her running outfit, wincing at the wrinkles. She did laundry pretty regularly since she only had limited things with her at the Coven. She was tired of washing her stuff so often. This week she'd left her clean clothes in the laundry basket and it clearly showed. Her entire outfit was wrinkled and frumpy. Well, she wasn't going to look good, she was going for a workout. It would do.

Twenty minutes later, she was at the Nature Preserve and ready to run. She decided she'd stick to the outskirts, maybe do some sprints or find a few small hills to work on her stamina. She could do whatever she felt like today, not having to worry about holding Daniel back.

Even staying on the outskirts of the Preserve, she could feel the low level pull of the lake. Jade sprinted a little faster, pushing herself despite the sick feeling growing in her stomach. This was total bullshit. She just wanted to run. She needed to do something she was good at, and running was usually it. She wasn't a great runner or a fantastic athlete, but she could put one foot in front of the other and when she was done, she'd feel proud about getting a workout in. That's all she wanted today. A happy, easy feeling. Instead, her head throbbed, out of step with her pace. Her lungs burned. Her breath came out wheezes. She turned up her music, wanting to drown out the sound of herself, but it couldn't drown out the pull of the lake. Tears sprung to her eyes and she dashed them away with her gloved fingers. She just wanted to get away, go away, be away.

A choked-off sob escaped her throat and she stopped, putting her hands on her hips, breathing hard as she tried to slow her heart rate down. Now she was crying in the middle of a running trail. Awesome. All it would take to make her day more fantastic would be if someone from the Coven were to come along and catch her having her little pity party in the middle of the woods. This was a total failure.

She headed home, not bothering to run, just keeping a steady walking pace. Her shoulder blades itched, like there was something watching her and she flexed her muscles trying to alleviate the sensation. Stupid fucking lake. It was like a bass note drawn out too long and deep - thrumming inside her chest.

Back at her cottage, she kicked off her shoes viciously, wincing when one left a scuff mark and small dent in the drywall. Perfect. Just perfect. Now she'd have to get some putty for that. She dragged herself up the stairs, her legs rubbery and her lungs scooped out and hollow. If she thought she could sleep, Jade would crawl back into bed. Forget groceries, forget cleaning, forget anything that wasn't just lying in bed with the covers over her head, pretending the rest of the world didn't exist.

She talked herself into a quick shower and got angry when she realized she was out of shower gel. Fine. Shampoo would work just as well for soap. Her skin felt weird and dry when she got out, but she could deal. She just had to pick clothes for the day and get going. She stared at her laundry basket and the wrinkly clothes within. She'd been wearing those things for weeks. They were wrinkled and they were worn and she was tired. She'd never gone back to get her things after she decided to stay at the Coven. She'd originally only brought a suitcase worth of clothes. Clothes that she was now sick of wearing. Clothes she might want to burn. She'd gotten some new things at the mall with Callie and Henri - some tops and a pair of pants, but she hadn't wanted to buy too much. She had clothes. Lots of clothes. She just didn't have them *here*.

She heard the 'thumpa-thumpa-thumpa' of Bruce coming into the bedroom before she felt the wet poke of his snout on her leg. He hopped up on the bed, his weight causing it to dip down. He looked up at Jade, his tongue flicking out.

"Pfffft."

"I don't have any of my things."

Bruce settled on the bed, going low to his belly, his eyes flickering at her. He looked at the laundry basket then back at her.

"Well, yeah, I've got that, but that's like... vacation shit. I miss my stuff." She took a deep breath. "I should go get it. Make it official. Move here. It's stupid to keep living like this. Like I'm stuck. Like I'm in two places." She toed the edge of the laundry basket. "Like I think I'm two people." Jade tried to swallow past the ache in her throat, looking up at the ceiling to keep the moisture in her eyes from turning to tears. Bruce shuffled closer to the edge of the bed, coming toward her.

"Pfffft."

"Crying isn't going to help anything. It doesn't get stuff done." She settled her hands on her hips and swallowed a few more times, taking a deep breath. Counting to ten. Not thinking about Lily.

"Okay." She breathed out on a long, slow exhale. "Okay," she repeated. "It might be nice to just get away for a bit. Clear my head."

Bruce's tongue flicked out again and Jade took a step toward the bed, settling her hand on his head, feeling the warm, supple scales under her fingers.

"Not from you, bud. I'd like to take you with me, but I'll need the room in my car on the way back for my stuff." Her heart clenched at the thought of leaving him. "You'll be okay while I'm gone, right? Hang out here and do lizard things?"

He blinked at her, pushing his head into her hand.

"If you need something, you can go to Paris' place." She paused. "You've got that whole 'magical creature' thing going on, I'm sure you could find it." His tongue came out and touched her hand and she took that as a 'yes.' Jade felt surprisingly confident in Bruce's abilities, perhaps more than her own. "And I'll only be gone long enough to pack some stuff and shut the apartment down. Just the weekend."

Bruce's tail thumped once on the bedspread and then wagged it a bit. Jade forced herself to take another deep, calming breath.

"So that's the plan."

#

Paris found it both amusing and somewhat irksome that members of the Coven seemed surprised to find him in the grocery store. Invariably, at least one person asked him, "What are you doing here?", to which Paris was forced to inanely respond that he was purchasing groceries. What else would he be doing in the supermarket? Hunting elephants? He was Coven Leader, but he was still just a person, subject to the same laws and rules as everyone else. That included grocery shopping.

It was also trying at times when people brought up work items when he was trying to run his errands. Not that Coven Leader was a position he ever truly left at the office. Indeed his mother often drilled into his head that Coven Leader was a 24/7 position. But, there were simply some matters that Paris felt were not pressing enough to be brought to his attention while he was in the dairy aisle. Like the strange smell coming from a neighbor's house - something that Janice Perkins was adamant was urgent business.

"I'm sure if you bring it up to your neighborhood Coven representative, they can investigate it, if necessary," Paris said, trying to keep his tone soothing and neutral.

"I've tried that, but there doesn't seem to be any sort of regulation on using cheap or fake essential oils," Janice argued. She was blocking the way out of the dairy aisle, her small five-foot-two frame doing a surprisingly apt job of keeping Paris and his cart in place. "Don't you agree that substandard ingredients are the sloppy witch's crutch? Sloppy in the spell is sloppy in the smell, my mother used to always say."

Paris did his best to school his features. "I appreciate that. However, as there is no official rule on the use of artificial scents, there's not much that can be done."

Janice's mouth twisted into a frown and she made a sort of 'harrumph' sound. "Well, I don't recall this being a problem when your mother was Coven Leader. I'm sure she had some sort of mandate or ban on it."

Perhaps she had, Paris thought. When he first became Coven Leader, he honestly wondered how his mother had done it and managed to raise him as well. She'd been a strong Coven Leader - well-loved, knowledgeable and firm. She'd been the same as a mother.

However, since finding the demon grimoires, he couldn't help but wonder how much there was that he didn't know about her. Maybe she had a ban out on fake oils. Or perhaps she'd cast some kind of spell to keep them from being used. Reading her demon grimoires and seeing her familiar handwriting detailing out darker spells and demon runes, it was quite possible. He wondered how many secrets she kept.

"I will look into that."

Janice screwed up her lips again, her face a moue of displeasure. "Well, I'll be following up."

I'm sure you will. Paris managed a polite nod of his head. "It's good of Coven members to stay on top of magic. We do best when we all work together."

She seemed satisfied by his platitudes, nodding her head firmly back at him before finally moving aside, allowing Paris to escape. He pushed his cart around the corner, stopping when he saw Callie in the next aisle, smirking at him. She waited a few minutes, listening to the sound of Janice's squeaky sneakers moving away from them before she spoke.

"The essential oils smell?" Callie asked, eyebrows raised. She hitched the small hand basket she carried, settling the weight of it on her hip.

"I take it you've heard."

"Oh, the entire neighborhood and half the Coven have heard. The thing is, I don't even think it's witchcraft. I think her neighbor has those fake scented pine cones from the craft store for decoration."

Paris' nose wrinkled as he thought of the false-spicy scent used in those items. "Why on earth would anyone want to have those?"

Callie gave him a knowing look. "That entire family's nostrils have been burned out by the dad's cologne. I think it's supposed to be spicy, but mostly kind of smells like salami."

Paris was sure his face was a mirror of the look of distaste on Callie's.

"I know," she said nodding. "But it's true. Salami." She paused a beat and then said, "I thought you'd be out with Jade this weekend working on her magic."

Paris frowned. "No, we didn't have plans. Why?"

"Oh, well, I tried calling her a couple times and there was no answer. I mean, it's not like she has a lot of places to go and she's pretty good at picking up her cell even when she's out and about." Callie shrugged. "I figured the only thing that would keep her from it was magic. She gets really focused on it."

"No, I've not seen her today and as I said, we didn't have plans. I thought I might stop by later, but I didn't set anything officially. Did you swing by her place?"

Callie made a so-so motion with her hand. "Kind of. She's got those demon locks and I can't get by them. Henri and I can usually make it partway up her walkway but after that, we get sort of stuck."

"I can swing by after I'm done here. The last time I was there, I think she spelled them to let me through."

Callie raised an eyebrow. "Oh really?"

"Yes. Don't give me that look. I happened to be there and she re-shuffled the magic at the time."

"I didn't say anything."

"You didn't have to. I've known you since you were four. I can read your face."

"And is it saying 'I think she likes you and you like her'?" Callie batted her eyelashes. Paris rolled his rolled his eyes.

"Of course we like each other. We work together and I'm helping her with her magic."

"That's not what I meant and you know it."

Paris ignored her comment. "I'll stop by and see if she's there. Perhaps her phone is off, or she's out running errands and forgot it at home or something simple."

"Okay. You'll let me know what you find out?"

"Of course."

"And you'll stop being such a chicken-shit and think about what I said?" Callie gave him a knowing look again.

"You're horrid to me," he said, his face deadpan. "I don't know why we're friends."

Callie took her middle finger and scratched up and down her nose, clearly making the rude gesture at him as she said, "Oh yeah? Can you tell what my face is saying now?" She couldn't keep a straight face, bursting out laughing as she flicked her hair over her shoulder. She maneuvered around his cart.

"Keep me posted," she called out over her shoulder, before disappearing down the aisle.

He finished up quickly, getting stopped twice more by Coven members with problems similarly as 'urgent' as Janice Perkins' odor issue. Finally, groceries packed in the car, he was ready to swing past Jade's house. He didn't figure it would take long - he'd likely find her in her cottage, her phone off or not charged. Or she wouldn't be at home, but he could set his mind at ease and check that her place appeared undisturbed.

When he got to Jade's and started up the walkway, the strange demon magic that she had securing her house parted for him, making him think of gears turning through thick molasses - heavy and slow. It seemed to take longer for the locks to recognize him, adjust and then let him through. The demon magic felt slightly dirty as well - like a slick oil or sludge he couldn't quite get off his fingers. Paris doubted that Jade felt that aspect of it. She seemed to rather like the demon magic, sometimes preferring it to other spells. For a moment, it was as though the spells broke, freeing the space around him before they snapped back into place. Whatever was wrong with Jade may be affecting her locks as well.

He knocked sharply on her door, waiting for an answer that didn't come. He knocked once more before trying the handle and finding it unlocked. He couldn't say he was surprised. Jade had such a preference for demon magic, he doubted she ever used her keys anymore, relying on the security of her demon locks instead.

Paris poked his head in through the door. "Hello? Jade? Bruce?"

Silence.

Stepping in, he closed the door behind him. Nothing felt wrong or amiss, but the place did have an empty feel to it. Paris stretched his magic out, searching for Jade's energy. He felt a slight pull from upstairs and called out again. After getting nothing in reply, he slowly made his way up the stairs.

He wasn't trying to be quiet, but he wasn't making an exceptional amount of noise either. Any minute now, Paris was sure Jade would pop out of one of the rooms upstairs.

Nothing happened. No Jade bursting out of a room. No yelling.

Although he did hear a thump from the bedroom.

Paris knocked and then opened the door slowly. He paused, feeling like a voyeur as he looked around her room.

A laundry basket was in front of the bed with some clothes strewn about on the mattress, but not the duvet or the pillows. Seeing some fabric peeking out from the closet, he stepped closer and pulled the closet door open. Inside he found the pillows and covering, bunched up like a nest. He glanced back at the bed and then the closet again, frowning, when it suddenly dawned on him. She was sleeping in the closet. But why?

Another 'thump' pulled Paris' attention away from the closet and he turned back to the bed.

Hearing the thump again, he knelt down, peering underneath the mattress.

Silvery-reflective eyes blinked back at him and he felt the lightening quick press of a wet tongue against his wrist.

"Hello, Bruce," Paris said quietly.

"Pfffft."

"Where's your mistress?" Now that he concentrated on it, Paris realized the sense of Jade's magic he'd felt downstairs was coming from Bruce. Paris squinted, trying to get a better look at the lizard. Bruce was curled around something, a box. Jade's shoebox, if he wasn't mistaken. Paris recognized it, having once seen Jade going through it, looking at a picture. At the time, he thought it was a picture of Jade as a young girl, but the girl in the photo had green eyes.

Green eyes like the shade Jade's eyes had turned after she defeated Dex. Like the apple-green that had been in Bruce's eye the other day. He thought back to the day he'd seen the picture.

"It looks like you but... Her eyes are green. Yours are grey. I didn't know you had any other family. A sister? That would explain why the demon couldn't pull you through the portal when it tried. You didn't say you had a sister." He flipped it over. *"'Lily. Six years old.'"*

"I don't. That's... That's just a photo. It's me. It's just...me."

"It says, 'Lily' on the back."

"I changed my name. So what? I have documents if you want to see."

Paris leaned down further, peering at Bruce, trying to get a look at his eyes. As he hid under the bed, it was hard to see his irises and Paris was loathe to reach in a try to pull him out. Bruce's tail, curled around the shoebox, flicked up and down. Paris hesitated, his eyes fixed on the shoebox.

"May I?" he asked Bruce. He wasn't truly expecting an answer, but Bruce was an intelligent creature, moreso than just a simple house pet. He'd shown quite a level of intellectual capacity before. Bruce's tongue darted out again, lightning fast and then his tail uncurled from the shoebox. Paris reached forward slowly, gingerly, in case Bruce changed his mind. His fingers settled around the cardboard and he pulled it out from under the bed.

If Paris opened it, he couldn't pretend it wasn't a violation of privacy. Until he opened that box, he was still working within the parameters of 'trying to find Jade.' Opening her little shoebox was definitely outside of that task. He was in Jade's house, in her bedroom, uninvited, looking at her things. But, he'd been avoiding his concerns for too long. Taking a deep breath, he flipped open the lid.

He didn't know what he was expecting. Paris opened the box with the same trepidation he would give to prying open an ancient sarcophagus, but there was no mad flash of light or billowing smoke. The first things he noticed were papers - scraps of things or handwritten notes. Some receipts. Some birthday cards. He carefully took one out and opened it, noting it had the obligatory reiteration of wishing a happy birthday to someone and then some initials scrawled at the bottom. He pushed some of the paper around slightly and found a small stack of photographs. They were old, or at least not very recent. Certainly taken before the use of digital photography was so prevalent. There were a lot of scenery shots, flowers, maybe vacation photos and then he found the one he'd seen before - a girl that looked like a young Jade but with green eyes. On the back of the photo, it said, '*Lily, six years old.*' Jade told Paris that she'd changed her name and he'd investigated it, finding paperwork that matched that assertion. Truth be told, he hadn't looked closely at his findings. He had the feeling he needed to take a second look. There were other photographs of Jade in the box. Some from when she was older, maybe about eight or so, and then a couple more from what looked like adolescence. She habitually wore a solemn expression, never truly smiling. He spread the photos out on the floor and looked at each one carefully.

In some her eyes were green and in others, grey. It was hard to tell and if he hadn't seen her eyes change to a striking, clear apple green himself, he would have said he was only guessing or it was a trick of the light in the photos. None of the other pictures had names or ages on the back. He picked up one of the middle ones, where she clearly had grey eyes. Jade's eyes were serious and grim, focused on the lens of the camera with a haunted look. He picked up another one where her eyes had a greenish cast. Nearly the same expression, but not quite identical. That wasn't surprising in and of itself - people wore different expressions all the time.

What did it mean?

Paris looked back in the box, saw some rocks and semi-precious stones. He recognized quartz, tiger-eye, amethyst and then a number of pieces of jade. He picked up some of the smooth, cold stones and turned them over in his hands, noting the distinct limey-green color in some and the darker, mossy shade of others. She had quite a collection, no doubt because of her name. He jangled the stones in his palm, hearing the click-clack of them as they rocked against each other. A flicker of movement from the corner of his eye had him turning his head. Bruce's snout stuck out from under the bed. Paris tipped his head down and made eye contact. Bruce blinked once and shifted.

"Are you trying to tell me something, Bruce?"

Bruce blinked again and then rolled onto his side, presenting the scaly patch of skin on his neck, just as he had done in Paris' office. Paris reached out and touched it, feeling the dry, cracked surface under his fingers.

"Yes, I can see it. But what does it mean?"

Bruce was silent as he continued to display the uneven patch of skin. Paris moved his hand from petting the afflicted area to soothing over the more supple part of Bruce's skin, just under his jaw. Bruce closed his eyes and let out a contented sigh. Paris looked back at the two pictures he'd lain out side by side. He was no closer to finding out where Jade was this afternoon, nor solving the mystery of her dual colored eyes.

His phone buzzed in his pocket and Bruce gave him a dirty look, as if chastising Paris for disturbing his naptime. As he answered his phone, Paris bit back the urge to apologize.

"Paris here."

"Hey, I was thinking," began Callie without hesitation. "Why don't we ask tech services to ping the GPS on her Coven phone? She might have that one on her or maybe it's charged even if her personal one isn't."

Paris felt relieved at having a path forward. "All right. What's her Coven cell phone number?"

There was a pause from Callie. "Why are you asking me? You should have it."

"I don't have it. Why would I have it?" Paris asked.

"Because you were the one that requisitioned it for her and took her to get it."

At his long silence, Callie sighed. "Shit. You didn't get her a Coven phone, did you?"

"It slipped my mind." Paris pinched the bridge of his nose.

"You know, you're a good Coven Leader and competent at managing large groups of people and all the busy work that comes along with being in charge, but you're shit at one-on-one management."

However true the comment was, it still made him bristle. "Yes, well, I'm sure you can make a note in my performance review at the end of the year."

"It's no wonder she feels left out of things, Paris. She *is* left out of things. She wasn't on the emailing list for weeks when she first got here and she didn't know about the Coven Ball. And now you tell me she doesn't have a Coven phone; which means she's probably not getting all the social media updates and just… the back and forth that we have."

"I'll get her a phone."

"Great," Callie said, sarcasm in her tone. "It can sit on your desk until we find her." Paris swore he could almost hear her roll her eyes. "Should we use magic? Is that an invasion of privacy? Maybe she's somewhere she doesn't want to be found? And it's not like she's missing, it's just we don't know where she is. But she's an adult; we don't have to know where she is. She could just be… shopping or playing mini-golf or at the library."

Paris looked at Bruce, stretched out with his head sticking out from underneath the bed. His eyes were drifting shut drowsily. He was still awake but obviously sleepy. Bruce didn't seem to be in any mortal peril - he had the strange scaly patch, but he wasn't violently ill. He was obviously concerned about something and trying to communicate it to Paris, but he wasn't anxious or overly agitated. He spared a thought for the demon Seth and his propensity for appearing in Jade's pantry. He worried that Seth could have something to do with Jade not being around, but looking down at Bruce again, dozing off, he reasoned it wasn't likely.

"I'm going to give it till the evening. As you said, she's an adult. She's under no obligation to tell us her comings and goings. Her things are here, as is Bruce, and nothing seems to be disturbed or out of place."

"Okay. Well, Henri and I will keep an eye out and an ear to the ground. So, if we don't hear anything by tonight, location spell?"

Paris nodded, momentarily forgetting he was on the phone and Callie couldn't see him. "Yes, I'll do a generalized one just to narrow down her whereabouts and at least rule out that she's not in danger. But I'll try not to disturb her privacy too much. As you noted, she may be somewhere she doesn't want to be found."

"All right. I'll call or text if anything comes up."

"Same here."

Paris hung up and pocketed his phone, absently petting Bruce's snout. Bruce's long tongue zipped out and lapped at his wrist bone before the creature smacked his chops and then gave a long, deep sigh.

"I'm sure there's nothing to be worried about."

Paris wasn't sure if he was talking more to Bruce or himself.

CHAPTER NINE

By eight o'clock that night, Paris was preparing a location spell for Jade. He and Callie periodically touched base throughout the day, along with Henri, and no one had seen or heard from Jade since yesterday. Paris was the last one to see her when he left her cottage on Friday night. As he gathered the materials for his spell, Callie chewed on the skin of one of her thumbs.

"Stop that, you'll make it bleed," Paris said quietly as he spread out his mortar, pestle and a map, weighting the four cardinal corners. They decided to go with the assumption that Jade couldn't be too far away and so they used a map of the local and immediate areas accessible by car or train. Paris assumed wherever Jade was, she got their on her own. He hoped.

"Nag." Callie pulled her thumb away from her mouth and dragged both of her sleeves down over her fingers. "I feel nervous. And dumb. Are we being dumb?" She hovered beside Paris' shoulder, watching him grind the herbs.

"We're simply being cautious."

"She doesn't have to check in with us. Still, it's weird that her cell phone's off."

Callie was so close that Paris felt her breath on his arm. The only way Callie could be any closer was if he raised his arm and she tucked in under it. "Callie," he said, looking at her pointedly about how close she was. He could hardly work with her nearly on top of him.

"I'm just worried, okay?" Callie took a step back and then another one when he raised his eyebrows.

"I'm sure we'll find Jade and she'll be in town somewhere, curled up with a book."

"If you really thought that, you wouldn't be doing the spell."

There was a downside, Paris thought, to being friends with someone for as long as he and Callie. You knew each other too well at times.

The scent from the spell ingredients washed over him with a rush of memory - this was the same spell he'd used to originally find Jade, before they knew who she was. Back then, they knew only there was a witch somewhere, outside the Coven, bleeding out magic. He'd created the spell from a combination of older ones, tweaking the ingredients until he'd gotten what he wanted. This time, on a whim, he turned to his spice rack and searched out his cloves - not for their magical properties, but because Jade's magic tended to smell like them. His mother had taught him to trust his magical instinct and as he ground the single clove into the mixture he'd already made, he could feel the spell settling into place.

As he had before, after grinding the ingredients into a fine powder, he smoothed out the map with his hand, imagining he was wiping the surface clean of all influence as he did. He paused and took a handful of the powder, holding it close to his lips before exhaling out sharply, blowing it into a cloud over the map. He focused his intent on Jade, expecting the cloud to react the same as it had the last time. Previously, when he searched for Jade, the powder hovered for a moment before snaking around lazily and then finally spiraling down and burning a small hole in the map at Jade's location. He thought it might be perhaps faster now that he knew Jade, knew her magic and how it felt.

To the contrary, despite Paris being better able to focus his energy and intent on Jade now that he knew her, the cloud of powder spun in a lazy ellipse, like a glass of liquid stirred quickly and then forgotten. Paris pushed at it with his magic, nudging it and the cloud moved in a sort of shimmy. In the center, a portion of the debris coalesced and gathered in on itself, amassing material. It broke off from the rest of the lazy, haphazard cloud, coiling in itself and zipping down toward the map, making a small, black dot at what was presumably Jade's location.

Paris stared at the rest of the mixture he'd made, hanging in the air, spinning slowly. He nudged it again with his magic. It shouldn't have separated out from the rest of the spell ingredients, but there it was, hovering above the map.

"What does that mean?" Callie asked, her voice quiet and small.

"I don't know," Paris replied.

The cloud of dust shimmied again and then fell out of the air, landing in disarray on the map.

"So, did it work?"

Paris checked where the spell had marked the map and quickly recognized the city Jade used to live in. "I think so. It looks like she went back home."

Callie blinked a few times in surprise. "What? Like for good? Why? Why didn't she say anything? Is she coming back?"

Frustrated at her questions, he said, "I know as much as you do right now, Callie."

In the way that only people who have known someone a long time can do, Callie pursed her lips and replied, "Excuse me." Her tone implied she wasn't apologizing for anything.

Paris cleaned up his spell work, taking the weights off the corners of the map and folding it up, careful to keep all the dust inside the folds. He was concerned about the way the spell misfired. The only thing he'd done differently this time was the addition of the single clove, and while any addition to a spell could alter its efficacy, he'd felt a resonating 'ping' in his magic when he'd added it. He'd been sure that it would only enhance the spell, not cause it to partially fail. Paris' magical intuition was rarely wrong, and when spells failed, they generally tended to fail as a whole, not just by bits and pieces. The powder split in two - half of it finding Jade and the other half falling apart.

"What are you going to do?"

Callie's question pulled him back from his musings. "I'm going to go see her and find out why she left."

"Do you want me to go with you?"

Paris paused in the middle of his spell clean up. He set the folded map down, careful not to jostle it too much and let the spell powder out. He fiddled with the mortar and pestle, picking the mortar up and wiping it meticulously with a soft cotton cloth. The weight of the mortar was heavy in his hands, the stone warm from his handling.

"I don't have to. I just thought if you needed the support, or if you wanted me to talk to her, I could," Callie continued.

Paris set the mortar down and picked up the pestle, giving it the same careful cleaning. "No, I think I should like to talk to her alone first." He had the fear that Jade suddenly decided to leave the Coven. It wasn't like Paris to jump to conclusions or to borrow trouble, but he worried that perhaps he'd completely missed something, the same way he'd missed little details about bringing Jade into the Coven fold. Or perhaps his avoidance of dealing with whatever was wrong with her had reached some kind of critical mass. He wasn't sure either he or Jade would want Callie there to hear what they may say.

"Okay," agreed Callie.

He wiped down the counter, being more meticulous and fussy than he normally was, stalling for time.

"So, are you going?"

Paris looked up, seeing Callie's expectant face. Her large brown eyes staring at him. He folded the cotton cloth and placed it off to the side.

"Yes. Yes, of course."

Callie nodded and then when Paris didn't move, she bobbed her head at him.

"Now?" she prodded.

"Yes, now, of course I'm going now." He walked out of the kitchen, Callie hot on his heels. He grabbed his car keys from the small counter next to the front door and his coat from the closet. He turned, seeing Callie on her smart phone, frowning slightly.

"It's a long drive - the train would probably be faster. There's one that leaves in an hour and half. Do you want me to book you a ticket?" She looked up from her phone, her eyes wide and helpful.

"Please." He shrugged into his coat, flipping down the collar. Callie nodded and pressed a few buttons, nodding again after a moment.

"Done. It's waiting for you at the station."

"I'll pay you back for it."

She grinned. "I used my Coven account. I'll get you to sign off on the expense report." She winked at him. "It's a Coven expense. You're following up on a Coven member."

As he and Callie left his house, Paris had once last thought. *I hope she's still a Coven member.*

#

After taking the train from the Coven and then starting to pack up the apartment, Jade felt like a worn, frayed rug - flattened, washed out and thin. She couldn't remember a Saturday that had been so long. Looking over her things while she packed had been comforting and disquieting. These were her creature comforts - clothes, trinkets, books. But they were also reminders of her life before the Coven. Both when she'd had Lily and then after, when Lily had been gone.

Jade gave up around one in the morning, hoping she was too tired to dream. She'd been wrong. She knew she was dreaming, but it had the tangible quality some dreams had - like everything was sharper and crisper than it should be.

They were in the closet. Jade tried to fit her long limbs comfortably in the small space without much luck. Lily was small again, a child, curled up against Jade's side. Lily turned her face up to Jade and in the dark light of the closet, Jade could only make out her small features.

"Tell me about the lake."

Jade turned away. "There's nothing to tell. I don't like the lake."

"Why?" Lily pushed.

Jade pulled back from her, unwrapping her arm from Lily's slight shoulders. "You know why."

"No, I don't. You avoid thinking about it."

Jade frowned. "No. That doesn't make sense. I only started thinking about the lake at the Coven. How could I avoid something I didn't think about before?"

"That's not true. The lake was always there."

A low bass note thrummed in Jade's head and in her gut. She turned and realized the back of the closet was also a door. The salamander charm around her neck went slightly hot and Jade held it between two fingers, fiddling with it. Lily's hand reached up and turned the handle on the door at the back of the closet, even as Jade reached out to stop her. The door swung open and they were at the Preserve with Lily walking ahead of her. She was an adult now - an exact replica of Jade. It was eerie, like watching herself from behind.

Jade wanted Lily to turn around, wanted to see her face, even though it would be the same as her own. It wasn't like she didn't know what Lily looked like. All Jade had to do was look in the mirror. But there would be something so different about having Lily in front of her, real and warm, instead of only a reflection in silver and glass.

"Are you real? Or am I going crazy?"

But Lily didn't stop, didn't slow down. "Would it matter what I answered?" she asked, not turning around. "If I say I'm not real, then you're going crazy. If I say I am real, you won't believe me and still think you might be going crazy." She kept making her way along the path, ducking under tree branches and pushing leaves aside, moving steadily forward like an unstoppable train.

Jade's stomach turned over as she realized they were at the lake. They broke through the foliage and Jade stopped short, pausing even as Lily kept moving toward the dock. The planks of it stretched out impossibly long and thin - the perspective all wrong - as though it went on for too far. Lily walked forward, the dock swaying slightly under her gait. Even though she stood on the solid ground of the forest, Jade could feel each sway and swag of the old wooden planks in her bones, as if it were her own feet on the dock. She didn't like Lily being so close to the water. Jade reached out a hand, opened her mouth to stop her, but no sound came out.

Lily turned around, standing at the edge of the dock, all at once far away and too close. When she spoke, her voice was clear and pristine - her words right in Jade's ear.

"You've always known this place. I could see it in your mind. But you never talked about it."

"I don't have anything to say," Jade lied, feeling anxious and sick. "Come away from the edge."

"Why?"

"You're going to fall in."

Lily shrugged. "I know how to swim."

"I don't!" Jade exclaimed.

The sun hit Lily's green eyes, making them seem like they were lit from within, greener than ever. "If I jumped, would you follow me?"

"I… don't know." Jade couldn't make her voice any louder and was terrified that Lily couldn't hear the quiet words.

"Come and get me, Jade."

Jade took a step forward as Lily turned away from her and then tipped forward, falling face down into the lake with a cracking sound.

Jade jerked awake, feet kicking out involuntarily, rattling the closet door. Last night she'd given up and had simply gone to sleep in the closet, feeling like if she chose to sleep there she could pretend that she was in control of it.

Another sharp sound rang in her ears and it took a moment to realize it was knocking on her apartment door. She pushed at the covers tangled around her limbs and stumbled out into the room. She'd left the bedroom light on and it was harsh against her eyes. She squinted at the clock as she passed it by. Seven in the morning. Freakishly early for someone to be at her door. Her hair fell in her face and she pushed it off to the side as she swung the front door open.

Paris stood there, looking like he was ready to bang the door down if necessary. His hair was sticking up, all out of place. He looked a little wrinkled, disheveled. She'd never seen him look so out of sorts.

"Paris? What the hell?" Jade rubbed at one of her eyes and then tugged at her t-shirt, pulling it down further.

"I should ask the same of you."

"What?"

"What are you doing here?" Paris hands were deep in his coat pockets and looking at him she got the impression of a border collie waiting for something - a direction, an order, a sheep to make a break for it. He was coiled energy ready to spring.

"Packing." Jade gestured in the mad and clumsy way of a person just out of bed.

Paris opened his mouth for a rebuttal and then, peering past her to the boxes she had strewn about, he stopped. "Oh. So you are." He deflated a little, his shoulders dropping. He shuffled his feet. "May I come in?"

Jade swung her arm wide again and he stepped past her. Her brain felt muddled and fuzzy, still ringing from her dream with Lily. She tried to focus on Paris instead. "It's seven in the morning, English? Are we under attack? Is this a fight?"

"We couldn't find you. No one knew where you were. We were worried. I thought - " He hesitated, his eyes darting away quickly and then back. "I thought perhaps you meant to leave the Coven."

Jade blinked, surprised. It hadn't occurred to her that anyone would notice she was gone, let alone that they might think she was leaving. "Why would I leave the Coven?"

"Well." Paris dug his hands deeper into coat pockets, as though he needed them to be doing something and that gesture would suffice. "I know it's not been easy for you and it seems as though lately, things have... been more unsettled."

"Yeah," she shrugged. "But I sort of live there now." Okay, it wasn't a ringing endorsement, but she was impressed she managed to get that many words out with the sleep debt she'd been accumulating and the late night she'd spent packing up boxes.

Paris again shifted his weight from one foot to the other. "We didn't know where you'd gone and then, when we did know, we weren't sure why."

"Are you using 'we' in the royal sense of the word, meaning just you?" Her brain-to-mouth filter was still not all the way awake.

Paris leveled her with a look, his blue eyes intense and sharp. Jade rubbed her nose, unaffected. "Don't look at me like that. It's a legitimate question. You like the third person and I can't tell when you mean it versus when you're just being English."

"I've been awake for twenty-four hours." His tone told her everything she needed to know about his mental state.

"Sorry," she said, trying to put some actual apology into the word. She managed to sound a little regretful, she hoped. "You could have called."

"I did. There was no answer on your cell phone and when I tried this number, the phone company said your line was disconnected."

Jade rolled her eyes. "You know it takes those fascists three weeks to set the thing up, but they can cut the line as soon as you ask to cancel it. Crooks." She looked around and spied her cell phone sitting on the floor, face down next to a box. She bent over and picked it up. Dead. Oops.

"I didn't know it died," Jade said, wagging it in the air, feeling sheepish. She glanced around at the mess of the apartment. "And I'm not sure where the charger is."

Jade watched Paris look around at the boxes, packing tape, packing paper and the remainder of her things strewn about. He tried valiantly to stifle a yawn, his face screwing up comically as he did.

"You need a nap? You could sleep on the couch," Jade offered. They both looked at the couch. It was short and a little lumpy. Jade knew from experience, it wasn't comfortable for napping.

Paris looked at her dubiously and she winced. "Yeah, it's about as comfortable as it looks."

"What about breakfast?" he asked.

She blinked back at him. "What about it?"

A ghost of a smile curled his lips. "If you like, I'll buy you breakfast."

"I never turn down free food," Jade answered easily. "Okay, let me just," she gestured down at herself, "get this presentable."

Back in the bedroom, she had to rummage around in half-packed boxes but found a warm, fuzzy sweater and leggings. She didn't know where her boots were, but she knew she saw a pair of runners last night. They weren't really appropriate for winter, but they would do. She'd been living out of her suitcase for so long at the Coven, she felt spoiled for choice knowing she could pick anything from these boxes. She yanked her hair back into a ponytail, wondering if she could get away without any makeup. She really didn't feel up to facing the mirror.

She poked around in her purse and used her compact to apply some blush and mascara. It was enough to make her look alive. Mostly.

Coming back out into the living room, Jade saw Paris peering carefully at some of the boxes. She didn't mind as much as she thought she might.

"You're close to being packed up then?" he asked.

Jade shrugged. "I guess so."

"What about your furniture?"

"My landlord and I worked out a deal where I don't have to pay the fine for breaking my lease if he can keep the place furnished and rent out as is." She sighed and looked around. "It's a total rip off in the long run, but it's not like I'm married to any of this stuff and the cottage at the Coven is furnished. Plus I can't be bothered to figure out what else to do with it."

Paris nodded at her. "I came by train and haven't a car. I assume you know some place we can dine?"

Jade smirked. "You trust me with that kind of power? I've got a cheap palate."

"Breakfast is difficult for most places to bastardize."

"You say that now..." She let her sentence dangle playfully as she led the way out of her apartment.

Jade took him to the local greasy spoon. The walls were done in dark wood paneling, with the windows tinted to keep out the bright morning sun. It gave the entire place a dark, cave-like feel. A row of video lottery terminals were lined up against one wall, on the side of the restaurant that was presumably a lounge later in the day.

"I know it doesn't look like much," Jade said, as she slid into a small booth and Paris took the other side, "but the food is good, the prices are cheap and it's impeccably clean. It's just old."

A waitress came by and automatically filled their coffee cups, dropping off some creamers on the table. Jade ordered off the top of her head, not bothering with a menu and was a little surprised when Paris did the same, opting for waffles with whipped cream.

"I forgot about your sweet tooth," Jade said after the waitress left. She watched Paris put four sugar packets in his coffee. Her teeth hurt just looking at it and thinking about him eating waffles after that. The coffee was so dark, she had to add three creamers before it turned a creamy beige shade. She watched Paris carefully, waiting for him to try it.

He took a careful sip and then coughed. "That is some coffee.".

Jade grinned. "It'll put hair on your chest." She took a generous gulp, rolling the almost smoky taste around in her mouth.

"Let's hope it doesn't do the same for you." He fiddled with his cup and she felt nervous and tense watching him. He had his 'serious' face on.

"Jade…" Paris began. His tone made her want to bolt. "You know you're part of the Coven, don't you?"

Oh, shit. Was this some kind of trick question? Jade knew she was part of the Coven - she was a witch and witches belonged in Covens. Okay, so she wasn't born into the Coven like everyone else, but Paris, Callie, Henri, heck even Daniel and Josef, had all been working hard at toeing the party line - Jade belonged at the Coven, whether the Coven wanted her there or not. Mostly the other witches seemed to kind of lean toward 'indifferent' or 'not.' Whatever.

"Um, yeah?" Crap, even she could tell that came out as a question.

Paris winced. "I know I've not done the best job of bringing you into the fold, but I hope you don't feel too separate from us."

Jade's eyes darted around, hoping for some kind of a distraction. Waitress coming back with refills, new patrons coming in, grease fire - she wasn't picky. The restaurant was quiet. Dammit.

"You got me a house, a job and I went to your Coven Ball thingy. I know I'm part of the group."

Paris took another careful sip of his coffee and then eyed sugar packets, like he wanted to add another one. "I'm concerned that you didn't feel it necessary to tell anyone you were leaving."

Jade narrowed her eyes. "Do I have to report in on where I'm going?" Suspicion curled in her gut.

"No, not at all. I'm just..." His voice trailed off and he sighed. "I just want to ensure you feel you belong with us."

Ugh. Feelings. Jade shrugged. "Okay. Sure." She could tell he wasn't thrilled with her answer. His lips thinned out and he looked grim. God, was he going to keep harping on this? She didn't know what else to say.

Paris exhaled sharply, watching her, his eyes bright and so blue. Jade tore at her napkin, leaving long trails of thin paper on the table.

"How much more work do you think it will be packing?"

Jade's stomach unclenched. Subject dropped, thank God. Breakfast was slightly stilted but not as bad as it could have been. Jade had some questions about spells she was looking at and although she had terrific recall for printed material, Paris didn't like going into too many details without seeing the books himself. It seemed to make him squirrelly that she could remember them so well - not that she would ever use that word in front of him. Sometimes she wondered what he thought. As if she would just blurt out some kind of spell while they were at a diner and bring the whole place to rubble. She felt a few times like he wanted to ask her something. He would pause and there would be an air of expectation in their conversation, but then he would only ask after something at Counter-Magic or Bruce's habits.

After breakfast, Jade put him to work packing up her apartment, which Paris seemed to find amusing. She had several boxes already sealed shut and she unceremoniously pointed to a stack in the corner and told him to put it in her car, handing him the keys and rattling off her license plate so he could find it in the parking garage. He must have been successful because he was back in her apartment a few minutes later taking another set of boxes down. Jade tried not to think as she worked, instead focusing on spatial relations - how many books would fit? Could she put this triangular shaped thing-y in with them? Was this box too heavy? She packed up books, knick-knacks, clothing, more books, odds and ends and a few coffee mugs, working like an automaton. *Don't think, don't think, don't think.* It felt like saying goodbye and she hadn't had anyone or anything to say goodbye to in such a long time. Not since she lost Lily. She cracked her neck, hoping to relieve some of the tension she could feel atrophying her muscles.

"Are you all right?"

Jade looked up from where she knelt on the ground to see Paris standing half in, half out of the doorway, a box of books in his arms. She nodded. "Yeah, just…packing sucks, you know."

He shifted the box and eyed her speculatively. "Is that all?"

She had a sudden urge to blurt her crazy words at him. *Hey, I know this will sound nuts, but an entire other person used to share this body with me and then she left, and now I think she might be back. Only I can't really tell and I don't know who I can ask because I don't think anyone's ever had this problem. I can't talk about how she left, and I don't even want to talk about when she used to be here because it makes me feel sick and empty. Like you know when you've forgotten to eat and you're so hungry you think you might vomit, even though you don't have anything in there? It feels like that. Any advice? No, really, I'm not crazy. You're probably worried about the demon grimoires you left with me, but I swear they're totally safe.*

Jade swallowed hard, forcing the words back. "That box must be heavy." She pointed uselessly at the one he was holding.

Paris didn't seem to mind the weight, shifting it again, coming back into the apartment and watching her with careful eyes. "It's not all that bad," he said. He paused, seeming to steal himself and then added, "I've not been carrying it long. Sometimes when you carry things for a long time, they seem heavier than they are. They can be hard to put down."

Her throat was tight and she blinked a few times, surprised by the sudden flood of moisture in her eyes. She looked away from him and as she did, she caught sight of her reflection in the glass panel of the TV stand. In that moment, it was like there were two of her in the room with Paris. She couldn't look away from the image of herself, doubled.

"Sometimes when you put something down, you can't pick it back up again. It would have been better to never stop carrying it." She watched her reflection open her mouth and speak, watched the slight way her head and body moved as she talked.

"Maybe you need some help carrying it."

The room was heavy and thick and she wanted to close her eyes, to look away from the glass surface of the TV case, but she felt stuck, unable to turn. There was a muffled roaring sound in her ears, viscid and soupy, like there was something in her ears.

Like she was underwater.

Paris said her name and it was far away, as though he were down a long, thin tunnel, speaking to her from a distance. There was a taut vertigo pulling at her and she knew if she just let go, if she just followed it, she would be dragged under. Or maybe something else would rise up around her, surrounding her. She felt a tug somewhere inside her and she wanted to pull against it, instinctively, like yanking a booted foot out of thick mud on a rainy day. There was so much pressure. Two sides of her pulling against one another.

There was a loud, sharp crack and she flinched. The glass door of the TV stand broke into a star-shape pattern - slender sliver spider webs branching out from the center of the glass, from the spot where her reflection had been. Jade's senses zoomed back to normal, her ears popping. Paris was saying her name.

She flinched again when she felt something touch her, looking up quickly at Paris, now by her side, hand resting carefully on her shoulder . The box he'd been carrying was on its side by the door and she had the sudden worry that something breakable might have been inside.

"Jade, your nose is bleeding."

She reached up and touched at the wetness she felt under her nostrils, her fingers coming back bright red. Her limbs felt heavy and slow - like she'd just woken up from a long nap. The smell of citrus filled her nostrils. Citrus and cinnamon.

"What happened?" Paris asked.

Jade looked back at the broken glass and then again at her fingertips. She shook her head. "I don't know."

She was stuck in place for half a second more before she realized if she didn't move, she was going to bleed all over herself. Her eyes cast around and she spotted a tea towel still hanging from the oven door. She moved to push herself to her feet, but pressure from Paris' hand on her shoulder kept her down. She tipped her head back, feeling the blood sluggishly start to run down her throat.

"I need that towel." She pointed with blood-covered fingertips at the kitchen.

Paris was quick, retrieving it and handing it to her in seconds. Jade had a brief thought that she hoped the blood would come out of the towel when she was done; it was a cute pattern with cherry blossoms. She wadded it up and jammed it against her nose.

"Perhaps we should call Dr. Gellar and get her to expedite your medical tests."

"Do you think Bruce is okay? Her voice came out muffled from her blocked nose and partially covered mouth. "Can you call Callie and ask her if she can go check on him?"

"I think I should call Dr. Gellar first."

Jade frowned. "I'm seeing her Monday anyway. But Bruce might need help now."

Paris frowned back at her. "I doubt Callie can make it past your demon locks."

Jade paused and then stretched out her magic, willing it to travel as far as it could. She should have changed her locks before to let Callie in. How else would Bruce get help if he needed it?

"I don't think using your magic is a good idea right now," Paris said, kneeling by her side and putting his hand back on her shoulder. She shamelessly pulled some his power, hearing him suck in a sharp breath when she did, but he didn't pull back, nor did he remove his hand. With that little boost, she could feel her locks even across the distance. Jade turned their tumblers in her mind, tweaking and reshaping the spell, feeling it slide into a new arrangement. The magic was still sluggish and slow. It had the sense of an old lace doily - fragile and flimsy. She reeled her magic back, releasing her grip on Paris' power at the same time.

"I think it will let Callie in now," she said. "Will you call her and ask her to check on Bruce?"

Paris looked displeased, his lips pressing together thinly as he stood, but he pulled out his phone and called Callie, quickly asking her to check in on Bruce and letting her know Jade's demon locks shouldn't be a problem. However, he then called Gellar and asked the doctor to request a rush on Jade's lab results.

Jade hit the side of his leg with the back of her hand. "You're such a tattletale," she said as soon as he got off the phone. She pulled the bloodied tea towel away from her nose and dabbed at her nostrils a few times, confirming the nosebleed had stopped. "It's just a nosebleed. I haven't had one in a while. I get them sometimes when I'm stressed, not only from magic stuff. It probably doesn't even have anything to do with-" she waved her hand around, not sure how to say, 'with all the crazy going on in my brain. You know, that crazy I haven't told you about.' "Stuff," she finished lamely.

"Then it should be simple enough for the good doctor to rule out anything once she gets your blood work. Which she'll get back sooner now."

Jade rolled her eyes, scrunching her nose as she did. It already had the dry, crusty sensation that would plague her all day due to the nosebleed.

"Besides, even if you do get them regularly," Paris said, eyeing her dubiously. "You also get them from too much magic." He pointed to the cracked glass pane.

"I'm going to have to ask the landlord to replace that now." Jade slumped as she sat. That was just one more thing to go on her 'to-do' list.

"That's hardly the most pressing concern of it." Paris paused, looking down at her. "What happened?"

Jade shrugged. "I don't know. I was just... thinking and it happened."

"Thinking of what?"

"Of things! Stuff and things and moving and packing and I didn't sleep well last night and-" she waved her hands around. She stopped, taking a deep breath. "Is there room in the car for the rest of these boxes?" Jade asked, wanting to change the subject.

Paris' jaw worked for a moment as he watched her before he darted his eyes quickly around the room. "Should be. Just enough."

"Then let's just finish and go."

She turned her back to him, moving toward another set of boxes. He didn't move from where he stood and she thought he would push her for more, but he only sighed. Moments later, she heard him pick up the box by the front door and head downstairs to the car. Her eyes drifted over to the doorway and she had to remind herself to get back to work.

It took two more hours of silence other than, 'pass me the packing tape gun' and 'no, that box doesn't look full, but it's heavy. That can't go in there,' before they were done.

Paris stood behind Jade in the hallway as she took a long, last look at the apartment. It didn't look much different, even with all her stuff gone. She felt transitory - like she was some kind of ghost, not a real person. Just an image moving from place to place without leaving any trace.

"Are you ready to leave?"

Jade nodded but didn't turn to leave.

"Come, Jade. Let's go home."

Home. To Paris, that's what the Coven was. Home. It wasn't quite that to Jade, but she didn't think this apartment had been either.

"I'm worried I'm forgetting something." Her voice sounded loud to her even though she barely put any effort behind it.

"If you are, we can always come back."

Jade nodded, but she didn't believe him. With a sharp tug, she pulled the door shut and locked it, shoving the key under the door for the landlord. Down in the parking garage, Paris handed her car keys to her before heading for the passenger side.

"You could have sent these things with movers," said Paris as he slid into the car. It had taken some serious work on his part to get all the boxes she had sent down with him into the backseat and trunk of her car.

She wrinkled her nose and then wiggled it a bit at the tight feeling inside it. "I don't like other people touching my stuff. It's weird. The things I'm taking are my important things. Things I like. Things I need."

"Even the coffee pot?" he responded dryly. "I know you have one back at the Coven."

She gave a weak smile, feeling like he was trying to humor her. "That coffee pot and I have been through a lot together. They don't even make that model anymore. If it clunks out, I'll never be able to replace it."

"And the pillows?" He gestured to some truly bland and generic throw pillows she had decided at the last minute to pull off the sofa and bring with her.

"Those are for Bruce! He likes to sleep on pillows."

Paris' lips curled up in small grin. "He's quite the creature."

"I hope he's okay."

"Callie will call or text as soon as she confirms that."

Paris seemed so sure of the answer. She wondered if he really was or if it was a sort of leader thing - the ability to fake the calm, cool exterior no matter what he believed. Jade liked to think she was getting to know him better, but she didn't know him well enough to tell if he was lying right now and trying to make her feel better.

She wanted to know him better, but maybe she wasn't ready. She gave herself a mental shake and focused on the task at hand - starting the car and driving back to the Coven. She had too much going on in her life at the moment for anything. Besides, Paris probably didn't even think of Jade that way. You know, in a relationship kind of way. Not that she thought of Paris in a relationship way. She just... sort of thought it might be nice to spend more time with him. Without magic or demons or hexes.

Just regular time where they didn't talk about the Coven, or Jade's magic or about some problem cropping up. Ugh. She was a mess. A relationship would be a horrible idea.

A sound from Paris had her glancing over even as she exited the underground parking garage of her (former) apartment, catching him yawning.

"I apologize. I'm quite tired." Out of the side of her eye, Jade could see him blinking and widening his eyes in the way people do when they are trying to wake themselves up.

"You look kinda shitty."

"Thank you."

"I'm just saying," Jade replied easily. *Great, win him over with your sweet talk*, she thought and then wanted to roll her eyes at herself. She'd just finished convincing herself that 'no relationship' was the path she was on. She again pushed those thoughts aside and stuck to stuff she did well. With one hand on the wheel she reached into the backseat and snagged a throw pillow. She pulled it forward, smacking it into his face a little as she did.

"Here," Jade said as she pushed it at him. "Catch a nap while I drive."

"But how will I ever tell Bruce that I stole one of his pillows?"

"He'll live. Besides, better make use of it now before he does some strange lizard thing to it. I don't think I'll get it back once it's his."

Paris pushed the pillow into the crevice between the seat and the window, slouching down a bit and tipping the seat back.

"If you need to switch off, wake me."

Watching him get comfortable, she felt a surge of… something. It made her feel good that he trusted her enough to sleep while she drove, that he felt comfortable enough to be unconscious in her presence. She tapped her fingers on the steering wheel. Maybe Paris was like this with everyone. Maybe it was nothing special. Just because it would mean something if Jade slept in front of him didn't mean it meant anything to him. She shifted her shoulders down and back, stretching her neck and getting comfortable for the long drive. Her eyes darted to the radio and she was just about to ask if he minded some music, but when she listened carefully, she heard his breathing already falling into that slow, steady, even breath that people get when they're asleep.

So, silence on the way back it was.

#

Paris didn't so much wake up as drift gently into consciousness. He became vaguely aware of the car engine humming and the slight bumps as it hit rough patches in the road. He swayed slightly as the road curved left and then right, the car easily following the turns. He opened his eyes, squinting as he shuffled himself upward in the seat. Jade turned her head to quirk her lips at him in a slight smile and then focused her attention back on the road.

"Hey. You napped for about two hours."

He looked down and saw a paper bag sitting on his lap. "What is this?"

"Snack. I thought you'd be hungry when you woke up."

"When did you stop?" he asked, amazed he had slept through it.

"About an hour ago."

He opened up the bag and smiled slightly when he saw what was inside. Double chocolate cookies.

"For your sweet tooth." She gave him another quick glance.

"Thank you." Paris wasn't sure if the cookie was warm because it was still slightly fresh or because it had been on his lap, but either way, he took a large bite of the chocolate goody and chewed thoughtfully. There were two coffees in the cup-holders on the dash and he made a sort of questioning noise as he reached for one.

"It's black but there are sugar packets and stir-sticks in the bag. I didn't know how many sugars to put in."

It was a slight juggle, which entailed holding the rest of his cookie with his teeth as he fixed his coffee. He heard Jade snort off to the side.

"There's gotta be some kind of magic spell to do that easier."

Paris secured the lid of the coffee and took the cookie out of his mouth. "Probably. But it's just as quick to do it the old fashioned way."

Paris settled back into the seat and focused on sipping the slightly cooled coffee and chewing the rest of his cookie. Though he was loathe to admit it, he had used the time at Jade's apartment to snoop a bit, looking for further information about her, her past and the mystery of Lily. He wasn't sure if he was relieved or perturbed that he'd found nothing. There hadn't been anything out of the ordinary. Not that he'd known what he was looking for, really, but it had just been an apartment with regular items - clothes, kitchen supplies, books. Although there had been a lack of personal pictures. Paris had seen the photos from her shoebox and he expected to see other ones around, or maybe a photo album. That in itself wasn't too strange - so many photos were digital lately that not many people took the time or effort to print them out. Still, after seeing the ones in the box, kept so safe and close to Jade at all times, he expected to find others. There had been none.

Jade seemed so lost and sad for a moment, staring off into space while they'd been talking about the box he'd been holding (while not really talking about the box at all). He'd not even felt her power surge up before it suddenly slapped out, cracking the glass of the TV stand. That had been surprising, as had been the scent of grapefruit, which he'd never associated with her before. Jade was usually quick with her magic, but Paris thought he should have at least had some warning before her power sparked out. It had felt different as well. It had been more like her magic from when she first came to the Coven. Unfocused, disoriented and disorganized. While Jade still had a lot to learn, she had made significant progress and her power felt cleaner and neater now. The sharp crack that had slipped out had been harsh and tangled.

"How is your nose? It hasn't bled again, has it?" he asked.

Jade shook her head, not taking her eyes off the road. "No. I told you, sometimes I get those things.

They're usually one-offs. Hey, can you check your phone and see if Callie said anything about Bruce?"

He did, passing along the message that Callie had found Bruce stretched out in front of an empty fireplace, napping. Feeling sorry for him, Callie decided to stay for a bit and conjure him a fire.

"She hopes you don't mind," Paris read from his phone, "but she's also eating a bag of chips she found in your cupboard."

Jade snorted. "She got suckered in by Bruce's puppy eyes." Jade frowned. "Lizard eyes, I guess. She can eat all the chips she wants."

Hearing her familiar was safe, Jade's shoulders relaxed, tension bleeding out. He could admit that he was relieved as well. Though he hadn't said it aloud, Paris had been concerned Jade's nosebleed meant they would find Bruce sick or hurt or... something. He wasn't sure what. It all made Paris wonder if he should ask Jade not to use any more magic until they sorted this all out. What ever 'it' was.

He was hesitant to bring anything sensitive up, however, while she was driving. The magical spurt that had caused the glass to crack back at her apartment had been out of control and he didn't like to think of what could happen if something similar should occur while they were on the road. Keeping to himself, they passed the rest of the trip in casual companionship with long bouts of comfortable silence. By the time they pulled into the driveway in front of Jade's small cottage, Paris had managed to get a few emails done on his smartphone.

Jade seemed anxious to be back; Paris wasn't sure why. Her mood lightened, though, when Paris spied a lumbering Bruce heaving his way out of a window on the main floor. Paris couldn't understand how the creature managed to hoist himself up and then out. He thought he sensed magic around the window and turned to ask Jade about it, but stayed silent when he saw the way her face lit up at seeing Bruce. He didn't think he'd ever seen her smile so open and wide. It made her appear years younger than she was. Bruce hobbled over and scratched at the car door and Jade quickly opened it up, not appearing to care about the paint job. Paris was certain if he looked, he'd find lovely gouge marks claw-distance apart, running down the entire door.

"Hey! There you are! Were you a good lizard while I was gone?" Jade's voice was higher - the pitch the people tend to use with pets. Bruce's butt did a sort of shimmy-wiggle that Paris assumed was his way of answering in the affirmative.

"And did Callie feed you some chips? I bet she did. I bet you totally conned her with your sad eyes."

Callie had indeed texted that as she left Jade's cottage, about an hour before, Bruce had been happily munching on some chips, still stretched out in front of the fireplace.

Crouched on the ground next to him, Jade went over his Elizabethan lizard collar and neck with careful fingers. Paris noticed when Jade found Bruce's scaly spot. Her smile faded and her eyes went tight at the edges. The spot looked as though it had doubled in size. From the look on her face, Jade had realized it too.

"I brought you pillows," she said conversationally, straightening up and smoothing out her jeans. "Pillows that are officially yours, so you can stop stealing mine."

"Pffffft." Bruce flicked his pink tongue out.

As Paris made his way around to their side of the car, Bruce waddled a few steps closer to him and presented his neck.

"Yes, Bruce. I see it," Paris said lowly, bending over to deposit a few light pets on his head. Out of the corner of his eye, he saw Jade biting her lip.

"Gotta unpack, Bruce," she said, her voice overly bright and cheerful. Bruce pushed past Jade and hopped into the front seat, grabbing the pillow Paris had used from the passenger side. He reversed out of the car, his butt waving side to side as he did, pillow firmly in his jaws.

Jade handed two boxes to Paris and took one for herself. She seemed to have a good idea of where things were in the car, despite not having been the one to load it up. Her directions were easy for Paris to follow - bring some items upstairs and leave that box close to the kitchen, put that box in the living room. They worked in relative silence, Bruce ever watchful from the fireplace, his chin resting on his new pillow.

Once the last of the boxes were in the cottage, Jade started a pot of coffee in the kitchen, using her older pot – the one she'd brought back with her. Bruce curled up under the kitchen table, his silvery eyes watching Jade as she moved around the kitchen.

"Hello, old friend," she said dramatically, petting the coffee machine as it spat and gurgled. Paris rolled his eyes, catching sight of the pantry door, slightly ajar.

"Have you received any more visits from the demon?"

Jade pursed her lips. Bruce snorted.

"Jade."

"It's not like I'm keeping them a secret. I just didn't get around to telling you because I know how you are."

"If you're not keeping them a secret, why are you so defensive?"

"Because this is how you are." She gestured at his tense posture and firm gaze, waving her hands at him. "Seth's just a creeper. A creeping creeper who creeps. He's not going to hurt me." She paused, leaning against the counter. "I don't think."

Paris took a seat at the kitchen table. "I would appreciate it if you kept me informed of his comings and goings. I don't fault you for his visits."

"I know." Her words said one thing, but her body language said another. Paris watched her for a few minutes and she was well aware of it - avoiding his gaze, picking at her cuticles and then finding an imaginary rough edge on the counter-top and worrying it with her fingernail.

"What happened at the apartment? With the glass?"

Jade shrugged, her shoulders going up and down in a sullen manner. "I don't know."

He got the feeling she wasn't being intentionally dense or surly. She really didn't know.

"What were you thinking of when it happened?"

The shoulder shrug came slower this time and he realized that he could read that gesture - that was her knowing what she'd been thinking of and not wanting to say. Paris thought of his next question carefully.

"Is that your first nosebleed since Bruce fell ill?"

"Yes," she answered easily and he took it for the truth.

Paris felt Bruce nudge at his foot under the table and wondered if it was by accident or design.

"And you've not had any others due to using too much magic?"

She shook her head. "I've been careful. I'm only doing small spells."

"When you stopped Dex, you bled from the ears."

Jade leveled him with a look. "You say that like I wasn't there. I remember what happened, English. Dr. Gellar said I was fine. No permanent damage. It isn't like I did that for shits and giggles. He was trying to whammy the whole Coven."

"I'm aware," Paris said, trying to placate her. Silence stretched out between them again as he flipped through what he knew.

"When we didn't know where you were, I cast a locator spell to find you."

"I said I was sorry about that. I didn't know you guys would be worried."

He held up a hand. "That's not why I'm bringing it up. What I meant to say was, I used a locator spell to find you, but it didn't work like it should have."

She slowly took a mug from the cupboard, giving him a quick glance and when he nodded once, taking one down for him as well. "What happened?" she asked, pulling the coffee pot out and pouring them each a cup.

"I don't know. It was like the spell only partially worked." Paris frowned. "Like it only half worked."

Jade turned to look at him, carafe in one hand almost forgotten. Her mouth moved like she wanted to say something, but wasn't sure what. "Did it...? How...?" She closed her mouth and swallowed, trying to find her words. "What do you mean half?"

"I used nearly the same spell to find you last night as I did when you first came to the Coven. It involves a fine powder created from some herbs and spices, along with a map, some weights and my own magic. I should have been better at it this time, more precise, since I know you now. I know your magic. But only half of the powder found you on the map."

"Who did the other half find?"

Her voice was quiet, like she was afraid to ask him the question and his brows knit together at her wording.

"No one," Paris said. She looked... disappointed. "Jade, who did you think it would find?"

Jade shook her head slightly, turning back to the counter. She poured two cups of coffee and pushed the carafe back with a slosh. She set his down on the table, pushing the small sugar dish over, but she didn't join him. Instead, after she'd fixed her coffee as she liked, she stayed standing, leaning up against the counter. The sound of the spoon clinking against the ceramic as he stirred sugar into his coffee was loud in the small kitchen. Under the table, Bruce pressed against Paris' leg again. He wasn't sure if that meant 'silly human, you should stop while you're still ahead' or 'keep going, you're getting there.'

"Jade, who is Lily?"

Jade watched the interior of her cup as though there were tea leaves inside, divining her future and past. Bruce got up from under the table and waddled over to her, falling over on his side and pressing his long, spiny back against her foot. She looked down at him and smiled before setting her mug on the counter and crouching down. She sat cross-legged on the kitchen floor, her hand swiping along Bruce's serpentine belly.

She took a long time forming her words and though he was generally a patient man, Paris found himself wanting to ask her more questions, prod her into an answer. But he also got the feeling that she was standing on a knife's edge and if he disturbed her at all in this moment, she would topple off, falling on the side of silence.

"My dad was a mean drunk and he drank a lot. He probably ended up with cirrhosis of the liver. I'm not sure. I haven't spoken to him or my mom since I left home. They could both be dead. Or they could both be as we left them; dad drunk, looking for something to hit and mom just… indifferent."

The small word 'we' caught his attention and he kept himself still so as not to distract her. Jade didn't look up as she spoke. She kept her head titled down, focused on Bruce. Bruce, however, had turned his head so that his eyes were solely looking at Paris. It was a very potent sensation. Paris kept his own gaze locked on Bruce, afraid that if he looked away, or stared directly at her, Jade would stop talking.

"I don't know which was worse, to be honest. I mean, my dad would hit, but my mom was checked out. She kept the house running, food on the table and liquor in the cupboards, but it was like she wasn't really there. Or like we weren't really there. I don't know if you've ever been ignored or not noticed." Jade didn't wait for him to answer - she wasn't really asking him a question so much as making a statement. "It really sucks."

Not only was Paris holding Bruce's gaze, he felt like he couldn't move. As though she had somehow spelled him into being still. In a way, she had.

"People say that kids act out sometimes because some attention, even bad attention, is better than no attention." She shrugged, one shoulder going up and down. "But what if we'd acted out and then she still didn't notice us? Maybe that would feel worse. So we were a good kid. We were a really good kid."

Paris noticed the subtle shift from the first person to the third and her mixing the two and his heart double-thumped in his chest. She must be talking about Lily. All this must be about Lily.

"With Dad drunk most of the time and looking for a fight and Mom there but... not...we were all we had. I had her and she had me and it was enough. We made it enough."

Bruce smacked his lips a little, like he was swallowing or working something in his mouth. It was an almost-canine gesture - one Paris had seen dogs do when they lie down to sleep. He still held Paris' gaze, his serpentine, reflective eyes easily resting on Paris and not looking away.

Paris had asked once if Lily was Jade's sister and Jade had said she wasn't. He recalled her words when he asked.

"You didn't say you had a sister."

"I don't."

She hadn't answered who Lily had been, only that she wasn't a sister. Now, with the way she spoke, he was more confused. Jade talked as though Lily had been there, together with Jade, as they grew up. If not a sister, then who? Or what?

"We used to sleep in the closet a lot," Jade continued, her voice low and almost dreamy. "Our dad wasn't a smart drunk. He'd come looking for us and if we weren't in bed..." she shrugged again. "I don't know why he never figured it out. It's not like you can go very far when you're young. But he didn't." Bruce's eyes were drowsy, starting to flicker closed as Jade continued to sweep her hand back and forth over his belly. But he kept his gaze focused on Paris, even as his eyes drifted shut.

"I've started sleeping in the closet again and I'm not sure why." Her voice was even softer now, like she was telling him a secret. "I don't mean to. I just wake up there. And sometimes, things have been moved that I don't remember moving." Her hand stopped moving over Bruce's belly and rested on his skin. "And I'm dreaming. Of water. Of Lily."

Paris wanted to say something, but wasn't sure what. Maybe that he was listening, that it was all right, that she could confide in him. But he was still afraid if he made a sound, he would break whatever impetus she was under to speak and she would lock her thoughts up tight again.

Suddenly, so quick that he flinched, both Jade and Bruce turned their heads toward the back door of the cottage. Bruce flipped up from his side to his belly, his eyes narrowing just as Jade's did, both of them staring at the door.

"My demon locks are unraveling," Jade said, a tone of dread in her voice.

"What?" Paris asked, sitting up right and staring at the back door. "How can you tell?"

"I can feel it." She pushed herself to her feet, taking a step closer to the back door and he reached out a hand to stop her, but she was out of his range. She didn't go any closer, frozen in place. Bruce's tongue flicked out and he spat, hissing at the door.

"Is your magic failing?" Paris asked, pushing his chair back and getting to his feet.

Jade shook her head, still facing the door, but her eyes were moving around like she was seeing something else. Perhaps she was. Her locks were a demon spell and she said she liked demon magic for its complexity and structure. Maybe she was looking at pieces of the spell in her mind.

"No, it's not my spell," she said, her fingers flexing slightly by her side, like they wanted to do something, but didn't know what. "Something... someone's taking it apart."

CHAPTER TEN

Bruce darted toward the back door, scratching the wood, leaving marks in the paint. When the door didn't open under his ministrations, he turned his head to look back at Jade. His expression clearly said to her, 'HUMAN WITH OPPOSABLE THUMBS, LET ME OUT.'

"Should I do it?" Jade asked Paris, not taking her eyes of Bruce. She couldn't tell what was out there, only that *something* was. Something or someone taking apart her demon locks.

"Do you know what's out there? Can you tell?" Paris asked. She felt him come up behind her, only slightly encroaching on her space. She didn't turn around; her eyes were focused on Bruce and the door.

"No. But Bruce really wants out." Bruce scratched at the door again, his claws leaving deeper grooves past the depth of the paint and into the grain of the wood. "The last time he wanted to go out like this, Dex and Veronica were outside my house. He scared them off."

"You never told me that," Paris said.

"It didn't seem important after it all had ended." Jade took a step toward the door, her hand reaching for the knob to let Bruce out.

"Wait. We don't know-" Paris began, but Jade had already opened the door, despite his warning. Bruce was like a cartoon character for a moment - feet moving so fast that they couldn't get purchase on the ground, and then he bolted out the door like he'd been launched. Jade wasn't sure she should follow him. She took another step toward the door, only stopping when she felt Paris' fingers lightly touch her shoulder once.

"We don't know what's out there."

"No. But... I trust Bruce," Jade said. She'd trust Bruce before any member of the Coven. Maybe even before Paris.

Between the bite of the winter air and the things she'd been telling Paris about her past, Jade felt vulnerable and unprotected standing in the cold air of the open doorway. Bruce has disappeared into the dark of the back yard, or perhaps even further still into the dense vegetation that lined the property. She couldn't see nor hear him. While Bruce seemed to be attuned to Jade's location, she didn't have the same connection back to him.

The demon locks were unraveling, like a knitted sweater with a loose, frayed end being pulled - slowly, methodically. They were coming apart. It wasn't a confused or scattered approach. It was smooth and seamless. On a whim, she sniffed the air and caught the scent of sage, vanilla and licorice. She knew it was the magic of the person taking the spell apart.

"Do you smell that?"

"What?" Paris asked.

"Their magic. I can smell it."

Paris sniffed the air next to her and despite the gravity of the situation, she thought he looked comical, delicately sniffing the air like a fancy dog. He blinked sharply and pulled back.

"Do you recognize it?" Jade watched his expression, but couldn't read it.

"No. I thought it reminded me of someone, but... no."

"Who?"

"It's not relevant."

Jade frowned at his answer. It could be relevant. She did best when she had all the information available - what might seem not important or incidental to Paris could still help. A rustle from further away caught her attention and Jade sighed in relief when Bruce sauntered back into the yard, no worse for wear. He trotted in like he hadn't a care in the world, which was confusing because Jade could still feel her spell, or rather the bits of what was left, falling away. And then, finally, suddenly, the spell was gone, like leaves the wind carried away. Her magic reached out for the last dregs of it, but couldn't catch anything. Bruce saddled up beside her, facing outside like she was, pressing himself against her leg.

"What did you find, buddy?" she asked, bending over to give him a solid pet, feeling better when she felt the weight of him under hand. "Did you see anyone? Did you scare them off?"

His tongue flicked out, toward the back of the yard, but he didn't make any other motions. Jade narrowed her eyes and then decided to go out in the yard herself. She thought maybe Paris would try to stop her, but he only followed right behind her. She was glad for his presence. She sniffed the air again, hoping to catch the scent of magic again, but there was nothing in the cold, crisp air - only the slightly spicy scent of nightfall. She reached the edge of her yard, where the dense foliage between the houses and the alleyway sprung up, closing off the views to other houses. There was a green space between the property lines - a little bit of a wild area where children could play relatively safely during the day without worrying about cars or traffic. It also meant there was plenty of space for someone to linger unseen.

Jade didn't hear or see anything. Bruce was sitting unconcerned by the back door. "I don't think there's anyone out there. Not anymore at least," Jade said. She was glad when she saw Paris nod beside her.

"Agreed. I don't think there's anyone. I don't think Bruce would have come back if there were."

Jade crossed her arms over her chest, cold, but not quite ready to go back inside. "You keep telling me no one else at the Coven practices demon magic."

"They don't."

She turned to face him, giving him her best, 'oh really?' face. "Someone just took apart my demon lock spell. The spell I use to keep my house safe. And they did it damn well. It just… fell apart."

"I don't know anyone that could do that. I don't understand your spell myself. I can't work demon magic like you can."

"Then who did this?" she asked, gesturing wildly with one of her hands.

"I don't know." Paris paused for a moment. "Is it possible…could it have been you?"

Jade hoped her expression conveyed the full force of her non-verbal, 'what the fuck?'

"I think you've been under extreme stress and your magic hasn't always been under your control." Paris' voice was low and gentle.

"I smashed some glass! That's the magical equivalent of throwing a hammer. This," she waved a hand around her gesturing to her house and herself, "is a little more fine-tuned than a hammer. It took me three hours to set up that spell and someone took it apart in two minutes."

"You managed to tweak it from your apartment, miles away."

Jade rolled her eyes. "It's not even the same thing."

"Forgive me for not knowing that. I already said I don't know the demon spells as well as you."

"Yeah, and every time you say that it sounds like some kind of accusation." Jade crossed her arms again, hugging them close to herself. She didn't want to fight with Paris. She was tired and feeling scared and there was a faint throbbing starting up behind her right eye. Jesus, what if she really was going crazy? What if Paris' question wasn't so far off the mark? Could she have done this?

But then she saw Bruce still sitting patiently in the doorway of her cottage and she knew it hadn't been her. If it had, Bruce wouldn't have been so keen to get outside and have a look around. She trudged back to the kitchen, hearing Paris following along behind her. She closed and locked the back door, hearing the inefficient slide of the deadbolt and sorely missing her demon locks already. She could try the demon lock spell again tonight, but it would take her time to set it up. Besides, what guarantee did she have that whoever took them apart wouldn't just do it again?

Paris asked another question. "Could it have been the demon? Seth?"

Jade's eyes darted toward the pantry. She was about to shoot off a quick negative response, but then paused to logically consider Paris' question. "No," she said slowly. "He just shows up if he wants to. And the demon locks don't work on him anyway. The warding does, or at least I hope it does." She felt another shiver at the thought of her demon warding being pulled apart like her locks. She reached out a tendril of magic and poked at a few of her wards and got a nice, resonant 'ping' back. "The warding feels okay. And if Seth did take apart my locks, I get the feeling he'd like to show up and tell me how he did it and maybe offer a deal on how to stop it in the future."

Paris' sharp blue eyes fixed on her quickly. "He's still pursuing a deal?"

Jade rolled her eyes. "Please, that's all he does." At the look on his face, she continued. "It's not like I'm taking him up on it."

Paris didn't look wholly convinced and she didn't have the energy to argue with him.

Jade leaned against the counter again feeling overwhelmed. Lily, her dreams, Bruce's scaly patch, moving and now the demon locks.

"I didn't want to mention this just yet, as you've a lot on your plate," Paris began and Jade felt her stomach sink. Ugh. This sounded like more bad news. "But there have also been some… reports of the area in the Preserve, out by the lake, of your magic."

"You mean complaints," Jade answered.

"I wouldn't necessarily call them that," Paris hedged diplomatically.

"You don't have to. I found the Counter-Magic log and read them."

"Oh, I see."

"I'm not doing that either," she said, but this time, she was sort of lying. While she knew she hadn't dismantled her own demon locks, she wasn't entirely sure that what was going on at the Preserve wasn't her fault. With the dreams Jade was having - dreams of her, Lily and some other presence - she didn't know if she was responsible for any magic out there or not.

"Would you be willing to go out there with me?"

Jade's knee jerk reaction was 'no.' Thinking about going out to the lake area made her stomach flip. She thought about how she felt when the mojo around the lake pressed into her. Cold, sick, heavy. Even now, it was like muscle memory took over and she got the same sensations.

"You clearly don't like the idea."

"Why do you say that?" she asked sharply, looking over at Paris.

"Your face. You had this look like you were about to be sick or perhaps that you'd eaten something rotten."

Jade was normally better at schooling her expressions. Just moments ago, she'd purposely given Paris a look, knowing full well the expression on her face. It bothered her that when she thought about the lake, she wasn't aware of what her face did.

"I don't," she answered honestly. "It makes me feel sick."

"Going there or thinking about it?"

"Both."

There was a long silence and she picked up her coffee cup, taking a sip and wincing when she realized it had gone cold. Gross. She was dreading the next words out of Paris' mouth. She was afraid he'd ask about Lily. For a moment, before her demon spell started unraveling, she'd been getting ready to tell him about Lily. Maybe not everything. Maybe not how Lily disappeared or what it had been like for Jade right after that. But she'd almost been ready to tell Paris about how she and Lily were the almost the same person, but not. How they had been two people living in the same body and that she knew it sounded crazy, but it wasn't. They could have silent conversations if they wanted, or just pass images and feelings back and forth.

Then the demon locks were falling apart and Jade had been jolted out of whatever calm space she'd been in. Now, only moments later, the thought of spilling all her secrets out made her feel cold and clammy. If Paris asked again, she didn't know what would come out of her mouth. It scared her, not knowing.

"I think we should go, to the lake," Paris said finally and God, that was just as awful of a thing to say as when he'd asked about Lily. Jade could feel her short, sharp fingernails biting into the flesh of her palm and she looked down and made a conscious effort to uncurl her fist. She didn't want to go and yet, she felt like she needed to. Maybe if Paris were there, it wouldn't be so bad.

"I'll think about it," she said quietly.

#

Paris was surprised when Jade agreed to think about going to the lake. While it wasn't a solid 'yes,' he feared he would have to do much more convincing to get even a soft 'maybe.' Looking at her in the kitchen, the way she stood holding her coffee cup close to her, she looked tired and worn. He wondered if taking her to the Preserve was a good idea, but truthfully, he wasn't sure what else to do.

"It's far too late to go today," he said, checking his watch and seeing the early evening hour. "But I can make arrangements to go tomorrow. I'm sure Josef won't mind if you're missing from work."

"No, I guess not. Not if half the complaints are about me anyway."

"They're not complaints. Not truly. People are concerned."

"Angry mobs with pitchforks and torches are also usually concerned."

"That's not what this is."

She sighed and turned, opening the microwave to put her cup of coffee in to warm it up a bit. "I don't think I'm doing anything, but... if I am, am I gonna get lynched?"

"No," Paris answered quickly. "That wouldn't happen."

She remained facing the microwave, watching her cup rotate lazily inside. He got the feeling she didn't believe him.

If Jade was responsible for something amiss at the lake area, Paris had no doubt the Coven may not initially take it well, given that it would indicate that Jade didn't have full control over her powers. However, she had recently done them a great service when she stopped Dex and Paris felt that they were warming to Jade, albeit slowly.

Besides, if Jade were responsible for what was happening at the lake, there was no law anywhere that said he had to make that public knowledge.

"Why don't you find my mother's demon grimoires and we can go over the spell you did for the demon locks and see if we can either reinstate it or find any holes or weaknesses in it?"

Jade took her cup out of the microwave and raised an eyebrow at him. "I thought you said you weren't good at demon magic?"

"I'm not, but I'm sure you can walk me through it."

She bit her lower lip slightly and then set her coffee cup down on the kitchen table. "Okay, I'll be right back."

As she left the kitchen, Paris felt something hit his leg and he looked down to see Bruce under the table, looking up at him and swishing his large, serpentine tail back and forth.

"Have I done well, Master Bruce?" Paris asked, petting him lightly on the head. Bruce's tongue darted out and touched Paris' hand and he took that as a good sign. "I think she was almost ready to talk to me about Lily, but then..." Paris sighed and Bruce turned and scowled at the back door. Paris wanted to laugh. "Yes, exactly. But you don't seem too concerned about what's out there, so I hope that's a good sign."

"Are you talking to Bruce?" Jade asked as she came back in the kitchen, cradling a demon grimoire and her tablet computer. "Because he doesn't talk back, you know." She set both items down on the table, waiting for Paris to take a seat before she took one herself.

"I know," Paris replied as he scooted his chair in closer to the table. "But there's something quite relaxing about him."

"Maybe you need a pet. I mean, I've got Bruce and Callie has her fat cat, although God knows you can't call him chubby in front of her."

"No," Paris mused. "She's quite blind to the bulk of Stuart."

"How does she not know that cat is fat? She must have to carry him to the vet. He's bigger than some dogs I've seen."

Paris smiled at the tone in Jade's voice, quite liking that it was back to her normal, sharper tone instead of the drawn out melancholy one she'd had earlier. "I'm not sure. Perhaps she's spelled his cat carrier so it's not as heavy."

Jade made a sort of 'harrumph' sound and then opened the demon grimoire, searching for her spell. As she did, a waft of scent came up from the books, mint, licorice and hickory. He wrinkled his nose. It was a heavier scent than he was used to from magic and he wondered if it was the smell of demon magic in general, or if this was the way his mother's demon magic smelled in particular. Though he hadn't mentioned it to Jade, the smell of magic outside had reminded him a little of his mother's magic - sage and vanilla. Hers used to also have a slight mix of peppermint as well. Now, smelling that peppermint on the grimoire, he wondered if it was due to his mother or if the smell of mint on her had been due to demon magic.

He pushed those thoughts out of his mind and tried to focus on what was in front of him. Jade had the grimoire open to the spell she'd used and was also scrolling through her tablet.

"Still trying to make a grimoire out of your computer gadgets?" Paris asked.

Jade made a so-so motion with her hands. "Meh. I like to take notes on the tablet, but sometimes I find I miss post-it notes or doodling. I may end up transcribing all my stuff. I don't know."

"If you'd like to start a proper grimoire," Paris said, ignoring when she snorted at the word 'proper,' "please let me know and we can go shopping for one."

"I figured you guys probably had a fancy shop for them or something. I've yet to see one that just looked like a regular notebook. They're all fancy with bindings and covers and such."

"Well, they're quite important to us. We like to have them done nicely. If you want one, let me know."

She shrugged. He was going to have to get better at reading that gesture on her, as she seemed to use it for a multitude of things.

"Yeah, okay."

Paris wasn't sure if that meant Jade wanted one right now or that she would let him know when she wanted to go. As he spoke, he looked down at the demon grimoires, his mother's books, and wondered if his mother had picked out something 'special' for these dark holders of demon magic with the same care and fastidiousness that she'd always shown picking out her other grimoires. He trailed a finger over the page, wondering when her life had been so split in two - Coven Leader by day and demon grimoire writer by night. Or if it had been that simple, or discrete.

He focused his attention back on Jade as she outlined what she had done for the demon spell and he was impressed. The original spell had been more like a ward than a lock, and she'd managed to slightly tweak it so that it worked more like the latter than the former. A ward worked like a magical 'area' or 'bubble.' It kept certain things out or in depending on the type of ward. But her locks,

Jade explained to Paris, worked more like a traditional deadbolt - they blocked off an area, without having to put out enough magic to work *inside* her house. They were a perimeter. It also enabled her to 'key' people, which she had done previously with Paris and then later on with Callie. She had enabled the demon lock to allow Paris and Callie in by focusing on their magical signature - something she was familiar with for both of them.

Looking at the demon grimoire in front of him and understanding what she'd done was one thing, but he would have never been able to do it himself and told her such. She blinked owlishly at him.

"But it's just like regular magic," she said.

Paris shook his head. "No, it's not. Looking at that spell, I wouldn't have had the first clue how to alter it. How did you know?"

"I dunno. I just thought about what I wanted the answer to look like and worked my way backward from there."

"But how did you know what your answer would look like," Paris pressed.

Jade looked down at the book and frowned. "I don't know," she repeated. "It's like… when I read the spells, sometimes I just know what the changes need to look like. Then I sort of fiddle around with things and when I get something right, it's like I feel better about it. Like it clicks. Then I know I'm on the right path."

"I get a similar sense with regular magic. I just 'know' it will work. But looking at these demon spells, even with all my magic and knowing they were written by my mother, I feel as though I'm reading another language and I'm never going to get the sense of it. Do you feel that way about regular magic?"

Jade pursed her lips together, thinking. "No, I feel like it's harder sometimes or not as logical. Here," she said pointing at the demon grimoires, "I feel like when I push left, things go left. With regular magic I feel like sometimes I push left and it goes upside down and I don't know how it happened."

Despite her knack for the demon magic, however, Jade was unable to re-cast the demon locks on her house. After three hours of trying, she was tired, Paris was tired and even Bruce was sacked out under the table on his side.

"It worked before! I don't know why it won't work now!" Long strands of hair were falling out of her ponytail and the remnants of her mascara were circling her eyes. She looked as though she might cry, pressing her fingers to her brow-bone and staring down at the page. Jade had been trying to cast the spell and hadn't been able to hang onto the magic long enough, losing it earlier and earlier each time she tried. At one point Paris had tried to help her, but he found the demon magic sticky and distasteful and she'd barked at him that his attitude was 'harshing her magic vibe.'

It had been after that sharp comment that she'd suggested another pot of coffee and he'd snapped that if she drank anymore, she could rival a harpy for attitude. She shifted in her chair, her foot kicking his leg, which she claimed was a total accident. Even Bruce looked suspicious at her words.

"You're too tired," he said honestly. "You were up late last night packing, we spent today moving and you drove all the way back to the Coven. Not only that, but you've been under significant emotional stress lately."

He could see tears pricking at her eyes. Jade was frustrated, exhausted and likely emotionally drained. Paris wasn't doing much better himself. He'd had a long night and longer day, but he'd at least caught a nap on the car ride home. Going back over in his mind what Jade had been telling him before they'd been interrupted, he had a better understanding of her now. It was no wonder she'd been so reluctant to join the Coven or to trust any of them - she'd been raised in an environment of distrust, fear and abuse. It must have seemed like some kind of strange joke or fairytale when Paris arrived and told her she was a witch and she belonged in a Coven. She rubbed at her eyes like a child and he spared another thought for the solemn-eyed girl he'd seen in her photos. He couldn't shake the feeling that it had been wrong of him to pry, but he was also glad he did it. Although, he didn't like the ideas that were starting to percolate in his brain. He didn't like hearing about her growing up in an abusive home, or about how her magic was flaring out now. Paris didn't know what they would learn when they went out the lake area, if anything. Maybe taking Jade out there would be a bad idea. But he didn't know what else to do - they needed more information.

"You should go to sleep for tonight. I'd like to go to the lake tomorrow and you should be well rested for that."

Jade fiddled with a worn edge of one the pages in the demon grimoire, her fingernail dragging over the point of the corner, fraying it. "Yeah," she said, half-heartedly. She quickly glanced under the table and Paris did the same, catching sight of Bruce stretched out on his side, eyes slit open. He kept opening his eyes as soon as they would drift shut, determined it seemed to stay awake as long as they did.

"Are you worried about going to sleep with your demon locks not working?"

Jade pursed her lips and he saw her shoulder start to hitch up in a shrug, like she wasn't going to answer verbally, but then she did speak. "Yeah. Kind of."

"I'm sure you're safe."

"I guess."

Paris tapped his fingers against the table, thinking quickly. "I don't mean to be presumptuous, but you've a spare room and I could stay, if you like."

She looked up at him, pinning him with her clear grey eyes. He swore he could see the wheels of her mind turning as she thought it over. He could see her hesitating and he took an educated guess at why.

"It's not an imposition. You're exhausted and your magic is probably feeling wobbly after attempting the demon locks for so long tonight."

She snorted. "Yeah, without success."

Paris tipped his head in agreement. He wondered if he was pushing his luck with his next words. "It's all right to want help. And to ask for it."

He thought his words had the exact opposite effect he wanted when he saw her eyes go glassy with a flood of moisture, but then she nodded.

"Okay."

"Why don't we check the physical locks down here and then call it a night?"

Jade blinked and shook her head, as though she was trying to clear it. He thought he might have to gently prod her to get up, but Bruce flipped to his feet and went to the back door, looking up at them expectantly. Jade checked the bolt and lock and then Bruce trotted toward the front door with Jade right behind him, where they went through the same routines.

"Go check your window," Jade said, her face tipped toward Bruce. He ambled over to one of the main floor windows, using his front feet to scrabble up the wall and then stick his snout all along the edge of the window. Paris watched in confusion and interest.

"It's spelled to let him in and out without actually being open. I just feel better when he checks it."

Now that she'd mentioned it, Paris could feel the faint impression of her magic in the area around the window. It was another impressive piece of magic. Very subtle, yet effective. He wanted to ask her about it, but didn't want her to think about magic anymore tonight.

Bruce came loping back, flipping his Elizabethan lizard collar up once before it smoothed down along his neck.

"All good?" she asked him and he snorted. "Okay," Jade said, starting up the stairs, Bruce waddling behind her, with Paris behind him. At the top, she pointed Paris toward the door opposite her own. "So, guest room, but I guess you kind of knew that since the Coven owns this place. Bathroom down the hall. It should be pretty clean since I use the master one mostly and no one ever comes over. Um, I might have a toothbrush still in the packaging?" She said the last bit like it was a question, looking at him expectantly.

Paris nodded. "Please, if you don't mind."

Jade disappeared into her room for a few minutes and he could hear her rummaging around in some of the boxes they had brought back from her apartment. She came back triumphantly holding a toothbrush, new in the package, and a small travel size container of toothpaste. The brush was fluorescent pink from the bristles all the way down the handle to the end.

"Er, sorry about the color. I like the bright ones."

"It's fine," Paris said, smiling at her expression. He took it from her and then they stood in the hallway, staring at one another awkwardly.

"Sooooooo," she said, drawing the word out. "Uh, good night. I guess."

"Good night."

Jade seemed stuck there for a moment longer until Bruce whapped her calf with his tail and she jumped. "Jeez. Fine! Good night," Jade said again, heading into her room and closing the door. He could hear her saying something to Bruce, but could only make out her tone (decidedly unimpressed with the lizard) and not the words. He hesitated a moment longer before stepping into the guest room.

Since he'd helped get the cottage set up for Jade when she first arrived, he was familiar with the room and noticed it hadn't changed at all since Jade had been living here. The room had a definite 'unused' feeling to it, along with a slight scent of dust and stale air. It wasn't unpleasant, but it didn't exactly welcome him in either.

It was of no consequence. He was only staying the night to put Jade's mind at ease since her demon locks weren't working. He made quick work of his evening ablutions, and then stripped down to his boxers, feeling strange about leaving his Henley on, but feeling even stranger about taking it off.

As Paris settled in the bed, he mulled over the list of problems Jade was having. Bruce was ill, Jade was having problems sleeping, a magical outburst at her apartment - different in feeling and scent from her normal magic - and now her demon locks taken apart. He readily admitted, he didn't know how it all fit in together. He thought about Lily - a girl who seemed to look remarkably like Jade, except for the color of her eyes. Jade had indicated she had no sister. Could she have lied? But to what end? The thing that troubled him the most was when Jade had been discussing Lily in the kitchen and her strange mixture of pronouns - first person and third person - 'I' and 'we.' Paris didn't like where that led his brain. What if Jade was significantly more ill than he'd realized, only her problems weren't physical? Paris knew little about psychology and psychiatry, other than the generic, general things that people got from an entry-level class. It seemed absurd to think that she might have some kind of mental disorder. Or did it? Jade had an abusive childhood - that much he knew. But could she have a psychiatric disorder from it? Did people really have multiple personalities, or was that all cinema and fiction?

He would continue on as he had been and gather more information. He and Jade would go to the lake, they would check the magic in the area. Then, they would follow up with Dr. Gellar and Jade's medical tests. Perhaps Paris could speak to Dr. Gellar about his concerns. No doubt she would chastise him for being so foolish and set him straight.

Paris resolved not to borrow trouble by imagining all sorts of outlandish and far-fetched scenarios. He took a deep breath, closed his eyes and was determined to sleep - stowing away his thoughts for the evening. He told himself by the time the sun rose tomorrow, in the clear light of morning, he would likely feel quite embarrassed at himself for his outlandish thoughts.

#

Again, Jade dreamt of the Preserve. Her limbs feeling heavy and thick as she walked and she could feel branches and twigs snapping under her feet. It was overcast, but bright - the kind of day that came about in the middle of February or March, where it seemed like it would be nice outside, but in reality, it was sharp and bitter. Out of the corner of her eye, Jade saw movement and she turned, finding herself facing a long, impossible wall of mirrors. The reflection of the Preserve surrounded her - bare trees, their empty branches crawling over one another. The grey sky punched through the empty spots, like spot lights. She studied her reflection, searching for anything amiss or out of place. Like one of those strange comedy shows, Jade raised her hand and her mirrored self did the same. Jade moved her hand back and forth and then tilted her head, keeping her eyes focused on the mirror. Her doppelgänger matched her motions. Jade stepped closer to the glass, reaching her fingers out, feeling oddly discomforted by the way it looked. It looked like she was reaching for herself.

Her fingers touched the glass finding it cold and firm. She breathed out a sigh. She wasn't sure what she expected. Maybe for her fingers to slip through the barrier and into the mirror. What would be on the other side, she couldn't say. More movement caught her eye and she turned from the glass to her left, seeing the winter trees of the Preserve stretching out before her again, stark and leafless. Jade squinted. She saw something in between the empty branches. Something, someone. A dart of movement, a flash of dark hair. She didn't get the sense that it was Lily. She always knew when Lily was there. The figure in the woods wasn't her.

Sparrow Lady. That's what Lily had called her. Jade looked up to the sky and saw sparrows high above her head, swirling and swooping, soundless. None came close to her like they had before.

Jade let her hand slide down the glass as she turned. The moisture on her fingertips caused a high-pitched squeaking sound, reminding her of the chirp-chirp of birds. She started walking in the direction from which she'd seen the figure. Her salamander charm was heavy against the notch of her collarbones. Beside her, her mirrored self kept pace, a silent shadow. Jade knew where they were going before the break in the trees revealed it.

The lake.

That was where Sparrow Lady had gone. Where she wanted Jade to go. It occurred to Jade that in all her dreams of the Preserve and the lake, Lily never spoke. Lily only spoke when Jade was in the closet.

Jade walked up the planks of the dock. The mirrored wall followed along with her, undulating with the motion of the old wood. Jade's ears were hypersensitive. She could hear the creak and groan of the wood as she moved. The surface of the lake was slightly frozen over and as the dock moved, the ice around it cracked and snapped. When Jade reached the end of the dock, she looked back to the mirror and this time, it wasn't her own reflection she saw in the glass. It was Lily. She was in jeans and a black sweater - one of Jade's favorites - the one that she liked to wear when it was cold outside and she didn't have anywhere to be during the day. Jade could curl up in a chair with a book and a pot of coffee and just read, feeling grateful not to be out in the cold. Lily's hand reached out, toward Jade, even as both of Jade's stayed by her side. Lily's eyes were bright green in the light of the day.

Jade reached out her hand, still surprised when she felt the unforgiving glass surface under her fingertips. Jade took another step closer to the mirror. As she did, Lily turned away from her and, as she had before, tipped forward, starting to fall into the lake. Jade jerked forward, feeling herself slide through the glass. Only she realized too late, it wasn't glass, it was ice and she was the one falling toward the water, slipping underneath the surface. Her salamander charm burned against her skin even as the water closed around her, ice cold.

Looking up, Jade could see the forest and sky - wavering lines of color and distorted shapes through the surface of the water. She was cold and in the dark, but she could see the daylight just beyond her reach. Her arms stretched up to the surface, but she didn't know how to swim. On the surface something blocked the light. Jade couldn't make out what. It was the shape of a person, a woman. Her dark hair fell around her face, blocking her features. She was a misshapen blob, looming over Jade. Jade felt her heart clench and her lungs burn. It was her own face staring down at her from above. Or Lily's face. Lily's hands plunged into the water for Jade and Jade reached back.

Just as Lily's hands gripped hers and started pulling her toward the surface, something grabbed Jade from below. Hard, unyielding pressure around her ankles, yanking down on her. The Sparrow Lady. Jade kicked and struggled. Lily's face went grim, her lips moving, but Jade couldn't hear her.

She was slipping away, falling out of Lily's grasp. Jade kicked again, looking down, her head moving slowly in the cold, thick water. Beneath her, in the murk, she could see blue eyes glowing - sharp and bright. Lily pulled harder, her fingernails digging into Jade's skin, painful and harsh. The hands belonging to the blue-eyed woman pulled back - talons digging into Jade. She was being dragged further down in the water, down toward the bottom, if there was a bottom to be found. The sky was going darker above her - only the shape of Lily remained and the green of her eyes. With a mighty tug from the Sparrow Lady, Jade slipped free of Lily's hands, and was dragged lower and lower and lower still. The sky was so far away - a small patch out of reach and growing smaller. She still felt herself being pulled or maybe she was only sinking now, she wasn't sure. She was moving away from the surface, away from her body and then just away from everything.

#

Paris didn't sleep well when he wasn't in his own bed. He was a light sleeper - one ear always listening for the phone in case the Coven had an emergency. At first, he wasn't sure what woke him and he was disoriented until he remembered that he wasn't at home. He was at Jade's cottage. The clock on the nightstand indicated it was just past two in the morning - he'd only been asleep for a few hours. He listened in the dark, trying to figure out what had woken him, when he heard footsteps on the stairs. Footsteps going down. Jade must be up. He wondered if something was bothering her. He flipped back the bed covers and grabbed his pants. He was still hitching them up as he opened the door to the guest room.

The door to Jade's bedroom was open and as he peered inside, he could see the bedclothes mostly off the bed. His eyes immediately darted to the closet, where the corners of several blankets and what appeared to be Bruce's tail were poking out. Whatever Jade was doing, her familiar was still asleep - curled up in the closet.

Quietly, swiftly, he started down the stairs. There were no lights on, but he didn't pause to fumble around for the light-switch. There was enough ambient light from the moon and the street-lamps outside for him to make his way. As he did, a cold gust of air hit his feet and he slowed slightly at the sensation. He was halfway down the stairs when he realized what it was - air from outside. He padded the rest of the way down, pausing to check the front door. Closed and locked. He made his way through the living room, stopping at Bruce's window. Finding it closed as well, he hovered a hand out in front of it in case the magic spell that Jade cast let air in. There was no breeze. Lastly, he headed for the kitchen.

It was cold when he got there and he could quickly see the reason why; the back door was open. Not just cracked open, not just open a sliver. It was wide open, as though someone had come in and forgotten to close it.

Or gone out.

He stepped up to the threshold and cast his eyes about in the backyard. He thought he saw something, movement, and he squinted.

It was Jade. She was out further than her backyard, walking slowly in the uninhabited area that settled in between the two rows of houses. He could just make out the white of her t-shirt in between the winter branches of the trees and bushes.

"Jade," he called her name, not quite a shout, but louder than a conversation. He was reluctant to start shouting in the middle of the night. He was sure he must have been loud enough for her to hear, but she didn't stop moving - travelling further away from the house, away from him. Frustrated, he raced to the front door, grabbed his shoes and slid them on quickly before returning to the kitchen and rushing out the back door.

Paris barreled unceremoniously through the bushes and trees, feeling the lower branches poke and scratch at his ankles. It was cold outside, his breath coming out in puffs, and he wondered if he should have stopped to grab his coat, or Jade's. He caught up with her easily. She was moving slowly - nothing like her usual hurried pace. He grabbed her arm, calling her name as he did.

She stopped where she was but didn't turn around.

"What are you doing?" Paris asked, catching his breath.

She didn't answer him. It seemed to him like she was looking at something ahead of her and she tugged on her arm almost lazily, like he was some kind of branch or hook she was caught on. A nuisance, nothing more.

"Jade," he said quietly. "What are you doing?" he repeated.

As she tugged again to go forward, he came up in front of her, blocking her way. She stopped short at his presence, but didn't alter her gaze, still staring somewhere in front of her. She was like a movie that had been paused. Set in stasis, her eyes focused past him. He moved closer, trying to get a better look at her face, or place himself in her viewpoint. She was passive, not moving away, but not doing anything else either. He laid his hands on her shoulders, feeling the chill on her through her t-shirt.

"Jade?" he asked, quietly, looking closely at her. He wondered if he could trust that her eyes were grey - in the half-light from the moon, partially blocked by the tree branches, he couldn't be sure. He cupped the back of her skull and exerted a gentle pressure to tip her head back slightly. It was like posing a doll. Jade moved her head without any resistance, her eyes opening up as her head moved back. The irises seemed grey to Paris, but it was dark outside and he couldn't be sure. He pushed his power out a bit, feeling for any sort of magic around her. Jade always had a lingering sort of magical presence, but right now it was dulled and almost dormant. He thought he might have sensed something else around her, but it was so faint he couldn't be sure. Was that licorice he smelled? Jade had been trying to work demon magic earlier and what Paris smelled could just be the remnants of that - slightly thick and cloying with a low scent of anise or licorice. He thought of Bruce, sleeping peacefully in the closet. As her familiar, he should have protected her from any kind of magical attack, or at the very least, would have some symptoms himself if Jade were under a magical influence. Or maybe the fact that he was still sleeping was how he was affected. Without Bruce, Jade would be down a level of protection.

"You're freezing out here." Jade was in a t-shirt and long flannel sleeping pants, her feet bare. Paris shivered with cold himself and he'd only been out for seconds. She'd been out longer than he had. He looked around in the lightly wooded area. It was dark and he couldn't see anything or anyone, but his mind was still on the unraveling of Jade's demon locks. Something or someone was likely out here. However, with Jade in her bedclothes and himself hardly dressed for the outdoors, there wasn't much he could do. Jades eyes were glassy and unfocused. He thought about her insomnia, about her emotional stress, and wondered if sleepwalking was just another symptom on the list.

"Alright," he said soothingly, rubbing her arm slightly. Even though she appeared not to hear him, he felt as though he should announce his intentions. "Let's get you back home." He slid one of his hands down her arm, feeling her chilled, goose-fleshed skin. He wrapped her cold fingers in his and pulled her slightly toward him. She resisted at first, standing still where she was, facing away from him. Her breath was light and shallow - he could barely see any of her exhalations on the cold night air.

"Come on, let's go."

Paris tugged at her hand again and this time, she fell into step behind him easily enough. He winced as he thought of her bare feet on the ground, but they were soon enough back in her yard and then making their way through the back door into her kitchen. Once inside, he let go of her hand, and closed the back door and locked it securely. He wondered if he should see Jade to bed and then head back outside to... what? Search in the darkness? He turned back to where she stood, waiting placidly in the center of the kitchen, eyes cast downward, expression blank. Perhaps he should wake her so they could talk about this?

Her head suddenly turned toward the pantry like she heard something and Paris found his gaze matching hers. There was a strange shimmer from the area and then a flash of light.

"Oh, I didn't know we had company."

The demon, Seth, stood in the pantry doorway, smiling.

CHAPTER ELEVEN

The last time Paris had seen the demon had been in the Coven library, months ago, when Jade was new to the Coven and trying to find out who meant her harm. The demon still looked the same as he did then - dark eyes and amused expression. He was definitely more 'casual' standing in Jade's pantry, wearing simple jeans and a t-shirt. He looked at Paris and smiled, showing off his glittering white teeth.

"A gentleman caller!" he said, one eyebrow going up. "At this hour?" He peered at his wrist where there was, in fact, no watch. The demon made a 'tsk-tsk' sound. "What will the neighbors think? You'll ruin our reputations."

Jade was stopped in the middle of the kitchen, facing the pantry and Paris had the urge to hustle her out of the room, but didn't want to give the demon the satisfaction of watching them make an escape. According to Jade, the demon showed up regularly. Was this how it happened? Without any warning or fanfare? He just... appeared? Paris wouldn't have liked any circumstances under which the demon appeared, but he certainly didn't like it at two in the morning with an unresponsive Jade.

"What have we here?" the demon said, eyes narrowing as he looked at Jade. He seemed to come to his own conclusions and then nodded like he understood. "Ah, the lights are on, but too many people are home."

"What do you know about it?"

Seth looked up at Paris with interest in his eyes. "My, my, you aren't very good at this, are you? Our little possum is much better at bantering. Hardly ever lets slip what she wants, but you? I'm here all of thirty seconds and you've just blurted out what you want to know."

Paris resisted the urge to dart his eyes over to where Jade stood, motionless. He kept his eyes on the demon.

"There you go," Seth continued when Paris remained silent "Better. Not as good as Possum, but then she's very rare. Though I suppose you knew that."

"What do you want from her?"

"I'm afraid that's between her and me. Despite my reputation as a demon, I'm not really into threesomes. Or foursomes as the case may be." Seth winked at Paris lasciviously. "Someone's feelings always get hurt."

Paris chose not to rise to the bait and instead went for another direct question. "Are you responsible for dismantling her demon locks?"

"That question is funny coming from you," Seth replied.

"What do you mean?"

Seth smiled. "No," he continued, ignoring Paris' question. "I felt demon magic working her locks from the other side and I admit, I do keep an ear, as well as several other appendages, to the ground where our dear Possum is concerned. Got a lot of potential, you know. I came to see what it was all about. I like to keep my eye on my investments. I've spent far too much time with her to have it all go pear-shaped."

Seth peered past Paris to where Jade stood. She was still motionless, asleep, Paris supposed, even though part of her attention had been caught by Seth's appearance. Paris wondered if it was simply the animal part of her brain recognizing a predator, even in her slumbering state.

Seth 'tsk-ed' again. "Neither a borrower nor a lender be, that's what I always say. She's in quite the pickle. I daresay she'll get herself out of it soon enough if she keeps getting pushed. Or pulled."

"I'm not pushing her," Paris said quickly and then immediately regretted it when Seth turned his attention back to him and smiled.

"I never said *you* were." Seth straightened up. "Well, it's not nearly as much fun when she's not here. Do tell her I stopped by. Or don't. I'm sure I'll be seeing her again."

"I could ward the pantry against you."

Seth shrugged. "You could, but it won't be as good as her wards, and she'd probably undo it. She won't admit it, but she likes to keep tabs on me as much as I like to keep tabs on her. I'm the devil she knows. She's got a bit more street-savvy than you do when it comes to this sort of thing, though I'm sure you're quite smart," Seth said dismissively and Paris bristled. "But books aren't everything." He waggled his fingers at Paris before disappearing in a shimmer of shadow and light.

Paris exhaled slowly, mulling over Seth's words as he tugged on Jade's hand, leading her out of the room. She followed him easily and he took a moment to note the irony. He doubted she would follow him so easily if she were awake. In her current state, she was silent and pliable. He didn't like it. At the stairs, she paused and he stood behind her, pushing once on her shoulder.

"Back to bed," he said, keeping his voice low. He was loathe to wake her. He thought perhaps you shouldn't wake a sleepwalking person, but he couldn't remember if that was an old wives' tale or not. Jade climbed the stairs easily, moving up them effortlessly. When she reached the top, she stopped again, as if she wasn't sure which way to go. He turned her shoulders slightly, directing her toward her bedroom, where he'd left the light on. As they entered the room, Bruce's head poked out of the closet, eyes blinking at the light, jaws stretching in a yawn. He shook himself like a dog, smacking his jaw.

"Next time, you might want to keep a closer eye on her," Paris said and then felt foolish for chastising her familiar. Bruce toddled over to Jade, sniffed her feet, and then her calf and then prodded at her leg with his snout. He exhaled a gust of air in a snort, like he was clearing his sinuses. Jade stepped toward the closet and Paris had a moment where he wondered if he should pull out all her blankets and put her to sleep in her bed, but she'd already dropped to her hands and knees, crawling back into the small space. Bruce was right behind her, nudging her hip with his snout. Without many clothes hanging on the rack, she had enough room to nestle down and make a little nest. As he watched, Jade curled herself as far into the dark corner as she could, settling all her pillows around her. Bruce squished in beside her, stretching out long, his tail curling over her legs. He looked up at Paris with a last look as if to say, 'thanks for bringing her back,' and then closed his eyes in dismissal. Jade's head already rested on her pillow, her eyes closed as well.

Paris wasn't sure how long he stood there, watching her sleep, thinking over Seth's words. Seth had echoed exactly what Paris had been thinking - too many 'people' in Jade's head. If Paris wanted to discuss this with Jade and, indeed, he felt he needed to, he knew he would have to be careful and sensitive. He may have to make some inquiries as well of specialized doctors and probably Hannah.

He felt like a failure of some sort. Not only had he failed Jade as a Coven leader, but he'd not even suspected she might be seriously mentally ill, despite the fact that she had all the traditional markers of it. Broken home, abused childhood, solitary life, difficulty making attachments. Paris supposed he was just another person in the long line of people that had failed her. He felt sad watching her curled up in the small space. As quietly as he could, he pulled the closet doors closed, shutting her in.

#

Jade woke the next morning in the closet, stiff, sore and hot. Feeling Bruce pressed up against her back, she pushed at him a bit, trying to get some wiggle room. He had his snout buried in the nape of her neck, his long body against hers. Every exhale wafted dampness into her hairline.

"Ugh, Bruce. Seriously?"

He snorted and she not-so-accidentally elbowed him in the gut. He snorted again, this time in disgust and pushed away from her, flipping onto his belly. The closet doors rattled as he did and she winced at the sound. She pushed them open and crawled out, frowning when she noticed one of her feet hurt. She squinted at it. Why the hell were her feet dirty? She looked back in the closet at Bruce, but he was already burrowing his way under the blankets to keep snoozing.

"Lazy bones," she muttered. Jade pushed herself to her feet, trying to roll out the kinks in her neck and shoulders. Given the size of knots she could feel, she was going to need a rolling pin to work out her back or for someone to put her through one of those old-time laundry-wringing machines. Looking around, she was surprised to see it was somewhat bright in her room. Dread coiled in her stomach and she turned to look at her alarm clock.

Shit. Seven thirty. She was totally late. How had she slept so late? Why didn't her alarm go off? Why didn't Paris wake up? God, if she was late, he was even later. He was always at the Coven before she arrived.

The sick, rolling feeling of being late for work had her darting out of her room and into the hallway to knock on the guest room door. She'd have to wake Paris up and hustle them both out the door, she guessed. Jade could skip a shower, but maybe Paris was one of those 'had to shower' people. Well, she could make coffee while he showered and that would save time and guarantee she still got her caffeine. What a disaster.

Her knuckles rapped hard on the guest room door and she paused, ear pressed up against the wood, waiting to hear some sounds indicating he was up. She didn't want to just barge in on him. He might be… disrobed. She couldn't even use the word 'naked' for him. People like Paris didn't get 'naked.' They were 'unpresentable' or 'dishabille.' People like Jade were 'naked' or 'without pants.'

Jade had to give a quick glance down to be sure that she actually wasn't missing pants. Sometimes if it was hot, she took her pyjamas off. Thankfully, today was not one of those days and she was still moderately, if not modestly, dressed.

She knocked again on the door and still heard nothing. God, did he sleep like the dead? Maybe he did sleep standing up like a horse, like Henri and she had joked that one time. Jade closed her eyes, clapping one hand over them to be sure she wouldn't see anything… 'disrobed' and opened the door.

"Hey, are you up? Are you… decent? We're late."

Silence. She squinted open one eye and peeked through two of her fingers. She was totally unprepared to find an empty room with the bed made. There was no sign that Paris had even been there at all last night, except for the toothbrush on the counter.

What the hell?

Standing there confused for a moment, she realized she could smell the faint scent of coffee. She sniffed the air like a prairie dog to confirm. Yep. Coffee. She made her way down the stairs with what she was sure was a suspicious look on her face. She knew she was wearing a frown as she walked into the kitchen and found Paris working on her laptop. He glanced up as she came in.

"Good morning."

Jade glanced over at the pot of coffee that was already done brewing and at his half finished cup. He seemed in no rush to go anywhere. She'd never seen him anything but clean-shaven and it was sort of a surprise to see him with five o'clock shadow. Or seven-thirty-the-next-morning-shadow as the case may be.

"Good morning," she said warily. "Aren't we late?"

Paris nodded. "I've called us both in absent today. I'd like to talk to you. Why don't you get a cup of coffee and have a seat?"

She slowly made her way over to the coffee pot and made herself a cup. She hesitated before coming back to the kitchen table, but realized she didn't have anywhere else to go. If Paris had called her in 'sick' for work, it wasn't like she could go to the Coven. She slid down into one of the chairs, leaning away from the table. Paris closed the laptop and turned in his chair to face her. While he still looked perfectly presentable, there was a more casual air about him than she was used to. Maybe it was his hair, slightly disarrayed, or his bare feet. Or maybe he was projecting a casual air on purpose, she didn't know. She wished Bruce were here.

"Last night, I found you sleepwalking."

Jade paused, in the process of taking a sip of coffee. Instead she set the mug down carefully, staring at it. Had she done something while she was asleep? Was that why Paris was all weird and 'wanted to talk' this morning?

"Okay."

"Do you have a history of it?"

Jade shook her head slowly, not yet meeting his eye. "No." She didn't add anything more and there was a long stretch of silence in the small kitchen. Her fingers twitched slightly before she finally spoke. "What did I do?"

It was his turn to shrug and the movement was economical and almost stately on him. "You left."

She finally flicked her eyes up to his. "Huh?"

"I found you outside, in the back yard."

"Where was I going?"

"I've no idea. Do you remember anything?"

Jade looked toward the back door as she thought. She remembered bits and pieces of her dream. The lake, the Preserve. A strange presence. "I dreamt, but…"

"But what?"

She didn't know what to say. Should she tell him about her dreams? Was it relevant? How could it not be? But telling him, telling anyone really, about her dreams would feel like taking off all her clothes in public - scary. But what if he could help? Jesus, what if after all this time, someone could help her?

"I have these dreams," she began, wrapping her hands around her mug. She cracked her neck and tried to ignore the gooseflesh she could feel rising on her arms. "I've been having them since we first went to the Preserve. Since we passed by the lake."

Jade chanced a glance at Paris. He appeared wholly invested in her, paying close attention. It didn't feel pushy or strange - he was just 'there' and he was listening.

"What happens in them?"

"I'm walking, near the lake. There's a dock. Sometimes I go out on the dock. I see my reflection a lot. In the water, or there are mirrors. Sometimes..." she paused not sure how to articulate it. "There's someone else there, but I don't know who. I don't see her. I just know she's there. I can see her in the trees."

"Is it Lily?"

Jade shook her head. "No. Sometimes she's there too, but it's not her out in the trees."

"What does the woman in the trees do?"

"She used to just be there and didn't really do anything, but last night..." she frowned, trying to recall the images. Last night Jade had been her own reflection until she hadn't been - then it had been Lily. There had been water, a lot of water, and someone holding Jade down. But not Lily. It wouldn't have been Lily.

Could it?

"Last night I dreamt she held me underwater. And I went away."

"Away where?"

She shrugged. "I don't know. Just away."

"Who is she? Do you see her face?"

She shook her head. "No. Just the shape of her. The water..." she waved one of her hands around. "It made everything wavy and weird. I couldn't see."

Stealing a glance at Paris, she could see him nodding thoughtfully. He took a quick sip of his own coffee and she hurriedly matched his movements, feeling better copying him, mimicking him - as though it made everything normal and sane.

"When I led you to back to bed last night, you went directly to the closet. All your bedclothes were already there. Last night you said you've been sleeping there a lot. That you used to do it when you were little. You and Lily."

"Yeah." She took a deep breath and tried to calm the pounding of her heart. She felt a little sick and shaky - an influx of adrenaline coursing through her body with no outlet.

"Who is Lily?"

Jade swallowed, feeling tears spring to her eyes. Her throat was tight. She wanted to tell him, but at the same time she didn't. Jade knew how it sounded. It sounded like she was crazy. That she had some kind of traumatic childhood and had a disorder and maybe made up an imaginary playmate to bond with. But that wasn't what happened. Jade couldn't remember how it happened - she just knew she never remembered a time when she didn't have Lily. Lily was always there, always present. When Jade tried to think if there was ever a time without Lily, there was just nothing. Darkness. And maybe sometimes the feeling of being cold. How could she say that to Paris? What made her think she could ever tell him? Tell anyone? She started to tell him last night about Lily. It seemed safer then, with Bruce pressed up against her. Now, in the brighter morning light with Bruce a whole floor away, she wasn't sure if she should have said anything at all. Ever. Maybe it was all a big mistake. Maybe...

She felt her power slipping out a second before it happened. The window over the sink broke with a mighty crack - a spiderweb of light and glass the spread through pane. Paris' magic settled over hers quickly, like a heavy, wet blanket. Her power bucked against it at first, but then Jade pulled it back, trying to get a hold of it.

"Sorry," she said. "I don't mean to."

"I know." His voice was the kind used on scared dogs or children. "It's just a window. It can be replaced."

There were several more seconds of her just sitting there, trying to think of what to say, of how to say it, or even if she should say anything at all.

"I don't know how to explain it. I don't know what to say."

"Is she you?"

"No," Jade answered quickly. Her eyes threatened to spill over when she added, "Maybe?" God, what if she'd been wrong this whole time? What if she really was just sick and she'd been deluding herself? Don't they always say crazy people don't think they're crazy? But then if she thought she could be crazy, did that mean she wasn't?

There was a popping sound as a small fire burst up on top of the table. Paris flinched back and Jade winced.

"Sorry," she said again. "I can put that out." She concentrated on the power burst, but found that she couldn't quite get a handle on it.

"It's fine," Paris said. "It's not actually burning the table. Or even putting out that much heat. I think your power just needs to breathe a bit. You can let it burn, if you like."

She stopped trying to put it out and just let it go, feeling the warmth on her face, watching the flickering orange and red flames. It was soothing to her.

A loud buzzing sound distracted her and she realized that it was coming from Paris. He frowned and reached into his pocket, pulling out his cell phone. The lines on his face deepened when he read what was on his screen.

"What?" Jade asked, warily, pulling back from the table.

"I asked Josef to keep me up to date on the Counter-Magic reports on the lake and to let me know if anything changed. He says there's been a rush of complaints this morning."

She curled backward in her chair. "From last night? From when I was dreaming?"

"Yes. You've noticed this trend?"

"I saw the log and I noticed that when I dream the calls come in."

Paris pocketed his phone. "There's more magic in the area than there should be." He looked at Jade and while it wasn't a harsh look, she still felt nervous meeting his eyes. "I think we need to go to the lake."

The flames on the table puffed out large in a big ball, like someone had let a bunch of oxygen into the room and then sucked it back out. It surprised Jade and she jerked back in her chair before she realized she'd even done it. She'd never been afraid of her own magic before. She quickly tamped down on her power, putting the fire out totally.

Jade put her coffee down, but kept her hands wrapped around the warm ceramic. She felt like she had to work really hard to push the next words out. "I'm afraid to."

"Why? What do you think will happen?"

I feel like something awful will happen, or something awful already happened. Jade shook her head. "I don't know."

"Do you trust me?"

"Yeah." Jade wasn't sure why that mattered. It wasn't Paris that she didn't trust. It was herself.

"Trust that I won't let anything happen."

"I don't know if you can make that kind of promise. I don't think it's up to you."

"Whom is it up to?"

Me. I think it's me. Or Lily. Or both of us. I don't know that anyone can stop it. She shrugged.

Paris reached a hand out toward hers, hovering slightly for a moment before he carefully set his hand on top of one of her own. She stared down at their fingers - his skin slightly darker than hers. Her fingers were white with how hard she was holding the mug. He put slight, even pressure on her hand and she slowly, so slowly, let go off the mug, her hand coming to rest on the table. He wrapped his fingers around her hand. She couldn't remember the last time someone, anyone, had held her hand. His hand was warm, almost hot on hers. She couldn't look up at him. It felt really intimate and she felt like if she looked at him, she'd have to pull her hand away. As long as she didn't look at him, as long as she only looked at his hand, then she could leave her own hand there, underneath his. Not trapped. Secured.

"Trust me, Jade. Trust that if something happens out there, I will help you figure it out."

Maybe that could be the difference. With Lily gone, Jade had been alone and everything rested on her. Even now, with Jade feeling like maybe Lily was coming back, she still felt this relentless pressure - a constant weight on her shoulders. She felt like she was carrying it alone.

"Okay. I'll go to the lake."

#

Jade had been waiting for so long to have her car with her and now that she did, she didn't want to drive it. Normally, having someone else drive her car would be anathema to her - her car was synonymous with her freedom, her independence. It meant she could go where she wanted, when she wanted. Today, though, she felt too tired to focus on the road or like she couldn't be trusted to get them to the Preserve. Perhaps at the last moment, she would suddenly turn the car around and drive as far away from the lake as possible.

Jade silently handed Paris the keys as soon as they stepped out of the little cottage. His eyebrows went up in surprise, but he took them without a word. Just as Jade was about to shut the front door, Bruce bounded out, looking a little anxious and nervous. He immediately made his way to the car and Jade opened the back door for him to hop in and stretch out. She hadn't thought about bringing him and felt a little unsure at his presence, but if he wanted to go, she wasn't about to leave him at home either.

Once Jade and Paris were both in their respective seats, Paris driving and Jade the passenger, Bruce's head came between the two of them, as if he wanted to ensure that they both knew he was there. This morning, in the closet, Jade hadn't had a chance to take a look at his scaly patch. Seeing it now made her think twice about taking him. The cracks were pink and raw, looking like gothic spiderwebs across his neck. She swallowed thickly as she stared at red lines, careful to pet only areas far away from them. Bruce's eyes slitted half shut at her attention for a moment and then he turned his head to Paris. Jade knew the moment Paris saw the sore spot. His eyebrows went in a bit and he looked even more serious and solemn.

"It's getting worse," he said, unnecessarily. "Hourly, it seems."

After getting some solid head pets from Paris, Bruce pulled away, into the back seat and stretched out along the width of the car, smacking his lips as he lay down.

"I looks like it hurts." Jade turned in her seat to stare at Bruce.

"I'm not sure about that. He doesn't seem to be in pain."

"He keeps showing it to us."

"Yes, but he's not overly careful of it when he lies down or moves. I don't know if it does hurt him."

Jade turned back around in her seat, buckling her belt and then crossing her arms over her chest. It was cold in the car. Or rather, it was cold outside and the car had taken on the ambient temperature. As Paris started it and pulled away from the cottage, the vents blew frosty air, making her shiver. It was a dry winter. There hadn't been any lingering snow yet, leaving everything in varying shades of brown. The grass, the trees, the hedges - all stark and spindly. While running in the Preserve with Daniel she watched fall turn to winter, but after skipping a few days, it was like her world changed overnight. It was kind of like that first day in fall when you noticed that suddenly, all the leaves were yellow. Only now, with winter settling in, everything was bare and barren. She sniffed, feeling her nose start to run from the dip in the temperature. She couldn't believe she'd been outside last night in the cold without waking up. What if Paris hadn't been there?

Would she have wandered around, getting hypothermia, until she possibly stumbled by someone? Or maybe she would have made her way to the Preserve and gotten lost in there? Maybe making it all the way out to the lake?

They stopped at Paris' place for him to grab more appropriate clothing for going out to the Preserve. While he'd been dressed casually, it wasn't casual enough for a hike in the woods. Jade declined to get out of the car, staying in and fiddling with the radio while he ran in and changed. Bruce poked his head up once or twice, sniffing the air and then hunkered down in the back again. Jade wished she could ignore what was happening to her and leave - turn around, go back to her cozy cottage and hide from the world. She tipped her head against the glass of the car window and sighed. The problem with that idea was wherever she went, there she was.

Paris was back in the car before she could pursue her mad thought of making a break for it. Although there was an entrance to the Preserve close to her cottage, where she and Daniel would go running, Paris drove them to another entrance further out. It was the same one they'd used when Paris had taken her out to work on her circle casting, the first day that Jade had passed by the lake. They had almost gone to the lake then, but as they'd gotten closer, Jade had felt sick and scared. It was hard to explain. Today as they drove through the entry gates to the area, she got the same feeling in her gut. It wasn't quite sickness, nor was it pain, but she didn't like it. It made her squirm in her seat.

"Are you all right?" Paris asked. She glanced over at him. He was focused on the road as he pulled into the area, stopping the car in a makeshift parking lot.

Jade snorted at bit. "Isn't that a loaded question? Aren't we here because I'm not all right?"

"I don't wish to force you into anything."

"We drove all the way out here. It would be stupid to go back now." She had to move before she could focus on the dishonesty in her own words. She pushed open the passenger door to let Bruce out of the back seat. He stretched his legs in turn, each one of his talons coming out and digging into the dirt. She should probably take him out here more. Maybe he needed to be walked, like a dog.

Paris moved slowly toward the trees and Jade knew he was taking his time on her account. She was reluctant to go to the lake, but she didn't know why. What did she think would happen when she got there? Would Lily come back? Wasn't that what she'd wanted ever since Lily left in the first place?

They started walking and Jade turned back when she noticed Bruce wasn't by her side. He was standing next to the car.

"Hey. You wanted to come out here. This is us. Out here," she said. He plunked his butt down decisively by the wheel well. Jade looked at Paris who shrugged. Jade turned back to Bruce. "So you're just going to sit there. By yourself."

Bruce's tongue flicked out and then he dropped his head down, resting his chin on the ground.

"Seriously?" Jade asked and then sighed. "Okay. Suit yourself." She gave one last look at

Paris who gave a sort of 'what shall you do' gesture.

Paris headed off into the woods and Jade followed. She stopped twice to check behind her in case Bruce changed his mind, but no such luck. They weren't going to break any speed records, but they weren't meandering either, making steady progress through the woods. A couple of times Paris paused and turned his head toward her, like he wanted to say something, but then he would start walking again.

Jade was thankful for the silence. Her mind was too cluttered and busy to focus on conversation. If Lily came back, would that mean Jade would go away? Lily had been gone for years. Would she expect Jade to 'leave' like she had? Or would she be okay with sharing, like they had before. Only… only before Lily had gone away, they hadn't been doing a good job of sharing - both of them jockeying for control of the body all the time, unable to stop. It wasn't that either one of them wanted the other one not to be there, but they both wanted to be in charge. It had been a long six years alone for Jade. Would she even remember how to share? Did she want to?

Last time, Jade had gone deeper into the Preserve before she felt the lake, but today, she felt it only minutes into their walk. It was a deep, solid tug on her brain and her chest. All her grey matter was a thick musical string that had been plucked once, decisively, by strong fingers. The vibration travelled through her body, settling deep behind her breastbone and left her vaguely nauseous. She wiped at her upper lip, feeling the chill of sweat cooling on her skin. Paris stopped and turned back to her.

"I'm okay," she said, cutting off his question before he could even ask it. "Keep going."

Jade focused on his shoulder blades, or what she could see of them underneath his jacket. He moved well through the woods. It was obvious he was fit, easily hiking up the sloping ground. The ground cracked beneath their feet, old, dead branches and fallen leaves crunchy from the dry winter. She swiped a hand across her forehead, feeling clammy skin.

As she walked, she thought about Lily.

"You know we're not normal."

"Normal's overrated," Jade said. "No one wants to be normal. Normal is beige. Or grey. Or avocado green. You put up with it, but you don't ask for it."

"Maybe I do, maybe I want to."

"If we were normal, we'd be alone."

Lily's silence said more than Jade had ever heard from her. For a finite moment, the inside of their brain felt vast and large.

"I know," said Lily, knowing instantly what Jade was thinking. "You don't mind sharing the body," she said quietly.

"No, I don't. I don't know why you hate it."

"I don't hate it," Lily said.

"Yes, yes you do. At least admit it out loud, because I can feel it in here."

"I remember what it was like to be alone. I remember before."

"I don't remember anything from before," said Jade sharply.

"I know." Lily sighed. "We aren't normal, Jade."

"I don't want to be normal. I just want to share."

"It's not that I want you gone. I just..." Lily trailed off.

"Want me gone", Jade finished.

Jade's breathing came faster the closer they got to the water. Bile rolled in her stomach, coming up her esophagus and sitting on back of her tongue, leaving her mouth sour and sharp. Paris stopped again and looked at her. She shook her head.

"Keep going."

He pursed his lips together, but nodded.

Jade tried never to think about the last day she saw Lily, about the way they had fought, the things they had said to each other. There were things they hadn't said aloud but, with their brains intertwined, they both knew the words that were held back. Barbed, edged things - words more like weapons that speech. Words meant to cut, meant to bruise. Words felt in anger and hurt, meant to cause anger and hurt in return. Words that cast blame, words that caused shame, words that could never be taken back and that was the only reason they stayed unspoken.

Only there never was such a thing as 'unspoken' between Jade and Lily.

Paris and Jade were closer now to the lake. The pull of it against Jade's insides was relentless, like meat hooks embedded in her chest, yanking and tearing at the flesh. God, and the chirping of those damn birds! She hadn't noticed when they started, but now it was all she could hear. Shouldn't they be gone for the season? It was winter.

"What?" Paris asked.

Jade hadn't realized she'd spoken out loud. She was surprised to see Paris stopped in front of her, closer than she expected him to be.

"Those stupid fucking birds," she said, bent over, hands resting on her knees. She felt sick. She might lose her coffee from the morning. She could feel the cream souring in her stomach and tasted it in the back of her throat and soft palate. Her head started throbbing. "That noise is scraping against me."

"There are no birds, Jade."

She tipped her head up at him, seeing him stare down at her with concern in his solemn gaze.

"The Sparrow Lady," she murmured, the name coming to her lips suddenly. She'd forgotten it until now. "She must be here."

Paris' eyebrows came together sharply. "Who is the Sparrow Lady?"

"She's the one in my dreams. She brings the birds. She holds me down. Lily warned me against her."

Paris looked back the way they had come and then toward the lake, and Jade knew he wondered if they should turn around. Jade looked forward, past him and she thought maybe she could see the lake through the trees.

"I've been here," she said, pushing herself upright and stepping past him. The chirping pounded against her eardrums and she squinted her eyes against the assault.

"In your dreams?" Paris asked, following her.

"Yes. No. Before that. I've been here."

Jade pushed through the dry winter branches and desiccated foliage. Her stomach somersaulted and she swallowed hard, feeling the burn of acid down her throat. She knew this place. Not very well, but enough that she knew what to expect as she walked through and then crossed the tree line into the lake area.

"How can it be exactly like my dreams?" she asked, saying the words out loud, but not really expecting Paris to have an answer.

"Maybe some kind of divination or clairvoyance."

Jade shook her head. "I don't have those things."

"It doesn't mean you won't or can't. Powers can evolve, like skills."

A flock of sparrows swooped down from the sky, flitting in front of her and then diving into the forest.

"Tell me you saw those," she said lowly, not daring to look at Paris.

She saw him nod out of the corner of her eye. "Yes. I saw them."

Jade's feet moved of their own will, one in front of the other, moving toward the lake. Her head throbbed in time with her footsteps, the same beat inside her ribcage, thick and heavy. A sharp stab of pain had her dropping her head into her hand, cradling her skull.

"Are you all right?"

Jade bent over and vomited up the morning's coffee. The sight of her own sickness made her want to vomit again and she couldn't stop, this time spitting up bile and saliva. She stumbled backward, away from the mess, feeling Paris' hands on her, keeping her from falling over.

Jade felt wetness on her hand and pulled back. Blood. She touched her nose and could feel the blood starting to drip out. Then she felt wetness trailing down the side of her neck, from her ear. Her hands shook.

"Jade," Paris said. He pulled her sharply back, away from the lake. "This was a mistake. I'm sorry, I'm so sorry."

He was pulling her back into the forest. She spun away from him and vomited again, gasping for air. She couldn't get enough, God it was like drowning, drowning, drowning. She was drowning, the sky going dark above her. Her ears roared and all she could hear were sparrows, sparrows, sparrows.

Jade had a sudden sense of vertigo and was confused when all she could see was sky going dark, so dark. She became aware she wasn't standing anymore, but she wasn't on the ground and she was still moving. It confused her until she realized she was being carried and she felt awful for Paris. She wasn't small and even though he was strong, there was no way he was going to be able to carry her back.

But then they were further from the lake and she blinked a few times, the sky above her blue again, the blackness bleeding away. The snapping sound of twigs and leaves under Paris' feet rushed into her ears and she no longer heard the awful sound of chirping. She could move her hand and she reached up clutching at Paris' lapel, leaving a bloody handprint on his jacket.

"Stop. Stop," Jade managed. "Put me down."

Paris immediately set her down and thank God her feet held under her although she needed his help to stay upright.

"Are you going to be sick again?" he asked, helping her tip forward in case she was about to vomit.

Jade shook her head, taking a deep breath and letting it out slowly and then doing it again. She swiped at her nose, her hand getting covered with blood again in the process. She looked down at her jacket and saw trails of wet, shiny, red blood down the front. She wiped her hand on her pants. She was a wreck, there was no sense in trying to keep her pants clean at this point.

"I think I'm better."

"You hardly look better," Paris said sharply.

Covered in blood, maybe vomit, hunched over and breathing hard? No, she probably didn't.

Paris was trying to hand her something, his scarf. Presumably to wipe herself off. She took one look and shook her head.

"Are you kidding me? I think that's cashmere."

"For the love of-" He exhaled sharply, only through his nose. "I don't care. You're covered in… fluids."

Jade unzipped her coat and used the bottom of her sweater to wipe off her face. Her nose was still bleeding, so it was kind of a lost cause, as she just ended up bloody again. She leaned forward and the blood dripped on the ground instead of on her.

The next thing she knew, she had a face full of navy blue cashmere, as Paris held his scarf to her nose.

"You'll never get this clean," she said, although with the scarf in front her face, it came out pretty garbled.

"Yes, I'm sure I'll lie awake nights bemoaning the loss of this scarf." She could hear the eye roll in his tone. She took the grip of the scarf from him and made to stand up. His hand on her back made her do so carefully, slowly. Her head pounded and the movement of her body made her feel tippy and twirly.

"I can carry you back to the car."

Jade hoped the look her eyes gave him over top of the scarf conveyed her opinion on that. "Are you crazy? I'm almost as tall as you and we had to hike in."

Paris pulled a phone out of his pocket. "I can call for assistance and we'll wait here."

"I can walk."

"You're bleeding from the nose and the ears and you vomited. You look like you should be hospitalized."

Jade fidgeted, feeling the undercurrent of the lake still pulling at her body. "Can we just go? I don't like it here."

Paris' lips thinned slightly and he studied her carefully.

"I can walk, I swear. I'll take breaks. I just... I just really want to go."

He harrumphed, like a disgruntled muppet. "All right. Please stay in front of me where I can see you."

#

Bruce was extraordinarily pleased to see Jade come the trees. He waddled up to her and seemed not at all surprised by the dreadful state she was in. Her nose had stopped bleeding part of the way back, but she had needed to rest twice, catching her breath along the pathway. Paris had been offered to carry her again, but she'd looked at him as though he were a lunatic. It did nothing for his ego. Yes, it was a long hike in and out, but if it had needed to be done, he could have and would have done it.

"Hey Bruce," Jade said, her voice sounding low and nasally, due to her sinuses suffering the leftover ravages of her nosebleed. Bruce's snout went up one of Jade's leg and then down the other. He sneezed and then spat on the ground next to her.

"Thanks," she said dryly.

"I'd like to get you to medlab and have Dr. Gellar look you over."

Jade looked like she was about to protest and then she glanced down at herself. She sighed. "Yeah."

In the car, she rested her head back against the seat and closed her eyes. Bruce poked his head between the seats, his long tail coming up between as well and resting against Jade's leg.

"How do you feel?"

Jade took a deep breath in and sighed it out, eyes still closed. "I'm tired. Really tired. My head hurts."

If Paris drove a little over the speed limit on the way to the Coven, it wasn't like anyone was going to ticket him. He was the Coven Leader.

When they pulled up to the Covenstead, Paris looked Jade over again. Her powder blue jacket was covered in blood down the front - blood that had dried a horrible brown-red. Jade took one look at his face as he ran his eyes over her appearance and then flipped down the visor to check herself, finding her face streaked with blood. She turned her head and he saw the moment she found the blood trails leaking from both ears.

"Jesus, I can't go in there looking like this." She flipped the visor back in disgust.

Paris shrugged off his coat, handing it to her. "Take yours off and put this on. Your face isn't... well. I was going to say it wasn't that bad, but it is. May I..." he hesitated for a moment.

"What?"

"May I perform a glamor on you? It will cover up the way your face looks."

"Sold," she said without hesitation. "What do I need to do?"

"Nothing, just... stay still."

He murmured a few spell words and concentrated, picturing what she normally looked like - her skin fair and maybe a bit uneven around her eyes. She wore makeup, but not a lot - not enough to make her look like she was wearing a mask. She blinked a few times, feeling his magic wash over her. He smoothed a hand over the space in front of her face, almost touching her, but not quite, pushing the glamor into place. She stayed dutifully still, only breathing lightly.

"There you go."

Jade looked herself over in the mirror again, taking in her normal appearance. "Wow. Thanks."

Paris had called ahead to Dr. Gellar on the ride in. All that remained was to get Jade into the Covenstead and directly to medlab. As soon as they entered the Coven, Henri looked up from his desk, a look of concern crossed his face. Paris was holding onto one of Jade's elbows, keeping her in a straight line as she walked. She was a little woozy on her feet and kept listing to the left.

"Are you okay?" Henri asked.

"Yeah, magical mishap this morning," Jade answered. "Minor snafu."

Paris was grateful Jade replied. He didn't think that it would look nearly as convincing if he declared Jade was fine.

"Are you hurt?"

Jade started to shake her head and Paris saw the exact moment she realized it was a bad idea. She squinted her eyes. "I've a headache. We're going to check in with Gellar, but she'll probably just give me some aspirin."

"Okay," Henri replied, still seeming suspicious. "Call me if you need anything."

"I will."

Paris hustled her up the stairs, finding that by the last two, he had to shift his grip - instead of just holding her elbow, he had to sling one of her arms over his shoulder. Thank God it was the middle of the morning and most people were at their desks or offices. The hallways were nearly empty. Knowing how fast Coven gossip was, when he did spot some witches coming toward them, he cast a quick glamor spell over both himself and Jade, blocking them from view. Jade stared at the witches as they walked by, completely oblivious.

"That is so cool. You have to teach me that one."

Her voice had a soft rambling tone to it and her steps were getting heavier and heavier. Paris was taking more of her weight. Her other arm sort of swung lazily by her side and she started to shuffle her feet instead of taking steps.

"I'll be sure to do that. Dr. Gellar," Paris said, greeting the doctor as she met them at the doors of med lab.

Dr. Gellar gestured to one of the side rooms where she had a bed waiting. Paris shuffled-carried Jade there, picking her up a bit with an arm wrapped around her side.

Jade clutched at his neck suddenly. "Don't let her cut my clothes. I hate when hospitals do that. I really like this sweater. I swear I can get the blood out."

"Of course." He got Jade seated on the bed and she sort of tipped backward, sighing happily as she did.

"Bed. Thank God."

Dr. Gellar picked Jade's feet up and put them on the bed, working on getting her shoes off. A nurse came into the room behind Paris and he flinched as he was moved out of the way.

"Paris, why don't you wait outside while we get her situated."

He didn't want to go, he wanted to stay to make sure she was all right, but it wasn't as though they needed assistance and they were starting to undress Jade and she would hate it if she knew he stayed.

"I'll be right outside."

Gellar nodded not even looking over as Paris left and shut the door behind him. He could go to the waiting area and get a magazine. Or he could take a seat and check his smartphone and start responding to emails that were likely stacking up in his inbox. Or he could call down to Josef in Counter-Magic and demand he send a team out to the lake immediately and start investigating.

He stayed where he was, standing outside the door.

A few minutes later, a ticky-tacking sound caused him to turn his head and he spotted Bruce lumbering into medlab.

"Oh. I'm sorry. We forgot you in the car." He wondered how the lizard had gotten out and if he'd done any damage to Jade's car in the process.

Bruce huffed at him and made his way over to the waiting area, hopping up on the sofa and stretching out across the entire length. He put his chin down and stared at Paris reproachfully, as if daring him to try and take a seat.

"I said I was sorry," Paris repeated quietly.

Paris thought Dr. Gellar was only going to get Jade outfitted in a gown and then come back out, but he was left standing there for several minutes. He paced a few short steps away, only to come back. He pulled his phone out of his pocket and then put it away again. He took a few steps toward Bruce and then turned back to the door to wait.

After ten long minutes, Dr. Gellar and her nurse came back out, the nurse ducking off to the side while Gellar shut the door behind her and turned to Paris.

"Is she all right?"

"She's no longer bleeding from the ears and nose, if that's what you mean. I was just taking some vitals and getting the details of what happened."

"I could tell you those. I was there."

Gellar gave him a sort of look. "It's better for me to get them from the patient first. I'm, of course, interested in your perspective on things, especially the magical elements, but I really needed to hear from Jade. She's the one living inside her body."

I'm just afraid she's not the only one, Paris thought, wondering how much Jade had shared with Dr. Gellar, and how much he should or could share.

"I'd like to run another scan on her brain, like the one Jade had when she first came to the Coven. First I want to have her do some simple movements and then I'd like to add in the magical elements and see how her brain responds."

"Is that a good idea so soon after..." he didn't know how to explain what happened at the lake. "Well, so soon?"

"She says she feels up to it," Gellar answered. "And I'd like to get a reading as close as possible after the incident."

There wasn't much he could say to that. Dr. Gellar was the doctor and Jade was in charge of herself. If she agreed, Paris could only offer support. While the nurse brought over the EEG machine and took it into Jade's room, Dr. Gellar had Paris run through his side of what happened at the lake. Paris found his attention distracted as he kept looking over at the door wondering how it was going inside the room.

"Okay, I think that tells me everything I need to know for now. I'm going to go start Jade's scan. I'll need you for the magical part, but let me just check if that's okay with her and see if you can be there for the first part."

He was worried Jade wouldn't agree, though he didn't know if that was a valid fear or just the tenseness of the situation. Dr. Gellar poked her head back out a moment later and ushered Paris in while the nurse left. Paris glanced over his shoulder at Bruce who was napping on the sofa. He seemed content where he was, so Paris decided to let sleeping lizards lie.

Jade was no longer on the gurney bed, but was seated in one of room's visiting chairs, electrodes already hooked up to her head. She was wearing Paris' coat overtop of her scrubs and she looked kind of sheepishly at him.

"I hope you don't mind. It's chilly in here."

"I don't mind."

"I tried to save your scarf, but I think it got taken out with the rest of my clothes and put in with the bio-hazard stuff."

"We'll have it put through with our medical laundry and then it will be returned," Dr. Gellar promised.

Jade winced at her and then looked back at Paris. "I don't think your cashmere will survive that."

"I told you, I don't care about the scarf."

Jade let out a jaw-cracking yawn, her face screwing itself up almost comically. "Sorry. I'm so tired." She blinked a few times, trying to open her eyes wide.

"I'm sure this won't take long and then you can have a nap."

Jade nodded.

Dr. Gellar went behind the machine and fiddled with some dials. Paris had no idea how it all worked, but was quite confident in her abilities. After a few more tweaks, Gellar looked up at Jade, smiled and then spoke.

"Okay, Jade, I'm going to ask you to go through a few motions. Please just do them as I ask, then return to your starting position."

"Okay."

Dr. Gellar had Jade raise one arm, then the other. Then one leg, then the other. She had Jade answer some memory questions about when she first came to the Coven, then had Jade do some simple tasks with her hands - non-magical things. Jade had to write on a note pad, do a little arithmetic, transfer an object back and forth - all things to test her hand-eye coordination and fine motor skills.

"Now, before we move onto the magical aspects, I want to ask you a few questions about some of the things you were telling me earlier."

Paris could hear the machine graphs scratching madly as Jade tensed up, her eyes darting over to him and then back to the Koosh ball in her hands.

"Did you want Paris to leave?" Dr. Gellar asked.

"No, that's okay," Jade answered. She didn't look up, just kept her gaze focused on the bright pink Koosh.

"We talked about your dreams, the ones of the lake, and others. Can you tell me about one of your dreams now?"

Jade took a deep breath, as though collecting herself. "I'm at the lake and I can see someone's on the dock already. I'm far away but I can tell it's Lily."

"And who's Lily?"

Paris felt his whole body tense, ready for the answer, even though he'd already asked the question.

Jade glanced again at him quickly and then looked away. "I don't know how to explain it. It's like she's me, but she's not."

"But she looks like you."

"I look like her," Jade corrected. Paris frowned. That wasn't necessarily a distinction but for some reason, Jade felt the need to make it.

"What does Lily do?"

Jade shrugged and the machine's needles went scratchy again as her brain processed the movement and the electrodes picked up the data. "She's just standing there, looking over the water. It makes me nervous and I want to go closer, but I'm afraid."

"Of?"

Jade squeezed the Koosh ball. "Of the water. And maybe of Lily and…" she breathed deep. "I don't know, I feel like there's someone else there."

"Who?" asked Dr. Gellar.

"I don't know. It just always feels like there's someone else there."

The Sparrow Lady, thought Paris, remembering Jade's words. She seemed reluctant to say it now.

"What happens?"

Jade's eyes were sort of unfocused, staring off into space. "Sometimes I go to the dock. Sometimes Lily falls in and I'm surprised she doesn't come back up because she can swim. She knows how. Sometimes I fall in, but I can't swim so I…" Jade paused and when she spoke again, her voice was soft. "I drown."

Jade blinked and then it was like her body *shifted*. Paris felt something… magical. He couldn't explain it. There was a different energy about her now. She looked down at her hands, dropping the Koosh ball in her lap and turning her palms over, like she wasn't sure her hands were hers. Her head turned and she looked around, as though checking herself.

When she looked up at him, her eyes were no longer grey, but green.

"Doctor," Paris said lowly. He couldn't look away from those green eyes, but he saw Dr. Gellar out of the corner of his eye, saw her look up and look at Jade.

"Yes?"

"Her eyes are green."

Jade tilted her head a little at his statement, like she was confused. She dragged her eyes from him to Dr. Gellar, looking her up and down like it was the first time she'd seen her.

"They're normally grey," Paris added. He took a step closer to the chair and Jade turned to look at him again, looking up at him as though studying him.

"Are you Lily?" he asked her.

She nodded and Paris felt like the air had been forcibly sucked out of his lungs. He pushed out a bit of his power at her, trying to find her magic.

Something pushed back, but it wasn't Jade's magic. Jade's magic was like an excitable puppy, flailing and romping, reaching out beyond her and then snapping back to its mistress. This was more like an owl - assessing, watchful, but still. Paris stepped closer and her eyes tracked his movements. She didn't seem scared or worried. Just cautious. Careful.

Paris pushed more magic at her, and again she pushed back, her power different from Jade's. He sniffed the air, smelling grapefruit and cinnamon. Not the floral and clove scent of Jade's power.

He took one more step closer and she leaned backward. She blinked several times and then cracked her neck, her eyes changing from green back to grey. She frowned at him, seeming wary at finding him so close.

"What are you doing?"

"Jade?" he asked.

"Yes." Jade looked from Paris to Dr. Gellar and back again. She paused, looking away for a moment, and Paris had this sense that she was searching her brain for something. "She was here. She was just here." Jade looked up at him. "Wasn't she? You saw her."

"Yes."

"Oh my God, she really is back."

CHAPTER TWELVE

Jade pulled the electrodes off her head, not caring that they were taking some hair with them as she did. She was tired. Tired and feeling soft and vulnerable, like the underbelly of a small forest creature, fallen from its perch and baring its underside to the sky.

"Are you all right, Jade? I'd like to run some more tests, but they can wait if you're not feeling up to it."

"I just want to go home."

Gellar pursed her lips. "I'd like it if you stayed, overnight if possible."

"I really want to go home." Jade looked up at Paris, expecting him to protest, but he stayed silent, watching her.

Gellar tapped a finger against her leg. "Will you at least stay for an IV and a nap?" Gellar bargained. "You had quite an incident out there at the lake and again in here. I don't know what's going on and while part of it seems magical, there's definitely a physical component."

Jade did still feel a little shaky. She nodded slowly. "Okay."

Gellar excused herself to get the necessary supplies and Jade chanced a sideways look at Paris.

He was going to want to talk about Lily. Of course he was. If Jade were in his shoes, she'd want to talk about it too. She'd be riddled with curiosity. All Jade could hope was that Paris gave her some time until he started bombarding her with questions. He probably wanted to know how Jade felt. That was a good question. One that Jade wanted the answer to as well.

Lily was back. Jade had felt her. Jade had seen through her eyes, like it had been before. They were never truly separate although they did switch control - each of them having turns at being 'outside.' But unlike the way people described dissociative identities, Jade and Lily were always aware of one another. There were no missing memories, no things they didn't know of happening, no surprises between them. When Lily was in control, Jade could watch, from behind, like being in the backseat of a car. Or she could sleep, going far away in their head and be totally unaware for the moment. But when Jade came 'back,' it was always easy enough to find out what had happened while she was gone. It was like watching a movie and leaving the room - when you came back, you could rewind and replay the parts you missed. Jade and Lily jokingly called it 'refreshing their cache,' -

going through each other's memories so that there was no uneven bits or blips.

It meant there were no secrets between them. Never. Every horrid thought, every embarrassing problem, every shameful thing they ever did or said, every joy or happiness they felt, everything was shared. Everything.

Having Lily back was exactly what Jade had wanted ever since she left. She thought she'd be happy, relieved, complete. Instead she was confused and conflicted. She pushed herself out of the chair, intending to head for the bed. Paris came beside her immediately and she didn't wave him off when he offered some help. His hand on her elbow was strong and warm. She should probably give him back his coat. If he asked for it, she would.

He didn't ask and she didn't say anything. She got into bed with it still on. The silence was starting to grate. She fidgeted with the blankets.

"Look, I know you probably have a million questions -" she began.

"I do," he said easily. "But they can wait until you've gotten some rest."

She relaxed further back into the bed. "Thanks. Don't let me sleep more than a couple hours. I don't want to spend the night here."

A sharp sound at the door had Paris frowning.

"Sounds like Bruce," Jade mumbled, her eyes already starting to close.

Sure enough, as soon as Paris cracked the door, Bruce nosed his way in, slipping underneath the medical bed. "He must know I'm having a nap here. Didn't want to miss out."

"Yes, he does look like he's settling in for the long haul," she heard Paris say. Her eyes were already closed and she could feel herself falling away. In that final moment before she fell asleep, she had one more thing to say and she knew it sounded crazy, but she had to say it.

"If Lily comes back, be nice. She's been gone a long time."

Jade must have dozed off quickly, because the next thing she knew, she felt a hand on her shoulder and heard Paris' voice calling her name.

"Jade, it's late afternoon."

She managed some kind of grumbling sound and blinked herself awake. She looked down at her arm, noting the bandage where an IV must have already come and gone. No dreams either - of the Preserve or the closet. She took a deep breath, waking up.

"How do you feel?" Paris asked.

"Groggy."

Paris went and got Dr. Gellar, who again iterated that she wished Jade would stay the night. Jade looked at Paris, almost challenging him, wondering if he would try to make her stay. Paris gave Jade a quick look and said that if both of them were amenable, he could take Jade home and stay with her in case anything arose.

Jade could tell Gellar wasn't happy with the answer, but she nodded anyway. Jade grabbed her shoes from under the chair. They were the only things that hadn't been taken away for cleaning, and probably the only things that didn't get ruined by blood. Bruce flicked his tongue at her quickly, almost like he just wanted to touch her to make sure she was still there.

"When we were getting here, it was like people in the hallway didn't see us," Jade said as she stuffed her feet into her shoes.

"Yes, I cast a quick glamor. I was nearly carrying you at that point and I wanted to avoid gossip and questions."

"Could you do it again on the way out?" Jade asked slowly, eyes darting up to him and then back down. "I just... don't feel like talking to anyone."

"Of course."

"It'll work for Bruce too?"

"Yes, although he'll have to stay close."

"You hear that, buddy?" Jade asked. Bruce slithered out from underneath the bed and stood as close as possible to Jade.

Paris' lips quirked in a smile. "That'll do, Bruce."

It was weird walking through the Coven without anyone seeing them. Jade dug her hands deep into the pockets of Paris' jacket, fiddling with the items he had in there. A few coins, an old receipt, a few wrapped pieces of fresh gum. He also had a small satchel and when she pulled it out and sniffed it, it smelled like wool, laundry and something else. Something faint.

"What's this?"

Paris' lips quirked. "An old gris-gris. My mother went through a phase where she was into Vodoun. Voodoo," he added at Jade's confused look. "Most witches don't practice it. It's not taboo, not like demon magic, but it is specialized."

"Is it like learning another language?" Jade asked, fingering the soft, worn cloth.

"Just so. She made that for me when I was younger. I've always kept it and it turns up in my things. Part of the magic of it, I suppose, although it's probably mostly worn out."

Jade squeezed it in her hand, feeling something grind together inside the small bag. "I dunno. It feels heavy." She sniffed it again. "Smells like…" she trailed off thinking. "Black licorice."

He turned to her sharply. "I never noticed that."

She shrugged, popping it back in the pocket of the coat. "You probably don't take your stuff out and sniff it. I'm like a squirrel in the forest, rooting around in your things." She hunched her shoulders. "Speaking of, do you want your coat back?"

"No, you can keep it for now."

No one so much as glanced their way as they walked through the Coven and Jade wondered how the spell worked. Did people notice the front door of the Coven swinging open as they left and think it odd, or was part of the glamor? Maybe the door appeared to stay shut. She thought about asking, but she didn't have it in her at the moment. She felt some kind of magical burst from Paris as they got in the car and figured he must have done something, maybe released the spell, as they drove off so that he didn't have to charm the entire car, or have people wonder why a car was driving itself.

Or maybe shit like that happened at the Coven. Jade had been taking public transit for so long, she had no idea what happened on the road.

Bruce stretched out in the back seat and Jade envied his relaxed pose, until she saw his scaly patch, more red and sore than before. She slouched down in the passenger seat and crossed her arms over her chest, warding off the chill. She closed her eyes on the drive home, focusing in on the rock and sway of the car as Paris drove. They were back at her cottage soon enough and as they walked up to her cottage, she missed the security of her demon locks. She had liked the way they whirred and rolled as she came home, letting her know that her place was secure. Sure the front door was still bolted, but that didn't mean anything to her anymore. It wasn't like the knowledge of 'safe' she got from her demon locks.

"I'm going to go take a shower. Do you mind putting on some coffee?" she asked, already heading up the stairs. Paris nodded and made his way to the kitchen. Bruce loped up the stairs behind her, his tail thumping a few times. Once in her room, Jade paused just to take a breath. Home. This was home now and things would be fine.

She took Paris' coat off and tossed it on her bed and then took off the medlab scrubs and threw them in the direction of her laundry pile. At least that was something different - she wasn't going to have to do laundry any time soon. She had all her stuff from the apartment now. No need to do laundry every three days.

All *their* stuff, she corrected herself. Her stuff and Lily's stuff. Jade wasn't by herself anymore.

Bruce dived under the bed immediately and started scratching at the wooden planks of the floor.

"Hey, stop that!" Jade hissed, getting on her hands and knees and peering under the bed. "What are you doing?"

Bruce scratched at the floor again, like he was trying to dig a hole out or something.

"Get out here."

He gave her a look and spat on the ground.

"Ugh, Bruce, c'mon, buddy. Don't be like this. I just got out of medlab and I'm gross and I just really want to take a shower."

Bruce blinked twice at her, and then the floor again, pawing at it.

"Please, Bruce."

He huffed and wiggled out from under the bed, popping on top of it and starting to nose at Paris' coat.

"Yes, have at it. Just don't eat it. I'm sure it's a very expensive wool coat and it will cost me a lot to replace. Other than that, go forth and do lizard things." Bruce shimmied down into Paris' coat like he was planning on a nap.

The shower was fantastic. She'd been grimy from the hike and being sick plus being medlab always felt like it left a layer on her. When she came back out, Bruce was still lying on top of Paris' coat on Jade's bed, his snout buried in the pocket. She shooed him away before getting dressed. Once presentable, hair wet and in a ponytail dripping down her back, she picked up the coat, intending to take it downstairs.

"We're not going to tell him you used this like a nap blanket," she said, folding it over her arm. Bruce flicked his tongue out at her. Jade hesitated.

She didn't suppose she could stay upstairs for the rest of the day. Paris was bound to come up and check on her. She was going to have to answer questions. Eventually. May as well be now. He'd seen Lily, had seen Jade change into her and back. It had always been her biggest secret and now, it was out there. Paris and Gellar had watched it happen.

It was sort of like falling. Liberating and terrifying. There was no going back now.

Jade inhaled the scent of brewing coffee and something else as she went downstairs. She hung his coat up by the door and then headed to the kitchen.

"Either you're making toast or we need to go back to medlab because I'm about to have a seizure," she joked.

Paris set a mug of coffee down on the table followed by a plate of toast.

Jade sat down in front of them and sighed happily. "What is it about toast when you don't feel good. It's... a happy-making food. Instant comfort."

"I'm glad you think so. I wasn't sure if you'd be up for eating."

A sip of her coffee informed her that Paris had made it to her liking and she smiled. "Thanks."

He had a mug for himself and a slice of toast as well.

"So, interrogation time?" she asked, taking a big bite of buttery toast.

"I hope not. I don't want to grill you. I'd hoped you'd feel comfortable talking to me."

Well, shit. Now she felt like a jerk. "No, I do, I mean, as much as I ever do. But that's more me than you. I guess I just don't know how or where to begin. It's like asking me how I feel about being a woman. I've always been a woman. I don't know how to explain it."

Paris chewed his toast thoughtfully for a moment. "Do you think you have a mental disorder?"

"Wow, okay, let's start with the big questions. No need to ease in."

"It is the elephant in the room."

"Yeah," she said, taking a sip of her coffee. "Yeah. I never thought of me, of us, as being a dissociative identity. I mean, I've read a lot about it, obviously, because what else should I research? But I don't feel like either one of us is an alter. And we have knowledge of each other. I know everything that happens when Lily's in control and she knows everything that happens when I'm in control. We're not unaware of each other."

"You did say you had an abusive childhood. Or rather, you've alluded to it."

Jade nodded. "I did. We did. But from what I've read the abuse has to be really severe for something like a dissociative identity to form and that just wasn't the case. Our dad drank. He knocked us around and it was really shitty. But not extraordinary? If that makes sense?"

"Do all your memories include Lily? There was never a time you were without her?"

"No, never." She shook her head. "She's always been there." Jade took another bite of toast while Paris thought of his next question.

"How do you switch? Where do you go?"

Jade shrugged. "I go away, or more to the back. I'm there but not. I can go to sleep if I don't want to do something. Like swimming. I don't like water and I can't swim. But Lily can and if she ever wanted to go, I would go to sleep. Or sometimes it was just… tiring being together all the time. So one of us would sleep."

"Her magic feels very different from yours."

"Lily has magic?" Jade sat up a bit.

"That surprises you?" asked Paris, his eyebrows going up.

Jade nodded. "Yeah. I don't know why, but I just… I didn't think she had magic. Huh. What's it like?"

Paris thought for a moment. "It's slower than yours. More sedate. Smells like grapefruit and cinnamon. You're more like flowers and cloves." Paris brushed the crumbs off the table and into his palm, depositing them back on his empty plate. "How did it work when you were younger?"

"You mean how often did we switch?" Jade asked and Paris nodded. "I don't know. It's not like there was a schedule. We both paid attention in school. That was helpful on tests. I've a better memory than her, so I did most of the reading. But she's better with people. She likes talking to them, getting to know them. She had more friends or, I guess, all the friends."

"Has no one else ever known about both of you?"

Jade shook her head. "No."

"But she hasn't been here while you've been at the Coven," Paris clarified.

"No. It's just been me for a long time. For about six years."

"Why? Where did she go?"

Jade thought about when Lily went away. Died. That's what Jade had thought it was. She thought Lily was dead, never to return. Only now she was back. Did she die? Could she die if Jade was still alive? Thinking of that day made Jade feel sick. She could still see it perfectly in her head - the white tiles of the bathroom, the water in the tub, and then blood, so much blood everywhere and Jade waking up alone. She'd been by herself and didn't know what to do, she'd always had Lily, always. Being alone was terrifying and awful.

"We don't have to talk about it right now."

Paris' voice cut through her thoughts and she looked down to see one of his hands resting on hers again, but his attention was focused on the flames burning in her sink. She didn't realize she'd lit them, her magic fuelling them a dark blue-green color. She took a deep breath and pulled them back, watching them die down slowly and then sputter out.

"If you don't want to answer something or can't talk about something, I won't make you," Paris said.

"I know," she answered. She felt raw - all her emotions too close to the surface. She knew she didn't have to answer his questions, but it was liberating to sit here and tell him things. "You've a nice face for talking to."

"How so?" he asked, his lips curling slightly in a smile. He kept his hand resting on hers. It was warm against her skin.

Jade shrugged, not meeting his eyes. "I don't know. You just don't look all judgy when I say stuff. You look like you're interested, but you're not hustling me along."

"You've carried these secrets for a long time. Secrets like that aren't easy to let go of."

She ate more of her toast and the kitchen was quiet. Not awkwardly quiet, but just silent save for the sound of her chewing.

"Where is Lily now?"

"Sleeping, I think," Jade said and then she let her mind drift, poking at the edges for where she used to be able to feel Lily. It wasn't quite like before, when she always knew Lily was there, but if Jade concentrated, she could feel Lily just out of her reach - on the perimeter, like a circumference around Jade's brain. "I think... I think coming back has been really tiring for her. I think she was really far away. Or really deep down. Like being underwater," she added, as an afterthought, thinking of the lake and its heavy, pressure-bearing weight. "I think she's been trying to reach me through my dreams. I think some of the dreams I've been having have been about her."

"Just some?"

Jade nodded. "Sometimes, in my dreams, I'm at home, where we grew up and Lily's there. She's there in the other dreams too, at the lake, but it's different there. There's someone else there with us, at the lake."

"The Sparrow Lady?" Paris questioned and Jade looked up at him sharply. "You mentioned her at the lake. You said Lily warned you about her."

"Lily said that it's easier to get to me in my dreams. For both her and the Sparrow Lady."

"Do you know who she is? Is she like Lily?"

"No," Jade said quickly, hoping her expression clearly stated what she thought of that idea. "Not at all. She's… there, but I don't see her face. I don't know her."

"What does she do?"

"She's just there. Although, once, I was underwater and she was pulling me down, toward the bottom only it never ended, I just kept going deeper and deeper." Jade shivered and took a sip of her coffee. It was cooling off and she wanted to microwave some warmth back into it, but she didn't want to get up.

"Is there anything you recognize about her? Is she a Coven member?"

"No, nothing. I don't recognize her shape or magic. I don't feel her when I'm awake. I don't know if that means anything."

"When you were trying to cast your dream spell and it wasn't working, I thought… I thought I felt someone working against your magic. I didn't tell you because I wasn't certain, or rather, I wasn't certain what I should do about it."

"Honestly, I should probably be really pissed at you for not telling me, but I'm so goddamn tired, I can't even be angry right now," Jade said, feeling the deep truth of her words. He shouldn't have kept it from her, but she didn't know if she would have been able to do anything with the information or if it would have been just one more thing overloading her mind. "Do you know who?"

"No. It wasn't anyone's magic that I recognized. I thought I smelled vanilla, but that's a rather common element to most people's magic, so it doesn't narrow it down."

"So if Sparrow Lady is the one hijacking my dreams, it sounds like she wants to keep hijacking them and didn't want me doing any magic to break that."

"Well, that can be resolved. If you're amenable, I'll cast some wards over you tonight, and I can stay here again if that's all right with you."

That sounded like a pretty great idea to Jade. Between Lily showing up and someone messing with her magic and her dreams, Jade didn't really want to be in the house by herself. Of course she had Bruce, but whatever this unknown woman was doing, he hadn't stopped her before, so Jade doubted Bruce would be much assistance.

"Yeah, I would appreciate that." She struggled getting the words out, feeling a little embarrassed at needing the help.

As if he read her thoughts, Paris leaned forward, his eyes bright blue and earnest. "It's not easy asking for help when you need it. Smart people are able to push past how they feel about it and ask anyway." He gave her hand a squeeze and she thought she might be blushing. Her face was hot and she felt nervous. "I should probably go to my place and pick up a few things. Are you okay to stay here by yourself for a short while? I could call Callie or Henri to come over. Or if you prefer, I'm sure Callie could pick up the things I need and I can stay."

"No, I'm okay now. It's light outside and I'm not planning on sleeping, so..." she shrugged.

"All right, I'll be back in an hour or so. I'm also going to email the Coven and tell them you're on a bit of a leave. And that I might be as well."

"Jesus, don't word it that way or people will think I've seduced you into leaving the Coven. That's all I need - they'll make me a scarlet letter to wear across my chest."

"I'm sure I can find a tolerable way to phrase it," Paris said, pulling his hand away and standing up. Jade's skin felt cold and clammy where his hand had been. "But if not, red is a charming color on you."

#

With Paris gone, Jade decided to busy herself by putting away more of her things. She'd set up the coffee pot when she'd arrived and unpacked her clothes, but everything else needed putting away. She was just finishing off her coffee, when the back of her neck itched. She groaned and looked directly at the pantry.

She could feel Seth coming.

Just as he appeared in the pantry, his eyes glittering and his teeth pristinely white and smiling, she murmured a quick wind spell. The door to the pantry shut in his face.

"I'm sure that was a mistake, Possum. I won't hold it against you."

"Go away," she yelled, getting up and putting her mug and plate in the dishwasher. She heard the loud thump of Bruce jumping off something upstairs and then the telltale sound of him scampering down the stairs. He showed up in the kitchen just as the handle of the pantry door was turning. Seth pushed it open and Bruce ran up to the doorway, spitting at him, Elizabethan lizard collar raised.

"Lovely to see you as well, Possum. And of course your horrid little lizard thing. And you're awake this time!"

Jade frowned. "What are you talking about?"

"Oh! Didn't your English boyfriend tell you? I felt some magic in your vicinity the other night and I popped by to see what all the fuss was about, but you were in the arms of Morpheus. Or perhaps Phobetor, he of nightmares. Tell me, which one was it?"

Seth had visited her? While she'd been asleep? Jade had thought she'd gotten used to being afraid of him, but knowing he'd seen her while she'd been asleep hit her freak-out-o-meter hard, burying the needle. But, if what he was saying could be trusted, Paris had been there.

So, Jade hadn't been totally vulnerable.

"What do you want?"

Seth shrugged one shoulder. "I told you. Wibbly-wobbly demon magic about. I like to keep tabs on it. And on you." He leaned forward, still trapped within the confines of her pantry, but as close as he could get to the barrier. He studied her, his dark eyes flashing gold for a moment. "Do you know, in some mythologies a person's doppelgänger is a harbinger of bad luck? Some even say it could mean death."

Jade's throat felt tight and she wished she had waited to eat her toast. What was Seth implying? Would Lily's return mean death for Jade? Would Jade have to go 'away' like Lily had gone away?

"So serious! Look at your face! I don't mean to scare you so, Possum. Just making conversation. I'm very proud of you, you know. You're holding up quite well given that you're being pushed and pulled at like taffy."

Bruce spat three times at the ground again and then looked at Seth with a challenging expression on his face.

Jade crossed her arms over her chest. "Who's doing all the pushing and pulling, Seth? You know, don't you?"

Seth tapped a finger against his temple. "I do, I do. But it's always tricky for demons you know. We've a lot of rules to abide by. Why do you think your legal system and lawmaking is so horrid? All based on demon rules and regulations. We were the first to go about making laws, statutes and edicts. Demons without rules are just a recipe for chaos." He sighed. "Ah, the good old days. But now," he rolled his eyes, "ugh, the paperwork, the red-tape. If I tell you too much, do you know how many forms I have to fill out? Preposterous. And not nearly as fun as dismembering souls or watching people suffer.

Torture for us is a trip to City Hall." Seth shuddered.

"So if you tell me who is behind this, that breaks a rule."

This time, Seth tapped his finger on his nose in a 'you got it' gesture.

Jade frowned, her memory percolating. "But the last time you said you couldn't tell me something, it was about Matthew, and you couldn't tell me because he'd made a deal with another demon."

Seth's eyes lit up and he placed his hands in front of him, as though he were an angel in prayer. He smiled at her and then raised his eyebrows, his face saying, 'go on.'

"You couldn't tell me about Matthew because you can't tell me about other demon deals, other than your own."

Seth clapped the tips of his fingers together in tiny applause. "Very close, just one more bit."

"So whoever is pushing and pulling at me," Jade said, "has a deal with another demon and it involves me somehow."

"Bingo! Oh, you're so good at this! I love playing games with you." Seth smiled and Jade had to blink against the force of his personality coming through.

"Sorry, possum. I got a little carried away there." He drew back on his power, and Jade didn't feel dizzy anymore.

"Is someone trying to steal my power again?" God, what was it with this Coven? Paris had said that witches didn't deal with demons, that it was taboo, but from Jade's vantage point, it was pretty regular.

Seth looked a little chagrined. "Can't say anymore."

"You haven't said anything!" Jade exclaimed.

"Tough break, I know. What can I say? I don't make the rules."

Out of sheer curiosity, she asked, "Who enforces demon rules?"

Seth's eyes went serious and settled on her. It was like a cold cloak had just been placed over her shoulders.

"You don't want to know. Suffice to say, no one breaks the rules if they can help it. No one. Well, I must be off. Don't worry, I've got my eye on you - I'll be keeping up on all your bits and pieces. I'm cheering for you, Possum. Rah-rah and all that." He raised a hand to his lips, kissing his fingers and then made a motion like he was going to blow it her way. Out of sheer self-preservation, she spat out the wind spell again, the pantry door slamming shut a second time.

Seth's laughter rang in her ears long after he disappeared.

CHAPTER THIRTEEN

Paris came back with an overnight bag and Jade marveled at how men could pack so easily and so quickly. She didn't consider herself high-maintenance by any means, but it did take her time to put together a suitcase or weekend bag - makeup, toiletries, clothes, electronics, chargers. But there Paris was with one very nice, not too large, leather satchel slung over his shoulder. He could probably live out of it for a week. He had a huge, ancient looking book tucked under one of his arms and Jade eyed it.

"Let me guess, light reading?"

His lips quirked. "No, it's one of my mother's grimoires. Not one of her demon ones," he added before Jade could interrupt. "She has a spell in it for calm sleep and I thought I would cast it for you. She used to cast it for me when I was younger."

"Did you used to have bad dreams?" Jade asked, following Paris up the stairs. He dropped his bag off in the spare room, keeping a smaller bag from inside it and the spell book with him, and paused in the hallway.

"Yes, but no more so than most children. Creatures under the bed and the like. May I?" he asked, indicating her bedroom.

Crap. Did she leave underwear out on the floor? "Just…" she said, holding up a finger for him to wait. She darted in, looked quickly around, kicked some clothing into the closet and closed the door to the main bath, where the mirror was still cracked and broken.

Jade opened up her bedroom door again. "Okay." She made a sweeping gesture with her hand, letting him know it was okay for him to enter. Paris didn't really look about, just took his little bag over to the bed and unpacked a few things from it, setting the book open to about three-quarters of the way through. It was clear the book was well-loved - the pages were dog-eared and worn, and as Paris flipped one or two, searching out the spell he wanted, the scent of sage, vanilla and mint wafted up. Paris put together a few ingredients on a scrap of fabric. Jade couldn't be certain, but it looked like silk. It was a lovely dark grey, like slate. He was murmuring to himself as he worked and she resisted the urge to stand closer and either listen in or read over his shoulder. She knew if she asked him to teach her the spell, he would, and that kept her from hanging over him, eager to see what he was doing.

Paris tied the little satchel together, saying more words that Jade couldn't make out and then he shook the little sack a bit at each of the four corners of her bed, before tucking it under her pillow.

"Was that Voudon?" she asked, reminded of the little sachet Paris had in his coat.

"Yes and no. It's a charm bag, which likely has it's roots in Voudon, but the actual making of this particular charm bag wasn't Voudon in nature. Just an older spell my mother knew. You just have to keep it under your pillow. If it doesn't work, we can try another combination."

Jade nodded and then came to the awkward-inducing realization that she was standing in her bedroom with Paris. It shouldn't have been suddenly weird, but it was and she froze, not wanting to look at the bed, but feeling like it was a magnet for her eyes.

A scratching sound caught her attention, breaking her immobility. "Bruce!" Jade hissed, bending over and sticking her face under the bed. "What has gotten into you, bud?"

Bruce glared at her once and then scratched at the hardwood again.

"Stop that! We discussed this!"

"What's he doing?" asked Paris.

"I don't know. Digging to China. He's scratching at the floor. Bruce! Come on, bud."

Bruce slunk out from under the bed, looking mulish.

"He may be more agitated than usual because you're highly stressed," Paris said.

Jade's shoulders slumped. Now she felt like a jerk. "Sorry, Bruce. My bad," she said, patting him on the head.

He tipped his neck back and showed her his scaly patch again. It was weeping a clear yellow-tinged fluid.

"Oh, buddy," Jade said quietly, taking a tissue off her nightstand and patting gently at it. Bruce's tongue came out and touched her once on the wrist while she carefully cleaned him up. "Do you want some more cream on it?" she asked and he shook himself like a dog, Elizabethan collar flapping wildly. "Is that a yes or a no?" she wondered aloud.

"Why don't we go downstairs and I'll flip through my mother's grimoire and see if I can find a poultice for him?"

Jade nodded. "Yeah. Okay."

Bruce loped out the door and Paris followed him, leaving Jade to bring up the end of their little trio. Once downstairs, Paris starting flipping through his mother's grimoire, while Jade decided to tackle unpacking some boxes. She only had a few books, having switched to an e-reader a while ago, but the books she did have, she liked to have out. She eyeballed the two boxes, trying to decide if she should keep to her former organizational set up (fiction by author and then non-fiction by subject) or if she should switch it up (fiction by genre, then author, and then non-fiction, still by author). The problem was always the genre-bending books.

Feeling eyes on her, Jade looked up and caught Paris watching her.

"Problem? You've shelved the same set of books three times."

"I just... don't know how I want them." She could always throw caution to the wind and sort by color. She sighed. She was too tired to make this kind of decision. She would just shelve them for now and think about it later. Decision made, she placed her stacks of books on the shelves.

"Problem solved?" Paris asked.

"Meh. Problem deferred."

Bruce sauntered over to the fireplace, kicked at the grate once and then gave Paris a pointed look.

"Message received, Master Bruce." Paris lips curled in a smile as he spoke a few words and a fire sprung up in the fireplace. Bruce fell over onto his side and then worm-wiggled his belly closer.

"You're going to burn yourself," Jade called from over by her books.

"Pfffft." Bruce smacked his lips and closed his eyes.

Paris did end up finding a poultice that he thought would work for Bruce and they moved into the kitchen, hunting for the right ingredients. Happy that she had them all, Jade listened attentively as Paris showed her the routine of making a poultice. It was like witchcraft and cooking mashed together and while she found it interesting, it wasn't as shiny and fun as demon magic.

Plus, it kind of stunk. Literally stunk.

Jade wrinkled her nose as she wrapped the poultice paste three times in cotton. It smelled moldy and wet - like moss or the forest gone bad which was weird because they hadn't used a lot of outdoors stuff. Paris tried to explain that was the magic combining with the ingredients and once it was ready, it wouldn't smell as foul.

Still, it stunk. Although if it helped Bruce, it would be worth it. It had to 'settle' or 'steep' over night, going through a cycle of the moon. Jade gently placed it in her fridge and then set up a little barrier of tin foil around it.

"For the smell," she said at Paris' wry look.

After that, her exhaustion caught up with her. She was ready for bed by nine.

"Okay, I'm not much of a hostess. You know where all my stuff is. Food, coffee, I think I even have some of that tea you like. In the cupboard. Way in the back. I'm going to bed."

Paris looked up from his laptop. The light of the screen highlighted his face and he looked tired. Not as tired as she felt, but he didn't look like he normally did, or should. He'd kind of had a tired look on his face ever since the whole thing with Dex and Veronica.

"Thanks," she said suddenly.

He frowned. "For what?"

"You know. Staying here. Helping out with my bag of crazy." Jade gestured at her brain. "I'm sure you have more important things to do. Like running a Coven."

"Your well-being is important to me. The Coven will be fine." He smiled. "It practically runs itself."

Jade laughed. "Yeah, that must be why you put in all those hours. Because it's a well-oiled machine." She wished she had something to do with her arms. She ended up crossing them over her chest. "Well, goodnight."

"Goodnight, Jade. Sleep well."

Jade really hoped she would.

#

Paris watched Jade go upstairs, his eyes lingering on the staircase long after she'd disappeared and he'd heard the door to her bedroom close over. She probably didn't shut it all the way in case Bruce wanted in later. He was still sacked out in front of the fireplace, belly soaking up the heat. He twitched when Jade went upstairs, his head moving slightly to watch, but he stayed firmly in place stretched out. When Paris finally looked away from the stairs to check back at Bruce, he was watching Paris. If a lizard could have a 'knowing' look, Bruce was wearing one.

"I'm worried."

Bruce's tongue flicked out, his 'pffft' sound familiar and comforting to Paris.

"Exactly."

Paris wasn't sure how he felt about his discussion with Jade earlier regarding Lily. Did he think that Lily was an alternate personality? A part of Jade's psyche, making her a very disturbed young woman? Strangely, no. He got the feeling he perhaps should. He should be asking Dr. Gellar for a psychiatric referral right now. Instead, he'd asked the doctor to keep what happened in Jade's medlab room, when Lily had shown up, out of her medical file. Dr. Gellar was going to review the scans from Jade's brain at the time and see what she could determine medically, but she'd agreed to wait before she put it in Jade's file.

There were several signs pointing to Jade's issue being magical in nature. While Paris hadn't necessarily made an ordered list in his mind, he did have some crucial points.

'Lily,' the other person Jade always referred to, had magic. While Paris would expect if a witch had a personality disorder that all personalities might have magic, Lily's magic did not feel like Jade's magic. A witch's magic was very holistic and homogenous. Paris had never known of it to be 'split' or 'divided' into separate and distinct components. The only variation he'd ever known of had been with respect to demon magic. Jade's demon magic was quite like her 'regular' or Coven magic, but Paris had read of cases where witches practicing demon magic had their power take on a taint or a sort of tarnishing. It was the only time he recalled from his magical studies that a witch's power could be altered.

Jade had also never mentioned any other distinct or separate individuals. Paris' understanding of dissociative identity was rudimentary at best, but he thought he'd read somewhere that a 'split' or alternate personality, where there was only the true personality and one other, was quite rare. He'd have to consult a specialist to be certain, as he doubted his rigorous reading of the internet's Wikipedia page made him an expert. However, Jade said that she and Lily shared memories and knew all about each other. Paris thought that secrecy and separation were key components of the disorder - one personality (or several) knowing parts of the abuse suffered, but not sharing with one another.

Jade never appeared to lose time and while he didn't always agree with how she approached things, he wouldn't call her unstable or erratic. She was quite methodical and rational when it came to her life and her magic.

Then there was the third player in Jade's dreams - the Sparrow Lady. Paris supposed she could be a third personality, but the way Jade spoke of her was very different from how she spoke of Lily. Jade spoke of Lily with fondness, regret or sometimes wistfulness. Jade spoke of the Sparrow Lady like it was the monster under the bed. Hushed tones, quiet words.

The sparrow had quite a few meanings, mystically and magically. It could mean joy, protection or creativity. Sometimes it was used as a symbol of small things being important. Sparrows could be seen as either good or bad luck - harbingers of death, soul catchers or symbols of love. He sent a quick email to Callie, asking her to research sparrows in their Coven library, but as he searched through the internet, his stomach sat uneasy. He found himself drawn to the darker stories containing sparrows - sparrows that pecked at animals and destroyed lives, sparrows that were omens of bad things to come, sparrows catching the souls of the dead to carry them to the afterworld.

Paris' eyelids were heavy. It had been a long day and he could only imagine how tired Jade must have felt if he was this exhausted himself. Bruce stretched on the ground in front of Paris, making little grunting and sighing noises as he did. There were a few more articles Paris wanted to read, but he found the words on the screen starting to swim in front of him. He sighed, thinking he would close his eyes for a few minutes, catch a catnap, and then send off a few more Coven emails before heading up to bed for the night.

As he stretched out on the sofa, something made him pause. He shouldn't be so tired. It had been a long day, but he'd slept the night before. Perhaps not all the way through the night, but he wasn't so old that a single night of poor sleep should wipe him out the next day. The faint scent of licorice drifted across his senses and he felt his heart beat twice hard in succession. He wasn't just tired. This was magic. This was witchcraft. Someone was making him fall asleep. He knew spells that would keep him awake, but he could feel his brain slowing down, his consciousness being dragged to sleep, his magic slipping through his fingers. His eyes closed and he felt the fabric of the sofa under his cheek. He was so heavy. He tried to move but couldn't make his limbs respond. He could feel himself falling further away from consciousness, tipping over the edge into sleep. He thought he felt something brush across his forehead - light and careful, and then he heard the quietest hint of words, like they were carried on light and shadow.

"You always were a good sleeper."

#

Jade thought she was awake. She got out of bed, out her bedroom door and went down the stairs. It was only when she got to the foyer and she looked over to the living room that she realized she must be dreaming. She saw Paris sleeping on the sofa and she thought perhaps she should go to him and put a blanket over him. But her legs wouldn't do what she wanted. Instead, she turned away from him, slipped her runners on, left her laces undone, and grabbed her coat. She must be dreaming. She had no reason to go outside, in her pyjamas, in the middle of the night, and surely Paris would hear her if she did. Her body felt far away - the connection between her mind and her limbs slow and thick. She was watching everything from the back of her mind - seeing things through a long, thin telescope, or down a deep, dark hallway with a light at the end.

She turned back to Paris. The Sparrow Lady stood next to the sofa where he slept. She wore a dark cloak - black or navy, Jade couldn't tell. She had the hood up over her head and she was like some bad, fairy tale monster hovering over a sleeping prince.

Bruce's tail thumped against the stone in front of the fireplace, like he was having a bad dream too. The Sparrow Lady walked toward Jade and Jade couldn't move as she did. She stood stock still as the Sparrow Lady came closer, and closer and then drifted past her, not saying anything.

Jade turned and followed her.

The Sparrow Lady walked out the front door, Jade right behind her, the night air cold on her face. Though Jade had slipped her coat on, it was undone and the air snuck in through the open zipper and curled around her thin sleep-shirt and pants, but she couldn't make her arms move to do it up. The Sparrow Lady had a car, and wasn't that strange? Something so ordinary. She got in the front seat and Jade got in the back - like the Sparrow Lady was a chauffeur and Jade was her charge.

Jade's body rocked slightly back and forth as the Sparrow Lady drove. She was talking. Talking to Jade. But her words were tinny and empty and didn't make any sense to Jade. Jade watched the Sparrow Lady for in the rear view mirror. She could just make out her eyes from inside the hood of the cloak. Light-colored. Blue. Blue like the summer sky. Like Paris' eyes.

Jade turned her head and looked out the side window, seeing her reflection in the glass. The moon was bright in the sky - not quite full, but Jade wasn't sure if it was waxing or waning. She never paid attention to things like that. Her face in the window was pale, her eyes glass. Behind her, she could make out another image of herself, just over her shoulder, glaring at her with green eyes. It was Lily. She looked like she was shouting, but Jade couldn't hear her. She could only see her lips moving.

Wake up.

Jade heard the words with her mind, not with her ears. Time was odd too, feeling as though it moved and shifted against the natural laws of science and nature. It seemed like only seconds and they were at the Preserve.

The Sparrow Lady was taking her to the lake. Jade shouldn't be surprised. That's where the dreams started. It made sense this one should end there. The Sparrow Lady got out of the car and as Jade's eyes followed her lazily, she again caught sight of Lily in the reflection of the glass, her hands on Jade's shoulders, her lips next to Jade's ears.

Wake up.

The Sparrow Lady opened the back door, breaking Jade's line of sight with Lily. It was cold as she followed after the Sparrow Lady. She wound and wove her way into the trees, moving silently. Her salamander charm was hot against her clavicle, a heavy weight resting against her skin. Jade's shoes were loose on her feet and at one point she stepped out of the right one and left it behind. Cinderella at the ball, she thought. Who would find her shoe and bring it back to her.

Don't lag behind, dear.

Not Lily's voice in her mind this time, but the Sparrow Lady, speaking again. Jade had to keep up, she had to keep following.

There were no sounds of sparrows at the lake this time. Maybe because Jade was with the Sparrow Lady. Or maybe because it was only a dream.

Not a dream. Wake up.

Again, Lily's voice in her head, or maybe from behind her. Jade wanted to turn around but kept moving forward, toward the dock. The Sparrow Lady pointed at the dock and Jade felt sick. Her stomach cramped and bile tickled the back of her throat. Her head hurt now too, an ice-pick poking around in her brain, trying to shuffle and stir things about.

Go to the end of the dock.

The Sparrow Lady's voice, calm and cold. Jade stepped up on the dock, losing her left shoe. Now she was barefoot. She hated dreams where she was missing her shoes. It was so ridiculous. Why would she go somewhere without shoes? But she didn't leave without them this time, she lost them along the way. Her toes hurt from the cold, feeling stiff and painful. The dock was more wobbly than it had been in her dreams. It was old, unused, with no one coming out to take care of it.

All the way to the end, dear.

Jade looked over the edge when she got there, her toes curling over the end. The moon was behind her shoulder, high in the sky, her body breaking its reflection. Her shadow was on the water - nearly perfect except for the slight ripples coming from the dock, breaking the surface making the outline of her shape wavy and indeterminate.

It was cold. The water would be colder. It had been so cold before. But that couldn't be right. She'd never been here before. But Jade remembered being shocked by the cold of it. So cold it stole her breath and she'd gasped, little lungs filling up with water and then...

I'm coming, Jade. I'm coming to help. Wake up.

In the lake beneath her, there was a shape. Rising slowly to the surface like it had been trapped at the bottom of the lake for years and someone, something, had finally cut its anchor and released it. The pain in Jade's head was worse and she felt the drops of blood fall from her nose before they hit the water and disturbed the surface. The color bled across the reflection of the moon, turning it pink.

The shape came closer to the surface - not just a shape, a little girl. Small. Smaller than Jade ever remembered being. A pale face, darkish hair - maybe dark blonde or light brown. Jade reached for her, like she had once reached for Lily in a dream, but the little girl's eyes didn't open. *Who are you*, Jade asked, although she didn't hear herself say the words out loud.

"Wait! Jade!"

So strange to think she could hear Paris' voice. He was never in any of her dreams.

Now, into the water.

No, that was a horrible idea. She couldn't swim. It would be so cold. And yet... the little girl was in the water. Her eyes were open now, looking at Jade and her lips were moving. She was alive, she was saying something. Something she wanted Jade to hear. But Jade was too far away. Jade leaned over, watching the girl. Her lips moved again and this time, Jade heard her words.

I'm you.

Jade fell into the water. Cold, it was so cold, just as it had been before. So cold it shocked her and stole her breath as she gasped, her lungs filling up with water. She couldn't swim, didn't know how and she was sinking.

I'm coming, Jade. I'm coming to help.

#

Paris blinked awake, wondering why he was on the couch, and why it was cold. Looking toward the direction of the draft, he saw the front door open. He was momentarily confused until he remembered the last few seconds before he fell asleep, or rather, was put to sleep.

Someone had spelled him unconscious. He remembered something else. A touch on his forehead and words - words he couldn't quite remember at the moment. Someone had been in the house, presumably the Sparrow Lady. Whoever she was, she had been in the house.

He called out Jade's name loudly as he ran upstairs, but his gut told him she wouldn't be there. Her bedroom door was open, the bed empty. Paris paused in the doorway, saying her name again in case she was in the master bathroom or closet, but there was no answer.

However, there was a scratching sound and then some animal grunts from under the bed.

"Bruce?" Paris asked, kneeling down. Under the bed, he could see Bruce's reflective eyes glinting back at him. Bruce was scrabbling at the hardwood, his long talons making gouges in the wood, almost like he was trying to rip up the planks.

"Bruce, where is Jade?" Bruce kept scratching away, not looking up. "Bruce! What are you doing?"

Bruce spat three times on the hardwood, ignoring him. Paris stood up, thinking to move the bed to get a grip on him. Paris would drag him out if he had to. Bruce helped Paris find Jade the last time he wasn't sure where she was, and Paris had faith he could do the same thing again. He pulled the queen-sized bed away from the wall to get at the lizard, who was hunkered down by the head of the bed.

After moving the bed about two feet, Paris stepped over to the headboard, intent on shooing Bruce out or grabbing him. He stopped when he saw markings on the wood. Dark black markings. Paris could see just parts of them - half-circles and the start of runes.

"What is this?"

Bruce was still hard at work, scratching at strange markings painted on the dark hardwood. Paris pushed the bed further away, exposing the remainder and stared down in awful comprehension.

It was a hex circle. Underneath Jade's bed, where she slept, was a complex, rune-ridden hex circle. Paris only understood a few of the runes - enough to make out the symbols for 'control' and 'unconscious.' Bruce was scratching at the symbols, trying to break the circle.

"That's what you were doing earlier this evening," Paris murmured. "You saw this when she didn't and you were trying to break it then. You're still trying to break it. Because it's working. Right now, wherever Jade is she's under someone else's control. The Sparrow Lady. Why, Bruce?" Paris asked, thinking aloud. "Why does she need Jade to be somewhere else? Where does she need Jade to be?" Paris was frozen for a moment before his brain made the necessary connections. "All her dreams are at the Preserve. The lake. Goddamit."

He ran downstairs, leaving Bruce to his mad scratching. He grabbed his coat, his shoes and ran out to his car, pulling his cell phone out as he did. He should have called 911 or Counter-Magic, but in that moment, he called the person he trusted the most.

"Callie," he began as soon as she answered, "I think Jade is at the lake, the lake in the Preserve, the one no one goes to anymore." He pulled the car out onto the street and floored it.

"What? Jesus, Paris it's three in the morning. What's going on?" Callie's voice had the sleepy, groggy tone of someone just woken up.

"I don't know what's happening. I just… I can't think." The only words going through his head were *drive, lake, water, I can't swim.* "Just. I need you to call help. I can't… I'm on my way, but I can't…"

"What?" Callie repeated and Paris wanted to shout at her, but then she took a breath. "Okay, okay, I think I got it. Lake, Preserve, Jade's in trouble, you're going there and you need me to call help. I can do that. Got it."

"Thank you."

"Be careful. I have to hang up now and call for help," Callie said and the phone went silent.

He sagged in relief. Callie would call for assistance, Callie would bring help. Paris just had to get there and… do something, he wasn't sure what, until help arrived.

The streets were dark and silent as he sped through them, the town and Coven asleep. As he drove, he started to doubt himself. What if he was wrong? What if Jade wasn't in trouble, or wasn't even at the lake? What if she was somewhere else and he was mistaken?

He wasn't sure if he was relieved or more worried when he arrived at the entrance to the Preserve and saw another car there, one he didn't recognize, with its front driver and rear doors still open. He left his car in much the same condition, his front door only getting a half-hearted push as he started running into the forest toward the lake. He didn't get far from the car before he realized his massive error in not bringing a flashlight. He quickly conjured a fire spell, hoping he had enough presence of mind to keep it from the dry timber of the Preserve and not set the entire area alight.

Paris tried to follow the pathway and was certain for a moment he was lost when he spied a running shoe on its side in the underbrush. Jade's running shoe. He left it where it lay and continued on. He moved as quickly has he could in the half-light, his flames as bright as he could make them. He wasn't nearly as proficient at fire as Jade was and certainly not while entirely distracted.

He broke through the tree line at the lake and paused, looking around for something, anything. Then he saw her. Jade, standing at the end of the dock, staring down into the water. She was too close to the edge for his liking. He moved toward the dock and found his steps sluggish and slow. The scent of licorice filled his nostrils. Magic - working against him. Strong magic, powerful magic. But not Jade's.

The Sparrow Lady.

Paris could see a figure standing at the land's end of the dock, watching Jade as she hovered with her toes hanging over the edge of the old wood. Paris struggled against the magic, calling on the sheer force of his power rather than any sort of spell he could think of at the moment. He was able to move forward a few steps, and then a few steps more. Jade leaned over, toward the water.

"Wait! Jade!" Paris yelled, not able to move faster - it was as though he were trapped in one of those horrible dreams where your body won't do what you want it to, not matter how much you will it.

He made it two more steps toward the docks and he knew he wouldn't make it in time. He knew what was going to happen before Jade moved again, before she started tipping forward, before she hit the water and he could hear her in his memory saying, '*I can't swim.*'

Even if Jade could swim, it was too cold. The water would be near freezing. Her body entered with a splash and she sunk under the surface. A strangled sound escaped his throat, as he fought against the magic holding him back. The licorice smell intensified, burning his nostrils. Underneath it, he could smell sage and vanilla and he knew that particular scent, but he couldn't spare the mental processing power to chase the thought.

A burst of magic tore through the night with a crack of sound and a burst of light. It blinded him and made his ears ring. The pressure wave of it brought him to his knees. It wasn't his magic and for a moment, he thought it was the unknown Sparrow Lady until he managed to look up and see her struggling on her knees as well. He'd never felt anything as powerful, hadn't even known magic could be so powerful without any kind of warning preceding it. The Sparrow Lady stumbled to her feet and disappeared into a flock of birds, the flock of them swooping into the darkness of the forest. No longer trapped by her magic, Paris pushed to his feet, breathing in the strong smell of flowers and cloves - Jade's magic. Linden blossom, his brain finally supplied. After all this time, he finally could place the scent of her magic. Linden blossoms and cloves. He staggered to the lakeshore and smelled grapefruit and cinnamon as well, only not as strong as Jade's magic. His gait was off and he fell to his knees in the shallow water, the shock of the icy temperature causing him to gasp. He didn't know what he thought he could do - in the cold, in the dark - only that he had to do something. He pushed to his feet again and yanked off his coat, throwing it to the shore. He sloshed further into the lake and was preparing to dive in when someone broke the surface, out by the dock.

It was her - Jade. She looked around, as though searching for something and then dived back into the water, gracefully, as though she knew how to swim, how to dive. Paris stumbled over the slightly rocky terrain, back out of the water and across the shoreline to the dock, running down the planks, his footfalls heavy and thick. He reached the end just as she broke through again, only this time, she wasn't alone. She had someone in her arms, their head hanging forward, face obscured.

She must have heard him because she turned toward him.

"Here!" she shouted, trying to heft up the unknown person she held. Unthinking, he reached out and grabbed the person, the woman, under her shoulders and heaved her sodden, soaking body to the dock, laying her down before turning back to Jade.

Her teeth were chattering and she had both hands up on the dock, already trying to kick herself out of the water. Paris reached down and hauled her up too. She crawled on her knees to the other body, pushing the long, dark hair from around the woman's face.

It was Jade.

They were both Jade.

Paris fell backward with a shock, landing on his ass hard. The body on the dock was prostrate, unmoving, but he could see in the silvery moonlight that blood was trickling from her ears and nose, running down the side of her head and into her hair.

The other woman leaned over the body and rested their foreheads together. She cradled the unconscious woman's face, her fingers running through her wet hair. She was speaking, despite her teeth chattering and her body shivering. For a moment, her words sounded jumbled and didn't make sense until Paris realized what she was saying.

"I'm awake now, it's your turn. Wake up, Jade. Wake up."

Paris swallowed hard and stared, open-mouthed at the woman who knelt over the body. She was kneeling over Jade, he realized.

"Who are you?" he asked, even though he knew what she would say before she spoke.

She looked at him and now that he was closer, he could see, even in the moonlight, the sharp green of her eyes.

"I'm Lily."

CHAPTER FOURTEEN

For a moment, Paris was at a loss. He stared at the two of them. Two identical women - one he thought he knew and the other an exact physical duplicate of her, who he did not know at all. Lily shivered, her teeth clacking together, and Paris could see her lips were slightly blue-tinged, as were her fingertips. She had pulled Jade partially into her lap and was holding her close, as though she had any warmth to give. Paris stumbled to his feet and ran back down the dock, to the lake edge, retrieving his coat. When he brought it back, he wasn't sure who to give it to, but Lily made the decision for him, taking it from him when he held it out wordlessly and draping it over Jade.

"She's breathing, but I can't get her to open her eyes," Lily said.

Paris knelt down and made a move to take Jade from Lily's arms and Lily reared back, clutching Jade closer to her.

"I mean to carry her," Paris clarified. "I hope you can walk?"

Lily nodded, but Paris began to doubt that she could with the way her body was wracked with cold. Her fingers were claws, digging into Jade's shoulders even as Paris tried to gently pull Jade away. He managed to get her from Lily's grasp and then heft her into his arms.

She'd been right before, she wasn't a slight woman, but he could carry her out of the Preserve if it was necessary, which it appeared it was. What he couldn't do was carry them both. Lily struggled to her feet, her teeth making horrible clacking sounds as they chattered. She started walking off the dock, Paris following her carrying Jade. Lily's feet were bare - her pale toes also blue and Paris remembered Jade had lost her shoes on the way to the dock. Lily was wearing an exact copy of Jade's outfit, even missing her shoes, as Jade was.

Jade was heavy in his arms and, though he was loathe to think it, all Paris could hear in his brain were the words, 'dead weight.' Jade was floppy, her body holding no position on its own and he had to keep a tight grip lest she simply slip out of his arms.

Christ, how the hell was he going to get them out of here?

A sound from the forest made both Paris and Lily turn their heads and he was confused when he saw bobbing lights and heard crunching footsteps along with voices. Then Callie broke through the trees with a headlamp on, followed by Josef from Counter-Magic, several other Counter-Magic agents and a two pairs of EMTs with medical bags and backboards.

The cavalry had arrived. Before he could open his mouth, Lily was hopping up and down on her bare feet.

"Here! We're here!"

Everyone headed over to them immediately and Paris was quickly and efficiently separated from Jade by two EMTs, who took her and expertly laid her out on a backboard before he even realized his arms were empty. He looked over and saw Lily with the other two EMTs, while the Counter-Magic agents were working a perimeter around the lake. Josef and Callie came up to Paris, Callie with her open, expressive face and Josef looking slightly grim.

"You said bring help," Callie said, shrugging a bit.

Paris lunged forward and hugged her tightly, so, so grateful for her friendship in that moment. He'd called her in a blind panic, not even knowing what to ask for and she came through for him, for Jade.

She patted him gingerly on the back. "Is everyone okay?"

He pulled away from her, looking at Lily as she was wrapped in several blankets and told to sit down despite her protests that she was fine. He then looked at Jade being strapped to a backboard, still unconscious.

"Holy shit!" Callie exclaimed, looking from Lily to Jade. "Who is that?"

It hit Paris that Callie was talking about *Jade* when she said that. She was staring at Jade unconscious on the backboard and Lily arguing with the EMTs. Callie just assumed the conscious woman, declaring she'd be fine once she warmed up, was Jade.

Josef edged closer to Paris. "Should I be working up some kind of containment spell right about now?" he asked, eyeballing an unconscious Jade. God, they both thought that Lily was Jade.

"Yes, I mean, no," Paris said. "Not for her, not for either of them. There was someone else here. I didn't see her face. She had Jade under some kind of a compulsion spell and was blocking me. I need your agents out looking for her."

"The Sparrow Lady," Lily interrupted, batting the hands of the EMT away and breaking free of them to come next to Paris. "She smells like licorice." She paused as though remembering something. "And she has blue eyes."

"Anything else?" Josef said to her.

She turned and looked at him, stopping stockstill and blinking, her eyes wide and bright. "I know you."

Josef smiled wryly at her. "I should hope so since you work for me."

Lily shook her head. "No, I mean, I know you from before."

Josef raised an eyebrow at Paris and he wanted to explain, but he didn't know how.

"I'm so glad you're okay!" Callie exclaimed, laying a hand on Lily's arm.

Lily looked down for a second, then up at Callie and then her whole body shifted slightly and she smiled at Callie. "Yeah, I'm okay."

"I thought you told Henri and I you were tired of saving the world."

"I am," Lily said easily, "I told you guys it was someone else's turn next, but I keep being the only one around when shit goes down."

Paris' mouth went dry. If he hadn't known she was Lily, if he couldn't still see Jade on the ground with EMTs by her side, he would never know this was Lily pretending to be Jade.

Callie lurched forward and hugged her and Lily hugged her back, just as Jade would - slightly awkward, but heartfelt.

One of the EMTs stood up from where he was kneeling next to Jade. "We have to get her to the medlab. She's hypothermic and in shock."

Lily pushed past both Callie and Paris. "I'm going with you."

"You don't even have shoes," Paris protested, following her.

"I have one," she said, holding up the one sneaker that had been on the dock. "I'll pick up the other on the way out."

The EMTs had already picked Jade up on the backboard and started carrying her out. Lily was hot on their heels, even only in one shoe, with Paris right behind her. He paused for a moment, torn between Josef and his Counter-Agents and following Jade. As Coven Leader, he should stay and try to find the Sparrow Lady. But he wanted to go with Jade.

"Go," Callie said, waving him on. "I can stay here and be an interim 'you.'"

"Thank you," he called, darting after Lily and the EMTs.

He caught up with Lily after only a few steps and placed a careful hand on her shoulder. She turned her head slightly but didn't break her pace, keeping up with the EMTs despite being soaking wet and in a blanket.

"You pretended to be her," Paris said, keeping his voice low enough that the EMTs wouldn't hear.

"What? Oh, back there? Yes, I did. I thought it would be easier than trying to explain."

"Don't do it again," he said flatly. He hadn't liked it. It had been flawless. If not for the color of her eyes and having her tell him not moments before that she was Lily, he doubted he would have known. It scared the hell out of him. She nodded once, in accession.

He wanted to start asking her questions, but hiking out of the Preserve wasn't exactly conducive to conducting an interview or an interrogation. Lily struggled to keep up with the EMTs, but she only paused once - when they came across the second shoe on the pathway and she picked it up, jamming it on her foot. They finally broke through the forest back in the parking area, where there were two ambulances and four cars.

The car that had been there when Paris arrived however, the Sparrow Lady's car, was gone.

The EMTs loaded Jade in the back of the ambulance and Lily scrambled in after her with Paris following a close second. They both got a look from an EMT but he said nothing.

"Can you tell me how she is?" asked Paris. Lily had the closer spot and had already tucked one of Jade's hands into her own. Paris felt a little like a third wheel, stuck at the end of the bed.

The EMT gave him the basics, which wasn't much. She was unconscious, she was unresponsive, she was bleeding from the ears and nose, and she was hypothermic. Their biggest concern was to get her warm and then get her to medlab, where Dr. Gellar would be meeting them. It wasn't anything that Paris didn't already know, but somehow hearing it come from professionals made it seem more real.

The remainder of the way to the Coven was silent with Paris unable to take his eyes off of Lily or Jade.

Dr. Gellar met them on the steps to the Covenstead, her small stature even more dwarfed by the building as it loomed behind her. The Covenstead was dark, with only minimum lighting this late at night, or early morning. Some decorative lighting, some spot lights for security and maybe one or two lights accidentally left on by a witch were the only illumination.

After the number of times Jade had required medical attention in the short time since she'd come to live at the Coven, you would think that Paris would be used to her being spirited away by medical personnel, while he was left to wait outside closed doors. Only this time, he wasn't alone. He had a companion.

Lily kept pace with him the entire way to medlab, brushing off a nurse who asked if she needed assistance. While she wasn't actively pretending to be Jade, Paris noted everyone just assumed she was. Who they thought the real Jade was, the one who'd been whisked in with Dr. Gellar, Paris could not say.

Lily disappeared for a few moments in medlab, causing Paris to wonder if she had somehow gotten to see Jade, until she came back in a pair of scrubs, drying her hair with a plain white medical towel. She smirked as she looked down at herself.

"What?" Paris asked.

She looked up at him, still partially smiling. "Jade's stolen a couple of pairs of these and wondered if she should feel guilty, but decided not to until her total reached five. I'll have to tell her to add one to her running count."

"You assume she'll be fine." Paris said it like it was a statement, but in his heart, he felt it more like a question. Lily didn't seem worried about Jade. Or rather, as worried as he thought she would be.

"Of course she'll be fine," Lily said, her voice steady and even.

Paris studied her. "How do you know? Can you feel something? Do you know something?"

Lily blinked, her eyes bright and clear. "No, not really, it's just... I'm here, so of course she will be too."

"I understood that she existed without you for many years."

"Well, yes. But I was just away." She frowned. "Or asleep, I suppose."

"And what if Jade sleeps now?"

"Why would she?" Lily seemed genuinely confused.

"Why did you?" Paris countered.

Lily's hands slowed from where they were towel-drying her hair. "We're not ready to discuss that."

It was odd the way she so easily made decisions on behalf of Jade, and yet Paris was certain that if Jade were here, she would have made the same choice. She'd not told Paris how she and Lily separated and Paris didn't think that Lily would tell him now either.

Lily went to the couches in the sitting area and dropped herself down on them heavily, still working on her hair with the towel. Paris stepped over to her slowly, cautiously.

"I don't bite," she said.

"You admit this situation is quite extraordinary."

"I suppose." At his look she continued. "I mean, sure, it's kind of weird, but we were always two people, stuck in one body." She shrugged. "Honestly, this is probably the most normal that I've felt in a long time. We're separate now." She paused, her eyebrows coming together slightly. "Kind of like we always should have been, I think."

"What do you mean?" Paris took a seat on the sofa gingerly, sitting further from her than he would if it were Jade. He could still feel her power, so different from Jade's. Lily's power was quite reserved and aloof. Paris wasn't sure if Lily herself were even aware of it.

"I'm sure you probably wondered at some point if this was some kind of dissociative identity, but it's not. I think you know about our childhood?" she asked and then nodded like she was answering her own question. If they shared memories as fully as Jade had indicated, she probably *was* answering her own question - flipping through their memories until she found what she was looking for. "Yes, she told you a bit about it. So, abusive childhood. It was awful and it sucked, but it wasn't personality altering. I am not her and she is not me." Lily sounded so sure, so absolute. "Jade told you that she never remembered a time before me, but I do remember a time before her. I remember when it was only me in the body and my memories of that are quite good. I was young, but I don't think dad drank then and mom was a real mom. I remember part of a birthday party and I got a yellow dress and I was really happy about it. Things like that. It was only after Jade showed up that things changed. Not before."

Paris moved, easing himself back on the couch. "What do you mean?"

Finished with her hair, Lily started folding the towel on her lap, fiddling with it. "When I remember it, one day I was alone and the next day I wasn't. Jade was there."

"Where did she come from?"

Lily shrugged. "I don't know. She didn't say. She didn't say anything for a long time. But it was after she came that things started going... badly at home. Not that she caused it," Lily clarified. "She didn't. I know she didn't. But it wasn't like that before. It all changed after."

Paris was surprised at how easy it was to get information from Lily. He asked and she answered. It was nothing like asking Jade questions.

"What do you mean, she didn't say anything for a long time?"

"She didn't talk. At the time, I didn't think it was strange. I mean, she was just there one day, in my head. Our head. I was six, so I knew she wasn't just some imaginary person. I had imaginary friends, but I knew they were fake. Like a teddy bear tea party. You know those bears aren't really drinking tea," she said to him, as though she expected him to have some experience with imaginary tea parties. Her eyes drifted off to the window in medlab, the one that looked out on the courtyard. It was too dark outside now to see anything, but she stared at it, or maybe past it. "Sometimes, if I sat next to a mirror, but didn't look directly at it, I could almost see her in the reflection. Or in a window, late at night when it's dark outside but you've a light on indoors, and the glass is reflective. I could see her sometimes then too. Only out of the corner of my eye. Never directly. She was this small girl. Smaller than me. Younger than me. We look like me now, but she didn't look like me back then. She had lighter hair. Done up in this really pretty braid." Lily shook her head a little as though clearing it. "I asked her a lot who she was, what she wanted. She didn't say anything. I just got this sense of her being scared and maybe lost. I don't know. Even though I felt big next to her, I was young too, so maybe I was wrong. But she seemed smaller, littler. I felt like a big kid next to her. I kept asking her what her name was. All I ever got was the letter 'J' so I named her Jade."

"You named her," Paris repeated.

Lily smiled. "Yeah. We have that rock collection, I think you've seen it?" Again, he could see she was filtering through information in her head, and then nodding to herself when she confirmed it. "I was big into rocks then. Still kind of am. I guess she's lucky she didn't get saddled with being called Quartz or Amethyst. I was a six-year old. God, I could have named her lapis-lazuli." She snorted. "What a disaster."

"What's her real name?"

Lily shrugged. "I don't know. She never remembered. We don't talk about that."

"Why not?"

"It's just one of the things we don't talk about."

"Is there a list?"

Lily looked like she was considering his question and then said, "Yes."

Paris wondered, if they had shared as much as both Jade and Lily had intimated, what kinds of subjects must be on the 'unspoken' list? What things were taboo between two people who shared so much? As intrigued as he was, he was torn about asking more questions, partially because he felt that asking Lily questions was a betrayal of Jade's privacy, but also, because he had other concerns.

"Who is the Sparrow Lady?" Paris asked.

Lily paused, thinking about the question. "I don't know."

"What do you know about her? Jade said you called her that."

"I guess I named her too," Lily replied. "I don't know when I started waking up, not exactly. I have this sort of sense that I was present for a while before I realized it. The first thing I remember, actually, is you."

"Me?" Paris repeated, surprised. "Why?"

"It was in the forest, after Dex. When Jade was trying to bind him. I was there. That was the first time I remember being aware. She needed help. Focus. I could always help her do that. I helped her that day. To focus her spell and try to bind Dex. But he disappeared before it worked and there was this... vacuum of her power. I think it pulled her away for a moment and pulled me to the forefront. I remember being in a circle, and you were there. I touched your coat. But I was tired. I was so tired and I had to close my eyes and then I was asleep again, I think."

Paris remembered that moment so clearly. It was Lily's green eyes he'd seen that day, only he didn't know what it meant then. He was still learning all it meant now.

"When did the Sparrow Lady arrive? What does she do?"

"I don't know when she showed up exactly. I felt like I was waking up, but it was slow. I was tired. Jade knew I was waking up, or rather, I think she hoped I was waking up. I can't imagine what it was like for her being alone, after I left. She'd never been alone." Lily stared at the window to the courtyard again, and Paris realized with a jolt that from where she sat, she would be able to see her reflection. Jade's reflection.

"I think the Sparrow Lady knows that. Somehow. She knows about me and Jade." Lily fidgeted with the towel on her lap. "And the lake," she added slowly.

"What about the lake?" Paris asked.

"Jade's been there before."

"Yes, with me. We passed by it on the way to work on her circles one day and also recently. She reacted very violently. She was ill, she bled from the ears and nose."

Lily shook her head. "No, before. She was there before."

"She'd been dreaming of it," Paris said.

Again Lily shook her head. "No, I think..." she laughed, "I was going to say, 'I know this sounds crazy,' but then I realized, we passed that station a long way back." She sighed and shook her head again, this time like she was clearing it. "Before Jade fell in tonight, she saw something in the water and I'm not sure if it was her or if it was the Sparrow Lady that made her see it."

"What did she see?"

"A little girl, underwater. And I think it was Jade. A long time ago, I think it was her."

#

Jade sat on the dock, her bare feet hanging off the edge and dipping into the water. She kicked them, watching the water ripple and swirl. She leaned back, resting her hands behind her. The sun was shining and she squinted as she looked up at the sky. Not cloudless, but she liked it better when there were big, fat, fluffy clouds drifting lazily along. She lay down on the dock, her feet still submerged. She closed her eyes, seeing red on the inside of her eyelids from the bright sun. Her face was hot, but her feet were cold. She inhaled and exhaled, breathing out long and even. She could hear the quiet lap, lap, lap of the water against the wood of the dock. It was a nice day.

But…

What if there were something under the water? What if something lurked in the deep, watching her feet from below? What if something dark and ugly lived down there, waiting to reach up and grab her around the ankles, pulling her down, into the cold? Was that just the watery currents trailing against the soles of her feet, or was it some unseen thing's hand, coming closer, closer, wanting to snatch her from the surface?

Jade pulled her feet up from the water sharply, sitting up like a jackknife. She looked down at the rippling surface, not seeing anything but the clouds in the sky and her own reflection staring back at her. A large shape loomed over her shoulder. Someone was standing behind her.

Jade turned, eyes narrowing against the sharp light of the sun. She raised her hand, like a visor over her eyes. The woman looked down at her. She seemed vaguely familiar. Jade had seen her face before, but couldn't place where. A flock of sparrows circled above her head, black spots against the blue sky.

"The Sparrow Lady," Jade said aloud.

She was beautiful. She had the kind of face that ages well - pristine, sharp bone structure. As she got older, her bones hadn't made her sallow or stark looking - only more refined. She looked to be in her forties or fifties, but with that bone structure, she could easily be in her sixties and just look that good. Her hair was still dark and Jade had the fleeting thought that it could always be from a bottle, but drugstore color didn't normally shine so bright in the natural light. She had lovely highlights - streaks of blue-black and deep mahogany, which both set off the blue of her eyes - deep and clear.

"I've seen you before."

She smiled at Jade. "Perhaps. It's hard to say."

She had an accent like Paris - British and slightly formal, her words clipped. She wore a dark cloak, the same cloak she'd been wearing in Jade's other dreams. Until that moment, it was as though her dreams were far, far away, but noticing the cloak, recognizing it as the same one she'd seen before, brought Jade's other dreams back to the front of her mind. Jade scrambled backward, mindful of the edge and got to her feet. The Sparrow Lady's blue eyes watched her, more like a hawk than her namesake.

Jade looked at the water, remembering being cold, remembering the sky being dark. She looked back at the Sparrow Lady.

"Am I asleep?"

The Sparrow Lady smiled and that too was familiar. "After a fashion. You're unconscious more than asleep. Slightly different, although both make it easier."

"Easier for what?" Jade asked warily, stepping around her, trying to move past her on the slender dock and get closer to shore.

She didn't answer. Jade started walking backward on the dock, moving closer to shore, while keeping her body facing the Sparrow Lady. Her bare feet made it easy for her to keep her balance, the soles of her feet finding their purchase better without shoes in the way.

"What do you want from me?"

"I need a favor."

As Jade stepped back, the Sparrow Lady stepped forward, keeping pace with Jade.

"You've been making me dream of Lily. Of the lake."

The Sparrow Lady looked contemplative for a moment. "Yes and no. You were already dreaming of the lake and of her. I just needed to push you a bit. And I needed you to come here."

"Why?" Jade stepped off the dock, feeling the solid ground beneath her feet. The sun-warmed rocks were smooth against her soles.

"There's magic here. There has been for a long time."

"I already had magic." Jade stepped sideways toward the treeline.

"Yes. Yes, you did. And I needed more for you. I needed more from you."

"Who are you?" Jade wanted to turn away from her and run, but she was afraid to take her eyes of her. Like a children's game, as long as Jade watched her, the Sparrow Lady couldn't dart forward and get her.

The Sparrow Lady paused, as if sensing Jade wanted to bolt. "My name is Sakkara."

Jade shook her head. "No, that's Paris' mother's name."

The Sparrow Lady, Sakkara, nodded once.

"She's dead," Jade continued and then a horrible thought. "Oh, shit. Am I dead?"

"No, dear, I told you. Only unconscious. Separating yourself from Lily and conjuring a body for her was quite taxing on you. I imagine you could sleep on your own for a little bit longer yet."

Jade continued to shake her head, as though by denying what she was hearing, she could make it untrue. Paris' mother, Sakkara, was dead. Paris wouldn't have lied to Jade about that. The Coven knew she was dead too. When she was spoken of, it was always in quiet, reverent tones.

"What do you mean, separating myself from Lily?"

Sakkara tipped her head. "Ah, of course. You wouldn't actually know what you've done yet since you're still unconscious. Lily. You've crafted her a body, from magic. It's quite impressive and I'm not sure I know any other witches that could do it. Although, you've got a bit of a boost working for you."

"What do you mean?"

Sakkara smiled. "All in good time."

"I've read your books," Jade blurted. "Your magic. Your demon grimoires."

Sakkara nodded. "I know. It took me a while to remember some of my hexes without my books."

Realization struck Jade. "You unraveled my demon locks."

"Well, technically they're my demon locks. But you altered them. You cast that spell very well. Better than myself, I daresay. It took me time to remember it, figure out what you'd done and then break them."

"Why? Why did you break them?"

Sakkara pursed her lips and Jade almost did a double-take. The gesture was so familiar - Paris had the same expression sometimes. "I needed you to come to the lake and my influence on your dreams wasn't strong enough. I had to enter your house to cast a dream hex."

"You did what? Where? How?"

"It's in your room, under your bed."

"But I did go to the lake," Jade protested. "Paris brought me."

"Yes, he did." Her tone softened as she spoke of Paris. "The talisman he made you is quite powerful." Sakkara tipped her head, eyes darting down to the salamander charm Jade wore. Jade automatically raised her hand, pinching the small charm between her fingers. "He imbued a considerable amount of magic in it. It was difficult to get around."

Jade fisted the charm, her fingers holding it tight. Even now, it was warm - far warmer than it should have been from only resting against her skin.

Sakkara took a breath. "But when he brought you to the lake, you didn't stay long enough."

"For what?" Jade asked suspiciously.

"For you to bring Lily back."

Jade shook her head. "I didn't bring her back. She came back. On her own."

"Did she?" Sakkara asked, a glint in her eyes. It was one of those questions that wasn't really a question. "You don't give yourself enough credit."

"What's going on? What do you want?"

"I told you, I need a favor. Or, rather, my mistress does."

"Who the hell is your mistress?"

"Another piece of information that will come in good time," Sakkara said, again with a slight smile. Her expression faltered and she looked sad, remorseful. "I'm so sorry. For everything. If I'd known... but you must understand, I thought I was protecting him. That's what mothers do, isn't it?" She looked at Jade beseechingly, her hand outstretched as though she wanted Jade to take it.

"I don't know what you're talking about and it's creeping me out," Jade said bluntly, taking another step back.

Sakkara's hand fell back to her side and she sighed softly. "No, I suppose you don't. You don't remember who you are."

"Of course I do. I'm me," Jade said simply.

Sakkara looked like she felt sorry for Jade and it scared her. "Perhaps now with Lily back, and the two of you separate again, you'll remember."

Jade's stomach rolled over. "I don't know what you mean."

"You've been here before. The Preserve. The lake."

Jade kept shaking her head even though she felt it was true. She wanted to disagree with everything Sakkara said. "No."

"The Coven," Sakkara continued.

"No," Jade repeated. "I'm the first witch born outside the Coven. I'm different."

"You are different. I made you different. We made you different. But you were not born outside the Coven."

Jade could feel her power swirling inside her gut. It roiled and rolled, twisting and turning her insides about. "Yes, I was. I had a mother and a father and they were shitty parents, but they were ours, Lily's and mine. And we grew up away from here. We didn't have magic."

"You always had magic." Sakkara paused, as though considering. "Lily has it now too, but I think that is a side effect of being tangled with you for so long. In a sense, *she* is the first witch born outside a Coven. As a result of her association with you."

Jade stumbled backward. "I don't know what you're talking about. You're crazy. Or I am. You're dead! I'm talking to a dead woman. Through a dream." God, maybe she really was crazy. She'd feared that being the answer, but it seemed more real than the convoluted mess she was getting from Sakkara.

"You remember being here before. Even when you were dreaming of the lake, you remembered it. You've always feared water."

A sound caught her ear and Jade turned. Off to the side was a little girl, toddler-aged. She wandered the rocky shore, her fat feet giving her that unsteady, drunken toddler walk that kids have. She had light brown hair in a mess of thin curls and a round belly poking out from the gap between her pink shorts and yellow shirt.

The sight of her made Jade feel dizzy and sick.

"There you are. See, you're already remembering."

Jade turned and ran into the forest, her legs going as fast as she could make them.

CHAPTER FIFTEEN

Lily turned her head quickly to the closed door, behind which Dr. Gellar was with Jade.

"What?" asked Paris. "What is it?"

"Jade's dreaming. Of the Sparrow Lady again."

Paris regarded her carefully. "How do you know that?"

Lily paused. "It's like… I can hear it. I can hear it happening in Jade's brain."

The door to the room opened and Dr. Gellar came out along with some nurses who discretely made their exit. Dr. Gellar came over to stand next to Paris, eyeing Lily.

"Dr. Gellar, this is Lily, Jade's…" he trailed off, not sure what Lily was. She wasn't Jade's alter, she wasn't Jade's family member.

"I'm just Jade's," Lily piped up amiably. She held a hand out for Dr. Gellar to shake, which she did, her eyes trailing over Lily with curiosity.

Paris looked around for a moment, ensuring they were alone, and then said lowly, "I believe somehow Jade brought her to life, but I'm not sure how just yet."

Dr. Gellar's eyebrows went up and she looked at Lily again, who only shrugged. Dr. Gellar turned back to Paris. "I look forward to hearing all about it. And I'd probably like to run some tests." She addressed Lily. "Are you all right? Is there anything I need to know right now?"

Lily shook her head. "Nope. I'm still a little cold, but I feel fine. How's Jade?"

Paris was grateful for Lily's change of topic and waited anxiously for Dr. Gellar's report.

"Still unconscious." Gellar's eyes darted over to Paris and he nodded.

"Anything you have to say about Jade can be said in front of Lily. In fact, she may be able to assist you."

Lily nodded. "Yeah, if there's something I can do, let me know."

"Well, as I said, Jade is still unconscious. I'm not sure if you know, but Jade has adverse reactions to using too much magic and it looks like tonight, whatever she did, presumably bringing you to life, overtaxed her. In the past, she's not done herself any permanent damage and I hope she hasn't this time, but we won't know for sure until she wakes up. I think that when she uses too much magic, her pressure spikes, which causes her to bleed from her nose and ears. Now that she's unconscious, her pressure's dipped down again and is rather low, probably as a result of her body being in shock." Dr. Gellar regarded Lily again. "Are you a double of her? A complete double?"

Lily blinked. "I think so?" she replied. "Did you want to run some tests to see?"

"Would you be amenable to that?" Dr. Gellar asked, her tone surprised. Paris knew how she felt. Jade was quite averse to medical attention and getting her to agree to tests was akin to pulling teeth.

Lily shrugged. "If you think it would help Jade, then sure."

With one more look to Paris, Dr. Gellar ushered Lily into the small medical room where Jade was. Paris craned his neck but only got a glimpse of Jade, her eyes closed and skin pale, before the door shut again.

"Okay, that's really creepy," Paris heard from behind him and turned to see Callie standing there. She still looked slightly sleep mussed and in disarray, but she was wide awake. "Obviously, asking at the lake was a bad time, but now that I'm here, why does it look like there are two of Jade?"

Paris directed her to the sofa, where Callie took up a perch, and he told her the bare minimum of what he knew - somehow, Jade had conjured Lily into being, but he wasn't sure how or why. Nor was he sure who Lily was. Callie bombarded Paris with a hundred questions for which he had no answers. How, why, why now, why the lake, what kind of magic was this, where did Lily come from, why did she look like Jade?

"I don't know," he kept repeating, tiredly, although, there were bits and pieces coming together in his mind and he was starting to have some suspicions. "Did you find anything else out by the lake?"

Callie shook her head. "No. Josef still has some witches out there, but we didn't find anything. But back to Jade. She's all right?"

Paris turned and looked at the closed door again. "I believe so. I haven't had a chance to go in and see her myself yet."

Callie rested her hand on top of his, giving it a squeeze. "I'm sure she's okay. Would you like me to go check on Bruce again?"

"I think she'd like that, when she wakes up. To know that someone looked in on him."

"I can do that. I'll even filch him some goodies from the fridge. Or maybe buy him a latte on my way over. I think the coffee shop should be opening up about now."

"Let me know how he's doing, please," Paris asked. Callie squeezed his hand again before standing. "Callie, did Josef come back with you?"

Callie nodded. "Yeah, I think he's down in Counter-Magic starting some paperwork and he's got about as many questions for you as I had."

"Thank you."

With the thoughts percolating in his mind, Paris supposed he should go down to Counter-Magic to see Josef right away, but he wanted to check some details first. He was certain Dr. Gellar would inform him immediately if there was any change, but he was still loathe to leave medlab. However, if he could answer some questions for and about Jade, it would serve her better than him sitting around waiting for her to wake up. He sent a quick email explaining his absence to Dr. Gellar, knowing she would likely check it once she realized he was gone.

The Coven was dark and quiet at this time of night. Or morning, Paris supposed it was now. He didn't expect to see anyone on the way to his office and he wasn't mistaken - the halls were empty. Sitting down at his desk, he logged into his computer, his fingers hovering over his keyboard for a moment, unsure. If his suspicions were correct, there would be no going back. He only delayed a minute longer before opening up the search tool for the Coven archives and entering in the keyword search terms - drowning, lake, Preserve, child.

It wasn't as though there were any other incidents of a child drowning in the Preserve, so Paris wasn't surprised when he got the results he wanted immediately. The archives confirmed what Paris recalled - it had been Josef's niece, four years old, death by accidental drowning. After that, the lake had a tainted energy about it - one that the Counter-Magic department at the time had been unable to do anything about. Coven members began avoiding the area. A formal investigation had been conducted that indicated no negligence on the part of the mother, Joseph's sister. However, the child's mother had fallen ill shortly thereafter, unable to stop blaming herself for not watching well enough over her daughter. The little girl had simply wandered away and fallen in, drowned before anyone noticed she was missing.

Paris wasn't sure how it was possible, but he was certain Jade was that same little girl.

The first time he'd taken Jade close to the lake, she'd had a strongly adverse reaction, which hadn't been all that unusual - many witches still disliked the lake area. But Jade had also admitted at the time that she struggled with her water powers. Paris had tried to get Jade to work on her water magic that day, and she'd spoken of it strangely.

"When I think about water, it's like… it's waiting for me, like it knows things about me. Sometimes… sometimes I think it wants me to belong to it."

It had been odd, but Jade had a different way of looking at magic, not having grown up in a Coven. Paris attributed her statements to her different point of view. But now, coupled with what Lily told him, he realized he'd been mistaken. Lily had said when Jade first 'arrived,' she'd seemed younger than Lily, smaller, and Lily herself had been six. A four-year old would definitely seem younger and smaller to Lily at that age. Jade hadn't remembered where she'd come from. A traumatic incident, like drowning, could have caused a memory block. Then, when Lily had asked her name, all she'd gotten from Jade was the letter 'J.' Paris had one more question he needed answered; an answer that wasn't in the archives. He picked up his desk phone and called down to Josef's office. He answered on the first ring.

"Just the person I was hoping to talk to," Josef said immediately. "I've got a lot of questions about what happened at the lake."

"I'm sure you do. Could you come to my office? I have one for you as well."

While Paris waited for Josef to come up, he wondered how he should phrase his question and by the time Josef arrived, Paris decided he would simply go for simplicity.

Josef knocked once before coming in and then took a seat in one of the chairs in front of Paris' desk. "So, did my old eyes deceive me tonight or do we now have two witches who look exactly like Jade?"

"Your eyes are correct. The second woman's name is Lily and she and Jade are interconnected. I'm starting to figure out how and why, although I fear it may lead to more questions than answers. I have a sensitive question for you."

"Ask away."

"Your niece, who died. If I remember correctly, she was your namesake?"

Josef had a sad smile on his face. "That's correct. Her name was Josefina."

\#

Jade was lost. She shouldn't be so scared or worried. She was only dreaming, but the feeling of being lost ate at her gut, making it rumble and roil. What if there was some other kind of hinky mojo happening? What if being lost in the dream meant she could never get out? She'd been in this part of the Preserve before and there should be pathways, but they were gone - overgrown and covered up. Or maybe they had never existed here in her dreams; Jade didn't know.

Every way she tried to go, every time she tried a new direction, she always ended up back at the lake. Jade crashed through the underbrush to find herself there again, with Sakkara standing calmly on the dock, looking at her expectantly. Waiting as though she had all the time in the world. The bright, sunny day had gone grey and ghastly, a chill seeping into Jade's skin and bones, settling down in her marrow and making itself at home.

"What do you want from me?" Jade shouted at Sakkara when she came out of the woods for the umpteenth time and found herself still at the lake.

"I told you, a favor."

"For you and your…" What was it Sakkara had said? "Your mistress. So, someone's pulling your strings."

Sakkara sighed. "My strings are quite tangled, yes."

"And you think I'll do you this favor why? Because you're Paris' mom? Because you say I'm part of your Coven?"

"Yes," Sakkara answered simply.

"Fuck you," Jade responded, hands falling to her side in defeat. She was a thousand percent done. She just wanted to wake up. Why wasn't she waking up? God, maybe she totally fried her brain. "Your Coven sucks. They don't like me. They're pretty elitist about me not being born there and now they're pissed their magic matches mine."

"They'll come around once they find out who you were. Who you are."

"I don't care."

"If you won't do it for them, then perhaps you'll do it for my son. For Paris."

Jade shrugged. "So he's Coven leader," she bluffed. "So what?"

"I think you harbor some affection for my son. I'm counting on it. I've been counting on it for years."

"You're seriously still creeping me out. I want to wake up."

"I can't let you do that. Not until you've agreed."

"You're keeping me here," Jade realized. "You're keeping me asleep."

"Yes."

"How?" Jade asked, eyes narrowing.

"The dream hex I cast on you is still in effect. You may not be in your bed any longer, but you're still under the spell. You can't wake up until I allow it."

The number one way to get Jade to do something was to imply that she would not be allowed to do it. Jade narrowed her eyes at Sakkara's words. "You won't 'allow' me," she repeated.

Sakkara shook her head. "I'm sorry."

Jade ran through a quick recap of what she knew. Paris' dead mom, not so dead. She needed a favor. She was keeping Jade asleep until Jade agreed. If Jade agreed just for the sake of getting let out, would she somehow be bound by the promise? Would this be like a demon deal? The thought that she might trap herself by agreeing, if only to escape, kept her from lying her way out of the situation. Jade thought about what she knew about Sakkara. In the Coven, she was spoken of reverently - a great leader, a wonderful woman. Jade had read her demon grimoires and thought about the magic contained within them. Powerful and elegant. Could Jade magic her way out of this? At best, all Jade usually had was brute force and while it worked with Dex, he'd been a little on the 'crazy' side, and that had worked in Jade's favor. Sakkara didn't strike Jade as unbalanced. Maybe she was crazier than a rucksack of angry cats, but Jade couldn't be sure. Sakkara was powerful, but she mentioned that it took her time to break Jade's demon locks. She didn't have quite as good of a memory as Jade herself and couldn't remember all the spells in her own grimoires. Jade might be able to best her simply because she could remember more demon magic.

Jade felt a tugging at her brain, like a string, just inside her head being plucked and vibrating.

Lily. Lily was still there. Different from before, but still present. Sakkara had said Lily was separate now, and the truth of that statement resonated with Jade. But, Jade could still feel Lily peripherally. Lily wasn't in Jade's head, not like she had been before, but Jade could sense her, hovering around the perimeter. Jade focused on that sensation. It was the same feeling she'd always gotten from Lily - a sense of calmness and safety. Like being a small bird tucked under a larger bird's wing.

Did Jade even need to use magic against Sakkara? Or could she use her connection to Lily?

Lily, Jade thought, trying to send the thought outwards, imagining it traveling with her intent to where Lily was. *Pull me out, wake me up*.

"What are you doing?" Sakkara asked. Her eyes sharpened, the bright blue of them (so like Paris' eyes) clear and piercing.

Jade took a step backward from the lake, into the forest, still thinking about Lily. *Wake me up, Lily.* Jade could feel the moment Lily's consciousness focused in on hers. She had been searching too, looking for Jade. Like two magnets put close enough together, they snapped into place. Jade felt her consciousness press up against Lily's. She was feeling double, like seeing double. Jade could see the lake and Sakkara in front of her, but also, if she concentrated, she could see the inside of a medlab room and... Paris, like she was looking through a filmy overlay. Paris said something to Lily and Lily answered him; Lily's words clear in Jade's mind. *I've almost got her.*

"Jade," Sakkara said, moving forward. "This is exactly why you're perfect for this favor, why she wants you to do it, *needs you* to do it. The things you can do, things like this... But I need you to agree. Please. Don't go just yet. Just... agree." Her voice was tight and somewhat frantic.

Jade took another step back.

"I will come back," Sakkara said sharply. "I may not have the dream hex, but I won't need such a powerful spell this time. You've already gone to the lake and separated from Lily. I just need you to agree. I'll keeping coming back."

"You can try," Jade said, taking another step backward.

Lily, Lily, come get me.

It was like being tugged softly at first, and then yanked hard. Like breaking the packaging on a cardboard envelope, she felt a sharp, strong pull, ripping through her brain with a tearing sound.

Then Jade was awake. Lying in medlab on a bed, squinting at the lights.

In front of her, leaning over her, for the first time ever in person, was Lily.

#

When Josef confirmed his niece's name, Paris wasn't sure if he felt victorious, feeling like he'd solved part of the puzzle, or if he was more confused than before. Josef had, of course, asked why Paris wanted to know. Paris wanted to tell him his suspicions, but at the same time, didn't want to say anything until he'd had a chance to discuss it with Jade. And Lily, he supposed. They were two of a kind now and even though Paris would like to speak to Jade privately, he doubted that would be possible.

Paris had indicated he was only certain at this point that Josef's niece's drowning and the lingering magical taint was somehow tied to the incident at the lake. Josef had questions himself as to what happened, who was involved and what sort of magical response from Counter-Magic Paris would be comfortable with at the moment. Now that Josef had finally been out at the lake, he'd found Paris' mother's old wards destroyed and was adding that to his list of concerns about the area. Paris wished he had more answers for him and let him know he was hopeful once Jade awoke, they could and would sort everything out.

Paris asked if Josef thought he could reset some wards at the lake, to try to contain any lingering magic, but Josef gave him another surprise.

"That's another thing I wanted to tell you," said Josef. "I don't get a linger sense 'wrong' or 'bad' from the area now. No one does."

Paris frowned. "Are you certain? No one feels anything?"

Josef shook his head. "I've had six Counter-Magic agents out there and I'm going to be calling in a random sample of witches today to do some testing. Well, I guess it's not exactly random. I'm calling in the people that have previously been extra-sensitive to the area. But so far, I don't sense anything anymore and neither do my agents."

Paris wondered if what Jade had done tonight, with the creation of Lily, and the resultant power surge, had finally burned out the lingering tinge of the area. Or was it more tied to Jade herself, having gone back to the area.

More questions.

Paris thanked Josef and let him know he'd be in touch when Jade was awake and up for some questions. Not wanting to sit in his office and ruminate, he headed back to medlab. As he walked through he hallways, he saw the Covenstead was slowly coming alive. It was still early morning, but the early birds were arriving to their jobs - those that preferred getting up and having their workday start at six o'clock were filtering in, coffee or other beverages in hand. He saw a few surprised faces as he walked back to the medlab. Paris was an early starter, but not as early as these rare folks.

Medlab was quiet when he arrived. The door to Jade's room was closed and Lily wasn't in the sitting area. Paris didn't see Dr. Gellar around and wondered if he should take a chance and peek in on Jade. He crossed to the door and knocked softly, his knuckles barely making a sound on the door. It opened rather quickly and Paris had to do a quick check on eye-color when he saw Jade's face.

Green eyes. Lily, then.

"Oh, hey, come in," she said, keeping her voice low. "She's still sleeping, but Gellar says everything seems okay."

As Paris came in the room, he was hit with a sense of low-level magic around Jade. It was the same magic he'd felt around her at the lake and he was confused.

"Did someone come by and cast a sleeping charm on her? To help her rest?"

Lily frowned and shook her head. "No, I mean, I don't think so. Gellar said she was sleeping, but didn't make a comment that they were making her or keeping her asleep. Why?"

Paris stepped closer to the bed. Jade's face was pale. Her hair should have been tangled from her fall into the lake and subsequent rescue, but it was nicely combed around her face. He spied a brush on the nightstand and assumed that Lily must have done it for her, as though Jade were some kind of maiden in a fairy tale.

Paris leaned over Jade, seeing her eyes flicker back and forth, dreaming. "There's definitely some kind of magic around her." He pushed his own magic out at it and was surprised when something lashed back at him - whip-quick and stinging, slapping his magic away. It was neither Jade's nor Lily's magic, but he recognized it - the same licorice tinged magic that had been surfacing around Jade lately.

Lily went to the other side of the bed and leaned over Jade as well. "How can you tell?" she asked and then her own eyes moved back and forth, like she was reviewing something in her mind. "Oh, I can feel it now." She looked up at Paris. "Jade knows how to poke stuff with her magic. I copied what she does. I guess that means I have magic too?"

Paris nodded. "Yes, I've felt your magic. Different from Jade's, but definitely there."

"It's not me, is it? I mean, I don't know how it could be, but I'm new to all this, so...."

Paris shook his head. "No, it's not you. I think it's your Sparrow Lady. The woman you say you see in the dreams. It feels the same as the magic I felt at Jade's, taking apart her demon locks, and then again when she was sleepwalking."

Lily's lips thinned. "Fucking Sparrow Lady." She sounded exactly like Jade and Paris wasn't sure why he was surprised, but he was. "What does she want?" The tone of Lily's voice suggested she was talking more to herself than to Paris. "You think the Sparrow Lady is keeping Jade asleep?"

"Yes. Of course, Jade was quite taxed after what happened at the lake. As near as I can figure, she conjured you a body. That's... I don't know anyone who's ever done anything that big before. I've read of it, but only in conjunction with blood or demon magic. There was a hex at Jade's cottage, under her bed and now, I can feel magic around her and-"

"And it's keeping her asleep," Lily interrupted, her voice a little far away. She looked down at Jade. "I think… It's like I can get a sense of her."

"Can you contact her?" Paris asked, intrigued. "If you can, we may be able to help her wake up, assist her or perhaps have her perform some kind of counter-hex from inside."

Lily leaned further over Jade, appearing to study her, but Paris got the feeling her mind was far deeper than just the surface.

"She wants me to pull her out," Lily said. "She knows she's dreaming." Lily blinked furiously, her eyes flickering back and forth. "She's dreaming about the lake and the Sparrow Lady is there."

"You can see this?"

"Yes." Lily tilted her head. "She's calling for me. She wants me to pull her out."

"Can you? Pull her out?" Paris asked.

"I think so." Lily nodded, going closer, bending over Jade further, her forehead almost touching Jade's. "I can almost get her," she whispered.

Paris could feel the moment Lily used her magic, intentionally, for the first time. He was overwhelmed by the singular mindset of it - Jade never had such clarity or pristine control over her magic. Lily's wasn't as strong as Jade's, but what she lacked in brute force, she made up for in perfect precision. Paris could feel Lily reach through the hex and *pull* on Jade. The scent of grapefruit and cinnamon wafted through the air.

"I've got her," Lily said, her voice quiet but strong. Paris felt another strong pull of Lily's magic, directed at Jade, and he felt a responding pull back, along with the scent of cloves and flowers.

Jade's eyes blinked open and Paris felt a sense of profound relief at seeing their clear grey color - so different from Lily's. He'd been half afraid Jade would open her eyes and they'd be yet another color - not that he'd know what it meant - only that it would somehow mean he didn't have Jade back. Not that she was his to have or not to have, only that he'd somehow be missing something if they hadn't been grey.

Jade's eyes were solely fixed on Lily and Lily looked down at her beatifically and smiled.

"Hi."

Paris wasn't sure what he thought Jade would do - smile back, or perhaps say something clever or teasing. He was completely unprepared for her entire face to crumble and for her to start crying.

"Oh, it's okay," Lily said easily, smoothing Jade's hair back, like a mother or a big sister would.

"I'm sorry, I'm so sorry, I didn't know, I didn't mean to," Jade babbled.

Paris took a step toward the door, wondering if he should make a discreet exit. The rational part of his brain said that yes, he should give the two women some time they obviously needed. But the not-so-rational part of his brain wanted to stay and talk to Jade himself to ensure that she was still *her* and that nothing about her had changed.

"No, no, I know. I know," Lily repeated. Paris wondered what they were referring to. It was clearly something they both immediately knew of without having to exchange any other words. "I never should have asked. You don't have to be sorry, I'm the one who's sorry."

Lily's words didn't seem to mollify Jade who continued to cry even as Lily soothed and shushed her. Paris took one more step toward the door, but Lily looked up and shook her head quickly and mouthed the words, 'it'll be fine in a minute.' He envied her in that moment. She seemed so sure that Jade would be better in a moment.

Paris guessed if anyone would know, it would be Lily. They'd been sharing a body for … well, years.

True to her word, in another minute or so, Jade calmed down - her crying shifting to the hitching breathing and stuttering breaths that often come after a hard jag - like a small child who has exhausted itself. Lily smiled at Jade again, tucking Jade's hair behind her ears and Paris recalled what Lily had said before, outside in the waiting area. Jade had been younger than Lily when she arrived. Lily herself had been around six, but Jade had felt younger. Josefina had been just shy of her fourth birthday when she drowned. That would mean that Jade, who Paris was certain was somehow Josefina, was actually at least two years younger than Lily's records would indicate she was. Suddenly viewing Jade as the younger, more child-like sibling, put a lot of her behavior into perspective for Paris. If Lily had always taken the role of elder sibling, of caregiver and protector, and if they had always been so intertwined, then Jade on her own would have been much like a child abandoned. Paris knew Jade had felt insecure when she came to the Coven, but now, framing it with his new knowledge of her, he realized how difficult things must have seemed to her.

"Okay?" Lily asked Jade and Jade nodded.

Jade finally looked over at Paris, her eyes rimmed red and her face all blotchy. "So you've met the person that used to share my brain," she said, tipping her head toward Lily.

Paris smiled at her wobbly tone, trying so hard to be light. "Yes, we've met."

Jade nodded. "I'm feeling a lot less crazy about the whole thing now that there's a person standing in front of me."

"Me too," Lily agreed. She and Jade shared some kind of look Paris couldn't decipher. He almost got the feeling they were having a conversation without saying anything.

"The Sparrow Lady," Jade said suddenly to Lily and Paris felt like his thoughts were confirmed.

"Can you hear each other thinking?" he asked.

They both turned to him and at the same time said, "Yes."

He blinked at their unity, about to ask something else when Lily turned her head sharply toward Jade.

"Are you kidding me?" Lily exclaimed, clearly to something Jade had 'said' mentally.

Jade's eyes darted over to Paris and then back to Lily and Paris knew he was missing something important, something Jade wasn't saying aloud on purpose.

"Why don't I give you two some time?" Paris said. He came closer to the bed, his hand hovering for a moment before coming down to rest lightly on Jade's arm. Lily seemed amused by the whole thing and stayed silent, even as Jade's eyes went to where Paris' hand touched her arm lightly.

"I'm glad you're all right. We'll get everything sorted out."

"Thanks," Jade murmured, her voice quiet.

Paris nodded at Lily, who gave him a perfect replica of a nod back, smiling as she did, as though she were teasing him.

It probably didn't bode well that he now had two new witches to contend with.

#

Jade couldn't stop staring at Lily. It was everything she'd ever wanted over the last few years. Lily, smiling in front of her. She'd been afraid upon waking up that she'd been mistaken - that maybe Lily wasn't there, that it wasn't real. Maybe she would wake up and find only Paris and possibly Dr. Gellar, and they'd tell her she was crazy and taking a trip to the institution, where they kept witches in her state. But now... Jade took a deep breath and focused on Lily's calm, easy expression.

We're creepers.

Creeping on each other.

Jade could hear Lily thinking and answered her mentally in return. It was just like before, when they used to 'talk,' only now, she could look at Lily while they did it. Jade thought of the Sparrow Lady and her identity; a thought she had just shared with Lily only moments before. Again, Lily's response was incredulous.

Paris' mother is the Sparrow Lady? Jade could feel Lily's disbelief and confusion, rolling over her like waves.

Yes. And she wants a favor.

Lily put a hand up to her head. "Ugh, this is actually getting confusing in here. It's like I have my thoughts and your thoughts and then my feelings and your feelings and they're jockeying for position. Out loud might be easier." She made a flapping motion with her hands. "Scoot over."

Jade slid over on the bed with jerky motions, making room for Lily. Her body felt stiff and sore and she had a headache at the back of her skull, one that throbbed in time with her heartbeat. It wasn't too bad until she moved her head, and then it would spike for a moment and before receding. She didn't want to mention it in case Lily would leave to bring Dr. Gellar back.

"I'm not going to rat you out to the doctor," Lily groused, sliding into bed beside Jade. "I don't like them either. Too many memories." She hip-checked Jade with her own hip and Jade wiggled over a bit more. They finally both settled, each one on their side, facing each other. A wave of affection rushed over Jade. She never thought she'd see Lily again. Jade didn't know what had happened to her when she left, when....

"Let's not talk about that," Lily interrupted. "We can't do anything about it now. It's over and done."

"Usually I'm the one that does that with things. Put them away. You usually want to talk about them."

Lily shrugged one shoulder. "Maybe you can teach a dog new tricks. Or maybe we've finally found something I don't want to talk about."

Jade looked away, another memory crawling into her brain, unbidden.

"Do you want to talk about that one?" Lily asked quietly, knowing which memory was flitting through Jade's brain.

"No," Jade said quickly. "We agreed. There are things we don't talk about."

Lily sighed. "You stated. I agreed." *Fine, fine,* she added silently, mentally holding her hands up in a gesture of surrender before changing to speaking aloud again. "Okay, Sparrow Lady. Paris' mother? As in his dead mother?"

"Not so dead as it turns out," Jade replied and she could feel suspicion about Sakkara and about Paris roll off Lily. "Paris doesn't know," Jade added.

"You're sure?"

"Yes." Jade was sure. Absolutely.

"Wow, I'm out of it for a few years and suddenly you're the trusting type. Who knew? Or maybe it's just for certain English men who run Covens and not everyone?" Lily poked Jade's shoulder with a finger, teasingly and Jade felt her cheeks blush.

"Stop it. We've got problems."

"All right, all right. So what does creepy Sakkara want? And what's with the birds? It's weird."

"It's not like I got a chance to ask her about the birds," Jade said dryly. "As for what she wants, I don't know. Some kind of favor. Which can't be good. People who pretend to be dead don't need normal favors like watching their house while their on vacation or watering their plants. She was going to keep me asleep until I said yes, but then-"

"I pulled you out," finished Lily. "I could feel you reaching for me and Paris said you were being kept asleep by magic. I can remember a lot of the stuff you've learned about magic. It's all-" Lily made a swirly motion with her fingers, "in there, but I don't know what I know until I stop to think about it. If that makes sense."

Jade could feel what Lily meant. It was as though she had a special window into Lily's brain, giving her access to thoughts and feelings and letting her own brain process them in a slightly different way. But she had to focus on it - it wasn't just there, Jade had to actively search it out and then work at processing the information.

"Yeah, that's totally it," agreed Lily. "It's like I have a dial-in to your brain, but I can turn it down or off if I want to."

"Sakkara said something about that. That she needed me, or us, I guess, because of what we can do. Because we can be in two places at once. She also said she's been hanging around my dreams because she needed me to go to the lake so this,"

Jade gestured between the two of them, "could happen. So that I could conjure you a body."

"Which makes you wonder, how did she know about us in the first place," Lily finished.

"Exactly. I don't like that she wants me, us, for some kind of chore or favour and it seems she's not above emotional manipulation to do it," Jade said, letting the memory of her conversation with Sakkara wash over Lily's brain, feeling when Lily had absorbed the information. "But it's weird that she knew it was even a possibility."

Lily nodded. "Yeah, like… she would have had to know about the two of us before."

"And she said," Jade began and then stopped, swallowing. She felt Lily's mind reach into her own and pluck out the next words.

"She said you used to belong to the Coven. Long ago. When you were little." Lily paused, thinking about that. "Before you came to me. You used to be part of the Coven."

Jade shrugged. "She could have been lying."

"She could have. But I don't think so, and neither do you. Not really. You saw a little girl in the lake. Before you dived in, that's what you saw in the water."

Jade nodded, looking down at the blankets and running her fingers over the threads.

"You saw her again, with Sakkara," Lily continued, Jade still feeling her brain brushing against her own, like fingers trailing lightly over a surface, leaving no imprints behind. It wasn't unpleasant - just a light touch, a feather against her grey matter. "A little girl, playing by the lake."

Jade's fingers clenched. "She could have made me see those things. It could have been more witchcraft."

"Yeah, but it wasn't," Lily said and Jade could feel the certainty that lay behind the words. She could feel the truth of them in her stomach. "You've always been afraid of water, just like you've never wanted to think about where you were before you were with me."

"I just…" Jade shrugged. "It makes me feel sick to think of it. I don't like it." Gooseflesh pebbled up on her arms.

"I don't know what happened, or how it happened. But somehow, I think you died. Your body died. But your spirit? Soul? Magic? Whatever you want to call it, found me."

Jade swallowed hard. *Found you and co-opted your body, your life, your everything. And then took it all when-.*

"No, it wasn't like that. I never felt that way," Lily said.

"Maybe you should have."

"Maybe. But I didn't. I don't." Lily took a breath, shifting on the bed and Jade realized that her neck was kinking up as they were talking and Lily's probably was too. "But, we've got other cats to whip."

"Ugh, I hate that expression."

Lily shrugged. "I know, but it's French. I love how ridiculous it is." Lily picked up a piece of Jade's hair and toyed with it, wrapping it around one of her fingers. "Sakkara," Lily began. "She's going to come back, isn't she?"

Jade nodded. "Yep. It's not like she'd do all this and then just stop because I said no."

"Are we going to tell Paris his much beloved dead mother isn't so dead?"

Jade sighed. "I don't see how we can not tell him. Or how I can not tell him."

"If you wanted to keep it a secret, I could. I would. I don't have to tell him."

It felt weird having Lily defer to her. That wasn't how it worked. Or at least, that's not how Jade preferred it to work.

Lily poked her in the shoulder again. "It's how it works now. You've been here longer than me. You know these people."

"You know everything I know."

Lily wrinkled her nose, making a face. "Yeah, but it's not the same. These people are 'your people.'"

This time Jade made a face. "Ew, that sounds like… I'm a tribal priestess or something. My people," Jade repeated almost comically. "Besides, most of them are definitely not 'my people.' I don't…" she paused, feeling embarrassed. "They don't really like me."

"They don't know you," Lily asserted. "And they're used to witches always being born in the Coven. Which you were. It's just that no one knew."

"Yeah, but I don't want to, like, advertise that." It would be like forcing her way in to what felt like an elite club. 'Oh, by the way, you can't dislike me anymore. I'm actually a full-fledged member of your Coven. Take that, haters.'

Lily laughed. "I can feel the distaste rolling off you. They can't all be that bad."

Jade thought of Callie, Henri, Josef, Daniel. Paris. "No. Not all of them."

Lily smiled knowingly. "I'm glad you have friends. Even if everyone else is a jerk, you have them. But, if you don't want to tell anyone about your past, I won't tell them either."

"I have to tell Paris about his mom. That's not something I want to keep from him. Even if…"

"Even if it probably breaks his heart. It's not going to be easy, finding out his mom has been lying about being dead. Kind of a biggie."

"Yeah," Jade said ruefully. It was so relaxing to talk to Lily. She didn't have to explain. She could just start a thought and let Lily finish it. "Then I have to tack on that not only is she not dead, she's the one who's been screwing with my head and wants a favor."

Sakkara was still out there somewhere as well, waiting for Jade to fall asleep again, presumably, or maybe once the cat was out of the bag, she'd just show up.

"I've got to tell Paris," Jade repeated. "Because if she just shows up here, and he finds out that way…" Jade shook her head. "That would really suck for him." Jade felt the flash of a dirty thought flit through Lily's brain having to do with Paris and Jade's choice of words.

"Oh my God, this is serious!"

"I'm totally being serious," Lily said, with a perfectly poised face. "This is our serious face. You should recognize it."

"I don't think of him that way."

"You know that saying 'you can lie to the world but you can't lie to yourself'? I'm as close to 'you' as a person can be. You can't lie to me."

"It isn't like that."

"It's exactly like that, it's just that you've shut down that part of your life ever since-"

"One of the things we don't discuss," Jade said hotly, feeling anxiety and avoidance flood through her body.

Lily pursed her lips together. "Fine. But if the lake has taught you anything, it should be that things won't or can't stay buried forever."

"Maybe they can if people stop poking at them."

Lily poked her in the shoulder a third time. "You know why I poke. I poke because I care."

Jade took a long, deep breath and let it out slowly. "I know."

A ruckus outside the door had them both turning their heads, Jade having to look over her shoulder to see.

"What the hell is that?" Lily asked.

"I think-" Jade started, only to be interrupted when there was a quick knock and then the door was pushed open a smidgen. It was then thrust open all the way and Bruce came darting into the room, leaping up onto the foot of the bed surprisingly well for his size.

"Bruce!" Jade exclaimed and Lily laughed. Bruce seemed torn between the two women momentarily, sniffing Jade, then Lily and then Jade again, before he wormed his way in between the two of them and collapsed dramatically, resting his snout on Jade's leg and exhaling loudly.

"I'm sorry, I've no idea how he got here," said Paris from the doorway. "But he burst into medlab and went immediately for the door and started pawing at it."

"It's okay," Jade replied as she pet Bruce on the head and then let her fingers trail down, trying to find his scaly patch. She frowned, feeling the dry, cracked skin. Bruce tipped his head up and Jade examined the area. It didn't look as bad as it had before. It was no longer weeping and it seemed like it was starting to close up some.

"It's looking better," Paris said, coming closer.

"Yeah, it is," Jade agreed. Bruce's tail thumped against Lily's legs and Lily patted his belly soundly in return.

"He seems really happy to see you," Lily said.

"Us, he's happy to see us," Jade argued.

Bruce stared up at Jade, eyes blinking a few times and then he scooted forward, trying to bury his snout in Jade's armpit.

Lily laughed. "I'm pretty sure it's mostly you."

Even though Jade didn't know what Sakkara wanted or how far she would go to get it, looking down at Bruce, hearing Lily laugh, having Lily beside her, made her the happiest she'd been in a long time.

Her headache throbbed, sending an ice pick of pain through her skull. Her brain felt soft and tender with the pain poking at it relentlessly. She winced, feeling like the lights in the room were suddenly too bright. Bruce flicked his tongue at her and made a quiet whining noise.

"What is it?" asked Paris immediately, coming further into the room.

"Her head," Lily answered for Jade.

"I'll get Dr. Gellar."

Lily's fingers were cool against the back of Jade's neck, as she tried to dig into the tight muscles. "This isn't just a headache," Lily said. Bruce pushed his snout further under Jade's arm and she wondered if he'd showed up right before it happened because he knew it was coming.

"Do you have one too?" Jade asked Lily, shutting her eyes tight and trying to stretch out her neck, hoping it might help.

"No, but it's like… I'm getting this feeling like my brain is bruised and I think it's from you."

Jade took a deep breath and exhaled it slowly. "I think I might have fried something this time. With my magic," she admitted, afraid to say it out loud.

"Well, maybe they can fix it with magic," Lily replied.

Jade didn't think it worked that way, but didn't say so out loud. Of course, with Lily able to read her thoughts, she didn't have to. Which turned out to be a good thing not two seconds later when she needed to throw up and Lily got a little plastic tub thing from the nightstand before Jade vomited all over herself.

Gellar was there a minute later asking questions and taking measurements, but she blissfully dimmed the lights so they were no longer assaulting Jade's eyes. Gellar didn't make Lily leave the room and Jade noticed Paris was hovering by the door as well. After her examination, she looked at Jade grimly.

"I scrambled my noodle, didn't I?" Jade said, her own voice making her head pound more.

"I think this is the start of a migraine and it's going to get worse over the next couple of hours. How much worse, I'm not sure."

"Because of her magic?" Paris asked from the doorway.

Gellar nodded, face grim. "Most likely." She faced Jade again. "Do you want some pain meds now or can you bear it?"

"Oh, meds, bring all the meds," Lily said and Jade scowled at her. "What? They don't hand out medals for not taking pills, you know."

"Lily is correct, Jade," said Paris carefully from the doorway. "If you're suffering, you should take something for it."

"Okay," Jade managed. Gellar was gone and back again in moments, injecting something into Jade's arm.

"We'll have to keep an eye on this. This may only be temporary or it could continue. I don't know enough about how your magic affects you to know at this point."

Jade wanted to nod or say something, but she also just wanted to close her eyes and pull a blanket over her head.

"We'll keep an eye on it," Paris answered.

Jade finally decided there was no reason not to pull the blanket up over her head, feeling like she wanted to shut the world out. Bruce wiggled, getting more comfortable and then gently put his foot on her shoulder, almost as if to say, 'I'll just be here.'

Jade felt the bed move as Lily got off and then she heard the low sounds of Lily and Paris talking. It was so weird. Hearing her own voice, only at a slightly higher pitch, coming from outside her ears instead of inside it. She heard the door open and shut again and then the bed dipped as Lily climbed back in.

"He's going to come back when you're feeling better. He's got stuff to talk to you about."

"Is that the official British term for it," Jade whispered, afraid her own voice would be too loud for her headache. "Stuff."

Lily chuckled softly. "I think he said there were some things of great significance and relevance that he needed to discuss with you." Lily paused. "He likes you."

"I think he likes everyone."

Lily made a low sound of partial agreement and Jade didn't have it in her to argue or say anything more. She started feeling the painkillers kick in and everything went soft and fuzzy.

CHAPTER SIXTEEN

"Why are you so nervous?"

Jade didn't answer Lily as she struggled getting her tennis shoe on. She got more and more frustrated when she couldn't wiggle her foot in without undoing the laces. She pulled the shoe off her toes and onto her lap, fighting with the knotted lace. Her fingers were thick and clumsy, a side effect of the headache that had turned into a truly spectacular migraine that left her bedridden for all of yesterday. She was feeling better today, the migraine receding to a low-level ache in her head that was more akin to having muscle strain. It was a thousand times better than the vomit-inducing pain she'd had for most of yesterday, even on pain meds.

Lily gently took the shoe out of Jade's hands and deftly undid the knot, handing it back to Jade. Jade was finally getting sprung from medlab, although she was under Dr. Gellar's orders to return if her headache got worse or turned into a migraine again. With both her shoes finally on, Jade paused, sitting on the medlab bed. Lily sat down next to her and waited. After a minute, Lily tapped her elbow against Jade's.

"They're your friends. You know them. They know you."

"Well, clearly they didn't know everything about me," Jade mumbled, giving Lily a significant look.

"No one knows everything about everybody," Lily answered. "Except you and me." Lily slung an arm over Jade's shoulder. "It'll be fine. We'll just have a coffee with them and then we can head home to the cottage. I'm looking forward to it."

"Coffee with Callie and Henri or seeing the cottage?" Jade asked.

"Both. Either," Lily answered. She'd stayed in medlab with Jade and hadn't seen anything of the Coven yet. Paris had brought by a bag of some clothes and toiletries for them, letting the women know that Callie was the one that thoughtfully packed it - including hand cream, lip balm, some fuzzy socks, pairs of sensible underwear - all the things that men generally didn't consider when packing. Callie had also included two full changes of clothes - presumably one for Jade and one for Lily. Jade didn't want to lie to Callie or Henri, so that morning, after waking up with her migraine receding, she'd texted both of them and asked if they'd like to have coffee with both Jade and Lily. Jade didn't think she was ready to face the cafeteria - not with Lily and the stares they'd surely get, so Paris had graciously offered up his office.

For now, after a discussion with Lily while Jade had been asleep, Paris had released a statement that Jade had a sister, a twin, formerly estranged, who was now back in Jade's life. Yes, her twin also had magic. Yes, her twin would also learn to control her powers by performing Coven sanctioned magic. No, Paris didn't think there were anymore lost leaves of Jade's family tree.

Jade imagined it was causing quite a stir in the Coven. It was probably their worst nightmare come to life. Not only was Jade still around, now she was bringing family members with her.

Lily hit her with her elbow again.

"Hey," Jade protested. "I'm recovering here."

"You're brooding and it's loud." Lily motioned her fingers around her brain. "It'll be fine," she repeated. "I don't know why you're so nervous."

Unbidden, the things Jade was afraid to say out loud started spilling forth from her brain and she could feel Lily pick up each thought, including the horrendously selfish ones. *What if they don't like you? What if they like you better than they like me? What if it's all weird now and ...*

Lily's arm tightened around Jade's shoulders. "I'm not nervous. From what I've seen in your head, I'm not nervous at all." *They're your friends. That won't change.*

Jade wished she could be as relaxed and calm about it as Lily felt. "Let's just go."

Lily stood, slinging the overnight bag over her shoulder. They ended up looking at each other, Jade checking Lily's appearance and Lily doing the same for her. Lily reached up and tightened Jade's ponytail a bit, noting it was sagging some.

"I might cut my hair," Lily said as they walked out of the room.

"What? Why?" Jade asked, immediately grabbing her own ponytail, liking the long feeling of it as it ran through her hands.

Lily shrugged. "I don't know. It might be nice to try something different. Or maybe I'll color it."

You don't like how I do our hair?

"It's not that. It's just... I thought it might be fun to try something else."

The Coven hallways were moderately busy - mid-morning traffic as people were at work and moving from department to department, grabbing coffee, showing up late, going to meetings. Jade thought she was used to the looks and the head turning, but it was more pronounced now with people openly watching her and Lily. Lily smiled at everyone. Some people looked away quickly, but others hesitantly smiled back. Jade kept her expression neutral - neither smiling nor scowling, which she thought was a pretty impressive feat.

Finally at Paris' office (where his assistant Suki still wasn't at her desk), Jade knocked once and waited for Paris to invite them in.

Callie and Henri were already inside, seated in the Queen-Anne chairs in front of the fireplace. Two more chairs had been brought in, making a small semi-circle around the hearth. Callie and Henri were already sipping coffee, with two more large coffees sitting on the small table in the centre of the semi-circle. Paris made a 'please, go ahead' gesture and then moved to leave his office. As he walked by, his hand reached out, almost like he would touch Jade's shoulder, but then he pulled it back at the last moment. Before she even realized she was doing it, Jade tugged at the sleeve of his shirt, by his elbow.

"Hey. Thanks for this," she said quietly and then wanted to pull the lame words back out of the air.

"My pleasure." He smiled at her and Jade heard Lily snort in her head. *I bet there's more he wishes was his pleasure.*

Jade turned to Lily, glaring at her with wide eyes. *Stop it!*

What? He can't hear me.

Jade rolled her eyes, hoping the gesture hid her embarrassment, as Paris closed the door behind him. She looked over at Callie and Henri who were watching them both carefully. She and Lily walked over to them, in unison.

"We brought coffee," Callie said brightly. "We know how Jade takes hers, but didn't know how you... that is... there's cream and sugar for you." Callie finished, gesturing to the small table where a pile of creamers and packets of sugar sat.

"Thanks," Lily said easily, grabbing the coffee marked 'black' from the table, fixing it up before she sat down. "I take mine just like Jade. Double cream."

Callie nodded, her smile overly bright and tight. Jade looked over at Henri, who was examining the air around Lily's head, probably reading her aura. Jade felt her stomach roll over in nervousness, but then, Henri seemed to relax back in his chair.

"So," Henri said with a grin. "Which one of you is the evil twin?"

A laugh escaped Jade, fueled by her nerves and anxiety. It came out with a strange 'bleat' sound, kind of like a goat. That set Callie off, who let loose with her indelicate snort, which in turn caused Lily to guffaw. Henri stuck his hand out, holding it in front of Lily.

"I'm Henri."

Lily took his hand and shook it heartily. "Nice to meet you, Henri. I'm Lily."

Callie put her hand out next. "Callie. I'm really glad to meet you."

Lily took hers as well, shaking it with a smile. "Me too."

Jade felt her insides relax and unclench. This was going to work out.

#

After a whirlwind couple of days, Paris stood on Jade's doorstep knowing he had to tell her what he believed about her past. He was certain that Jade was Josef's niece - the little girl who drowned at the lake all those years ago. He worried about telling Jade for many reasons. He still didn't understand or know how it had all happened, only that it *had* happened. Somehow, Jade was Josefina - a young Coven member they believed had died. Her essence or soul had escaped and found a home with Lily, in Lily's body. Paris didn't know how Jade would react. Would she be angry? Sad? Would she believe him? He squared his shoulders and knocked soundly on the door, waiting. When it opened, in the fading light of the day, he couldn't tell who it was that answered - Lily or Jade?

"Oh, hey. Come on in. We're just hanging out doing magic."

Paris felt a surge of worry at the tone and also at the fact that he still couldn't tell whom he was addressing. He followed 'her' in, not sure who she was. She rested a hand on the banister and shouted up the stairs, "Jade! Your Englishman is here!"

Lily, then.

Paris took off his coat, hanging it up neatly, and then his shoes, placing them on the mat by the door. Jade came down the stairs, as always like a herd of elephants, Bruce hot on her heels, adding to the noise.

"Hey, we're hanging out doing magic," she said, a near replica of what Lily had told him.

"So I hear," he replied wryly. He caught the scent of Jade's magic, linden blossom and cloves, mixed in with Lily's, grapefruit and cinnamon. "Fire spells?" he guessed.

Jade smiled. "Yep."

"I'm not as good at fire as Jade is," Lily added as the three of them made their way to the kitchen.

"She's better at air," Jade said.

"You don't have to try to make me feel better about it," Lily said good-naturedly. "I'm not as powerful as you. I don't think I ever will be. I'm just... not the same. But I don't mind."

Given the look Jade gave Lily, Paris gathered it was Jade who minded, or was bothered by their differences. Lily didn't seem to be bothered by it.

Before he could lose his nerve, Paris spoke. "That might be tied to what I wanted to discuss with you. With Jade, rather."

Jade turned and looked at him. "You can say anything you want in front of Lily. I'll tell her anyway."

Paris glanced up at Lily and she must have seen the hesitation on his face. "You know," she said, "why don't I take Bruce for a walk in the Preserve? I can start collecting rocks. Jade's going to help me make my own rune collection," she added for Paris' benefit.

Jade frowned at her. "I want you to know whatever it is."

"And I will. But maybe you should take some time for yourself. We don't always have to share."

Jade looked confused at the statement and Lily darted forward quickly and gave her a hug. It was strange to see someone touch Jade without Jade flinching slightly or pulling back. Stranger still to see Jade hug Lily back, tightly and easily. Jade was more comfortable around Lily than Paris had ever seen her with anyone.

Lily headed back toward the front door, making a sort of 'kiss-kiss' sound to call Bruce. Bruce flicked his tongue at Jade, his customary 'pffffft' sound coming out low and soft before he trotted after Lily. Paris turned to look at Jade, whose eyes darted to the coffee pot and back to him again.

"You can start a pot if you'd like. If that would make you feel more comfortable." He knew, for Jade, the ritual of coffee was just as important as the beverage itself. He took a seat at the kitchen table and watched as she went through the familiar motions - emptying, rinsing, filling and then starting. When she was done, she hesitated before sitting down at the table as well.

"I've something I need to tell you," he began.

"Me too," she interrupted and he blinked in surprise. She'd just blurted it out and seemed as startled as him that she'd said anything. "I mean, there's something you should know."

"May it wait?" Paris asked. "This is quite important."

"My thing is really important too," Jade replied, squirming in her seat. "But, uh, you go first," she waved a hand. "We'll get whatever out of the way and then I'll tell you my thing."

Paris frowned. He didn't think that they'd just be able to brush past what he was going to say, but they'd cross that bridge when they got there.

He took a deep breath. "You know, of course, about the death at the lake, many years ago." Jade's shoulders stiffened slightly. She sat with her hands in her lap, under the table and he wished that she'd rested them on the table. He thought perhaps he would have liked to touch one as he spoke.

"Yeah, I know. Little girl."

"I believe that little girl was you."

She didn't say anything - didn't jump up and start denying it, didn't look askance at him, didn't even look shocked.

"You don't seem surprised."

"I'm... I don't know what I am." Jade looked down at her hands.

"Lily told me you saw a little girl, in the water, in your dream. Before you fell or jumped in."

"I didn't jump," Jade said quickly. "I was… compelled to? Not like magically compelled, but I felt I had to do it. I don't know why."

"Nor I. But I think you saw yourself, perhaps in a memory, perhaps as imagery in your dream, or perhaps as something more, I don't know. But you were that little girl."

"Yeah. But I don't know how it's possible."

"Nor I. But I believe it to be true. I'll help you figure out what happened, how it happened. We can and will figure it out."

Under the table, he felt one of her socked feet bump into his and then rest against his instep. It wasn't a huge or overt gesture, but it warmed him just the same.

"What-" she began and then paused to clear her throat. "What was her name? My name. Do you know?"

The kitchen was silent except for the spitting and hissing of the coffee pot. At her question, and emboldened by her foot resting against his, Paris reached down into her lap and took one of her hands. She held his loosely, letting him pick her hand up and cradle it between his palms and then rest it on the kitchen table.

"Her name, your name," Paris corrected, "is Josefina."

Jade's nose wrinkled slightly. "Like my boss at Counter-Magic?" He could almost see the wheels turning in her head. "Oh my God, Daniel… Daniel told me that girl that drowned was Josef's niece."

Paris nodded. "Yes."

"That's me? I'm... her?"

"Yes."

She took a slow, shuddering breath, blinking suddenly. Her hand was stiff and tense in his and he worried that she would pull it away and he would have to let her go. Instead, it felt as though she willed herself to relax, her joints slowly going soft. "Have you... have you told him?" She looked up at him, her eyes wide and clear - perfectly grey with a dark circle around the iris. Having looked at more Coven archives over the last couple of days, he could now see the resemblance to Josef's sister, her mother. But only in her eyes. The rest of her face was Lily's.

Paris shook his head. "No, I haven't told anyone. I wanted to talk to you first and find out what you'd like to do."

Jade looked down at their hands, hers held between his, and then toward the coffee pot. Her eyes went unfocused as she thought.

"I think," she began slowly, her words halting and carful, "that I'd like to tell Josef. If you think, I mean, that is, if you think he might-"

"I think he'd be quite pleased."

Jade shrugged. Although the gesture should have implied she didn't care one way or the either, Paris could tell that it mattered a great deal to her. "I guess. I mean, he might think it's weird or creepy."

"I think he'll be happy to know his niece is alive," Paris said. "And that it's you. I think he's fond of you anyway."

Jade looked over at Paris, somewhat shyly. "Yeah?" she asked, like she couldn't trust his words completely.

"Yes."

Jade nodded and took a deep breath. "Okay, then I'd like to tell Josef. But, not the rest of the Coven."

"All right," he readily agreed. "May I ask why?" He couldn't say he was surprised at her decision, but he was curious to know her reasons.

"I know that I'm not the most liked person here and that I'm, like, odd witch out, or whatever. Maybe if people knew who I used to be, that might change. But, I'm not that person. Or I guess, I'm not the same person I would have been if I grew up here. I'm still the same person they've been wary of and kind of shady to and I don't think I want that to change because they suddenly think they know me." Jade paused, looking down at their hands again. The skin between her knuckles was smooth and soft - softer than he thought it would be since she didn't seem like the type who cared about keeping her hands safe or well kept. He ran his thumb over the space between her second and third knuckle. "They don't know me," she continued. "I don't want them to feel like they do just because they maybe knew who I was when I was four." She looked back up at him. "Does that make sense?"

It was his turn to nod, slightly touched by the raw honesty in her answer. "I will abide by your wishes."

She smiled. "That sounds like the closing line of historical letters. Next you'll be saying you remain my most humble and obedient servant," she teased.

Paris smiled back, feeling his lips curve up. "That too."

Jade fidgeted again and Paris could feel the tension come back into her hand, her joints going stiff with it. He waited for her to speak, sensing that she was gathering her words.

"Are you... Do you understand why I didn't tell you?"

"About Lily?" he asked and she nodded, again casting her eyes away from his.

"I thought about telling you. Maybe it would have changed the way it all turned out. Maybe not. I don't know. But I... no one had ever known. And I thought... I mean I didn't know what to say. I was scared and..." Her eyes went glassy with moisture and she blinked furiously.

"I understand," he said, even as he wondered if it was true. He supposed it was true. He understood why she didn't confide in him, but at the same time, he wished she had. He wished she had felt comfortable enough, safe enough, to come to him with the truth. Whatever she thought it had been at the time. He gave her hand a soft squeeze and she smiled at him - quick and easy. "Would you like to be there when I speak with Josef?"

"Uh, no. What if... I mean, it's been a long time and even if he likes me fine at Counter-Magic, that's totally different than finding out I'm related to him. Whatever." She was trying so hard to act as though it didn't matter to her. He was astounded how at times, she could mask her feelings completely from him and how at other times, like now, it was painfully obvious how much she cared.

"It's your decision. I'm happy to do whatever you wish."

Her lips quirked. "Don't let Lily hear you say that."

"Why not?" he asked, intrigued.

Jade shook her head. "Nothing."

"How is Bruce?"

Jade's eyes lit up and she sat back, pulling her hand from his as she did. He found he missed it as soon as it was gone from his grasp. "His scaly patch is almost gone," she answered, motioning with her hands around her own neck. "It's just a little flaky now. Even though it was starting to get better after Lily and I separated, I put that poultice that we made on it. It didn't smell nearly as bad after it had 'sat' in the fridge for a while and Bruce really seemed to like it."

"They tend to smell better after all the ingredients have had time to settle." He could see from her expression that although he'd mentioned that to her before, she'd doubted his words until she'd seen it for herself.

"I put some cream on him too. He came into our room after digging out my purse cream and I figured he would know best what would be good for his skin, so..." she trailed off, giving a half shrug that seemed to say, 'whatcha gonna do.'

Paris smiled. "It's charming how you refer to it as your shared room. You and Bruce."

Jade's eyebrows came together. "I meant me and Lily."

Paris thought about the arrangement upstairs in Jade's cottage. "She didn't take the guest room?"

"Why would she take the guest room?"

"Did you move the bed over?" he asked, trying to figure out how the spatial arrangements would work. The master bedroom was roomy, but not enough for two queen sized beds.

"No." The way Jade answered his question clearly implied she thought he was a little strange for even asking. "My stuff is her stuff. It's just... our stuff. Our things."

"Oh. I see. My mistake." Paris couldn't think of anything else to add. He quirked his lips in a slight smile.

"Are you staying for a cup of coffee?" Jade asked, getting up from the table and heading to the cupboard with her mugs.

"I should be off. I was hoping to speak to Josef today. I don't feel right about keeping this from him longer than necessary."

"Oh. Yeah." Jade held her mug close to her chest. "I guess... I'll wait to hear from you then."

Paris stood and stepped over to her, carefully resting a hand on her shoulder.

"He'll want to talk to you. He'll be happy. I know it."

She nodded, but he could tell she didn't believe him.

He squeezed her shoulder. "I'm sure I'll be calling you shortly to arrange something."

"Okay.

"I'll see myself out."

It didn't occur to him until he'd already left Jade's cottage that she'd not had a chance to bring up what she'd wanted to discuss with him. He supposed whatever it was, it could wait.

#

Paris thought it was a good idea for both Josef and Jade to 'sit' with the news about Jade's past for twenty-four hours before seeing each other.

"Blah, blah, blah, something about processing and getting used to it. Blah, blah, blah, something, something about not getting caught up in the moment so we could better appreciate it," Jade said, waving her hand as she paced back and forth in her living room. Josef was supposed to be on his way over. She chewed at her cuticle, pulling a flap of skin off that made her finger bleed slightly. She winced as she looked at it, grabbing her purse from the foyer table to find her small manicure set.

Lily swiped her finger on her tablet, not looking up from her magazine. "He's a smart guy." Lily's hand dropped down to rest on Bruce's head. Bruce looked about as agitated as Jade felt. His tail was swishing back and forth, his tongue kept poking out and he'd kept making his 'pfffft' sound with no provocation.

"I'm not saying it was a bad idea, just… a day is a long time to sit around and think about stuff," Jade replied, trimming her cuticle and then tossing all her stuff back in her purse without putting it away properly. Lily got up from the couch and took Jade's purse from her, organizing her things correctly before slinging it over her own shoulder.

"I'm going to head out. Take the car and grab some stuff from the store."

"What? But he's coming over right now!" Jade exclaimed.

Lily's face softened. "And he's here to see you."

"But, we're, I mean, you and me…"

"Are separate now," Lily finished for her. "And we can do separate things. I think this is one of them."

"He probably wants to meet you too."

"He will. I'm living here now."

"But-" Jade began again, feeling unsettled in her stomach. Lily darted forward and hugged her tightly. Jade took a deep breath at the feeling - safety, security and warmth all at once.

"I'll give you guys about an hour. Text me if you want me to stay out longer."

"I won't," Jade replied quickly as Lily pulled away. Lily put on the one pair of tennis shoes they had and their one winter coat.

"We have to go shopping," she said ruefully.

Lily's face brightened. "Good idea! I'll text Callie and Henri and see if they want to come with."

Jade made a face. "Ugh, it'll take all day if there's four of us." She crossed her arms, the words she was thinking about saying sitting heavy on her tongue. She looked up at Lily - her eyes patient and relaxed, knowing what Jade was about to say, but waiting until she was ready to say it.

"Maybe… maybe you guys should go without me," Jade said carefully.

"Maybe," Lily hedged. "Or maybe I could promise to keep it to two hours and entice you a little by mentioning those boots you wanted are in the store at the west mall in our size."

"In that distressed brown color?" Jade asked.

"Yep."

"Sold. Two hours and we're getting those boots."

Lily waggled her fingers at Jade and then was out the door. Jade resisted the urge to rush after her and ask her to stay. That would be ridiculous. Jade knew Josef. She liked Josef. She liked working for him. She saw him every day at Counter-Magic. It was absurd that she should be standing in the middle of her foyer, feeling like she was about to break out in a cold sweat.

Absurd.

The tickety-tack of Bruce's talons on the floor announced his presence moments before he listed to the side and rested his weight against Jade's leg, letting his butt hit the ground with a thud. She looked down and he peered up at her - his hooded eyes looking large and solemn. His tail swished back and forth, the arc so large that he hit the small stand where she kept her keys, some spare change, and the detritus that ended up in her pockets. The table wobbled, sending some coins and a gum wrapper to the floor. Bruce looked over at it, startled, and then back at her sheepishly.

"It's okay, I'll clean it up."

Jade was about to bend over to get the coins, when there was a knock at the door and she froze. Her heart thumped in her chest - uncomfortable and thick. Bruce tapped his tail against the back of her calf and it was enough to jar her into action. She reached for the door handle, hand hovering for a moment as Bruce pressed up against her leg and she took a deep breath.

Josef stood on the doorstep, eyes meeting hers immediately. Considering they saw and spoke with each other every day at Counter-Magic, it was almost comical that neither one of them seemed able to say anything.

Almost comical, but not quite. Jade nervously tried to read his expression. Did he look happy? Regretful? Sad?

Wary, she supposed. If she had to put a word on his face, it would be wary. She felt the same way.

"Uh, come in, I guess," she said, having to clear her throat when the words got caught. Though she invited him in, she didn't budge from the doorway until he raised his eyebrows at her and leaned slightly forward, broadcasting his intentions to step inside. "Sorry," she blurted, stepping aside and letting him in. A 'swish-swish-swish' sound had her looking down at Bruce to see him wagging his tail, the serpentine length of it sweeping across the floor.

"Hello, Bruce," Josef said, bending down to pat Bruce on the head. Bruce's tongue came out and landed on Josef's hand and then Bruce preened, closing his eyes as Josef pet him. Josef stood and then took his coat off and Jade had a momentary panic that she didn't have a hanger for it until Bruce snatched it from Josef's hands and darted out of the foyer and into the living room, stealing the coat.

"Bruce!" she hissed after him before turning back to Josef. "Sorry, I don't know why... ugh. Bruce!" Not quite knowing if it was the 'right' or 'okay' thing to do, Jade rushed after Bruce, finding him already in the living room, in front of the fireplace, using Josef's coat as a blanket. He was nestling down in it, almost doing a wiggle-shimmy as he got comfortable.

"Oh, wow, I'm... he usually doesn't... Bruce, give him his coat back."

Josef laughed and Jade felt some of the tension leave her. "It's all right," he said. "Actually, I'm flattered." He came to stand by her, the two of them side by side, watching Bruce settle in for what looked like an epic nap. Bruce gave Jade a significant look, looked at the empty fireplace and then back at her.

Jade rolled her eyes. "Fine," she said, drawing the word out like it was two syllables. She snapped her fingers and flames lit up in the fireplace.

"That's a neat trick."

Jade could hear how careful Josef was being. His tone was an almost too perfect mix of curiosity and flattery, all very casually delivered.

"Um, thanks. I figured out how to shortcut some small spells with gestures. Finger snaps for the fireplace. Some tongue clicks for lighting candles. Hand claps for lighting some bigger flames. Like for a campfire or something." Jade didn't look directly at him as she spoke, instead, trying to keep her posture easygoing and her tone light.

With a mighty sigh, Bruce didn't so much roll over as fall over onto his side, belly exposed to the fireplace, his jaws smacking as he soaked up the warmth.

"He's so spoiled." Jade shook her head fondly.

"My grandmother had a familiar who was equally as spoiled," Josef said quietly. "Your... great-grandmother."

Jade's felt her stomach clench at his words. Josef's grandmother. Her great-grandmother. Her family.

"Did she?" Her words came out so quietly she was afraid at first that maybe Josef hadn't heard them. She licked her lips and was about to try again when he continued.

"Yes. An owl."

"Did it," she began, having to clear her throat again. "Did it have a name?"

Jade could see Josef's lips curl a bit, out of the corner of her eye. "She did. Cyclo."

She finally turned to look at him, knowing she wore a questioning look.

Josef shrugged. "She had only one eye." He closed one eye, squinting it shut in a prolonged wink. "Like a cyclops."

"You're making this up."

"'Fraid not."

Jade laughed, feeling even lighter when Josef joined her.

"It seems like ..." he said, hesitating for a moment, "the women in the family aren't too creative when it comes to names." He tipped his head toward Bruce and Jade startled for a moment when she realized he was including her in that sentence, just like he had when he talked about his grandmother. Jade's great-grandmother. She was part of his family. It was surprising every time she thought it, but not in an ugly or scary way. It was like opening up a box and finding cake and coffee inside or putting a hand in a coat pocket and finding a twenty-dollar bill. It was bright and shiny.

"If...we weren't creative," she said slowly, testing out the word 'we' between her lips. It felt smooth and easy and she saw Josef smile again when she said it. "They'd be named Owl and Lizard."

Josef laughed. "I suppose you're right." He nodded to himself, still watching Bruce.

"Do you want to have some coffee?" Jade asked, still slightly afraid he'd say no. "Maybe... maybe you could tell me more about Cyclo? It might be helpful for me and Bruce and... I'd like to hear it." The last words rushed out before she could think too much about them and stop herself.

"I'd like that."

#

Paris didn't lie to himself that he wasn't checking in on Jade and Lily in Counter-Magic. That was exactly what he was doing. He'd managed to keep his distance all day and finally gave in by five o'clock. He peered into the Counter-Magic office's, trying to be discreet and could see them both, Lily and Jade, sitting at Jade's desk. Jade looked like she was going through some spell work, Lily at her side taking notes in a spiral book. Lily stopped Jade by resting a hand on her arm, then pointing at the screen. Jade pointed at something else quickly and Lily nodded, making another note.

The entire thing happened without them saying a word to each other. It was strange and bewitching (for lack of a better word) to watch them communicate with one another. Suddenly, Jade spoke aloud, saying, "Yeah, half and half, too. Ours is old," and Lily scribbled something on another note pad. A grocery list, Paris realized. They were having more than one conversation at once. Jade paused, tilting her head a bit and Lily watched her for a split second, before they both turned to the doorway and caught him staring. The smiles on their faces were nearly identical. Nearly, but not quite. His eyes flicked back and forth, trying to study the almost infinitesimal differences. He still couldn't tell them apart without context. Or without getting close enough to see the color of their eyes.

"Is this an official part of your job description? Creeping?" Jade asked, a smile curving her lips.

Something flashed between Lily and Jade; Lily smirking a bit while Jade… blushed? Paris wondered what on earth had just transpired.

"Yes, this is how I supplement my meager income. Extra monetary incentive for checking in on new witches," he replied, coming into the room.

Josef looked up from his desk in his office and Paris gave him a slight nod, receiving one in return. He turned back to Jade and Lily.

"How are things?"

Lily shrugged while Jade answered. "Good. Counter-Magic log. Still resetting spells and fixing hexes since you reset Coven magic."

Paris looked to Lily. "Are you able to assist with that?"

"Yes," Jade answered at the same time that Lily said, "No."

"You're helping," Jade protested.

"I'm taking notes," Lily clarified. She turned to Paris. "I can follow along, but can't contribute."

"Yet," Jade added, sounding defensive.

"It doesn't bother me," Lily said. "I like learning even if I can't help."

It clearly bothered Jade, her eyebrows coming together in a frown. Lily checked her watch. "But we should get going. We told Henri we'd drive."

"Oh, right," Jade said, her voice flat and monotone. She wasn't happy about something.

Lily laughed at her expression, turning at Paris. "Booty yoga," she said, as though it should mean something to him.

"Is that code for something?" he asked.

"Don't I wish," replied Jade.

"Yoga's good for you." Lily hitched a purse up on her shoulder. "Helps loosen up those running muscles."

"Well, I was just coming by to check up on you and see how things were going," Paris said, watching as Jade put her coat on and hefted her own purse on her shoulder. She paused, looking at him and then Lily slowed her movements too, looking back and forth between Jade and Paris. Jade turned to Lily and Lily nodded.

"You know, why don't I take the car and catch up with Henri and you can maybe get a ride home?" Lily raised her eyebrows at Paris.

"Of course," he said, addressing both of them. "I don't mind driving you."

Lily's smile was wider and brighter than Jades, but Paris found Jade's was just as sincere, if slightly more circumspect. "Great," said Lily. "I'm going to go catch up with Henri. I'll see you at yoga, or... not." Lily placed a hand on Jade's shoulder and then let it run down her arm. Jade grabbed her fingers as they reached her own palm and gave them a quick squeeze and then Lily was gone.

"Is something wrong?"

Jade shuffled. "No... not really. I just... never got a chance to talk to you the other day. About that thing I wanted to tell you."

Well, that was unhelpfully vague. Paris studied her. She stared at him with solemn, serious eyes. "And you'd like to discuss it now?"

"Well, if you're free. I mean, I don't want to assume..."

"I'm free," he replied, perhaps a bit too quickly. "Would you like to go to your place first?" he wondered if she would like some privacy. She seemed rather hesitant and perhaps nervous.

"Um, yeah. My place is good." Jade nodded, seemingly more to herself than him.

"All right."

Jade popped her head into Josef's office before leaving and they exchanged quick but pleasant words, with them making plans to have dinner on the weekend.

"He's going to bring some pictures," Jade said, looking bashful as she and Paris left the Counter-Magic offices.

"I'm sure that will be lovely."

"Yeah." Her voice had a slightly far away quality to it and she seemed lost in her thoughts.

They kept an even pace with each other as they left the Covenstead, a comfortable silence between them even as they got in Paris' car and drove. Jade looked out the window as he drove, not saying much, something clearly on her mind.

Once at her cottage, Bruce came stampeding down the walkway to see them and Jade laughed at his exuberance.

"I just don't get that kind of reception anywhere else, buddy," she said, petting him soundly on the head as they walked up the steps into her house. Paris felt a slight touch of demon magic as he passed the threshold.

"Are you casting your lock spell again?"

Jade moved slowly, taking off her shoes and coat and it was obvious she was stalling. "Yes and no. It's not the same spell as before."

"I can feel that. Why not?"

Jade took a deep breath and settled her hands on her hips, almost like she thought she was preparing for battle. "Because the Sparrow Lady unraveled that one. And she'd just do it again if she wanted."

He frowned while he took off his own coat and shoes. "We've not yet had a chance to discuss her in great detail. Is that what you wanted to talk about?"

She winced. "Yes and no," she said again. She was about to say something else when she and Bruce both turned their heads sharply toward the kitchen. An instant later, they heard the deep, succulent voice of the demon.

"Possum! I know you're here."

Jade's lips curled in disgust and Bruce hissed.

"And your Englishman!"

Jade swore quite loudly and they could hear Seth laugh from the pantry. Bruce darted into the kitchen and Paris could hear him spitting and hissing. Squaring her shoulders, Jade set off for the kitchen, Paris following behind.

"Horrid thing! Where is your mistress? Stop spitting at me. It comes through the warding, you know. I go home smelling of lizard spittle."

Once in the kitchen, Paris spotted Bruce. His Elizabethan collar was raised and he had one foot up in the air, making a kind of clawing motion at Seth. Jade, stood next to Bruce, crossing her arms over her chest. "What do you want? I'm busy."

"Call off your lizard thing. It's unseemly for me to be treated this way."

Jade didn't say anything and Bruce spat three more times. Seth's nose wrinkled in distaste.

"You're lucky she's fond of you," Seth said to Bruce. "You wouldn't stand a chance anywhere else."

"Don't talk to him that way."

Seth raised his eyes to look at Jade and for a moment, his gaze made Paris dizzy. If it did the same to Jade, she hid it well. Paris shook his head a bit and the feeling passed. Seth's eyes narrowed as he stared at Jade and then he peered closer at her, studying her. He smiled brightly. The flash of his teeth was dizzying. "Look at you! Little bit lonely in your brain now? Allllll byyyyy yoursellllllllf," he sang off key. "Where is your other-but-not-necessarily-better half?" Seth craned his neck, dramatically looking around the empty kitchen.

Jade rolled her eyes. "Get to the point, Seth." Bruce flicked his tail.

"Oh, Possum. That's what I'm here for. Front row seats." His eyes moved past Jade and Paris, peering behind them toward the front door. Paris turned his head toward the front of the house, even as he told himself he shouldn't take his eyes of the demon. He saw Bruce turn his head as well, as though he heard something. He bolted out of the kitchen, claws scratching at the floor as he did.

"Bruce! What-?" Jade clearly wanted to go after him, but stayed put, watching Seth.

There was a knock at the front door, the sound of it loud enough to carry into the kitchen. Paris' feet moved of their own volition, taking two steps away from Jade and back toward the door. He knew he was moving and struggled, forcing himself to stop. A thick feeling rolled through his stomach. Again, like when he'd been compelled to sleep, this was magic. He was being drawn to the door.

"Jade," he said, wanting to reach for her, feeling somehow that if he could touch her hand, her magic might be enough to break the compulsion he felt. Unease clutched his chest and squeezed.

"Listen, Possum, I just popped by to remind you how near and dear we are. We've shared things, you and I. *I've* disfigured people, *you've* disfigured people. I was there when you made that witch gouge out his own eye and then you almost lost your heart to a demon. Those were good times," he said fondly. Paris cringed at his tone, hating that he had his back facing Seth but not able to turn around. "So, now that you're getting more popular and moving on up, I just want to remind you of our bond."

"Our what?" Jade said, her voice going up an octave at the end.

"Our fellowship, our affiliation. Our *tendre*."

Paris felt a stronger pull toward the front door, his feet moving again even as he tried to remain still.

"Jade," he repeated. "I have to answer the door."

"What?" Out of the corner of his eye, he could see her look him up and down, see her frown. "What's wrong?"

"I have to answer the door," he said again, leaving the kitchen and heading back toward the front of the cottage. He heard her follow him and felt grateful.

"Go away, Seth," Jade called back to the kitchen. "I'm busy." She followed Paris' wooden steps as he kept moving forward.

"Should I be ready to fight? Bruce, are we fighting?"

Bruce was already at the front door, tail swishing back and forth. His collar was still up, but he wasn't spitting. Paris wasn't sure what that meant.

"Remember all we've shared!" Seth called out. "Don't be swayed by a pretty face and a tragic back-story!"

"Get bent!" Jade shouted, Paris felt her hand grab his elbow, felt her magic rush through him and although it lessened the heavy tug in his chest, he couldn't stop. Her magic was like fire in his veins - burning through his being hot and quick. It collided with the magic pulling at him and there was a whip crack backlash from the unknown magic - hard and vicious against Jade's power. Her feet stumbled and her fingers tightened on his elbow. Jade poured more power into him. He'd never felt such power before. He had no idea this was what her magic truly felt like - molten and thick. As powerful as she was, though, she was only brute force. The other magic was methodical, calm and calculated. He could feel it pushing back against Jade's power and the response surging through him from Jade - all power and no finesse. It made his stomach clench.

"Stop. You can't help just by forcing it. Not by sheer strength." Jade was a demolition force against a lightening storm - powerful but ineffective against such an onslaught.

"Sorry." Jade's voice was quiet and although her magic stopped rushing through him, she didn't take her hand from his elbow, keeping pace with him. She kept a low-level stream pulsing into him, not trying to stop the magic compelling him, but merely making its presence known to the unknown witch. Her magic seemed to say, 'I'm still here and that won't change.'

Paris was at the foyer now, crossing the tile floor, his hand reaching out toward the front door. Her fingers tightened around his elbow once, before sliding up his arm and resting on his shoulder. Her magic was a warm beat in his veins. She stepped close to him, her face next to his, although he couldn't make his head turn to look at her. "Should I get some more Counter-Magic Agents, or call a priest or stop you from answering the door?"

"I don't know. Someone wants me to answer the door." Paris cocked his head, feeing the magic that was compelling him. "It feels familiar… but impossible."

"Impossible how?" Jade asked, her voice wary.

"It feels like my mother's magic."

The look on Jade's face and how her countenance went grey made his stomach turn over.

"Oh, shit. Remember that thing I needed to tell you?"

Paris remembered; it was why they were meeting - to discuss it. "Yes, of course." His hand was on the door handle, turning it, pulling the door open. A woman stood before him in a dark cloak, the hood of it obscuring her face. She reached up and drew the hood back, exposing her countenance.

"Hello, my dear."

Standing in front of him was his mother. But that was impossible. She was dead. Dead for over fifteen years. Dead and gone, leaving the Coven to him. And yet it was her. Her face was more lined, but her hair was still dark, her bone structure impressive, her posture perfect, as always. Her magic embraced him like an old, familiar blanket, wrapping around him, surrounding him in the scent of vanilla, sage and mint.

With a touch of licorice.

"She's the Sparrow Lady," Jade said, her fingers tightening on his shoulder, her other hand coming up to rest against the center of his back, as though he needed bracing and she could give him strength.

"Mother."

AUTHOR BIO

Margarita loves the art, creativity and romanticism of storytelling. Sometimes, however, the act of putting pen to paper proves challenging. She works to develop genuine, relatable characters which grow in the hearts of her readers. From that foundation, the stories flourish into a warm friend.

She enjoys pursuits which blur the lines between the analytical and creative sides of her brain. This includes her day job in electronic data management, where she uses her creativity to solve logical problems, and also her lessons learning to play the cello, where she finds beauty in the structure of music and the instrument. She believes there is a place for both logic and imagination to work together. When they do, the results are magical.

The 'label' she identifies most with is 'storyteller.' According to Wikipedia, storytelling is the conveying of events in words, and images, often by improvisation or embellishment. It seems to fit pretty well with how she feels about her work.

At www.margaritagakis.com, you can sign up for her newsletter to get updates on her current work and upcoming releases.